MARGARET:

A TALE OF THE

REAL AND THE IDEAL, BLIGHT AND BLOOM;

INCLUDING

SKETCHES OF A PLACE NOT BEFORE DESCRIBED,

CALLED

MONS CHRISTI.

IN TWO VOLUMES.

REVISED EDITION.

"It is the vernal season; for the heart is every moment longing to walk in the garden, and every bird of the grove is melodious in its carols as the nightingale; thou wilt fancy it a dawning zephyr of early spring, or new year's day morning; but it is the breath of Jesus, for in that fresh breath and verdure the dead earth is reviving."—SAADI.

BY THE AUTHOR OF "PHILO," AND "RICHARD EDNEY AND THE GOVERNOR'S FAMILY."

VOLUME I.

BOSTON:
PHILLIPS, SAMPSON, AND COMPANY.
1851.

AUTHOR'S NOTE.

It is now more than ten years since "Margaret" was commenced. To-day is the revision of the work ended. Not without sensibility has such a retrospect been gone through with. Old acquaintances and familiar scenes of the imagination are not less impressive than those of the actual world. The author cannot retrace the gronnd of these pages without being reminded of some things he would forget, and others that he is too fearful of losing. The book was written out of his heart and hope. Has a decade of years and experience vitiated or overset aught of that heart and hope?—Going over the book at this time is not precisely like a call on old friends; it becomes a species of self-examination.

In the result, as to the general character and drift of the work, the author finds little to alter. Not that he could write just such a book again—he could not. But he cleaves to the ideas according to which, and the objects for which, this was written.

In the revision sentences have been changed, not sentiments, and the expunging process has respected words more than things.

"Margaret" was never designed for railroads; it might, peradventure, suit a canal boat. Rather is it like an old-fashioned ride on horseback, where one may be supposed to enjoy leisure for climbing hills, and to possess curiosity for the trifles of the way.

It is proper that some answer be given to observations that have been freely, and it will not be doubted, kindly bestowed on the author and his labors.

"He is too minute; he seems to be making out a ship's manifest, instead of telling a plain story."—This book was written for the love of the thing, and each item has been introduced with a love of it. Every bird has been watched, every flower pursued, every footpath traversed. No author can, indeed, expect the public to share his tastes or join his recreations; he does solicit a charitable construction of his spirit and purpose.

"He is vulgar."—A popular tradition declares tastes to be indisputable, and imparts to them an authority which belongs only to revelation. We are inclined to think there is a dispute about them; and the issue may as well be made up first as last. Is what we call common life, are what pass for illiterate, uncultivated, ignorant people, their properties and reminiscences, here in New England, to be regarded as vulgar?—using the word in a certain odious sense. To take an instance from the following pages—and that is where the question is carried—is Obed vulgar? We aver that he is not. He is an unrefined, rude, simple youth; but in all his relations to Margaret, in all the little part he acts in the scene, he is courteous, gentle, delicate, disinterested, pure. At least he seems so to us. We may have failed to report him fairly. But, allowing him to be such, are we justified in pronouncing him vulgar? Is Nimrod to be accounted a vulgar-spoken youth?

"He is unequal, grotesque, mermaiden, abrupt."—Here are involved the same questions as before, What is vulgar, and what refined, what noble, what mean? There are standards of taste valid and needful. But is not the range of their application too limited? May not rough rocks have a place in the fairest landscapes of nature or art? May not a dark pool of water in a forest, with its vegetable and animal adjuncts mirror the stars? Have we not seen or heard of a cascade that starts, say, from the blue of the skies, pours down a precipice of rusty rock, and terminates in drift-wood and bog? Is that water *bathetic?* These are questions we do not care to argue here and now. Are they not worthy of considration? Have they no pertinence to the subject in hand?

"He is no artist."—If what every body says be true, and what almost every body says be almost true, to this iterated charge, we ought to gasp out a *peccavi*, and be silent. But, good friends all, a moment's indulgence. May there not be a moral as well as a material plot—a plot of ideas as well as of incidents? "Margaret" is a tale not of outward movement, but of internal development. An obvious part of its plan is the three epochs of the life of its principal personage. Another part is the times in which the scene lies. Rose belongs to the plot of the book, so does the Indian. Master Elliman has been called a sort of a diluted imitation of Dominie Sampson! The plot of the book involved this, that while Margaret grew up in, or contiguous to, a religious and civilized community, she should remain for the most part unaffected by these influences; yet that she should not mature in ignorance, but should receive quite an amount of a species of erudition. To effect this the Master is introduced. The management of this part of the tale, it need not be said, was one of the most difficult problems the author had to encounter. To the general thread of the drama a variety of things are attached, not one of which, in the main, is not conceived to be tributary to the gradual evolution of the whole. The purely material accessories of the story being deemed quite insubordinate, are thrown in corners by themselves.

The book takes our country as it emerges from the Revolution, and does not bri g it down to what now is, but carries it up, or a portion of it, to what it is conceived should be; and the final *denouement* may be found in the last Part. In all this is system, arrangement, precedent, effect, and due relation of things. We have wished herein to be artistical; certainly our feelings are not whimsical, neither is our method governed by any conscious caprice. How far we have succeeded it is not for us to say. We would thank certain ones, assayers of literature, at least to consider what we have attempted to do.

To those who have been glad at what the author has written he extends the hope that they may never regret their gladness.

Those that disrelish his productions he knows can find things enough in the bookstores to their liking; and he is sufficiently generous to wish them joy in whatever line of reading their fancies or feelings may adopt.

Riverside, Augusta, May 12, 1851.

CONTENTS OF VOLUME I.

PART I.—CHILDHOOD.

PART II.—YOUTH.

PART I.

CHILDHOOD.

PART I.

CHAPTER I.

PHANTASMAGORICAL—INTRODUCTORY.

We behold a child of eight or ten months; it has brown curly hair, dark eyes, fair conditioned features, a health-glowing cheek, and well-shaped limbs. Who is it? whose is it? what is it? where is it? It is in the centre of fantastic light, and only a dimly-revealed form appears. It may be Queen Victoria's or Sally Twig's. It is God's own child, as all children are. The blood of Adam and Eve, through how many soever channels diverging, runs in its veins, and the spirit of the Eternal, that blows everywhere, has animated its soul. It opens its eyes upon us, stretches out its hands to us, as all children do. Can you love it? It may be the heir of a throne, does it interest you; or of a milking stool, do not despise it. It is a miracle of the All-working, it is endowed by the All-gifted. Smile upon it, it will smile you back again; prick it, it will cry. Where does it belong? in what zone or climate? on what hill? to what plain? It may have been born on the Thames or the Amazon, the Hoan Ho or the Mississippi.

The vision deepens. Green grass appears beneath the child. It may, after all, be Queen Victoria's in Windsor Park, or Sally Twig's on Little Pucker Island. The sun now shines upon it, a blue sky breaks over it, and the wind rustles its hair. Sun, sky, and wind are common to Arctic and Antartic regions, and belong to every meridian. A black-cap is seen to fly over it; and this bird is said by naturalists to be found in both hemispheres. A dog, or the whelp of a dog, a young pup, crouches near it, makes a caracol backwards, frisks away, and returns again. The child is pleased, throws out its arms, and laughs right merrily.

As we now look at the child, we can hardly tell to which of the five races it belongs; whether it be a Caucasian, Mongolian, American, Ethiopian, or Malay. Each child on this terraqueous ball, whether its nose be aquiline, its eyes black and small, its cheek bones prominent, its lips large, or its head narrow; whether its hue be white, olive, or jet, is of God's creating, and is delighted with the bright summer light, a bed of grass, the wind, birds, and puppies; and smiles in the eyes of all beholders. It it God's child still, and its mother's. It is curiously and wonderfully made; the inspiration of the Almighty hath given it understanding. It will look after God, its Maker, by how many soever names he may be called; it will aspire to the Infinite, whether that Infinite be expressed in Bengalee or Arabic, English or Chinese; it will seek to know truth; it will long to be loved; it will sin and be miserable, if it has none to care for it; it will die.

Let us give it to Queen Victoria. "No," says Sally Twig, "it is mine." "No," says the Empress Isabella, "it is destined to the crown of Castile." "Not so shure of that, me hearty; it is Teddy O'Rourke's own Phelim." "Ha," laughs a Tahitian, "I left it playing under the palm trees." "What presumption!" exclaims Mrs. Morris, "it is our Frances Maria, whom the servant is airing on the Common." "I just bore it in my own arms through the cypresses," observes Osceola, quietly.

It seems to be in pain. "Mein Gott! gehet eilend hin." "Poor Frances Maria!" "Paneeweh htouwenaunuh neenmaumtehkeh!" "Per amor del Cielo!" "Jesus mind Teddy's Phelim." "O Nhaw nddg erm devishd!" "Wæsucks! my wee bonny wean, she'll die while ye are bletherin here." "Bismillahi!" "Ma chere enfante!" "Alohi, Alohi!" "Ora pro nobis!" "None of your whidds, dub the giggle, and take the bantling up." "Highder davran under!"— What a babel of exclamations! What manifold articulations of affection!— How the motherly heart bursts forth in a thousand tongues! But hold, good friends, may be the child does not belong to you.

The scene advances. Two hands are seen thrust down towards it, and now it smiles again. Near by discovers itself a peach-tree. Where does that belong? Not like the black-cap every where. In the grass gleams the golden eye of a dandelion; the skin of the child settles into a Caucasian whiteness, and its fat fingers are making for the flower. Be not disappointed, my friends, your children still live and smile; let this one live and smile too. Go, Mongolian, Ethiopian, American, or Malay, and take your child to your bosom, and it will remind you of this, since all children are a good deal alike.

Now the child crawls towards the peach-tree. Those two hands, that may belong to its brother, set the child on its feet by the side of the tree, as it were measuring their heights, which are found to be the same. Yellow and brown chickens appear on the grass, and run under the low mallows and smart-weed. A sheet of water is seen in the distance, spotted with green islands. Forest trees burst forth in the rim of the picture — butternuts, beeches, maples, pines. A sober-faced boy, seven or eight years old, to whom the two hands are seen to belong, sits down, and with a fife pipes to the child, who manifests strong joy at the sound. A man in a three-cornered hat and wig, with nankeen small-clothes, and paste buckles, takes the child in his arms. Where is the child? A log cabin appears; a woman in a blue striped long-short and yellow skirt comes to the door. An Anglo Saxon voice is heard. If you were to look into the cabin or house, you would discover a loom and spinning-wheels, and behind it a larger boy making shingles, and somewhere about a jolly-faced man drinking rum. The woman, addressing the first boy as Chilion, tells him to bring the child into the house.

This child we will inform you is MARGARET, of whom we have many things to say, and whom we hope to reveal more perfectly to you. She is in the town of Livingston, in that section of the United States of America known as New England. And yet, so far as this book is concerned, she is for you all as much as if she were your own child; and if you cared any thing about her when you did not know her, we desire that your regards may not subside when you do know her, even if she be not your own child; and we dedicate this memoir of her to ALL who are interested in her, and care to read about her. In the mean time, if you are willing, we will lose sight of her for seven or eight years, and present her in a more tangible form, as she appeared at the end of that period.

CHAPTER II.

WORK AND BEAUTY.—AN IMPRESSION OF THE REAL.

THE child Margaret sits in the door of her house, on a low stool, with a small wheel, winding spools, in our vernacular, "quilling," for her mother, who, in a room near by, is mounted in a loom, weaving and smoking; the fumes of her pipe mingling with the whizz of the shuttle, the jarring of the lathe, and the clattering of treadles. From a windle the thread is conducted to the quills, and buzz, buzz goes Margaret's wheel, while a gray squirrel, squatted on her shoulder, inspects the operation with profound gravity.

"Look up the chimney child," says the mother, "and see what time it is."

"I don't know how," replies Margaret.

"I suppose we must get the Master to learn you your *a b c's* in this matter," rejoined the mother. "When the sun gets in one inch, it is ten o'clock; when it reaches the stone that bouges out there, it is dinner time. How many quills have you done?"

"The basket is full, and the box besides. Chilion said I might go and sail with him."

"We have a great deal to do. Miss Gisborne's flannel is promised the last of the week, and it must be drawn in to-morrow. I want you to clean the skans; there is a bunch of lucks down cellar, bring them up; get some plantain and dandelion on the smooth for greens; you must pick over those beans; put some kindlers under the pot; then you may go."

"I had a dream last night."

"Hush! You are always dreaming. I am afraid you will come to a bad end."

"It was a pretty dream."

"I can't help your dreams; here, pick up this."

The woman had broken a thread in the chain, and while Margaret was helping repair the accident, she looked into her mother's face, and, as if following out her thoughts, said, "A woman came near to me, she dropped tears upon me, she stood in the clouds."

"I can't stop to hear you now," replied her mother. "Run and do what I have told you."

When Margaret had finished the several chores, she went to the Pond. She was barefooted and barearmed. She wore a brown linen gown or tunic, open in front, a crimson skirt, a blue checked apron, and for head covering a green rush hat. By a narrow foot-path, winding through shrubbery and brambles, and defiling along the foot of a steep hill that rose near the house, she came to the margin of the water. Chilion, her brother, who was at work with a piece of glass, smoothing a snow-white bass wood paddle, for a little bark canoe he had made her, saw Margaret approach with evident pleasure, yet received her in the quietest possible manner, as she leaped and laughed towards him. He asked her if she remembered the names of the flowers; and while he was finishing the paddle, she went along the shore to gather them. The Pond covered several hundreds of acres, its greatest diameter measured about a mile and a half; its outline was irregular, here divided by sharp rocks, there retreating into shaded coves; and on its face appeared three or four small islands, bearing trees and low bushes. Its banks, if not really steep, had a bluff and precipitous aspect from the tall forest that girdled it about. The region was evidently primitive, and the child, as she went along, trod on round smooth pebbles of white and rose quartz, dark hornblende, greenstone, and an occasional fragment of trap, the results of the diluvial ocean, if any body can tell when or what that was. In piles, among the stones, lay quivering and ever accumulating masses of fleece-like and fox-colored foam; there were also the empty shells af various kinks of mollusks. She climbed over the white peeled trunks of hemlocks, that had fallen into the water, or drifted to the shore; she trod through beds of fine silver-gray sand, and in the shallow edge of the Pond she walked on a hard even bottom of the same, which the action of the waves had beaten into a smooth shining floor. She discovered flowers which her brother told her were horehound, skull-caps, and Indian tobacco; she picked small green apples that disease had formed on the leaves of the willows; and beautiful velvety crimson berries from the black alder.

When all was ready, she got into her canoe, while her brother led the way in a boat of his own. With due instructions in the management of the paddle, she succeeded tolerably well. Chilion had often taken her on the water, and she was not much afraid. The pond was commonly reported to have no bottom, and it possessed the minds of the people with a sort of indefinable awe: but this Margaret was too young to feel; she took manifest delight in skimming across that dark, deep mystery. She toppled somewhat, her canoe shook and tilted, but on it went; there was a thin wake, a slight rustle of the water; her brother kept near her, and she enjoyed the fearful pastime. Reaching the opposite shore, Chilion drew up his boat, and went to a rock, where he sat down to fish with a long pole. Margaret turned into a recess where the trees and rocks darkened the water, and the surface lay calm and clear. The coolness of the spot was inviting, birds were merry-making in the underwood, and deep in the water she saw the blue sky and the white clouds. "That looks like her," she said, calling to mind her dream. She urged her canoe up a shelving rock, where she took off her hat and apron; and, the process of disrobing being speedily done, waded into the water. She said, "I will go down to the bottom, I will tread on the clouds." She sunk to her neck, she plunged her head under; she could discover nothing but the rocky or smooth sandy bed of the pond. Was she disappointed? A sand-piper glided weet weeting along the shore; she ran after it, but could not catch it; she sat down and sozzled her feet in the foam; she saw a blue-jay washing itself, ducking its crest, and hustling the water with its wings, and she did the same. She got running mosses, twin-flower vines, and mountain laurel blossoms, which she wound about her neck and waist, and pushing off in her canoe, looked into the water as a mirror. Her dark clear hazle eyes, her fair white skin, the leaves and flowers, made a pretty vision. She smiled and was smiled on in turn; she held out her hand, which was reciprocated by the fair spirit below; she called her own name, the rocks and woods answered; she looked around, but saw nothing. Had she fears or hopes? It may have been only childish sport. "I will jump to that girl," she said, "I will tumble the clouds." She sprang from the canoe, and dropped quietly, softly, on the bottom; she had driven her companion away, and as she came up, her garlands broke and floated off in the ripples. Wiping herself on a coarse towel her mother wove for her, see dressed, and went back to her brother. A horn rang through the woods. "Dinner is ready," he said; "we must go."

Returning, they came to the greensward in front of the house, where was a peach-tree.

"I remember," said her brother, "when you and that were of the same size; now it shades you. It is just as old as you are. How full of fruit it is."

"How did it grow?" asked Margaret.

"I put a peach-stone in the ground one winter," replied her brother, "and it sprouted in the spring."

"I was an acorn once," rejoined the child, "so Obed says, and why did'nt I grow up an oak-tree?"

A dog bounding towards them interrupted the conversation. This animal had enormous proportions, and looked like a cross of wolf and mastiff; his color was a brindled black, his head resembled the ideas we have of Cerberus, his legs were thick and strong, and he was called Bull. Following the dog, approached the jolly-faced father of Margaret from the barn, where he had been swingling flax; his hat, face, and clothes were dangling and netted with tow and whitish down, but you could see him laugh through the veil; and the glow of his red face would make you laugh. He caught Margaret and set her on the dog, who galloped away with his load. They encountered her older brother coming in from the woods, where he had been burning a piece; his frock crusted with ashes, his face smirched with coals. He spoke tartly to Margaret, and contrived to trip the dog as he ran by, and throw his sister to the ground.

"Don't do so," said she.

"Let Bull alone," he replied, speaking in a blubbering, washy manner, which we cannot transcribe. "You'll spile him; would you make a goslin of him? Here's your sticks right in the track;" saying which he scattered with his foot a little paling she had constructed about a dandelion. She must needs cry; the dog went to her, looked in her eyes, lapped her tears, and she put her arms about his neck. Her brother, who seemed to be a kind of major domo in the family, whistled the dog away, and ordered his sister into the house to help her mother.

Her father and older brother wore checked shirts, and a sort of brown tow trousers known at the time—these things happened some years ago—as skilts; they were short, reaching just below the knee, and very large, being a full half yard broad at the bottom; and, without braces or gallows, were kept up by the hips, sailor fashion. Neither wore any coat, vest, or neck-cloth. Her father had on what was once a three-cornered hat, but the corners were now reduced to loose ragged flaps; a leather apron completed his suit. Her brother had a cap made of wood-chuck skin, steeple-shaped, the hair of which was pretty well rubbed off. They went to the cistern on the back side of the house, washed and rinsed themselves for dinner. The father discovered a gamesome expression of face, shining scirrous skin, and a plump ruby head; his eyes were bloodshot, his cheeks whealed and puffed, and through his red lips his laughter exposed a suite of fair white teeth; his head was nearly bald, and the crown showed smooth and glairy; and under the thin flossy wreath of hair that invested his temples, you would not fail to notice that one of his ears was gone. Her brother had a more catonian look; thick locks of coarse black hair kept well with his russet, sunburnt face, and his lips, if by nothing else, were swollen with large quids of tobacco.

The dinner-table, appropriate to the place in which it was set, consisted of boards laid on a movable trestle without a cloth. A large wooden dish or trencher contained, flummery-like, in one mass, the entire substance of the meal—pork, potatoes, greens, beans. There were no suits of knives and forks, and the family helped themselves on wooden plates, with cuttoes. A large silver tankard curiously embossed, and bearing some armorial signets, formed an exception to the general aspect of things, and looked quite baronially down on its serf-like companions. This filled with cider constituted their drink. They sat on blocks of wood and rag-bottom chairs. Margaret occupied a corner of the table near her younger brother Chilion, and had a cherry plate with a wolf's bone knife and fork he made for her. They all ate heartily and enjoyed their meal. After dinner, Chilion went with his gun into the woods, the father and elder brother returned to their respective employments, her mother resumed her smoking and weaving, and Margaret had a new stint at quilling.

CHAPTER III.

LOCALITIES DESCRIBED.—THE FAMILY MORE PARTICULARLY ENUMERATED.—OBED INTRODUCED.

THE house where Margaret lived, of a type common in the early history of New England, and still seen in the regions of the West, was constructed of round logs sealed with mud and clay ; the roof was a thatch composed of white-birch twigs, sweet-flag and straw wattled together, and overlaid with a slight battening of boards ; from the ridge sprang a low stack of stones, indicating the chimney-top. Glass windows there were none, and in place thereof swung wooden shutters fastened on the inside by strings. The house was divided by the chimney into two principal apartments, one being the kitchen or commons, the other a work shop. In the former were prominently a turn-up bed used by the heads of the family, and a fireplace ; the last, built of slabs of rough granite, was colossal in height, width, and depth ; stone splinters filled the office of and-irons. A handle of wood thrust into the socket of a broken spade supplied the place of a shovel. The room was neither boarded nor plastered ; a varnish of smoke from tobacco pipes and pine-knots possibly answering in stead ; and the naked stones of the chimney front were blackened and polished by occasional effusions of steam and smoke from the fire. The room also contained the table-board, block, and rag-bottom chairs, and little stool for Margaret before mentioned. In one corner stood a twig broom. On pegs in the log, hung sundry articles of wearing apparel ;

sustained by crotched sticks nailed to the sleepers above, were a rifle and one or two muskets ; a swing shelf was loaded with shot-pouches, bullet-moulds, powder-horns, and fishing tackle, &c. ; on the projecting stones of the chimney were sundry culinary articles, and conspicuously a one-gallon wooden rum-keg, and the silver tankard. In the room, which we should say was quite capacious, hung two cages, one for a robin, the other with a revolving apartment for a gray squirrel, called Dick. You would not also omit to notice a violin in a green baize bag, suspended on the walls, which belonged to Chilion, and was an important household article. On a post, near the chimney, were fastened some leaves of a book, which you would find to be torn from the statistical chapters of the Old Testament. The floor of the room was warped in every direction, slivered and gaping at the joints ; and, being made of knotty boards, the softer portions of which were worn down, these knots stood in ridges and hillocks all over the apartment.

The workshop, of smaller dimensions, was similar, in its general outline, to the kitchen ; it contained a loom, a kit where the father of Margaret sometimes made shoes, a common reel, hand reel, a pair of swifts, blades, or windle, a large, small, and quilling wheel, a dye tub, with yarn of all colors hanging on the walls. The garret was divided by the chimney in a manner similar to the rooms below ; on one side Margaret slept, and the boys on the other ; her bed consisted simply of a mattrass of beech leaves spread on the floor, with tow and wool coverlids, and coarse linen sheets. The ascent to this upper story was by a ladder.

In rear of the kitchen was a shed, a rough frame of slabs and poles. Here were a draw-shave, beetle and wedges, hog and geese yokes, barking irons, a brush-bill, fox-traps, frows and sap-buckets; this also was the dormitory of the hens. At one corner of the shed was a half-barrel cistern, into which water was brought by bark troughs from the hill near by, forming an ever flowing, ever musical, cool bright stream, passing off in a runnel shaded by weeds and grass. On all sides of the house, at certain seasons of the year, might be seen the skins of various animals drying; the flesh side out, and fastened at the extremities; foxes, wood-chucks, martins, raccoons, and sometimes even bears and wolves; the many-colored tails of which, pendant, had an ornamental appearance.

The house was on the west side of the road, and fronted the south. Across what might have been a yard, saving there were no fences, was a butternut tree—the Butternut *par excellence*—having great extension of limb, and beautiful drooping willow-like foliage. Beyond lay the eastern extremity of the Pond. On the north was a small garden enclosed by a rude brush hedge. On the east side of the road stood a log-barn, covered with thatch, and supported in part by the trunks of two trees.

The name of the family whose residence we have explored was Hart, and it consisted essentially of six members; Mr. and Mrs, Hart, their three sons, Nimrod, Hash, and Chilion, and Margaret. We should remark that the heads of this house were never or rarely known by their proper names. Mr. Hart at some period had received the sobriquet of Head and Pluck, by the latter part of which he was generally designated; his wife was more commonly known as Brown Moll. Mr. Hart had also a fancy for giving his children scriptural names; his first-born he called Nimrod; his second, Maharshalalhashbaz, abbreviated into Hash; and for his next son he chose that of Chilion. It must not be thought he had any reverence for the Bible; his conduct would belie such a supposition. He may have been superstitious; if it were so, that certainly was the extent of his devotion. The subject of this Memoir was sometimes called after her mother, Mary or Molly, and from regard to one long since deceased she had received the name of Margaret. Her father and mother were fond of contradicting each other, especially in matters of small moment, and while the latter called her Margaret or Peggy, the former was wont to address her as Molly.

Nimrod, the oldest son, was absent from home most of the year; how employed, we shall have occasion hereafter to notice. Hash worked the farm, if farm it might be called, burnt coal in the fall, made sugar in the spring, drank, smoked, and teased Margaret the rest of the time. Chilion fished, hunted, laid traps for foxes, drowned out woodchucks; he was also the artisan of the family, and with such instruments as he could command, constructed sap-buckets and spouts, hencoops, sleds, trellises, &c. He was very fond of music, and played on the violin and fife; in this also he instructed Margaret, whom he found a ready pupil; taught her the language of music, sang songs with her; he also told her the common names of many birds and flowers. He was somewhat diffident, reserved, or whatever it might be; and while he manifested a deep affection for his sister, he never expressed himself very freely to her. Mr. Hart, or Pluck, if we give him the name by which he was commonly known, helped Hash on the farm, broke flax, made shoes, a trade he prosecuted in an itinerating manner from house to house, "whipping the cat," as it was termed, and drank excessively. Mrs. Hart, or Brown Moll, carded, spun, colored and wove, for herself and more for others, nipped and beaked her husband, drank and smoked. At the present time she was about forty-five or fifty ; she had seen care and trouble, and seemed almost broken down alike by her habits and her misfortunes. She was wrinkled, faded and gray ; her complexion was sallow, dark and dry ; her expression, if it were not positively stern, was far from being amiable ; she was a patient weaver, impatient with every thing else. Her dress was a blue-striped linen short-gown, wrapper, or long-short, a coarse yellow petticoat and checked apron ; short grizzly hairs bristled in all directions over her head. If in this family you could detect some trace of refinement, it would not be easy to discriminate its origin or to say how far removed it might be from unmixed vulgarity.

The term Pond, applied to the spot where this family dwelt, comprised not only the sheet of water therein situated. but also the entire neighborhood. In the records of the town the place was denominated the West District. Sometimes it was called the Head, or Indian's Head, from a hill thereon to which we shall presently refer, and the inhabitants were called Indians from this circumstance. An almost unbroken forest bounded the vision and skirted the abode of this family. They had only one neighbor, a widow lady, who resided at the north about half a mile. A road extending across the place from north to south terminated in the latter direction, about the same distance below Mr. Hart's, at a hamlet known as No. 4. In the other course, directly or divergingly, this road led to sections called Snakehill, Five-mile-lot, and the Ledge. On the south-west was a plantation that had been christened Breakneck. The village of Livingston, or Settlement, as it was sometimes termed, lay to the east about two miles in a straight line. If a stranger should approach the Pond from the village he would receive the impression that it was singularly situated up among high hills, or even on a mountain, since his route would be one of continual and perhaps tedious ascent. But those who abode there had no idea their locality was more raised than that of the rest of the world, so sensibly are our notions of height and depression affected by residence. From the village you could descry the top of the Head, like a tower upon a mountain, elevated far into the heavens.

On this hill, it being a striking characteristic of the Pond, we must cast a passing look. A few rods back of Mr. Hart's house the ascent commenced, and rose with an abrupt acclivity to the height of nearly one hundred feet. Its surface was ragged and rocky, and interspersed with various kinds of shrubs. From the edge of the water its south front sprang straight and sheer like a castle. The top was flat and nearly bare of vegetation, save the dead and barkless trunk of a hemlock, which, solitary and alone, shot up therefrom, and was sometimes called the Indian's Feather. This hill derived its specific name, Indian's Head, from a rude resemblance to a man's face that could be traced on one of its sides. This particular eminence was not, however, a detached pinnacle ; it seemed rather to form the abrupt and crowned terminus of a mountainous range that swept far to the north, and ultimately merged in those eternal hills that in-wall every horizon. Behind the hill at the northern extremity of the Pond proper, where its waters were gathered to a head by a dam, and a saw-mill had been erected, was the Outlet; which became the source of a stream, that proceeding circuitously to No. 4, and turning towards the village where it was again employed for milling purposes, had been denominated Mill Brook.

Mr. Hart had cleared a few acres for corn, potatoes and flax, and burnt over more for grain. He enjoyed also the liberty of brooks and swamps, whence he gathered grass, brakes and whatever he could find to store his barn. Beyond the barn was a lot of five or six acres, known as the Mowing or Chesnuts. It was cleared, und partially cultivated with clover and herdsgrass. This consisted originally of a grove of chesnut trees, which not being felled, but killed by girdling, had become entirely divested of bark even to the tips of the limbs, and now stood, in number two or three score, in height fifty or seventy-five feet, denuded, blanched, a resort for crows, where woodpeckers hammered and blue-linnets sung.

When Margaret had done her task, she was at liberty to repair the effect of Hash's spleen and attend to other little affairs of her own. Obed Wright, the son and only child of their only neighbor, was at hand to assist her. She had hops and virgin's bower trained up the side of the house, and even shading her chamber window. To prevent the ravages of hogs and geese, Chilion had fenced in a little spot for her near the house. Obed brought her new flowers from the woods, and instructed her how to plant them. He was thirteen or fifteen years of age, homely but clever, as we say, a tall, knuckled-jointed, shad-faced youth; his hair was red, his cheeks freckled; his hands and feet were immense, his arms long and stout. He suffered from near-sightedness. He was dressed like his neighbors, in a shirt and skilts, excepting that his collar and waistbands were fastened by silver buttons; and he wore a cocked hat. It seemed to please him to help Margaret, and he staid till almost sunset, when Hash came in from his work. Hash hated or spited Obed, partly on Margaret's account, partly because of misunderstandings with his mother, and partly from the perverseness of his own nature; and he annoyed him with the dog, who always growled and glared when he saw the boy. But Margaret stood between him and harm. In the present instance, she held the dog by the neck, till

Obed had time to run round the corner of the house and make his escape.

Margaret seated herself on the door-step to eat her supper, consisting of toasted brown bread and watered cider, served in a curiously wrought cherry-bowl and spoon. The family were taking their meal in the kitchen. The sun had gone down. The whippoorwill came and sat on the butternut, and sang his evening note, always plaintive, always welcome. The night-hawk dashed and hissed through the woods and the air on slim, quivering wings. A solitary robin chanted sweetly a long time from the hill. Myriads of insects revolved and murmured over her head. Crickets chirped in the grass and under the decaying sills of the house. She heard the voice of the waterfall at the Outlet, and the croaking of a thousand frogs in the Pond. She saw the stars come out, Lyra, the Northern Crown, the Serpent. She looked into the heavens, she opened her ears to the dim evening melodies of the universe ; yet as a child. She was interrupted by the sharp voice of her mother, " Go to your roost, Peggy ! "

" Yes, Molly dear," said her father, very softly, " Dick and Robin are asleep ; see who will be up first, you or the silver rooster ; who will open your eyes first, you or the dandelion ? "

" Kiss me Margery," said Chilion. She climbed into her chamber, she sank on her pallet, closed her eyes and fell into dreams of beauty and heaven, of other forms than those daily about her, of a sweeter voice than that of father or mother.

We conclude this chapter by remarking, that the scenes and events of this Memoir belong to what may be termed the mediæval or transition period of New England history, that lying between the close of the war of our Revolution and the commencement of the present century.

CHAPTER IV.

THE WIDOW WRIGHT.

MARGARET was up early in the morning, before the sun. She washed at the cistern and wiped herself on a coarse crash towel, rough, but invigorating, beautifying and healthy. She did her few chores, and, as she had promised, started for the Widow Wright's. Hash was getting ready his team, a yoke of starveling steers, in a tumbril cart, the wheels of which were formed from a solid block of wood. He set her in the cart, he desired to show his skill in driving, perhaps he wished to tease her on the way. "Haw! Buck, hish! Bright, gee up!" Vigorously plied he his whip of wood-chuck skin on a walnut stock. The cart reeled and rattled. It jolted over stones, canted on knolls, sidled into gutters. Margaret held fast by the stakes. "Good to settle your breakfast, Peggy. Going to see Obed, hey? and the Widder? ask her if she can cure the yallers in Bright." Margaret was victimized and amused by her brother. She half cried, half laughed. Her brother came at last to the lot he was engaged in clearing. He lifted Margaret from the cart. She went on, and Bull followed her. Hash called the dog back, and in great wrath gave him a blow with his whip. The animal leaped and skulked away, and joined again with Margaret, who patted his head as he ran along by her side. She entered woods; the path was narrow, grass-grown. She followed the cow-tracks through thickets of sweet fern almost as high as her head. The road descended to a brook crossed by a pole-bridge. The dog stopped to drink, she to look into the water, Minnows and pinheads were flashing and scudding through the clear, bright stream. There were hair-worms fabled to spring from horse-hair, in black lines writhing on the surface ; caddice-worms clothed with shells and leaves, crawling on the bottom ; and boat-flies swimming on their backs. The water made music with the stones. She waded in, and sported bare-foot on the slippery pebbles. She looked under the bridge, and that shaded spot had a mystery to the child's mind, such perhaps as is more remembered in future years than commented on at the time. She pursued a trout, that had shown its black eye and golden-spotted back and vanished. She could not find it. On she went towards Mrs. Wright's.

This lady had lost her husband a few years before. He left her in possession of a small farm, and a large reversion in the medicinal riches of the whole district. It had been a part of Dr. Wright's occupation to gather and prepare herbs for the sick. His *materia medica* was large, various and productive. He learnt as he could the nature of diseases, and was sometimes called to prescribe as well as sell his drugs. When he died his wife came in full possession of his secrets and his practice. She gathered plants from all the woods, sands and swamps. She knew the quality of every root, stalk, leaf, flower and berry. Her son Obed she was instructing to be her servitor and aid, as well as the successor of his father. The lady's habits were careful, saving, thriving. She cultivated, in addition, a few acres of land. Her house was neat and comfortable. It was a small frame building, clap-boarded on the sides and roof. It had a warm sunny position, on a southern slope, with rocks and woods behind. It stood in the centre of a large yard, surrounded on all sides by a fence of hemlock stumps, with their large, spreading, tangled roots, like the feet of giants, turned towards the street, making a grotesque but complete barrier. You entered the yard by a stile formed of the branches of these roots. Within the enclosure were beds of cultivated herbs, caraway, rue, savory, thyme, tansy, parsley and other aromatic and medicinal plants. Obed was at work among the beds. Margaret climbed the stile. Bull leaped up after her. When Obed saw Margaret his dull face emitted rays of joy which were succeeded by a cloud of dismay.

"Bull won't hurt you Obed. He's a good dog," said Margaret. "Put your hand on his head."

"He's a great dog," said Obed. "He's got dreadful big teeth. Hash's allers makin' him bite."

The dog taking no notice of these insinuations, retired to the shade of the fence. Margaret proceeded to assist Obed weed his beds, then she walked through the little aisles her kind friend treated with so much care. The atmosphere was charged with the perfume of the flowers. Margaret shook the thyme-bed, and a shadowy motion, like the waving of a cloud, floated over it. Bees, flies, beetles, butterflies, were bustling upon it, diving into every flower, and searching every cup.

"What d'ye think of the yarbs, Moll?" said the Widow, calling to Margaret from the door of the house.

"They look pretty," replied Margaret.

"Not looks, child, 'tis use. We'll get a hundred bunches, this year. The saffron we cut to-morrow, and the balm'll be ready soon."

"You are not going to cut all these flowers, are you?"

"Yes. Them's for medicine. Wait till the flowers is gone, they wouldn't be worth more'n your toad-flax and bean vines. They wouldn't fetch a bungtown copper. See here, that's sage, good for tea. That's goat's rue, good for women as has little babies. Guess you was a little baby once. I've known ye ever sen ye warn't more'n so high."

"Was I so little?" asked Margaret.

"Yes, and pimpin enough. An I fed yer marm with rue, and comfrey-root, or ye never'd come teu this. Ye was thin and poor as a late chicken."

The Widow Wright was dressed in the costume of the times, a white linen short-gown, checked apron and black petticoat. She wore on her head a large brown turban. Her eye was black and piercing, and she had a singular power of laughter, which was employed to express every variety of emotion, whether pleasure or pain, anger or complacence.

This lady possessed a fine colony of bees, and Margaret approached their house. These orderly and profitable busy-bodies seemed like a rain storm blowing from all points of the compass, and the child looked as if she was out in it. The ominous drops fell on her head, and she appeared to be catching some in the bare palm of her hand; some lit on her hat, and crawled over her neck. Not one offered her harm; she was not stung.

"A marvellous wonderful gal," uttered the Widow to herself, as she surveyed the scene from the door. "Pity 'tis she's Brown Moll's child."

Margaret had an errand, to get honey for a bee-hunt Chilion had in prospect, and stated her desire to Mrs. Wright. There was an old feud between the two families, not affecting intercourse and acquaintance, so much as matters of interest. The widow received the message rather coldly, and beginning in unwillingness, ended with invective

"He's a lazy, good for nothin' feller, Chil is. He's no better than a peakin' mud-sucker. He lives on us all here like house-leek. He's no more use than yer prigged up creepers. He is worse than the witches ; vervain nor dill won't keep him away. I tell ye, Chil shan't have no honey."

Margaret was abashed, silenced. She could understand that her brother would feel disappointed ; that he was not so bad. Beyond this she did not discriminate.

" Chilion is good," she stammered at last.

" Good ! what's he good for ? " rejoined the woman, " Does he get any money ? Can he find yarbs ? He don't know the difference between snake-root and lavender."

" He's good to me," said Margaret. This was an appeal that struck the woman with some force. She seemed to soften.

" Ye are a good child ; ye help Obed."

" Yes," said Margaret, as if watching her cue, " I will help Obed. I'll mind the beds when the birds are about. I'll go into the woods and get plants. I'll keep Bull off from him."

" Bein' ye'll help Obed, I'll give ye the honey. But don't come agin."

Margaret, taking the article in question on some green leaves, went merrily home.

We cannot dismiss this chapter without remarking that the Widow Wright revered the memory of her husband. It was certainly of some use for her to do so, as his reputation had been considerable in the line of his practice. The representation of the deceased, which she herself bore, she designed by degrees to transfer to her son. The silver buttons, which shone on Obed, as well as other articles of dress he occasionally wore, belonged to his late father. With all her thrift and care, the lady liked our Margaret very well. " She was so feat and spry, and knowin, and good-natered," she said, " she *could* be made of some use to somebody."

CHAPTER V.

THE BEE HUNT. — MARGARET GOES FARTHER INTO NATURE. — SHE SINS AND REPENTS. — THE MASTER.

THE next morning, Chilion and Margaret, joined by Obed, started on a bee-hunt. Obed was to remain with them till the chase was over, when Margaret promised to aid him in collecting plants for his mother. They took with them honey, leather mittens for the hands, screens for the face, brimstone and other requisites. They entered the woods lying to the south of the Pond, an unlimited range, extending in some directions many miles. The honey being placed on a stump, several bees, springing up as it were from vacuity, laded themselves with the fatal bait, and darted off. Our hunters pursued, watching the course of their flight, and were conducted by the unconscious guides to their own abode, a partially decayed tree. A few strokes of the axe brought it crashing to the ground. It was a more difficult task to possess themselves of the honey. The outraged and indignant insects spurted out from their nest like fire; their simultaneous start, their mixed and deepened huzz, their thousand wings beating as for life, made a noise not unlike a distant waterfall, or the hidden roar of an abyss. The persecutors speedily covered their faces and hands, and waited for the alarm to subside. Margaret said she thought they would not hurt her, as those at the Widow's did not. It is said there are some persons whom bees never sting. She kindled the brimstone each side of the tree. The bees within, called out by a rap on the trunk, and those without, flying and crawling about their nest, fell dead in the smoke. Chilion cut a passage to the cavity where the comb lay. Margaret, looking in, and seeing the beautiful chambers of these sylvan operatives seemed struck with remorse. She had eaten honey and honey-comb. She had seen bees, but she never had associated the two together in such a touching, domestic and artistical sense. She saw the bees lying dead in heaps. She had killed them. Some not quite dead, lay on their backs, their feet convulsed and arms quivering. Others were endeavoring to stretch their wings. She could render back no life ; she could set not a muscle in motion ; she could re-form not a filament of a wing. They would visit her flowers no more ; their hum would blend never again with the sounds she loved to hear. Whether the reflections of the child were just of this sort, order and proportion, we are not told. The bees were dead, and she was sad. She had seen dead squirrels, raccoons, partridges, pigeons. But they were *brought in* dead ; she had not killed them. What is the child's first sense of death? She would have given all her little heart was worth, could she restore the life she had so thoughtlessly taken, and see them again busy, blithe, happy about her house. Tears ran down her cheeks, the unconscious expiation of Nature to the Infinite Life. Chilion and Obed were apparently too much occupied to notice her agitation, nor would she have dared to speak to them of what she felt.

The tall gawky form of Obed went before through the woods. The lad's trousers, through which penetrated his lean dry shanks, gave him a semblance to a peasant of Gascony on stilts. His shovel hat skewed on this sideand that, and bobbed up and down among the branches. It was, as we might say, a new scene to Margaret. She had never gone so far into the forest before. She was susceptible in her feelings, and fresh as susceptible. The impression of the bees somewhat abated, though its remembrance could never be stifled. The woods, — where Adam and Eve enjoyed their pastime and sought their repose; where the Amorites and Assyrians learned to pray, and the Israelites to rebel; where all ancient nations found materials for sacrifice and offering; where Hertha, the Goddess of the Angles, had her lovely residence; where the Druids "thought every thing sent from Heaven that grew on the oak;" the religion and worship of the old Germans, Italians and Gauls; where Pan piped, the Satyrs danced, the Fauns browsed, Sylvanus loved, Diana hunted, and Feronia watched; whence Greek and Saracen, Pagan and Christian derived architecture, order, grace, capitals, groins, arches; whence came enchantment and power to Shakspeare, Milton, Wordsworth, Scott, Cooper, Bryant, Titian, Claude, Allston; where "the stately castle of the feudal lord reared its head, the lonely anchorite sang his evening hymn, and the sound of the convent bell was heard," and the fox and stag-hunter pursued their game; where Robin Hood and his merry men did their exploits, and king Rufus was slain; the enlivenment and decoration of the Feast of Tabernacles, May-day, Whitsuntide, Christmas; the ward of dryads, the scene of fairy revels, and Puck's pranks, the haunt of bul-beggars, witches, spirits, urchins, elves, hags, dwarfs, giants, the spoorn, the puckle, the man in the oak, will-o'-the-wisp; the opera-house of birds, the shelter of beasts, the retreat of mosquitoes and flies; where sugar was made, and coal burnt; where the report of the rifle was heard, and the stroke of the axe resounded; the home, manor, church, country, kingdom, hunting-ground and burial place of the Indian; the woods, green, sweet-smelling, imparadisaical, inspiring, suggestive, wild, musical, sombre, superstitious, devotional, mystic, tranquilizing;—these were about the child and over her.

That we must know in order to know, that we must feel in order to feel, was a truth Margaret but little realized. She was *beginning* to know and to feel. Could the Immortal Spirit of the Woods have spoken to her?—but she was not prepared for it; she was too young; she only felt an exhilarating sensation of variety, beauty, grandeur, awe. She leaped over roots, she caught at the spray above her head, she hid herself in thickets, she chased the birds. Yet with all that was new about her, and fitted to engross her vision, and supplant her recent sorrowful impressions, there seemed a new sense aroused, or active within her, an unconscious instinct, a hidden prompting of duty; she trod with more care than usual; a fly, beetle, or snail, she turned aside for, or stepped protectingly over; she would not jostle a spider's web.

"It won't hurt ye," said Obed. "It brings good weather."

"I know that," replied Margaret, "but I don't want to kill it.

Obed was homely and clever, as we have said, simple and trusting. He never argued a point with Margaret; he was glad to have her help him, and glad to help her. He held back the low branches for her to pass, he assisted her over slippery trunks, he lifted her across the narrow deep stream of Mill Brook. He brandished his spade, and said he would keep off the snakes; Margaret replied that she was not afraid of them. They came to a sunny glade in the woods, tufted with black and white moss, shaded by huckle-berry shrubs, and sown with checker-berries, whose fruit hung in round crimson drops, and little waxen flowers bloomed under the dark shining leaves. Margaret sat down and ate the sweet berries and their spicy leaves. The shadows of the forest vibrated and flickered on the yellow leaf-strewed earth and through the green underwood ; the trunks of the trees shot up, in straight, rough, tapering stems clear through to the sky.

This particular patch of woods was of great age, and the trees were very large, and the effect on Margaret's mind was like that of a child going into St. Peter's church at Rome. But there were no bronze saints here to look down on her ; a red squirrel, as she came in sight, raised a loud shrill chattering, a singular mixture of contempt, welcome and alarm. She made some familar demonstrations towards the little fellow, and he, like a jilt, dropped a nut into her face. She saw a brown cat-headed owl asleep, muffled in his dark feathers and darker dreams, and called Obed's attention to it.

"That's an owl," cried the startled lad ; "it's a bad sign ; Marm says it will hurt."

"No," replied Margaret ; I've seen them on the Butternut a good many times." Knowing that as Obed never reasoned so he could never be persuaded, Margaret joined him in leaving the ominous vicinage.

"That's saxifax," said her companion, striking his spade into the roots of a well-known shrub. "It's good teu chaw ; the Settlers eats it—take it down, and they'll give ye ribbons and beads for it." Wisping the top together, and bending it over, he bade Margaret hold on, while he proceeded with the digging. The light black mould was removed, and the reddish damp roots disclosed. "Taste on't," he said, "it's good as nutcakes." Margaret loitered, wandered, attracted by the flowers she stopped to pick. "Marm won't let us," said Obed, "them ant yarbs, they won't doctor, the Settlers won't touch them. Margaret, whether convinced or not, yielded, and ran on before, apparently the most anxious to discover the plants desired.

"That's um!" cried Obed.

Margaret was bounding through a wet bog, springing from one tussock of sedge to another. She, too, had espied it, and in sight of its beauty and novelty forgot every thing else. It was a wake-robin, commonly known as dragon-root, devil's ear, or Indian turnip. Margaret broke off the flower, which she would have carried to her nose.

"Don't ye taste on't!" exclaimed Obed, "it's orful burnin; put it in the basket." So the plant, flower and all, were deposited with the rest of their collection.

It was time to go home. They had reached the edge of the woods whence they started.

"That's him!" cried Margaret, clapping her hands.

"It's the Master!" echoed Obed, quite disconcerted.

There appeared before them a man, the shadow of whom they had seen among the leaves, about fifty years of age, and dressed in the full style of the times, or we should say of his own time, which dated a little earlier than that of Margaret. He wore a three-cornered hat, with a very broad brim tied with a black ribbon over the top. His coat, of drab kerseymere, descended in long, broad, square skirts, quite to the calves of his legs. It had no buttons in ront, but in lieu thereof, slashes, like long button holes, and laced with silk embroidery. He had on nankeen small-clothes, white ribbed silk stockings, paste knee and shoe buckles, and white silk knee-bands. His waistcoat, or vest, was of yellow embossed silk, with long skirts or lappels, rounded and open at the bottom, and bordered with white silk fringe. The sleeves and skirts of his coat were garnished with rows of silver buttons. He wore ruffle cuffs that turned back over his wrists and reached almost to his elbows; on his neck was a snow-white linen plaited stock, fastened behind with a large silver buckle, that glistened above the low collar of his coat. Under his hat appeared a gray wig, falling in rolls over his shoulders, and gathered behind with a black ribbon. From his side depended a large gold watch-seal and key, on a long gold chain. He had on a pair of tortoise-shell bridge spectacles. A golden-headed cane was thrust under his arm. This was Mr. Bartholomew Elliman, the Schoolmaster, or the Master, as he was called. He was tall in person, had an aquiline nose, and a thin face.

"Ha, my Hamadryad!" said he, addressing Margaret; "salutem et pacem; in other words, how do you do, my girl of the woods?"

"Pretty well, thankee," replied Margaret.

"I thank you, Sir," said he, amending her style of expression.

"I forgot," she added, "pretty well, I thank you, Sir."

He nodded to Obed, who stood aloof in awkward firmness; besides there were signs of uneasiness or displeasure on the faces of both.

"How came the Pond Lily in the woods?" said he.

"I am after herbs," replied Margaret; "and I have some flowers too," added she, taking off her hat.

"Flowers, have you? You are a noble specimen of foliacious amfractuosity — a hortus siccus of your hat! Would I could send you and your flowers across the waters to my friend, Mr. Knight, the great botanist, nox semperlucens."

"He shan't hurt Molly," interrupted Obed. "He'll drown her, he'll pull her teu pieces. Marm says he spiles every thing. He wants to pitch Molly into the Pond."

"Don't be alarmed, my glandulous champion, no harm shall come to this fair flower."

"He 'll git um all, Molly; don't ye let him have any."

"I tell you," responded the Master, "Margaret is a flower; she is my flower."

"She an't a flower," rejoined Obed, "she 's Pluck's Molly."

Obed became quite excited, and spake with more than his customary freedom. It needs perhaps to be explained, that Master Elliman and the Widow Wright were somewhat at odds. He was in pursuit of science, she of gain. They took a common track, plants and flowers; their ends essentially diverged. They frequently encountered, but they could never agree. Margaret herself was another point of issue, the Widow being jealous of the child's attachment to the Master. The impression that Obed on the whole derived, was, that he was an evil-disposed person, and one whose presence boded no good to Margaret.

The Master proceeded in the examination of the flowers Margaret gave him.

"I have another one," said she; and thrusting her hand into Obed's basket, drew out the wake-robin.

"An Arum!" said the Master, "the very thing I have been written to upon."

"Tan't yourn, Molly; it's Marm's," said Obed, seizing the flower and replacing it in the basket.

Here was, indeed, a mistake. Margaret had unreflectingly given the flower to Obed to carry, at the same time thinking it belonged to herself. She did not know the value attached to it by Obed, whose mother had enjoined him to get one if possible, for some particular purpose of her own. At last she said, —

"I can get more; I know where they grow."

"Can you, can you?" said the Master, "their habitat is sphagnous places, what you call swamps. It is impossible for me to reach them. Stultiloquent yarb-monger!" he broke out, speaking of or to Obed; "son of a helminthic android! you ought to be capistrated."

"That's hocuspocus, Molly," said the lad: "Marm says 'tis. He 'll hurt ye, he 'll hurt ye."

"I will get some for both of you," said Margaret; "I will go to-morrow."

"You don't know the way," rejoined Obed, "snakes 'll bite ye; there's painters in the woods, and wild cats, and owls."

"I 'll take Bull with me," answered Margaret.

This allusion to the dog renewed Obed's trouble. He feared his mother, who he thought would not wish the Master should have the flower; he dreaded the dog, he disliked the Master, he loved Margaret; he *was* in a quandary. He stammered, he tried to laugh, he put his hand on Margaret's head, he yerked up his trousers, he looked into his basket. He leaned against a tree, and dropped his face upon his arm. Margaret ran to him, and took hold of his hand. "Don't cry Obed," she said; "poor Obed, don't cry."

The Master, seeing the extremity of affairs, told Margaret not to care, that he presumed she would be able to get the flower for him, and took her hand to lead her away. She clung to Obed, or he to her, wholly enveloping her little hand, wrist and all, in his great fist. Thus linked, sidling, skewing, filing as they could through the trees and brush, they soon emerged in the road. The Master went on with them to the house, and Obed continued his course homeward. Master Elliman was evidently not a stranger to the family. His visit seemed welcome. Even the hard muddy features of Hash brightened with a smile as he entered. The dry, pursed mouth of the mother yielded a pleasant salutation. Chilion offered the best chair.—Pluck was always merry. Margaret alone for the moment, contrary to her general manner, appeared sorrowful.

CHAPTER VI.

WHY MARGARET WAS SORROWFUL. — DREAMS. — LIVINGSTON.— A GLIMPSE AT "THE WORLD." — ISABEL. — NIGHT AND OTHER SHADOWS.

After dinner, hospitable as it was rude, of which the Master partook with sensible relish, Pluck proposed that Chilion should play.

"The rosin, Margery," said her brother.

"I have some rosin in my pocket," said the Master, at the same time producing a pint flask, which he set upon the table. "A bibilous accompaniment," he added, "I thought would not be out of place."

"Good enough for any of their High Mightinesses!" ejaculated Pluck, drinking, and returning the bottle to the Master.

"Nay, friend," replied the latter; "Femina et vinum make glad the heart of man. Let her ladyship gladden her own."

Mistress Hart also drank.

"Now, he who maketh speed to the spoil, Maharshalal-hashbaz," said the Master.

"Not so good as pupelo," replied Hash.

"A rightly named youth," said Pluck, who, receiving the bottle to return it to the Master, perceived its contents nearly exhausted.

"Mea discipula," said the Master, addressing himself to Margaret, "you must be primarum artium princeps."

"No thankee, — thank you sir," replied she.

"Well done, well done!" exclaimed he,

"What! would you not have the child exhilirate and spruce up a little?" cried the father.

"You mistake me, friend," said the Master, "I approbated the girl, not that she did not receive this very genial beverage, but that she manifests such improvement in speech."

"Let her drink, and she will speak well enough," rejoined her father. "She won't touch it! She mopes, she nuzzles about in the grass and chips. She is certainly growing weakling. Only she sings roung after dark, like a thrasher, and picks up spiders and pismires, like a frog."

"This is none of your snow-broth, Peggy," said the mother, "it's warming, it's as good as the Widow's bitter-bags."

"Don't you touch it," said Chilion, who had been screwing and snapping the strings of his violin.

"Yes, drink Peggy," said Hash, thrusting his slavery lips close to her ear. "He'll bring some more, he likes ye. He wants ye too."

Margaret started from him. "I can't," she said; "it won't let me."

"What won't let you, dear?" asked her father, drawing her between his knees, and patting her head.

"She's always a dreaming," said her mother; "she is a born bat, and flies off every night nobody knows where. And in the day time I can't get her to quilling, but she's up and away to the Widow's, or to the Pond, or on the Head. She gets all my threads to string up her poses; she's as bad as a hang bird that steals my yarn on the grass."

"Did'nt I do all the spools?" inquired the child.

"You did indeed," responded the father, "you are a nice gal. Hush! Let us hear our son Chilion; he speaks well."

Chilion played, and they were silent.

"Now it's your turn, my daughter," said Pluck, "you will play if you won't drink."

Margaret taking the instrument executed some popular airs with considerable spirit and precision. "Now for the cat, child;" so she imitated the cat, then the song-sparrow, then Obed crying.

At this, and especially the last, there was a general shout. The Master seemed highly surprised and pleased. "A megalopsical child!" he exclaimed. Margaret with blushes and tremors, glad to have succeeded, more glad to escape her tormentors, ran away and amused herself with her squirrel, whom she was teaching to ride on the dog's back. The flask having been drained, the keg was brought forward from the chimney wall.

"Here's to Miss Amy," said Pluck, ogling the Master.

"Mehercule!" exclaimed the latter, "you forget the propitiatory oblation. We must first propose his Majesty the King of Puppetdom, defender by the grace of God of England, France, and America; the most serene, serene, most puissant, puissant, high, illustrious, noble, honorable, venerable, wise and prudent Princes, Burgomasters, Councillors, Governors, Committees of said realm, whether ecclesiastical or secular; and the most celebrated Punch and Judy of our worthy town of Livingston, Parson Welles and Deacon Hadlock, to whom be all reverence."

Pluck. "Amen. I stroke my beard and crook my hamstrings as low as any one."

The Master. "Your promising daughter, Mistress Hart."

Mis. Hart. "Long life to you, and many visits from you."

Hash. "I say yes to that; and here's for Peggy to Obed."

The Master. "Miss Sibyl Radney."

"How you color, Hash!" exclaimed his mother.— "Hang your nose under your chin, and it would equal old

Gobbler's wattles. Put you into the dye-tub and Peggy won't have to get any more log-wood. There now she must go down for some copperas this very afternoon."

"Odzbodkins! You won't spoil our sport," cried her husband. "Your crotchets are always coming in like a fox into a hen-roost."

"I have work in hand that must be done," replied his wife. "Trencher worm!" she exclaimed, raising her voice with her fist, "what do you do? lazying about here like a mud-turtle nine days after it's killed. You may whip the cat ten years, and you won't earn enough to stitch your own rags with.—I have to tie up your vines, or you would have been blown from the poles long since."

"Dearest Maria," began Pluck.

"Don't deary me," said Brown Moll; "you had better go to washing dishes, and I'll take care of the family."

While Mistress Hart was entertaining her spouse in this manner, for it seemed to be entertainment to him, the Master called Margaret and asked her to spell some words he put to her, which she did very correctly. "You must certainly have a new spelling-book," said he. "And now I want you to repeat the 'Laplander's Ode.'"

She began as follows:—

I.

"Kulnasatz, my rein-deer,
We have a long journey to go;
The moors are vast,
And we must haste;
Our strength, I fear,
Will fail if we are slow;
And so
Our song will do.

II.

"Kaigé, the watery moor,
Is pleasant unto me,
Though long it be;
Since it doth to my mistress lead,
Whom I adore:
The Kilwa moor
I ne'er again will tread."

The Master, having expressed his delight at this, said he must return to the village.

"I will go with you," added Margaret.

"Here are the eggs," so her mother instructed her, "Deacon Penrose must give a shilling a dozen. One pound of copperas, six skeins of No. Nine, half a pound of snuff, the rest in tobacco."

Margaret, wearing in addition to her usual dress a pair of moccasons which an Indian who came sometimes to the Pond gave her, called Bull and started off. Hash, in no unusual fit, ordered the dog back.

"Woman! woman!" cried Pluck, "the keg is out, it is all gone."

"Let the yarn go," said her mother, "and get it in rum."

"She will bring home some of the good book," said Pluck to Hash, "the real white-eye, you know. Let her take the dog."

Her brother yielded, and she went on with Bull and the Master; the latter, having grown a little wavering and muddled by liquor, taking the child's hand.

There were two ways to the village, one around by No. 4, the other more direct through the woods; the distance by the former was nearly four miles, by the latter, as we have said, about two; and at the present season of the year it was the most eligible. This they took; they went through the Mowing, traversed a beautiful grove of walnuts, black-birches, and beeches, and came to the Foot-bridge made of a large tree lying across the small brook Margaret encountered on her way to the Widow's. This stream, having its rise among the hills on the north of the Pond, at the present point, flowed through a deep fissure in the rocks. The branches of the tree rose perpendicularly, and a hand rail was fastened from one to another.

"Danger menaces us, my child," sighed the Master.

"Give me one of your hands," said Margaret, "hold on by the rail with the other, shut your eyes, that is the way Pa does."

"How it shakes!" exclaimed the Master. "It would be dreadful to fall here! How deep it is! My head swims, my brain giddies, I am getting old, Margaret. Tempora mutantur et nos. When I was young as you I could go any where. Facilis descensus—."

"You can hold on by Bull, he'll keep you steady. Here, Bull."

The well-trained dog came forward, and the Master leaning on this tri-fold support, the child's arm, the rail, and the animal's head, accomplished the pass. Their course was downward, yet with alternate pitches and elevations, now by a sheep's track, now across a rocky ledge, anon through the unbroken forest. The fumes of the liquor subsiding, and the path becoming more smooth and easy, the Master spake to Margaret of her dreams.

Master. "Dreams come of a multitude of business, says Solomon."

Margaret. "What, Solomon Smith? He says that great folks come of dreams, that children will die, and some be rich; and people lose their cows, and have new gowns, and such things. I dream about a great many things, sometimes about a pretty woman."

Mas. "A pretty woman! Whom does she look like?"

Mar. "I don't know, I can't tell him."

Mas. "*You;* always say you to me. The juveniles and younkers in the town say him. How does she seem to you?"

Mar. "She looks somehow as I feel when Ma is good to me, and she looks pale and sorry as Bull does when Hash strikes him."

Mas. "Where do you see her?"

Mar. "Sometimes among the clouds, and sometimes at the foot of the rainbow."

Mas. "That is where money grows."

Mar. "Not money, it is flowers, buttercups, yellow columbine, liverleaf, devil's ears, and such as I never saw before."

Mas. "Arum, the Arum! Your covetous friend Obed won't like it if you get those flowers."

Mar. "His mother wants to know what the woman does; if she makes plasters out of the flowers, and if they will cure worms."

Mas. "Caustics of aures diaboli! The Devil is no vermifuge, tell the Widow. Ha! ha!"

Mar. "But she don't speak to me; she stands on the flowers, and breaks them off, and they fly away like little birds; she pricks them into the rainbow, and they grow on it."

Mas. "Are you not afraid of her?"

Mar. "She tells me not to be."

Mas. "You said she did not speak to you."

Mar. "She don't speak, but she tells me things, just as Bull does. He don't speak, but he tells me when he is hungry, and when there is any thing coming in the woods. Sometimes she kisses me, but I don't feel her. She goes up on the rainbow, and I follow her. I see things like people's faces in the sky, but they look like shadows, and there is music like what you hear in the pines, but there are no trees or violins. She steps off into the clouds. I try to go too, and there comes along what you call the egret of a thistle, that I get on to, and it floats with me right into my bed, and I wake up." So they discoursed until they issued from the woods, in what was known as "Deacon Hadlock's Pasture," an extensive enclosure reaching to the village, which it overlooked.

The village of Livingston lay at the junction of four streets, or what had originally been the intersection of two roads, which, widening at the centre, and having their angles trimmed off, formed an extensive common known as the Green. In some points of view, the place had an aspect of freshness and nature; extensive forests meeting the eye in every direction; farm-houses partially hidden in orchards of apple-trees; the roads rough, ungraded, and divided by parallel lines of green grass. Yet to one who should be carried back from the present time, many objects would wear an old, antiquated and obsolete appearance; the high-pitched roofs of some of the houses, and jutting upper stories; others with a long sloping back roof; chimneys like castles, large, arched, corniced. Here and there was a house in the then new style, three-storied, with gambrel roof and dormar windows. The Meeting-house was not old, but would now appear so, with its slim, tall spire, open belfrey, and swarm of windows. There were Lombardy poplars on the Green, now so unfashionable, waving like martial plumes; and interspersed as they were among the spreading willow-like elms, they formed on the whole not a disagreeable picture. South of the Green was the "Mill" on Mill Brook, before adverted to; this was a distinct cluster of houses. Beyond the village on the east you could see the River, and its grassy meadows.

Livingston was the shire town of the county of Stafford, having a Court-house, square yellow edifice with a small bell in an open frame on the roof; and a Jail, a wooden building constructed of hewn timber. The Green contained in addition a pair of Stocks, a Pillory and Whipping Post; also, a store, school-house tavern, known as the "Crown and Bowl," and barber's shop. The four streets diverging from the centre were commonly called the North, East, South, and West Streets. A new one had been opened on the west side of the Green, and received the name of Grove Street. Let us observe the situation of the principal buildings. The Meeting-house stood at the north-west corner of the Green; in the rear of this were the Horse-sheds, a long and conspicuous row of black, rickety stalls, having the initials of the owner's name painted in a circle over each apartment; at the east end of the sheds was the School-house; and behind them terminated an old forest that extended indefinitely to the north. The Tavern occupied the corner formed by the junction of the West street with the Green, a few rods from the church. Below the tavern, flanking the west side of the Green, in succession, were the Court-house, Jail, and Jail-house, the jail-fence being close upon the highway. The Pillory with its adjuncts stood under the trees in the open common fronting the Court-house.

Master Elliman lodged with the Widow Small, who lived on the South Street. In this street reappeared the small stream they had so much trouble in crossing; to which, we may add, the Master, from some fancy of his own, gave the name Cedron; and the path by which they came through the woods he called Via Dolorosa.

Children were playing on the Green, the boys dressed in "tongs," a name for pantaloons or overalls that had come into use, and roundabouts; some in skirt coats and breeches; some of them six or eight years of age were still in petticoats. The girls wore checked linen frocks, with short sleeves, and pinafores. All were bare-footed and most of them bare-headed. "He's coming!" "The Master!" was a cry that echoed from one to another. They dropped their sports, and drew up in lines on either side as the object of their attention passed; the boys folding their arms and making short quick bows; the girls dove-tailing their fingers and squatting in low courtesies. Margaret, with Bull at her heels, kept at a respectful distance behind. "Moll Hart," exclaimed one of the boys. "A Pond Gal." "An Injin, an Injin." "Where did you get so much hat?" "Did your daddy make them are clogs?" So she was saluted by one and another; but the dog, whose qualities were obvious in his face, if they had not been rendered familiar in any other way, saved her from all but verbal insolence.

The Master's was a ground room in an old house. It was large, with small windows; the walls were wainscoted, the ceiling boarded, and darkened by age into a reddish mahogany hue. The chairs were high-top, fan-back, heavy, mahogany. A bureau desk occupied one side, with its slanting leaf, pigeon-holes, and escutcheons bearing the head of King George. On the walls hung pictures in small black frames, comprising all the kings and queens of England, from William the Conqueror to the present moment. Margaret's attention was drawn to his books, which consisted of editions of the Latin and Greek classics, and such school books as from time to time he had occasion to use ; and miscellanies, made up of works on Free-Masonry, a craft of which he was a devoted member ; books of secular and profane music, a science to which he was much attached ; various histories and travels ; the works of Bolingbroke, Swift and Sterne ; the Spectator and Rambler, the principal English Poets ; Wolstoncraft's Rights of Women, Paine's Age of Reason, Lord Monboddo's works ; Tooke's Pantheon ; Burton's Anatomy of Melancholy ; the Echo, by the Hartford Wits, the American Museum, and the Massachusetts Magazine ; Trumbull's McFingal, The Devil on Two Sticks, Peregrine Pickle ; Quincy's Dispensatory ; Nurse Freelove's New Year's Gift, the Puzzling Cap, the "World turned upside down." He gave Margaret, as he had promised, "The New Universal Spelling Book," by "Daniel Fenning, late School master of the Bures in Suffolk, England."

The Store, to which Margaret next directed her steps, was a long old two-story building, bearing some vestiges of having once been painted red. The large window-shutters and door constituted advertising boards for the merchant himself, and the public generally. Intermixed with articles of trade, were notices of animals found, or astray ; sales on execution ; beeswax, flax, skins, bristles and old pewter, you were informed would be taken in exchange for goods, and that "cash and the highest price would be given for the Hon. Robert Morris's notes." One paper read as follows : "You, Josiah Penrose, of, &c., are hereby permitted to sell 400 gallons W. I. Rum, do. Brandy, 140 Gin, and 260 pounds of brown Sugar, on all of which the excise has been duly paid, pursuant to an Act of the Legislature.

(Signed) } Collector of excise for the
WILLIAM KINGSLAND, } County of Stafford."

There was also on the door a staring programme of a lottery scheme. Lotteries, at this period common in all New England, had become a favorite resort for raising money to support government, carry on wars, build churches, construct roads, or endow colleges. There was one other sign, that of the Post-office. Entering the store you beheld a motley array of dry and fancy goods, crockery, hardware, and groceries, drugs and medicines. On the right were rolls of kerseymeres, callimancoes, fustians, shaloons, antiloons, and serges of all colors ; Manchester checks, purple and blue calicoes ; silks, ribbons, oznaburgs ticklenbergs, buckram. On the left were cuttoes, Barlow knives, iron candlesticks, jewsharps, blackball, bladders of snuff ; in the left corner was the apothecary's apartment, and on boxes and bottles were written in fading gilt letters, "Ens Veneris," "Oculi Cancrorum," "Aqua æris fixi," "Lapis Infernalis," "Ext. Saturn," "Sal Martis," &c. On naked beams above were suspended weavers' skans, wheelheads, &c., and on a high shelf running quite around the walls was cotton warp of all numbers. The back portion of the building was devoted to a traffic more fashionable and universal in New England than it ever will be again ; and a long row of pipes, hogsheads and barrels, indicated its extent. Above these hung proof-glasses, tap-borers, a measuring rod, and decanting pump ; interspersed on the walls were bunches of chalk-scores in perpendicular and transverse lines. Near by was a small counter covered with tumblers and toddy sticks ; and when Margaret entered, one or two ragged will-gill looking men stood there mixing and bolting down liquors. Had she looked into the counting-room, she would have seen a large fireplace in one corner, a high desk, round-back arm-chairs, and several hampers of wine.

Margaret sat waiting for two young ladies, who appeared to have some business with the clerk. These were Bethia Weeks, the daughter of one of the village squires, and Martha Madeline Gisborne, the daughter of the joiner. The clerk's name was Abel Wilcox.

"For my part," said Miss Bethia, "I don't believe a word of it."

"He has kept steady company with her every time he has been in town," responded Miss Martha Madeline.

"As if every upstart of a lawyer was to Captain Grand it over all the girls here," added the clerk.

"I don't think the Judge's folk are better than some other people's folk," said Martha Madeline.

"Susan is a nice girl," rejoined Bethia.

"I should not be surprised if they were cried next Sabbath," said Martha Madeline.

"I guess there will be more than one to cry then," added Bethia.

"Now don't; you are really too bad," rejoined Abel.

This conversation continuing some time, was unintelligible to Margaret, as we presume it is to our readers, and it were idle to report it.

"How much shall I measure you of this tiffany, Matty?" at length asked Abel.

"Perhaps I shall not take any now," replied the young lady. "You give three shillings for cotton cloth, and this is nine and six, a yard; I declare for't I shall have to put to; and I must get some warp at any rate. We have been waiting for some we sent up to Brown Moll's to be colored, and I don't think it will ever be done."

"There's young Moll, now," said Abel, pointing to Margaret.

"Has your Marm got that done?" asked Martha Madeline.

"She has not," replied Margaret.

"A book, a book!" exclaimed the same young lady. "The Injin has got a book. She will be wise as the Parson."

"Can you say your letters?" asked Bethia.

"Yes," answered Margaret.

"Who is teaching you?"

"The Master."

"Pshaw!" ejaculated Martha Madeline, "I never was at school in my life. Now all the gals is going; such as can't tell treadles from treacle have got books. And here the Master goes up to that low, vile, dirty place, the Pond, to larn the brats."

Margaret came forward and stated her errand to the clerk.

"Yes, I dare say, she wants rum," added Martha Madeline. "Daddy says there is no sense in it; they will all come to ruin; he says Pluck and his boys drink five or six glasses a day, and that nobody should think of drinking more than three. Parson Welles says it's *a sin* for any family to have more than a gallon a week. There's Hopestill Cutts, he has been kept out of the church this ten months because he won't come down to half a pint a day."

"Never mind," interposed the clerk, "I guess they will find their allowance *cut* short this time, ha! ha! Here ain't eggs enough, gal."

"Ma'm says you must give a shilling a dozen," replied Margaret.

"Perhaps your Marm will say that again before we do," rejoined the clerk. "Eggs don't go for but ninepence in Livingston or any where else."

Margaret was in a dilemma; — the rum must be had, the other articles were equally necessary.

"Pa will pay you," she bethought herself.

"No he won't," answered the clerk.

"Chilion will bring you down skins, axe-helves, and whip-stocks."

"I tell you, we can't and won't trust you. Your drunken dad has run up a long chalk already. Look there, I guess you know enough to count twelve;—twelve gallons he owes now. You are all a haggling, gulching, good-for-nothing crew."

"I will bring you chesnuts and thistle down in the fall," replied Margaret.

"Can't trust any of you. What will you take for your book?"

"I can't sell it; the Master gave it to me."

"If he would teach you to pay your debts he would do well."

A little girl came in about the age of Margaret, and stood looking attentively at her a moment, as one stranger child is wont to do with another; then lifting Margaret's hat as it were inspecting her face, said, "She is not an Injin; they said she was; her face is white as mine." This little girl was Isabel Weeks, sister of Bethia.

"Ha, Belle!" said the latter, "what are you here for?"

"I came to see the Injin. Have you got a book too?" she said, addressing herself to Margaret. "Can you say your letters?"

"Yes," replied Margaret, "but they want it for rum."

"That's wicked; I know it is. Ma wouldn't let me give my spelling-book for rum. I have threepence in my pocket—you may have them."

"Save a thief from hanging and he will cut your throat," said Martha Madeline.

"Can't bore an auger hole with a gimlet," interjected Abel; "two threepences won't be enough, Miss Belle."

"Judah has got tenpence, I'll go and get them," answered Isabel.

The dog at this moment seeing the trouble of his mistress began to growl and the young ladies to scream.

"Out with your dog, young wench, and go home," cried the clerk.

"Lie down Bull!" said Margaret. "Here, sir, you may have the book."

The bargain being completed, Margaret took her articles, and left the store; and Isabel followed her.

The two children went across the Green in silence. Isabel said nothing, but with her pinafore wiped the tears from Margaret's eyes. She was too young, perhaps, to tell all she felt, and could only alleviate the grief she beheld by endeavoring to efface its effects.

Margaret, happy, unhappy, fagged up the hill; she had lost her book, she had got the rum; she was miserable herself, she knew her family would be pleased; yet she was wholly sad when she thought of the Master and then of her book. She left the highway and crossed the Pasture. The sun had gone down when she reached the woods; she feared not; her dreams, her own fresh heart, and the dog were with her. The shadow of God was about her, but she knew Him or It not; she was ignorant as a Hottentot. She came to the bridge; the water ran deep and dark below her. Who will look into her soul as she looked into the water? Who will thread the Via Dolorosa of her spirit. For the music, the murmurs of that brook, there were no ears, as there were none for hers. Yet *she* looked into the water, which seemed to hiss and race more merrily over the stones as she looked. She heard owls and frogs; and she might almost have heard the tread of the saturnine wood-spider, at work in his loom with his warp-tail and shuttle-feet, working a weft which the dews were even then embroidering, to shine out when the sun rose in silver spangles and ruby buds ; and her own soul, woven as silently in God's loom, was taking on impressions from those dark woods, that invisible universe, to shine out when her morning dawns. Alas ! when shall that be ; in this world, in the next ? Is there any place *here* for a pure beautiful soul ? If none, then let Margaret die. Or shall we let her murmur on, like the brook, in hopes that *some one* will look into her waters and be gladdened by her sound ? She ran on through the Chesnuts, the strange old bald trees seeming to move as she moved, those more distant shooting by the others in rapid lines, performing a kind of spectral pantomime. Run on, Margaret ! and let the world dance round you as it may.

When she reached home, she found the family all a-bed, excepting Chilion, who was sitting in the dark, patiently, perhaps doggedly, waiting for her.

He gave her somewhat to eat, and she went to bed, and to that forgetfulness which kind Nature vouchsafes to the most miserable.

CHAPTER VII.

RETROSPECTIVE AND EXPLANATORY.

At this day of comparative abstinence and general sobriety, one is hardly prepared to receive the accounts that might be given of the consumption of intoxicating liquors in former times. In the Old World, drinking was cultivated as an Art; it was patronized by courtiers, it fellowshipped with rustics; it belonged to the establishment, and favored dissent; it followed in the wake of colonial migration, and erected its institutions in the New World. Contemporary with the foundation, it flourished with the growth and dilated with the extension of this Western Empire. Herein comes to pass a singular historical inversion; what we rigorously denounce as "distilled damnation," the Puritans cheerily quaffed under the names of "Strong Water," and "Aqua Vitæ." While we expel rum from our houses as a pestilence, an earlier age was wont to display it with picturesque effect, and render it attractive by environments of mahogany and silver.

In Livingston there were five distilleries for the manufacture of cider-brandy, or what was familiarly known as pupelo. There was also consumed a proportionate quantity of alcoholic liquors of other kinds. The amount annually required for a population of about twelve hundred could not have been less than six thousand gallons. It found its way into every family, loaded many sideboards, filled innumerable jugs; all denominations of men bowed to its supremacy. In the account kept with Parson Welles at Deacon Penrose's, rum composed at least one half the items. Master Elliman, as we have seen, was not exempt from the habits of his age. He drank constantly, and at times excessively. To the cheer prevailing at the Pond he was no stranger. His botanical excursions were enlivened and relieved by the humor of Pluck and the liberality of his entertainment. There were other causes operating to bring together these two persons of qualities and manners in some respects so apparently opposed. On these we must beg the patience of the reader while we briefly delay.

The first permanent settlement in Livingston was effected in the year 1677, at the close of the war of King Philip or Pometacom, the chief of the Wampanoags. The original inhabitants came partly from the old colonies, and were reënforced by migrations direct from Europe. A one-story log-house with thatched roof constituted the primitive church edifice; a tin horn, in place of a bell, being used to summon the people to worship. What is now known as the Green early became the centre of the town, and on the four streets before mentioned many of the planters established themselves. The town underwent and survived the various incidents and vicissitudes that belong to our national history; Queen Anne's war, Lovell's war, the Seven Years' war, incursions from the Indians, drafts of men for the frontiers, small-pox, throat-distemper, Antinomianism, New-lightism, Scotch Presbyterianism, an attempted "visit from Whitefield," settling ministers, the stamp-act, succession of sovereigns, kings in England, governors at home, earthquakes, tornadoes, depreciation of currency, taxes, etc., etc. A period of more exciting interest approached. The question of a final separation from the mother country engaged all minds. Committees of Safety, Inspection, Vigilance or Correspondence, whatever they might be called, were formed in every village; these cöperated with the County Committees, which in their turn became auxiliary to those of the State. "The towns," say our historians, "assumed, in some respects, the authority of an individual community, an independent republic. The Committee met daily and acted in a legislative, executive and judicial capacity. All suspicious persons were brought before them, and if found guilty were condemned." "Numerous arrests, imprisonments and banishments were made." "The Committee was empowered to use military force. Many tories and their families were expelled the State, and others required to give security to reside in prescribed limits; and occasionally the jails, and even the churches, were crowded with prisoners, and many were sent for safe-keeping to the jails of neighboring States." An "Association," as it was termed, covenant, or oath, was prepared and offered for the signatures of the people of Livingston. The sessions of the court, which had been interrupted elsewhere, received little or no disturbance in this town. Judge Morgridge, a resident of the place, who received his commission under the king, and faithfully administered the old laws of the State, was equally devoted to the interests of the people. News of the battle of Lexington had arrived; Tony, the negro barber, fiddler and drummer, had gone through the streets at midnight, sounding alarms from time to time.

Court week came, and in addition to such scenes as for many years had characterized that occasion—huckstering, wrestling, horse-racing—at the present moment there assembled great quantities of people, from Livingston itself, and the neighboring towns, who were animated by unusual topics. There was little business for the functionaries of law, and more for the officers of the people. The County Committee was in session. Numbers of delinquents were brought from various parts, and lodged in the jail. The Crown and Bowl was filled with people, among whom was Pluck. While others were drinking to the Continental Congress, he toasted the king; when rebuked, he replied in some wanton language. This, in addition to other conduct of a suspicious nature, exposed him to the action of the Committee, before which he was taken; that body consisting in part of his fellow-townsmen, Deacon Hadlock and Mr. Gisborne the joiner. The proceedings in his case may be known by the subjoined extract from the records:—

"*Livingston, August 28th,* 1775.

"Didymus Hart being summoned to this Committee, on the information of sundry witnesses, that the said Hart on the 27th day of this month, had violated the laws of the Continental and Provincial Congress, and done other acts contrary to the liberties of the country, appeared, and after due proof being made of said charge, the said Hart was pleased to make a full confession thereof, and in the most equivocal and insulting manner attempted to vindicate said conduct, to wit:—

1st. "Working on the Public Fast recommended by the association of ministers.

2d. "Speaking diminutively of the County Congress, in which they recommended to the people not to take Hick's and Mill's paper.

3d. "Not sufficiently encouraging people to sign the Covenant.

4th. "Saying that his wife had bought tea, and should buy it again, if she had a chance.

5th. "At the Ordinary of Mr. Abraham Stillwater, with

a bowl of grog in his hand, drinking to the success of the king's arms.

6th. " Saying, ' by G—d if this people is to be governed in this manner, it is time for us to look out; and 'tis all owing to the Committee of Safety, a pack of supple-headed fellows, I know two of them myself.

" These charges being proved and the Committee having admonished said Hart, but he continuing his perverse course, it was voted that said Hart is an enemy to his country, and that every friend to humanity ought to forsake said Hart, until he shall give evidence of sincere repentance by actions worthy of a man and a Christian.

(Signed) "JAMES GISBORNE, *Clerk.*"

The next day an event occurred that aroused the people still more against Pluck. Another individual in town had rendered himself obnoxious to public sentiment. This was Colonel Welch, a brother-in-law of Judge Morgridge, who had derived his title for services against the French in the Seven Years' war. He occupied a large house at the head of the West Street, near "Deacon Hadlock's Pasture." He refused to sign the Association, and used language which gave the people cause to doubt his patriotism. He declined also accepting a command in the Continental army, and intimated that his present commission could not be supplanted or nullified. He had already been summoned before the Town Committee, where his replies were not satisfactory. Further measures were proposed.

At this crisis of affairs, late in the evening, Judge Morgridge visited his brother-in-law, and informing him of what was in progress, suggested that he had no other alternative but recantation or flight. The Colonel replied that the former he would not do, and if it came to the latter, that should be done ; and with his family made hasty preparations for departure. In the middle of the night he left Livingston, went to New York, whence he ultimately sailed for Nova Scotia. When the two families had indulged those tokens of regret, speedily finished, which were natural to the occasion, and the Colonel was on the point of starting, it was discovered that one horse delayed, and the cause was soon obvious. Cæsar, a servant of Judge Morgridge, was found clinging passionately to Phillis, the servant of the Colonel. Such a moment for the expression of what they might feel was certainly most inopportune, and the lovers were unceremoniously parted. The next morning, Pluck understanding from Cæsar what had happened, and withal as we say now-a-days, endeavoring to make capital out of the fellow's distress, appeared on the Green, and more than half in liquor made boast of toryism, applauded the conduct of Colonel Welch, and declaimed on the cruelty practised towards the negro. Already sufficiently odious, he would have done better not to trifle with an indignant populace. He was declared not only inimical but dangerous, and by order of the Committee was confined in jail.

Among a multitude of fellow-prisoners Mr. Hart found one of whom till that moment he had known but little ; this was his townsman and subsequent acquaintance, Master Elliman. This gentleman, inveterately attached to olden time, without reverence for the people, and as his subsequent conduct would indicate, with no other regard for kings than what consisted in a preference for an old and long-established state of things over any new projects that might be started, possibly unwilling to have his quiet disturbed, perhaps averse to receiving dictation from those whose children he had flogged, or who themselves may have been under his thumb; certainly we have reason to believe, from no conscientious scruples ; this gentleman, we say, received the Committee who waited upon him with an irritating indifference, and refused to sign the oath. It was considered unsafe to have him at large, and he was thrown into prison.

Thus commenced an intimacy that in the result proved not unfavorable to one as yet unborn, Margaret. Whatever points of resemblance might exist between Pluck and the Master, these became strengthened by their confinment together, and contrariety was forgotten in a sense of common sorrow. The cells of the jail were crowded, comforts did not overflow, and whatever relief could be had from an exchange of sympathies the convicts would naturally betake themselves to. In the end it appeared that Pluck and the Master became very good friends, and the visits of the latter to the Pond, originating in the double cause which has now been related, were in after years not infrequent. Add to this a deep and ingenuous interest in Margaret, and we shall understand why he came so often to her house, and exerted himself so readily for her instruction. The durance of these recusants lasted no more than two or three months.— Pluck, as being of less consequence, was released almost on his own terms. In the Kidderminster Chronicle appeared the following, which relates to the Master:—

"Whereas I, the subscriber, have from the perverseness of my wicked heart maliciously and scandalously abused the character and proceedings of the Continental and Provincial Congress, Selectmen of this town, and the Committees of Safety in general, I do hereby declare, that at the time of my doing it, I knew the said abuses to be the most scandalous falsehoods, and that I did it for the sole purpose of abusing those bodies of men, and affronting my townsmen, and all the friends of liberty throughout the Continent. Being now fully sensible of my wickedness and notorious falsehoods, I humbly beg pardon of those worthy characters I have so scandalously abused, and voluntarily renouncing my former principles, do promise for the future to render my conduct unexceptionable to my countrymen, by strictly adhering to the measures of Congress, and desire this my confession may be printed in the Kidderminster Chronicle for three weeks successively.

"BARTHOLOMEW ELLIMAN.

"Test,

Abraham Stillwater,
Josiah Penrose,
Nathan Hadlock.

"*Livingston, Nov. 23d,* 1775."

CHAPTER VIII.

MARGARET'S OLDEST BROTHER, NIMROD, COMES HOME. — HE PROPOSES A VARIETY OF DIVERSIONS.

NIMROD made his annual visit to his father's. Where he had been, or what he did, none asked, none knew. His appearance would indicate the sailor and the horse-jockey; he wore a tarpauling and blue jacket, high-top boots with spurs, and leather trousers; he flourished a riding stick, commonly known as a cowhide, and had large gold rings dangling in his ears. He rode a horse, a cast-iron looking animal, thin and bony, of deep gray color, called Streaker. He seemed to have money in his pocket, as he evidently had brandy in his saddle-bags and humor in his soul. He brought one or two books for Margaret, to whom he showed great attachment, and whose general management seemed surrendered to him, while he was at home. These books were Mother Goose's Melodies, National Songs, and Bewick's Birds with plates. He gave her, in addition, a white muslin tunic with pink silk skirt. Nimrod was tall in person, with bluish, lively eyes, light hair and a playful expression of face. All the family seemed delighted with his return; Pluck, because his son's temper was congenial with his own; his mother, for some presents; Hash, because of the brandy; Chilion was happy to see his brother; and Margaret for obvious reasons. He leaped from his horse and ran to Margaret, who met him at the door; raised her in his arms, kissed her, set her down, took her up again, made her leap on his horse, caught her off and kissed her a second time. "Can you spell Streaker?" said he, which she did. "Ah, you little rogue!" he added, "you are spruce as a blue-jay."

"Has the Indian come yet?"

"He was here last week."

"An't you afraid of him?"

"No. The little girl that was with him gave me some apples."

"That's you, for a broad joe! Never be afraid of any body, or any thing, two-legged or four-legged, black, white, blue or gray, streaked or speckled, on the earth or in the air. I have learned that lesson. How is our other Margaret, the Peach tree?"

"Don't you see what beautiful red peaches there are on it?"

"Yea, verily," as the Master says, "this is like a woodchuck in clover. These are sweet and luscious as your cheek, Margaret."

Nimrod ran into the house, and out to the cistern, and towards the Pond, and up the Head. He shook his father's hand heartily; to his mother he made a low bow; Hash chuckled and grinned at sight of him, and Nimrod laughed harder in response. Chilion greeted him cordially, but said little. Bull he held up by his paws, made sundry bows and grimaces to the dog, and talked to him like an old friend, so that Margaret declared the animal laughed.

If Nimrod were enjoying a furlough or vacation, or any thing of the kind, it seemed to be his purpose to make the most of it. He talked of the meeting in the woods, a turkey hunt the next moon, a husking bee, thanksgiving ball, racing, and a variety of things. In whatever he undertook, Margaret was his constant attendant; and at some risk even, he carried her into all scenes of wildness, exposure and novelty; nor can it be said she was loth to go with her brother.

The meeting in the woods was the first in order of time. This practice, imported from England, began to flourish incipiently in our country. From the suburbs of old cities, from church-yards, court-yards, gardens, the scene was transferred to pine forests, shady mountains, and a maiden greensward. Heptenstall Bank was revived in Snake Hill. The scoffing Kentishmen appeared in the "Injins," No. 4's and Breaknecks. What lived in Europe must needs luxuriate in America. The jumpers of Wales were outdone by the jerkers of Kentucky.

The meeting was to be held in the district we have before spoken of as Snake Hill, lying four or five miles north of the Pond. Nimrod started off horseback, with Margaret behind him on a pillion. Hash and Bull went afoot. At the Widow Wright's, they found that lady with her son mounting their horse,—a small black animal resembling the Canada breed, called Tim,—and just ready to proceed on the same excursion. The Widow was solemn and collected, and she greeted Nimrod, for whom she had no love, with a smile that a susceptible eye might have construed into coldness. Tim, the horse, had a propensity for dropping his ears, biting and kicking, when a stranger approached. He began some demonstrations of this sort as Nimrod came up. Whether Nimrod regarded this an insult on Streaker, or was nettled at the manner of the woman, or to gratify his own evil taste, he dealt the horse a smart blow with his cowhide. Tim darted off at full jump; insomuch that Obed and his mother, with all their use to his back and manners, had much ado to keep their seat. Nimrod ambled forward about a mile to a house known as Sibyl Radney's, where he overtook the Widow breathing her beast. Sibyl lived alone with her mother in the woods, cultivated a small farm, kept a horse and cow, mowed, cut wood, and did all her work without aid. Her face and neck were deeply browned, her arm was like that of a blacksmith. She was also getting ready for Snake Hill. Nimrod contrived to stimulate the three horses into a race, which was executed in a manner a fox-hunter might have envied, through brambles, over stumps, across ditches.

The spot to which these riders directed their way was in a forest on the crown of a hill. A circular opening had been cut among the trees for the purposes of the meeting. At one end of this amphitheatre was the pulpit, constructed of rough boards ; about the sides were arranged the tents or camps, made for the most part of hemlock boughs. Slab seats filled the area between. In the centre of the whole was a huge pile of wood to be kindled in the evening for warmth if need be, or for light. There were also booths on the outside for the sale of cider, rum, gingerbread, and the practice of various games. Here were assembled people from twenty different towns. Nimrod fastened his horse to the trees amongst scores of others. The Widow reminding Nimrod of the circumstances of the place, admonished him of his recklessness. "I cal'late God is here," said she, "and you had better not be pokin' your fun about." Compassionating the dangerous situation of Margaret, she requested that she might be delivered to her care. Nimrod, knowing he should find entertainment of a sort that would not be agreeable to the child, yielded her to the Leech. He and Sibyl went towards the booths, and Mistress Wright, leaning on the arm of her son, leading Margaret, entered the encampment. Three men in black occupied the pulpit, their heads powdered, with white stocks and bands, and straight square-cut collars. One of them, a tall bronze-complexioned man, was addressing the congregation.

"The sacred flame," said he, "has spread in Virginia. Brother Enfield, the assistant in the Brunswick Circuit, conjectures that from eighteen hundred to two thousand souls have been converted since the middle of May. Twelve hundred experienced the work of grace in Sussex; in Amelia half as many more. Many Christians had severe exercises of mind respecting the great noise that attended this work of God. Some thought it was not divine; yet from its effects they dare not ascribe it to Satan; but when the Lord broke in upon their own families, they saw it at once, and began to bemoan their own hardness of heart. Many gospel-hardened, old, orthodox sinners, have, as mighty oaks, been felled; and many high-towering sinners, as the tall cedars of Lebanon, bowed down to the dust. As many as fifteen or twenty commonly gave up in a day under Brother Staffin's preaching, who is indeed a Samson among the Philistines. It is no strange thing now for children down to seven years of age to come in."

The Preacher then digressed in a strain of exortation designed to reproduce effects similar to those he had recounted. A thunder cloud gathered in the sky, and buried the woods in darkness. "That," said he, "is the shadow of hell. It is the smoke of torments that ascendeth up forever and ever." The thunder burst upon the camp, its hollow roar reverberated among the hills. "Behold!" he exclaimed, "God proclaims his law in fire and smoke!" It began to rain, "What!" continued he, "can you not endure a little wetting, when you will so soon call for a drop of water to cool your parched tongues?" Lightnings blazed through the trees. "The great day of the Lord is coming, when the elements shall melt with fervent heat; the heavens shall pass away with a great noise, the earth also shall be burned up." There was a movement in the congregation. "Oh my soul!" "Jesus save!" "Glory! glory!" rang from seat to seat. "It is the Lord's doings, and marvellous in our eyes," exclaimed one of the men in the pulpit. Nimrod and his confreres from the booths ran in to see what had befallen. There sat Obed waving to and fro in his seat, groaning, and calling upon his mother. "Yes, my son," exclaimed the latter convulsively, "its an orful time. God has come, we are great sinners. I han't done my duty by ye. Parson Welles would let us all go teu hell together." "What a mercy," exclaimed another, "we can come where the gospel is preached!" "O Lord, forgive me," cried a third, "for going to the Univarsal up to Dunwich; I do believe there is a hell, I do believe there is a hell." "I have been down among the Socinians," echoed a fourth. "God be praised I have found where there is some religion at last. Glory, glory!"

The Preacher, the storm and the effect increased. Some of the congregation foamed at the mouth, others fell to the ground in spasms; the color of their faces fluctuating from white through purple to black; one appeared to be strangling and gasping for life, another became stiff, rigid, and sat up like a dead man on his seat; there were sobs, shrieks, and ejaculations. The thunder crashed, as if the heavens had split and the earth would give way. There was a stifled groan, a shuddering recoil among the people; the Preacher himself seemed for a moment stunned. Margaret screamed to the top of her voice, which sounded like a clarion over an earthquake. Nimrod impulsively rushed among the people, dashed Obed from his seat, seized Margaret and drew her out.

The Preacher recovering himself as he observed this movement, "Son of Belial!" he broke forth, "thinkest thou to stop the mighty power of God? Will he deliver that child into thy hand as he did the children of Israel into the hand of Chushan-rishathaim? Stop, on thy soul, and repent, lest ye die."

"I guess I shan't die before my time," retorted Nimrod, "nor any sooner for your croaking, old Canorum. The child is getting wet, and she is sca't. I han't lived in the woods to be skeered at owls."

"A scoffer!" "A scoffer!" one or another exclaimed. The people began to look up and about them. The tide of feeling was somewhat diverted. "O, there will be mourning, mourning, mourning," &c., was pealed forth from the pulpit, and a full chorus of voices chimed in. The Preacher renewed his exhortations, and the attention of the assembly was regained. Groans and sobs began once more. "This beats the Great Earthquake all hollow," exclaimed one of the congregation. "Yes," echoed the Preacher, "what a rattling among the dry bones." "O Lord!" cried one of the assistants, "send an earthquake, shake these sinners, send it quick, send it now. There were near four hundred converted at the last earthquake in Boston." "O, what a harvest of souls we should have, brother!" rejoined the Preacher. "Help me with your prayers, brethren, as Aaron and Hur did Moses."

In due time these exercises closed. After supper in the evening the pile of wood was kindled, pine knots were lighted at the corners of the pulpit; the horn blew and the people reassembled. Margaret ran off into the woods with her dog and laid down under a tree, her head resting on the flanks of the animal, and her feet nestling in the soft moss. Nimrod was drinking and roistering at the booths.

At the close of the evening service, the people dispersed to their tents. A middle aged man, Mr. Palmer, from the Ledge, happening in the woods, saw Margaret asleep under the trees, took her in his arms, carried her into one of the tents, and gave her in charge of his wife. The good woman with one hand patted Margaret on her head, while with the other she tended her own with a pinch of snuff, and asked her if she didn't want to be saved. Margaret replied that she didn't know.

"The spirit is here mightily," said the woman, taking a fresh pinch, "won't you come in for a share?"

"It won't let me," replied Margaret.

"You may lose your soul."

"I haven't got any."

"Mercy on me!" exclaimed the woman, "Don't you know the devil will get you if you don't come in?"

"It won't," replied Margaret, "Bull won't let it."

"What will you do when all the little boys and gals goes up a singing?"

"I'll stay at home and hear Chilion play on the fiddle, and read my new books."

"Luddy mussy! can you read? Where do you live?"

"Down to the Pond."

"Han't they got any of the religion at your house?"

"No, Ma'm, they drink pupelo and rum."

"A born fool!" ejaculated the woman with herself.—"But she can read, she must be knowing. Wonder if the power is'nt in her? She will certainly die, and she an't no more ready than our Rufus."

The people began to crowd into the tent, among whom were Mistress Wright and her son Obed. The widow made immediately for Margaret, who with Mistress Palmer, was sitting on the straw in a corner apart. She heard the latter lady's soliloquy, and added, " O no, I'm afeered she an't."

"What's the matter of the child?" asked Mistress Palmer.

"Don't know Marm," replied the Widow. "I wish sutthin' could be done for her, she's bred in orful wickedness. Any sick up your way, Miss Palmer ? I've brought a few yarbs with me. If we could only keep the poor sinners alive long enough teu save their souls it would be a marcy."

The speakers were interrupted by noises in the tent, into which a large number of people had found their way, who began to sing, exhort and pray. They had Obed down flat on his back. The mouth of the lad was open, his eyes shut; he shook spasmodically, he groaned with a deep guttural guffaw. Men and women were over and about him; some praying, others crying, "Glory!" The Preacher came in, a bland smile on his face, rubbing his hands; "Good!" he ejaculated with a short, quick snap of the voice. "The Lord is here, Miss Palmer," said he.

"Yes in truth, you told us we should have a great time," rejoined the woman. "But see this gal, I wonder if any thing can be done with her."

"Ah! my little lamb," said the Preacher, taking Margaret's hand and drawing her gently towards him. "Hope you have found the Savior, you are old enough to repent." Margaret wrested herself from him. "What's the matter, dear?" inquired the man. "You are not one of the wicked children that reviled the prophet, and the bears came out of the woods and tare them in pieces?"

"I an't afraid of the bears," replied Margaret pettishly.

"A mazed child! a mazed child!" exclaimed Mistress Palmer.

"Don't you want to be converted?" asked the Preacher.

"I don't like you, I don't like you," replied Margaret. "You hollered so and scared Obed, he's scared now. They are hurting him," she said, pointing where the youth lay. Darting from her company, she penetrated the crowd and knelt down by the side of Obed. "Poor Obed!" she said, "dont make such a noise, Molly is here."

"I am going to hell," hoarsely and mournfully replied the boy.

"The arrows of the Almighty are thick upon him," ejaculated the Preacher.

"If the Lord would only grant him deliverance!" said his mother, looking through the crowd.

"Pray, brother, pray, sister," said the Preacher, addressing one and another. "Jacob wrestled all night in prayer with God. The Ark is now going by. Three have already closed with the offers in Dunwich tent."

"Don't cry so, Obed," said Margaret. "They shan't hurt you."

"The devil is in that child, take her away," said the Preacher.

Some one endeavored to pull her off. "Let me alone, she exclaimed, "I can't go, I won't go," and she adhered to the boy, whose arm had become closed about her neck as that of a man in a fit.

There was a hubbub of voices; men and women reeking with excitement, and vieing one with another who should pray the most importunately.

"What are ye doing here?" shouted a still louder voice over the heads of the crowd. It was Nimrod, who half intoxicated thrust himself among them. "Bite um Bull, bite um," he rubbed the dog's ears and holding him between his legs, teased him into a piercing yelp and howl that startled the people.

"Bull! Bull!" shrieked Obed. "He's comin', he'll bite." The lad sprang to his feet staring wildly about.

"Satan has come in great wrath," cried the Preacher.

"And I guess you know as much about him as any body, old Cackletub!" rejoined Nimrod. "You set them all a-going, and then snap them up like a hawk."

"Hoora!" shouted another of the scoffers from the others' side of the tent. "I hearn him comin' down a tree jest now; look out or he'll be in your hair, white-top."

Meanwhile the uproar deepened, profanity and fanaticism, like opposing currents of air, meeting in that confined space, wrapped the scene in confusion and dismay; lights were extinguished, friends and enemies tore at each others' throats; Sibyl Radney, alone collected and resolute, drew Margaret from the midst, and returned with her to the Pond.

CHAPTER IX.

MARGARET SUCCESSFUL IN A NOVEL ADVENTURE.

A FEW days afterwards, there came to the Widow Wright's Mr. Palmer from the Ledge, the man who found Margaret in the woods and delivered her to his wife. He purchased of the Widow a prescription for his daughter Rhody, who he said was not in strong health, and then stated that his family had been troubled for want of water, and intimated a conjecture of his wife that Margaret was one in whom resided the faculty of discovering it, and asked the Widow if she would accompany him to Pluck's, and aid in procuring the services of the child for the purpose indicated. They went to the Pond, where Mr. Palmer gained the consent of the family to his object, and especially that of Nimrod, who evinced a positive delight in the project, and even volunteered to be Margaret's gallant on the occasion. They all proceeded together, accompanied by the Widow, who suggested that her personal attention might be of benefit to Rhody. The Ledge was six or seven miles from the Pond. It was properly speaking a marble quarry, and belonged to Mr. Palmer, who with his sons, in addition to a large farm they carried on, sometimes worked at gravestones and hearths.

Mr. Palmer was in popular phrase a forehanded man, his house and barns were large, and his grounds indicated thrift. He had three sons, Roderick, Alexander and Rufus, stout, vigorous boys; and one daughter Rhody, about seventeen, a fair-looking, black-haired girl.

This family were obliged to fetch their water from a considerable distance, not having been able to find a spring near the house. Agreeably to the doctrines of rhabdomancy, formerly in vogue, and at the present moment not entirely discarded, a twig, usually of witchhazle, borne over the surface of the ground, indicates the presence of water to which it is instinctively alive, by stirring in the hand. The number of persons would seem to be small in whom this power is lodged, or through whom the phenomenon exhibits itself. It appeared that the neighborhood had been canvassed for an operator, but none succeeded. It occurred to Mistress Palmer, at the camp, that Margaret might be endowed with the rare gift, and she was accordingly sent for.

The family at the Ledge showed great joy on the arrival of the party from the Pond. Mistress Palmer took a pinch of snuff, and helped Margaret from the horse, and even received Nimrod kindly, although his pranks at the meeting might have operated to his prejudice. The large pewter tankard of cider was passed round, but Margaret refused to taste, saying she should prefer water. "Dear me! we hav'nt a drop of decent water in the house," exclaimed Mistress Palmer. "The gal shall have some milk, the best we have; Rhody get some of the morning's; pour it out cream and all." Of this Margaret drank freely. "Poor thing!" ejaculated the lady, "she don't know as she has got a soul, and our Rufus is nigh as bad, for he won't do nothing to save his."

"I tell you what it is, Marm," rejoined Rufus, her youngest son, about twelve or fourteen years of age; "I an't going to have that old preacher whining and poking about me. I believe I can get to heaven without his help; if I can't, then I am willing to stay away."

"Well, well, child," replied the mother, "I shall not care how, if you get there at all, only I want you to be a good boy." She took a large pinch of snuff. These preliminaries being settled, and Margaret having received her instructions to hold the stick firmly and tell when it moved, proceeded on her duty. She made sundry gyrations, she traversed the grounds about the house, she tried the garden, but effected nothing. "It is too wet," said one; "it is too cold," said a second; "it is too dry," said a third; "it is too warm," said a fourth. Mistress Palmer took a pinch of snuff. Another trial was proposed. The child went farther from the house, and perambulated the orchard. All looked on with a breathless interest; she moved about slowly and carefully, the stick held horizontally forward in her two fists — a little diviner, in green rush hat and Indian moccasons; the wind shook her brown curls, her blue checked pinafore streamed off like a pennon. Did they do wrong to use a little creature so? Yet is not God useful? Is not Utility the sister of Beauty? At last she cried out that it moved. Mr. Palmer hastened forward and struck his spade into the spot; Margaret ran off. Presently there were signs of water, then it bubbled up, then it gushed forth a clear limpid stream. Mr. Palmer praised God. The boys hoora'd. Mistress Palmer took a pinch of snuff.

"Taste on't, Alek," said Rufus.

"No," replied the father. "It belongs to the finder to be the first taster. The gal, where is she?"

Rufus was despatched for Margaret. He found her at the quarry trying to get a harebell that grew far above her head. The boy crouched under her, and she, stepping on his shoulders, reached the flower. When she would have descended, Rufus fastened his arms about her and bore her off on his back, pappoose-like. Approaching the spot where the water was found, she leaped down and scampered around the house; Rufus pursued, she laughed, he laughed, and full of frolic, he brought her to the spring. She said she was not dry and would not drink, and would have run away again; when Nimrod prevailed with her to the end desired. Then they all drank, and pronounced it excellent water. Mistress Palmer said it was soft and would wash well; Mistress Wright declared it was nice to boil mint in; Alexander didn't care if he hadn't to lug any more from the brook. All were satisfied, and Margaret became a wonder.

A sumptuous home-made dinner, with suet Indian-pudding and molasses for dessert, was served on bright pewter plates with stag-horn knives and forks. After this, Rufus brought Margaret a marble flower-pot he had made, also a kitten very well executed, which he had cut from the same material. Rhody gave her a root of the Guelder rose. Mr. Palmer paid the Widow handsomely for her visit to his daughter, whose case she elaborately investigated. He offered money to Nimrod, who refused it. Mistress Palmer presented Margaret with a roll of beautiful linen of her own manufacture.

"Thank Miss Palmer," said Nimrod to his sister.

"O no!" exclaimed the lady. "Take it and welcome, and any thing we have got. But do, my young friend," she added as he was mounting his horse, "do think on your ways, strive, strive, who knows but you may find the good thing at last? And the little gal—she is a good child as ever was. It was very kind of her to come all the way up here, and do us a service. She is worth her weight in gold. I hope she will have a new heart soon. "Here," she continued, "let me help you on." Margaret, scarcely touching the woman's hand, sprang to the pillion. "Why, how she jumps! She is as spry as a cricket. How pretty she does look up there behind you; I must have a kiss at her,—there—remember thy Creator in the days of thy youth—and don't you forget, my young friend.—Good day."

"I want Rhody to kiss me," said Margaret.

"Run Rhody," said her mother.

"Did Rhody kiss you?" asked Nimrod, when they had gone on a while without saying any thing.

"Yes," was the reply.

CHAPTER X.

THANKSGIVING, OR NEW ENGLAND'S HOLIDAY.—MARGARET HAS HER DIVERSION.

It is noticeable that we of the present age have fewer holidays than our puritanical ancestors. "The King's Birth Day" was formerly celebrated with great pomp; in addition there were enjoyed "Coronation Days," the "Birth of a Prince," Accessions and Burials of Governors, Victories in War, Masonic Festivals, to say nothing of Military Reviews, Election Days, Ordination of Ministers, Executions for Murder; and at a still later period Washington's Birth Day, now almost forgotten, and the Fourth of July, at present diverted to a Sunday-school or Temperance Festival. But of Thanksgiving; a day devoted to mirth, gratefulness, hospitality, family love, eating, drinking; a day sometimes externally snowy, drizzly, benumbing, drenching; internally so elastic, smiling, lark-like, verdant, blithe; it is not sanctified or squandered like Merry Christmas in the Old World: it has no gooding, candles, clog, carol, box, or hobby-horse; it has no poetry or song; does not come in the calendar, only by the Governor's proclamation; New Englanders can sing with Old Englanders, *mutatis mutandis*:—

"Now thrice welcome Christmas,
Which brings us good cheer,
Minced pies, plum porridge,
Good ale, and strong beer,
With pig, goose and capon,
The best that may be."

They cannot add, —

"With holly and ivy
So green and so gay,
We deck up our houses
As fresh as the day,
With bays and rosemary
And laurel complete."

Our houses and churches are brown and sear as the gardens and orchards about them. The cedar may be green in the woods, the box-tree, the fir and the pine together, we never use them. In both cases, there is, or was, an abundance of wassailing, dancing, gaming, shooting, and if one pleases to say, "Heathenrie, Divelrie, Dronkennesse, Pride." We have no budding oak or holy-thorn, which sprang from the staff of Joseph of Arimathea, and bears milk-white blossoms every Christmas day, in the forests of Glastonbury; although no doubt such trees might be found in our woods. Unlike Christmas, bread baked Thanksgiving Eve moulds never the slower. Yet, bating ecclesiastical days and a few calendar superstitions, which the dissenting Colonists left behind, how much did they not bring with them from their native soil! "We owe," says the Democratic Review, "our political institutions, and nearly all the arrangements of our public, social and domestic life, to our English ancestors." In addition to religion, language, habits, costume, fashions, science, art, architecture, agriculture, the military and naval art, horses, carriages, cows, sheep, grass, bells, knives and forks, glass ware, apples, etc., etc., there floated across the sea, and has descended the stream of Time, idiosyncrasies of temper, idioms of speech, rhetorical figures, colloquial metaphors, an entire dialect of vulgarisms, ballads, madrigals, maxims, witticisms, witchcraft, bigotry, omens, a thousand and one fanciful calculations on the moon, the weather, beasts, birds,—a whole argosy. Some of these may be traced to the Saxons and Britons, in unbroken succession. They still exist in England, Germany, Sweden, nay, every where. We must look perhaps for some great Oriental centre, some fountain head beyond the Indus. The fathers of the Sanscrit, the authors of the Vedas, the original Brahmins, whoever they may have been, possibly the step-sons of Noah, seem to have given population, language, law, philosophy, superstition, and, saving Christ, religion to the world.

John Bull and Brother Jonathan, a North Briton and a Yankee, have the same flesh and blood, the same corpuscular ingredients, the same inspiration of the Almighty. The latter differs from the former chiefly in this, breadth; his legs are longer and his feet larger, because he has higher fences and steeper hills to climb, and longer roads to travel; he is more lank because he has not time to laugh so much, since it takes him so long to go to mill, to pasture, and the neighbors; he is less succulent and oozy because he gets dry and hardened in the extensive tracts of open air he has to traverse; he is more suspicious because in his circuits he meets with more strangers; he is more curious for the same reason; he is more inventive and calculating for this same breadth, having no aids at hand, and depending entirely on himself; his eye is keener because he sees his objects at a greater distance; he is more religious because he has farther to go for his religion, that is to say, to meeting; men valuing what costs them much; —the whole difference is breadth, interminable forests, rivers, mountains, platitudinous farms, families reaching from the Madawaska to the Yazoo. The same cause operates to distinguish the Kentucky hunter from the Yankee, cypress swamps, alligators, catamounts, the Indians, the Mississippi. Sam Slick is an elongated and skinny John Browdie, and David Crockett is the same "critter," knobbed and gnarled.

Thanksgiving was an anti-Christmas festival, established as a kind of off-set to that. Yet both are a fealty paid to the universal gala sentiment. We cannot always work, we cannot always pray. So say young and old, grave and gay. Hence, Hindoo Doorga, Celtic Juul, Jewish Succoth, Japanese Majira, the Panathenæa, Fete des Fous, Volks-fest, Carnival, Halloween, Christmas, Thanksgiving.

Thanksgivings have been observed—what do we say? The first Thanksgiving must have been of God's own ordaining about the beginning of the new year 1621, that is to say, the 25th of March, at New Plymouth, after a dismal winter of destitution, disease and alarm, when the snows were melting, and "brooks of sweet fresh water" broke loose, the children found a new May-flower peeping from the dead leaves, the buds of the dogwood began to swell and the birds to sing, the "sick and lame recovered apace," and the Colonists saw something that looked like living and home. The first Thanksgiving "by authority" was, if we are agreed, June 13, 1632. We can hardly call that a New England Thanksgiving, inasmuch as it embraced but a handful of the people. The Indians must have kept it as a Fast.

Thanksgivings were appointed for "the removal of sickness," "the precious life of our Sovereign;" "success of the king of Prussia," "the conquest of Martinico," that "God had been pleased to support our most gracious Queen in the perils of childbirth," "for success against the Indians, so that scarce a name or family remain in their former habitation," "the suppression of rebellion in Great Britain," "the near view of peace." Fasts, the antipodal holiday, were proclaimed by reason of "the small-pox," earthquakes, inundations, and other calàmities in Europe," "distressing Indian wars," "that we may be preserved against the rage of the heathen," "the great number of insects," "drought," "unseasonable rains," "divisions in our churches," the "Ranters and Quakers," "the low estate of the people of God," "some heathen yet in hostility," "the great distresses of Ministers, their salaries being paid in depreciated paper."

Thanksgiving was at hand for Livingston, the Pond, Nimrod, Margaret. Its succedanea, as respects the latter, were a turkey shoot the next day and a ball in the evening at No. 4. If Margaret had lived in the village, or almost any where else than the Pond, she might have enjoyed the meeting of families, parents and children, grandparents and grandchildren, uncles, cousins; she might have united in the consumption of turkeys, chickens, plum-pudding, pumpkin, mince and apple pies, beer, cider, flip; she might have gone to church and heard a discourse from Parson Welles on the distressing state of the times, and the imminent danger from French influence, and learned what a Philistine Napoleon Bonaparte was; she might have gone to a party of boys and girls at Esq. Weeks's and played "blind-man's buff," "run round the chimney," and "button, button, who's got the button;" but she did not. Yet she was quite busy at home. Two or three of the preceding days she spent riding about with Nimrod to invite company and arouse interest for the ball. They went to Mr. Pottle's at Snake Hill, and Mr. Dunlap's at Five-mile-lot, where they also encountered the camp Preacher sedulously disputing the field with them. They went also to the Ledge, where the Preacher followed.

But Mistress Palmer decided the question by saying that Roderick, her oldest son, had professed a hope and would not think of going, but that Rhody had not come forward at all, and she thought the exercise would do her good, and that Rufus, if he had been serious, had lost his impressions, and it would not harm him to go.

Thanksgiving Eve was kept at the Pond in this wise: their candles were pine torches, which they flourished about the premises in pursuit of hens and turkeys; their clogs were large clumps of bark crowded into the immense fire-place; their carol consisted of oaths, smirks, songs; for ale they had an abundance of cider brandy. No St. Nicholas watched about the chimney during the night, or filled Margaret's stocking in the morning. Who is the patron saint of Thanksgiving? Only Chilion made her a present of a beautiful blue-painted sled to coast with when the snows came, and named Humming Bird. They had stewed chicken and crust coffee for breakfast, and for dinner chickens roasted by strings suspended before the fire, potatoes, brown bread and cider. Pies and cakes were wanting. The remainder of the time was occupied in preparing for the events of the next day, scouring guns, polishing buckles, and the like. Nimrod took occasion to renew his instructions to Margaret in the dancing art, and Chilion intimated some of his best tunes.

No. 4, to which the attention of the family was now directed, lay in a valley below the Pond, formed by the passage of Mill Brook, and was enriched by nature with fine intervals and excellent drainages. The approach to the place was by a narrow, woody, rocky road or lane. Here was a large tavern, known as Smith's, and a distillery owned by the same gentleman. In the language of a writer of the times, this hamlet presented a spectacle of "houses without windows, barns without roofs, gardens without enclosures, fields without fences, hogs without yokes, sheep without wool, meagre cattle, feeble horses, and half clad, dirty children, without manners, principles or morals." The people were loungers about the tavern, which seemed to have exhausted the life of the place, and to have diffused over it instead, indolence, dreariness and sterility.

To this hamlet Nimrod bore Margaret, and Hash carried his turkeys. The day was chilly and drizzling, and Margaret was deposited in the kitchen of the tavern, where she had a chance to become acquainted with Mr. Smith's daughters, the Gubtailes, Hatchs, Tapleys, from the neighborhood, Paulina Whiston, Grace Joy and Beulah Ann Orff from Breackneck. The bar-room was filled with men and boys, fumes of rum and tobacco, and a jargon of voices; the air about was charged with the smoke of powder; there were the report of rifles, the running to and fro of men and boys, disputes about the shots, wrangling, and wrestling; in all which Margaret had no share. Thus passed the fore part of the day.

In the evening, Nimrod, as one of the masters of arrangements, with Margaret, came early to the tavern. Soon the ladies and gentlemen began to assemble. Of the number were Pluck and his wife, the Widow Wright and Obed, and Sibyl Radney. Abel Wilcox, the clerk, and Hancock Welles, grandson of the Parson, from the village, constituted the principal loafers. The hall was a long unfinished upper room, having its naked timbers and sleepers garnished with pine and hemlock. Tallow candles in wooden blocks effected a rude illumination. The ladies' dresses presented considerable variety; some had made requisition on the wardrobes of their grandmothers, some had borrowed from their neighbors, servants from their mistresses; in a few appeared the latest style of the cities; several wore gowns of their own manufacture, striped or checked linen, with flowers elaborately wrought with the needle. There were sacques, trails, and one or two hoops. All had necklaces of gold, glass, or waxen beads. The coiffures were equally diversified, consisting of tye-tops, crape cushions, toupees, sustained and enriched with brass and gilt clasps, feathers and flowers. Their shoes were striped with a white welt. There was an agreeable intermixture of old and faded brocades, rustling padusoys, and shining lutestrings. Many wore ear hoops of pinch-beck, large as a dollar.

The gentlemen exhibited a similar blending of old and new patterns. If Joseph's coat of many colors had been miraculously enlarged, and cut into separate garments, it would form the appropriate suit of this assemblage, in which red, blue, yellow, chocolate, butternut, green, and all hues but black, were represented. Their hair was powdered, and done in tyes, queues, frizzes. Margaret wore the new dress Nimrod brought her, and her moccasons. Pluck retained his leather apron, his wife had donned a clean long-short. Chilion, the chief musician, had on a pearl-colored coat, buff swansdown vest, white worsted breeches and ribbed stockings. Tony Washington, the negro barber from the village, and assistant violinist, appeared in powdered hair, a faded crimson silk coat, ruffle cuffs and white smalls. It was a singularly freaked and speckled group. There were burly, weather-beaten faces under powder and curls; broad, hard hands in kid gloves; thewy, red elbows that had plied brooms, shuttles, cards, in lace ruffles; there were bright eyes, smiling faces and many pleasant words.

Chilion, whose general manner was reserved and obscure,

grew animated as the dance began. Margaret, omitted at first, was presently called up by Rufus Palmer. None were so young and small as she; but she enacted her part with vigor and precision. Her father asked her for a partner, and it gave her new life when she saw she pleased him. She was, for the most part, among strangers, in a strange place and strangely occupied. The lights, the open fantastically shadowed garret above, the evergreens, the windows shining with the dew of so many breaths, the mystic motion, steps which one takes and comprehends not, balancing, gallopading, confusion harmonized, oiled intricacies, plough-boys graceful and boors mannerly, earnestness of participation, so earnest that even in the height of the sport no one smiles; and then more than this, the clear, exhilarating, penetrating notes of the violin, and Chilion's violin, that she always loved to hear, played in its best way; the life of all this life, the motion of this motion, the inspirer and regulator of this maze,—as to all these things, she felt grateful to her brother, and for the rest, she seemed to enjoy it with a deep unconsciousness of joy.

One might have noticed her brother Chilion peculiarly employed. He not only controlled the action, but seemed to gratify himself in varying and modifying it. He evidently fantasied with the company. He made them move faster or slower as he pleased. He might have been seen watching the effect of his viol, or his own effect through it. Whatever power he possessed he exerted to the utmost. He seemed to be playing more upon the dancers than upon his instrument. In the midst of a figure he would accelerate the parties, and whirl them to the end with frantic rapidity and bewildering intent. In a contra-dance, to the "Campbells are Coming," never did plaided Highlander leap down his native rocks with more headlong step than those same pied bumpkins sprang over that hall floor. He slackened the motion at the close, and dismissed them quietly to their seats. In one of the intermissions might have been seen entering the place the indefatigable Preacher. He stole through the crowd, erected his tall dark form on a bench, and taking advantage of the pause, broke upon them like a thunder gust. His loud, guttural, solemn voice rang through the room:—

"Thus saith the Lord God, thy pomp shall be brought down to the grave, and the noise of thy viols!"

"A sermon! a sermon!" cried Abel Wilcox.

Preacher. "You look fair and seemly, but you are stench in the nostrils of the Almighty."

Crowd. "Another set, who'll lead off?"

Preacher. "The Lord will take away the bravery of your tinkling ornaments, your cauls and round tires like the moon, your chains and bracelets and mufflers."

Pluck. "Let us praise God in the dance, praise him with the stringed instrument. Let us, as David did, dance before the Lord."

Preacher. "This place shall be as God overthrew Sodom and Gomorrah; owls shall dwell here, and satyrs shall dance here."

Crowd. "Peggy and Molly!" "The Haymakers," "Here's Zenas Joy and Delinda Hoag want 'Come haste to the Wedding!'"

Preacher. "You stand on slippery places, your feet shall stumble on the dark mountains."

Crowd. "Chorus Jig! Hoa! Chilion!"

Chilion. "Take your partners."

The words of the Preacher, as not unusually happens, were disregarded. He pitched his voice still higher. They danced the faster, Chilion played with the greater energy. The Preacher himself, exhausted or discouraged, became at length a listener, and finally his eye was riveted to the scene before him. Chilion played on almost wildly. Tony seconded the purposes of his master to the best of his endeavors, his teeth and eyes shone with a terrified whiteness, and the powder from his hair ran in chalky streams down his face. Chilion was unmoved in the storm he raised. Curls uncurled, ruffles were ruffled, trains trailed; but the game went on. Margaret revelled in the movement; she danced as to the winds; she knew her brother, she loved his power, she leaped out his spirit and tones. She sprang through the figure like a shuttle, she spun round and round like a top. Chilion, in his own time, softened the measure, and suffered the piece to glide away in the gentlest pulsations. The night waxed and waned. The Preacher and spectators had gone; most of the dancers left.

Here we must recede a moment to relate that in the forenoon, Hash, the brother of Margaret, and Zenas Joy, a resident of the place called Breakneck, had a serious misunderstanding about a shot the latter made at a turkey set up by the former. Numbers came forward to the arbitration, and in the result it happened that the interests and jealousies of all parties became joined in issue, and the strength and prowess of the several neighborhoods were marshalled under the respective standards of the Pond and Breakneck. It was proposed to adjust the difficulty by a champion from each side in a wrestling match. A rain, however, separated the combatants, and broke up the ring. At the supper-table in the evening, the subject was renewed. Again at this late hour of the night, there were not wanting causes to stimulate the feud in such as remained. Mr. Smith, the tavern-keeper, brought forward a fresh supply of liquors, of which both gentlemen and ladies freely drank; and the two young men from the village had no other business than to foment and egg on the rivalships or the several districts. A final dance was called for; but there appeared little self-possession either in respect of temper or limb. Chilion played a while, and then relinquished his instrument. Zenas Joy seized Hash by the collar; Joseph Whiston tripped Obed, who, poor youth, was already nearly down with liquor; Abel Wilcox spurred Rufus Palmer to tread on Beulah Ann Orff's trail; Grace Joy taunted Nimrod with a false step Margaret had taken; Sibyl Radney rushed into the fray, pounced upon Zenas Joy, and sent him whirling about the room, as she would a spinning wheel. So one and another were engaged. Margaret, who had left the floor, was standing by the side of Chilion. She looked at the quarrellers, and then at her brother. He snapped his viol strings, and was silent.

"Sing, Margery," at length he said. He began a familiar tune, "Mary's Dream,"—he played and she sang. This twofold melody, sweet and plaintive, seemed to touch the hearts of those excited people. They stopped to hear, they heard to be won. They moved towards the music; they were hushed if not subdued, they parted in peace if not in harmony. Thus ended their Thanksgiving, and we must end ours, and turn to other times and scenes.

CHAPTER XI.

A REVISED ACCOUNT OF NIMROD AND HIS DOINGS.

We shall omit the wild-turkey hunt of a bright autumnal moonlight night in the woods, exciting and engaging though it was, and the race with Streaker, in which Margaret bore no part, while we proceed to enumerate some particulars of her eldest brother, that have a relation to herself. Nimrod evinced a volatile, roving, adventure-seeking habit from his boyhood. The severe waspish temper of his mother he could not abide, the coarse, dogged despotism of Hash he resented; Chilion was only a boy, and one not sufficiently social and free; with his father he had more in common. At the age of fourteen he became an indented apprentice to Mr. Hatch, the blacksmith at No. 4. But of the different kind of blows of which he was capable, he relished those best that had the least to do with the anvil. He liked horses well enough, but preferred their hides to their hoofs; and became more skilful with the fleam than the butteris. He left his master in a rage, himself in good humor. He next let himself at the Crown and Bowl in the village, where one might fancy he would find his element. He was hostler, bar-tender, errand-boy, farrier, mistress'-man, waiting-maid's man and every body's man by turn. He entertained traveller's at the door, girls in the kitchen and boys on the stoop. He was quick but he always loitered, he was ingenious yet did nothing well. It would not seem strange that he should prove a better auxiliary to every one's taste and fancy, than to his employer's interest. He hung a flint stone on the barn-door to keep the devil from riding the horses in the night; but this did not prevent indications of their having been used at unlawful times and in unlawful ways. He was dismissed. While he served others at the bar he must needs help himself, and he became at an early age an adept in what an old writer denominates the eighth liberal art. At the close of the Revolutionary war, it became more difficult to fill vacancies in the army than it had been originally to form companies. There were "Classes" in Livingston, as every where else, instituted to furnish a certain number of soldiers, as exigency required. By one of these, Nimrod, not yet fifteen years of age, but of due physical proportion and compliance, was hired. He joined a detachment ordered on the defence of our northern frontier.

But even military discipline was insufficient to correct his propensities, or reform his habits. He deserted, and crossed the Canada line. He joined a band of smugglers that swarmed in those quarters, and during the spring of the year 1784, we find him in New York city aboard a sloop from up river. The vessel was anchored in the stream not far from the Albany Basin. She had a deck-load of lumber, and wheat in her hold, the ordinary supply of the country at the time; her contraband goods were stowed in proper places. Government, both state and national, was pressed for means; the war, taxes, suspension of productive labor, had heightened necessity and diminished resource. Duties were great, but legislation was irregular. The city held in its bosom many who had suffered during the late contest. The general amnesty, while it retained the disaffected, failed in some cases to reconcile them. Hence smuggling, while it grew to be a most vexatious practice, was one of tolerably easy accomplishment.

Late in the evening the cabin of the sloop was visited by an elderly gentleman in buff coat and breeches, having an eagle holding an olive branch wrought on his left breast. He was addressed by the Captain as Mr. Girardeau. He complained bitterly of the times, the rise of taxes, financial depressions, the decline of real estate and sundry misfortunes. He said that his clerk, meaning thereby his daughter, had eloped, and that his old servant Samuel was dead. He had evident connection with the private objects of the vessel, and under his supervision preparations were made for carrying the contraband articles to his own store in the city. These, consisting of silks, ribbons, laces, &c., were laid in coffin-shaped boxes, and Nimrod with another of the crew was detached as porter. They rowed in a small boat as far as the beach in Hudson Square, threaded a lane along the woods and hills of Grand Street, came down through the marshes and fields of Broadway, till they reached a small wooden house lying under a hill back of the City Hall, the residence of Mr. Girardeau. They encountered several of the police stationed on the skirts of the city, one of whom they frightened by intimations of the small-pox; another they avoided by slinking into the shadows of trees; a third they stupefied by drafts of rum, a supply of which they carried in their pockets. Nimrod recounted his adroit passages to Mr. Girardeau, who seemed pleased with the success if not with the character of the youth; and, in fine, hearing him highly recommended by the Captain, he the next day engaged him, under the assumed name of Foxly, to fill the place recently held by his deceased servant.

Nimrod was nothing loth to exchange masters and enter upon new scenes. Mr. Girardeau's quarters comprised both his store and dwelling-house. The building was one of the old style, having its gable to the street. In the rear of the shop-room was a kitchen, and above were sleeping apartments. In the first instance, Mr. Girardeau intimated to Nimrod the necessity of a change of apparel, and that he must wear one of a color like his own. He himself had been a resident in the city during the war, while the British had possession, and at that time wore a scarlet coat, with the arms of the king. At the peace, he changed his hue and badge. In the next place, he undertook to indoctrinate his new servant in the secrets of his business, and to impress upon him a sense of the responsibleness of his vocation. "I—I should say we—'tis all one concern, one interest," so his employer unfolded himself, "we are poor, we are embarrassed. You, Mr. Foxly, perhaps know how awful a thing poverty is. You can understand me. We are opposed, we are maltreated, we are vilified. Enemies beset us night and day; even now they may be listening to us through the walls."

Nimrod, who was not without a tincture of the superstition of his times, notwithstanding his ordinary display of fearlessness and daring, started. "They won't take us off in the night, will they?" exclaimed he.

"Yes, in the night," replied Mr. Girardeau.

"Then I may as well be a packing," said Nimrod. "I can't stay here. I thought you hadn't any of them in the city."

"Why the city is full of them," replied Mr. Girardeau, "hence we see the necessity of care, confederation and secrecy."

"But they come in any where," answered Nimrod. "They'll whisk you right out of your bed. Aunt Ravel had seven pins stuck into her in one night. Old uncle Kiah, that used to live at Snake Hill, was trundled down hill three nights agoing, and his skin all wore off, and he grew as lean as a gander's leg."

"Mr. Foxly!" interrupted Mr. Girardeau, "you misunderstand me,—I see you are from the country, a good place,—but you misunderstand me. It is men I mean, not spirits. We have no witches here, only hard-hearted, covetous, ignorant, griping, depraved, desperate men."

"Sho! it's humans you are speaking of," replied Nimrod; "I an't no more afraid of them than a cat is of a wren. I like them, I could live among them as well as a fish in water."

"Mr. Foxly!" continued Mr. Girardeau, solemnly, "we *have* something to fear from men. Here likewise you mistake. I fear you are too rash, too headstrong."

"Any thing, Sir," answered Nimrod, "I will do any thing you wish," he added more soberly. "I will serve you, as they did the troops in the war, work for nothing and find myself."

"You may well say so," added Mr. Girardeau, Samuel was faithful, he spared himself to provide for me. We are in straits, we must live frugally. Persecution surrounds us. We have enemies who can do us a great injury. I can be made to injure you, and you to injure me. We need circumspection; we are, if I may so say, in one another's power. There are those who might take advantage of my necessities, to compel me to surrender you to the rigor of unjust laws, and you might end your days in a prison. My whole life has been one of exposure and want, labor and toil." Thus was Nimrod addressed. In the third place, added Mr. Girardeau, "I must admonish you, Mr. Foxly, and most rigidly enjoin, that on no account are you to have conference, or hold any relations with a certain young woman, that sometimes comes here, whom I will point out to you."

Nimrod found upon the premises a little black-eyed boy eight or nine years of age, whom he took for the grandson of his employer. This boy was sent to school, and when at home played on the hill back of the house, and slept in a room separate from Nimrod's, with whom Mr. Girardeau did not seem anxious that he should have much intercourse. These three constituted the entire family. Nimrod became cook, washerman, porter, and performed with alacrity whatever duty was assigned him. How Nimrod relished his new service and new master *for a while,* we need not relate. He could not fail however to be sensible that his food was not quite as good as that to which he had been accustomed, and to see that his master did not prove exactly what he expected. He found Mr. Girardeau to be, to say the least, harsh, arbitrary, exacting; he began to suspect something worse than this; he believed he told him falsehoods; that he had money, and that in abundance. As he lay on the counter, where he usually slept at night, he was sure he heard the sound of coin in the room overhead. Of the young woman, respecting whom he had been cautioned, he saw nothing, till one day he heard voices in the chamber. He listened at the foot of the stairs, and distinguished a female's voice. There were sharp works, severe epithets. Presently a woman came hurriedly down, and passed into the street.

"Did you see that girl?" asked Mr. Girardeau, descending immediately afterwards.

"Yes, Sir," replied Nimrod.

"She is my daughter," added Mr. Girardeau. "Yes, my own flesh and blood. You know not the feelings of a father. She has been guilty of the greatest of crimes, she has disobeyed me, she has violated my will, she has endangered my estate. She has married to her own shame, and my grief. I have borne with her, till forbearance becomes a sin. She would strip me of my possessions. The author of her degradation she would make the pander to her cruelty. I am doubly beset, they are in a conspiracy against me. Heed her not, listen not to her importunity, let her suffer. I have no feelings of a father; they have been wrenched and torn away; I cannot own a viper for a child."

Nimrod thrust his fists in his waistcoat pockets, where he clenched them angrily. He was silent. He listened as to an unanswerable argument; he believed not a word. In the mean time let us refer to some events wherein his own interest began to be awakened; and which we shall embody in a new chapter, with a new title.

CHAPTER XII.

THE STORY OF GOTTFRIED BRÜCKMANN AND JANE GIRARDEAU.

Among the Mercenaries, popularly known as Hessians, employed by England against America during the war of our Revolution, was Gottfried Brückmann. He was, properly speaking, a Waldecker, having been born in Pyrmont, an inconsiderable city of that principality. From what we know of his history, he seems to have shared largely in the passion for music, which distinguishes many of his country. To this also he added a thirst for literary acquisition. But a peasant by caste, he encountered not a few obstacles in these higher pursuits. He became bellows-boy for the organ in the church of his native town, and availing himself of chance opportunities, attained some skill on that instrument. He played well on the harpsichord, flute and violin. In the French language, at that time so much in vogue among the Germans, he became a proficient. Nevertheless, he fretted under the governmental yoke that lay so oppressively and haughtily upon the necks of that class of people to which he belonged. His conduct exposing him to suspicion, he fled into the region of country described as the Hartz Mountains. Whatever of romance, literature, poetry, descended into the mass of the population; whatever of legendary tale or cabalistic observance was cherished by the common heart; whatever of imaginative temper, ideal aspiration, or mystic enthusiasm has ever characterized any portion of his countrymen, Brückmann possessed; and in the vicinity where he now found himself, there was a supply of objects fitted to animate the strongest sentiments of his being, and scenes and associations that were congenial with his inclinations; —forests of oak and beech, fir and pine; every kind and conformation of rock; birds of all descriptions; cloud-piercing hills, unfathomable chasms; lakes embosomed in mountains; waterfalls; mines and smelting-houses, with the weird and tartarean look of the workmen and their operations; gorgeous sunsets; dense and fantastic fogs; perennial snows: points of local and traditionary interest; the Altar and Sorcerer's Chair, the seat of the festival of the Old Saxon idol, Crotho; the grottoes Baumanshole and Bielshole; a cave reputed at the time to have no termination; wildness, irregularity, terror, grandeur, freedom and mystery, on every side. In addition, were little villages and clusters of houses in valleys embowered in forests and overshadowed by mountains, into one of which Brückmann's wanderings led him, that of Rubillaud, through which runs the Bode. Here in the midst of almost inaccessible rocks and cold elevations, he found fruit-trees in blossom, fields green with corn, and a small stone church surmounted with a crucifix, a May-pole hung with garlands, around which the villagers were having their Whitsun dances. In this place he remained a while, and was engaged as a school teacher for children, the parents of whom were chiefly miners. Here he became warmly attached to one of his pupils, Margaret Bruneau, daughter of the Pastor of Rubillaud, who was a Lutheran. In her he found tastes and feelings like his own. With her he rambled among mountains, penetrated caves, sang from rocks; and had such an intercourse as tended to cement their affection, and prosecuted whatever plans were grateful to their natures.

But in the midst of his repose came that cruel and barbarous draft of the British Crown on the German States. Some of the inhabitants of Rubillaud, who were subjects of the King of Hanover, were enlisted in this foreign service. Requisition was made on several provinces then in alliance with England, Brunswick, Hesse Cassel, Hanau, Anhalt and Waldeck; and on Brückmann's native town, Pyrmont. The general league formed among these princes against the peace and liberty of their people, would not suffer that Brückmann should escape. He was seized, as if he had been a felon, and forcibly taken to Rotterdam, the place of embarkation. The reluctance with which this body of levies contemplated the duty to which they were destined, will be understood when it is told that they were obliged to be under guard on their march to the sea-coast; that many of them bound hand and foot were transported in carts; some succeeded in deserting; others making the attempt were shot. Brückmann, for some instance of insubordination, received a wound at the hand of his own Captain, from which he never entirely recovered. Swords ruled souls. Their avaricious and tyrannical lords let them out as slaves, and had them scourged to their tasks. Brückmann and Margaret parted in uttermost bitterness of spirit, and with the fondest expressions of love. They wafted their adieus and prayers to each other across the bridge of the Bode, over which he was rudely snatched to see her in this world no more forever.

We shall not follow him through the fortunes of the war; but hasten to its close, when he was stricken and overwhelmed by the news of Margaret's death. A strong bond, and perhaps the only one that attached him to his native country, was broken; and in common with many of his countrymen, he chose to remain in America after the peace.

These Germans, such as survived,—more than eleven thousand of their number having perished during the war,—disposed of themselves as they could; some joined the settlements of their brethren in Pennsylvania, others pushed beyond the Ohio, a few sought the New England States. Brückmann took up his abode in New York. Those who returned to Germany he bade plant Margaret's grave with narcissus, rosemary and thyme, and visit it every Whitsun Festival with fresh flowers; while he would hallow her memory with prayers and tears in his own heart. He was disappointed in purpose, forsaken in spirit, broken in feeling. Contrary to the usual maxim, he loved those whom he had injured, and was willing that whatever of life or energy remained to him should be given to the Americans, while he remembered the land of his birth with sorrow, upbraidings and despair.

Owing to our numerous and profitable relations with France at this time, the French language had arisen in the popular estimation, and was in great request. He would teach it, and so earn a livelihood, and serve the land of his adoption. Music too, the musical spirit of Margaret and of his native country, that which survives in the soul when every thing else is prostrate, came over him. He would live again in song. He would recall the scenes of the past. Margaret would reappear in the tones of their love and their youth; her spirit would echo to the voice of his flute; in song, like night, they would meet again; by an invisible pathway of melody they would glide on to the grave. Poor Brückmann! Poor America! What with his deficiency in our tongue, and his former services against our liberties, he obtained but few scholars. Superior and more agreeable Frenchmen were his rivals. Music! How could we pay for music, when we could not pay our debts? The crescendo and diminuendo were other than of sound our people had to learn. He grew sicker at heart, his hopes had all fled, and his spiritual visions seemed to grow dimmer and dimmer. He sat by the narrow window of the small unlighted room he rented, in the night, and played on his flute to the darkness, the air, the groups of idle passers by, to memory and to the remote future whither his visions were flying and the fair spirit of his reveries had betaken itself. Yet he had one and not an unconcerned listener, and perhaps another. These were Jane Girardeau and her father. Mr. Girardeau had discovered the sound of the music proceeding from the hill behind his house, and his daughter listening to it. He called her in; she would go up to the chamber window, and repeat her curiosity. He ordered her to bed; she would creep from her room, and sly into the street that she might hear it. He detected her, rebuffed her, and locked her into her room. "Can you indulge such extravagance?" was the language of Mr. Girardeau to his daughter. "Can you yield to such weakness? Will you waste your time in this way? Shall I suffer in you a repetition of all your mother occasioned me? Will you hazard your reputation? Why will you so often break my commands? I will have none of this. You are impudent, beastly."

His daughter ill brooked such treatment. To the mind of her father, she was rash, turbulent, inordinate, selfish, lavish, insensible. She was lavish, but only of her heart's best affections; she was rash, not in head, so much as in impulse; she was insensible, but only to the demands of lucre; she was troubled, not turbulent; she was inordinate, for no want of her heart had ever been supplied; she was selfish in the sense of obeying her nature, while she disregarded the behests of stupidity and meanness.

Jane had rebelled under the iron jurisdiction of her father. Like the hidden fires of the earth she broke out wherever she could find vent. She was held down, not subdued. She was too elastic to flatten, too spiritual to stagnate. She rebounded with a wild recoil. Her fits of anger, or sallies of spirit, whatever they might be called, were frequent and energetic. As she grew older, she became more sensible of her degradation and wrongs, as well as more capable of redressing them.

She was the only child of an ill-assorted marriage. She became of some service to her father. Her personal beauty was an attraction to customers, and he valued her aid as shop-girl. She presided over the department of the store devoted to the sale of fancy goods, which, obtained in various ways, afforded enormous profits, and became an item of trade, that, notwithstanding her father's extensive and multifarious business, he could not well forego. She was also a good accountant and book-keeper. Brückmann was straitened for means. His quarterly rent was due. He would make one effort more; and that perhaps the most dangerous for a poor man; he would borrow money. He knew of the broker near by, and his reputation for wealth. He had no friend, no backer. He obtained a certificate ftom the parents of one of his scholars, to the effect that he was believed to be an honest man. He presented himself at the store of Mr. Girardeau. Jane was there; she recognized in him the flute-player, whom she had sometimes seen in the streets, or at his window. Brückmann was a Saxon throughout; his eyes were full blue, his complexion was light and fair, his hair was of a sandy brown, thick and bushy. Dejection and disappointment were evidently doing their work upon him. His face had grown thin, his eyes were sunk, and his look was that of a sick man. He addressed Mr. Girardeau in broken English. "Speak in your own language," said the latter gentleman, "I can understand you." He stated briefly his object. Mr. Girardeau looked at the note, and replied in German, "Hard times, sir, hard times; securities scarce, liabilities uncertain, business dull, great losses abroad, foreigners do not appreciate our condition." He then proceeded to interrogate Brückmann on his business, circumstances, prospects. There were two listeners to the answer, father and daughter, both intent, but in a different manner. The old gentleman ordered Jane away while he transacted a little private business. She retreated to the back part of the store where she persistingly stood; and it was obvious, although the stranger spoke in his own tongue, she comprehended what he said. From one thing to another, Brückmann was led to recite his entire history; his birth, his retreat to Rubillaud, his interest in Margaret, his enlistment, his service in the war, Margaret's death, his present method of support. Mr. Girardeau replied, in brief, that it was not in his power to accommodate him. The agitation of Brückmann was evidently intense at this repulse; and there seemed to be aroused a corresponding sympathy of distress in the heart of Jane. The story of the stranger interested her, it took strong possession of her imagination. As he left, her thoughts followed him with that most agonizing sense of powerless compassion. Could she but see him, could she but speak with him, she would bestow upon him her condolences, if she could offer him no more substantial aid.

Jane studied day and night how she might encounter the unhappy stranger, the enchanting musician. To perfect her for his purposes, her father allowed her to do a little business in her own name. These earnings, ordinarily devoted to some species of amusement or literary end, she now as sedulously hoarded as increased. She discovered where Brückmann had some pupils in a private family. Thither, taking her private purse, she went; sought her way to his room, and seated herself among the scholars. She heard the recitation, and the remarks that accompanied it. She discerned the originality of Brückmann's mind, as she had formerly been interested in the character of his sensibilities. He spoke in a feeble tone, but with a suggestive emphasis. She knew well the causes of his depression. He sang also to his pupils one of his native hymns; she admired its beauty and force, and perhaps more the voice of the singer. She staid behind when the scholars left. He spoke to her. She replied, to his surprise, in his own language, or something akin to it. She told him who she was, that she had heard his story, and she compassionated his wants, that her father was abundantly rich, and that from her own earnings she had saved him some money. She pressed upon him her purse, which neither delicacy demanded, nor would necessity allow that he should refuse. She told him how much she had been interested in his history; she desired him to repeat it.

She was reproached and maledicted by her father, on her return, although he knew not where she had been. An idea had seized her, and for that she was willing to sacrifice every thing. It had neither shape, nor color, nor definition, nor end. She thought of it when she went to bed, she dreamed of it, she awoke with it. She would see the stranger. She went again to his school-room. She walked with him on the Parade. "Tell me," she would say, "more about Margaret. How old was she? How did she look? How did you love her? Why did you love her?" He would rehearse all he had said before, and discover new particulars each time.

"Were her parents rich or poor?" asked Jane.

"Poor," replied Brückmann.

"Happy, happy Margaret! O if my father was poor as the sheerest mendicant I should be happy."

"You may be able to do much good with your money, sometime or another."

"I see nothing before me but darkness and gloom," replied Jane. "My father,—you know what he is. My dear, dear mother, too fond of her child, too opposed to her husband, too indulgent, too kind,—she has gone from my love and my approach forever. I may be in the midst of affluence, I am cursed, blighted by a destitution such as you know nothing of. Gold may be my inheritance, my prospects are all worthless, fearful, sombre. You say you will meet Margaret in heaven!"

"Speak freely with me," said Brückmann, "I love to hear, if I cannot answer. Margaret and I often talked of what we could not comprehend. We strove to lift each other up, even if we made no advance. She had a deep soul, an unbounded aspiration. We sang of heaven, and then we began to feel it. We were more Sphinxes than Œdipuses. Yet she became heaven to me, when there was none in the skies. She was a transparent, articulate revelation of God."

"How I should love Margaret!" said Jane to him one day. "What was the color of her hair? like yours?"

"No," replied Brückmann; "as I have told you, she was not of German origin. Her ancestors came from Languedoc in the Religious Wars. She was more tropical in her features, and perhaps in her heart, than I. She had black hair and eyes; she resembled you, Miss Girardeau, I think."

"How I wish I could see her!" replied Jane. "You say she does come to you sometimes?"

"Yes," said Brückmann," and since I have known you she comes more frequently, more clearly. My perishing heart had scarce power to evoke her. My song became too faint a medium. You have revived those visions, and refreshing communions."

"Then I am happy," said Jane; "I knew not that I had such a power. You, sir, know not the misery of being able to make no one happy. I torture my father, I plague Samuel. I am of use to no one. And my poor self answers not for itself!"

"How could you fight against our poor country?" she one day asked him.

"I never did," he said; "my heart was with the Americans. I was forced into the work. I was bayoneted to the lines. My musket shared the indisposition of its owner, and shot at random. Wounds that had been spared by those against whom I was arrayed were anticipated by my own officers. At this moment I am sensible of the pain."

"Yet you might have been killed in battle," said she, "and I, poor, ridiculous, selfish me! should never have seen you."

"Nor I you," he rejoined; "I know not which is the most indebted."

These interviews could not be repeated without coming to the knowledge, or kindling the indignation of Mr. Girardeau. He noticed the frequent, and sometimes protracted absences of his daughter; he traced them to the indigent German, whose application for money he denied, to the villanous musician that had given him so much annoyance. His passion had no bounds. He ceased to expostulate; he raved, he threatened; he shut Jane into her chamber, he barred the door and declared he would starve her. As Jane had never learned filial obedience, so she had not disciplined herself to ordinary patience. Even in matters that concerned her interest and happiness most vitally, she was impetuous and inconsiderate. She could bear imprisonment, she could bear starvation, she could bear invective and violence; she could not endure separation from Brückmann. She experienced, in respect of him, new and joyous sensations that enchained her existence. She looked on him as a superior being. She felt that he alone could understand her, appreciate or sympathize with her. She felt that of the mass about her, he only seemed to have a common nature with her. She thought not of his poverty or his dejection. She thought only of his soul into which she could pour her own. She was eager for him, as a child for its mother's breast. His love for Margaret Bruneau only heightened his value in her eyes. He seemed for his devotion to Margaret Bruneau, purer, greater, diviner He and Margaret constituted to her mind a delightful company. She entered a magic circle when she came into their communion. She became one of a glorious trio. Then she saw herself interpreted and symbolized in Margaret; and she acted as a conjuration to bring that delightful vision from the shades. Brückmann she assisted, encouraged, enlivened; she rendered him more hopeful, more happy. And she herself had no life, except as he was able to explain that life. His soul seemed to respond to hers, and her own grew serener and stiller as it received that response. "He, too, will suffer," she said to herself, "if he sees me not. His own heart will break again Margaret Bruneau will come to him no more;" and every thought of his uneasiness or suspense vibrated, like a fire, through her sensations.

Mr. Girardeau waited to see some tokens of his daughter's repentance and amendment, but none appeared. The more completely to secure his purposes, he instigated a prosecution against Brückmann, on the score of debt, and had him thrown into the City Jail. The old gentleman then approached his daughter, apprised her of what had befallen her friend, and announced his final decision. He told her if ever she saw Brückmann again, if ever she communicated with him by word or letter, he would turn her into the streets, close his doors upon her forever, and cast her out to utter shame and wretchedness. With whatever tone or spirit this sentence may have been distinguished, and there could be no mistake as to its general purport, its effect on Jane was scarcely perceptible. Her die was cast, her resolution taken. She undid the fastenings of her room and escaped into the street.

Going to the jail, she obtained access to the cell and was locked in with Brückmann. Through his drooping heart and wasting frame he received her with a bland, welcome smile. She fell at his feet, and vented herself in a torrent of tears. His kindness reassured her, and she told him what had transpired. "But," she continued, "Gottfried, I must see you, I must be with you, I cannot live away from you, I die without you. Existence has not the faintest charm, not a solitary point of interest, if I am separated from you. You have awakened within me every dormant and benumbed faculty. You have spread over time the hues of a higher being. You have given back to my soul the only answer it ever received; with your eyes I have looked into myself and discovered some beauty there, where before was only a deep and frightful chaos. In a world of shallowness and stupidity you alone have anticipated, understood and valued me. I repose on you as on the breast of God. You have introduced me to an elevated communion; you have welcomed me to the participation of yourself and

Margaret; you have inspired me with a desire to know more of the laws of the spirit's life. For all this I have made you no return. I am little, how little! to you. You owe me nothing, I owe you every thing."

"Jane,—" said he.

"Do not interrupt me now," she continued. "Let my poor soul have its say. It may be its last. I have now no home on earth but you. May I remain with you? May I hear your voice, look into your eyes, be blessed and illumined by your spirit?"

"Is it possible," asked Brückmann, "that your father will never relent? He needs you, his own fortune is under obligations to you."

"*You know not my father*," was the decisive reply. "He is fixed, inexorable, as the God he serves. I look to you, or to vacancy, to nought, to the sepulchral abyss of my own soul, to the interminable night of my own thoughts To be poor is nothing, to be an outcast is nothing; to be away from you is worse than all calamities condensed in one blow. Do not be distressed, my good Gottfried. I will not embarrass you. Gottfried—I will marry you—I do embarrass you. I do distress you—I will not. No! I go away—I leave you.—Farewell, Gottfried!"

"Stay!" replied he, "do not go away."

"Speak to me," she said. "Chide me, spurn me. I can bear any thing. I will not stir, nor wince, nor weep, I can stiffen myself into insensibility. I will sit here unmoved as a curb-stone. Speak, Gottfried, speak, if you kill me."

"Jane," said he, very kindly, "you have nothing to fear from me, we have nothing to fear from each other. We know each other too well to be alarmed by surprises, or perplexed at disclosures. We have no secrets to keep or to reveal, no hopes to indulge or disappoint. Our natures are bared to each other; our several destinies too well understood; a word, the faintest expression of a wish is sufficient. You know Margaret, I need not——"

"No, Mr. Brückmann, you need not——"

"Call me Gottfried. Margaret called me Gottfried. You must never call me any thing else."

"O," said she, "if I could do Margaret's least office for you, if I could ever remind you of her! And this assimilates me nearer to her. It gives me a prerogative, which, with all my rashness, I should hardly otherwise dare to claim. But you need not speak to me of her. I know all about it, and you, and her. Yet not as a beggar, not as a friend, not as one who has the slightest demand on your notice, yet I say, obeying an impulse which I know how neither to control nor define, but which is deep as the central fires of my being, I ask for entrance, for a home, in that which you are, for fellowship with you and all your life. Tell me more of Margaret; I will grow up into her image; I will transmute myself to her nature. You shall have a double Margaret; no, not double, but one. Nay, if needs be, I will go out of myself; I will be the servant of you both. Call me your child, your and Margaret's child, your spirit-child, and so love me. And when we get to Heaven, you may do what you will with me. Sure I am, I shall never get there if you do not take me. I cannot sing, as you say she could. But my soul sings. I can describe with my sensations as many octaves and variations as you on your flute; and with your nice ear perhaps you could hear some pleasant strains. Away from you, I am all discord, a jangling of broken and bewildered emotion."

"Have you thought," asked Gottfried, "how we should be situated. This prison is my home now, and I have no better prospect for the future."

"I have enough in my purse," said Jane, "to release you. You can teach as you have done. I perhaps could give instruction in the more popular branches."

"Dear Jane!" said he, "you are dearer to me than all on earth beside. But how fade all earth scenes from my thought! I feel myself vanishing into the spirit-world. Daily I perceive the hand of destiny lying more heavily upon me. Hourly invisible cords are drawing me away. The echoes of my song sound louder and louder from the shadowy shore."

"Ah, dearest Gottfried! if you die, I will die too. I cannot live without you; I cannot survive you; I perish with you. I will be absorbed with you into the Infinite. All your presentiments I share."

"We will be married," answered Gottfried. "I have loved you; I will still love you; you deserve my love. Margaret Bruneau too will love you; and the heaven-crowned shall bestow her blessing on the earth-worn."

Jane procured his release from prison, by paying debts and costs of suit. They went to the house of the Rev. Dr. ———, a kind and benevolent old clergyman, by whom the marriage ceremony was performed, the wife and daughter of the rector being present as witnesses. They knelt on a couch for an altar; the long black hair of the bride gathered loosely about her temples and skirting a clear marble neck, and her dark eyes, contrasting the light thick hair, deep blue eyes, and flickering pale face of the groom, produced a subdued and sad impression in the mind of the observer; yet the evening light of their souls, for such it seemed to be, coming out at that hour, shed over them a soft, sweet glow. The old man blessed them, and they departed.

They sought lodgings in a quarter of the city at some

distance from their former abode. Brückmann was enabled to form a small class in French. If female education or the employment of female instructors had been as common in those days as at the present time, Jane might have directed the powers with which Nature had enriched her to some advantage. She secured, in fact, but a solitary pupil, and that one more anxious to be taught dancing and dressing than to advance in any solid acquisition. She found a more satisfactory as well as promising task in perfecting Brückmann in the English language. This difficulty once surmounted, she fancied he would be able to pursue his practice to any desirable extent. So five or six months passed away.—Whether it was the seeds of disease constitutionally inherited, the effect of disappointment, want, heartache, he had been called to endure, the internal progress of his wound, or his own presentiments acting upon an imagination sufficiently susceptible—Brückmann fell sick. He lay upon his bed week by week. Jane abandoned every thing to take care of him.

"Jane," said he, "I must die."

"I know it," she replied, "you told me you should soon die. I believed it then, I am prepared for it now."

"Voices," he added, "are calling me away."

"I know that too," she rejoined; "I hear them."

"An inward force propels my spirit from me."

"Yes," said she, "I feel it."

She bent over him, not as over a sick and dying man, but a convalescing angel. He seemed to her not to be wasting to skin and bones, but to spirit and life. His eye brightened, his smile was sweeter, as he grew paler and thinner.

"I wish you would sing to me, Jane."

"I am full of music and song," she said, "can you not hear me? All that you have ever played or sung, or spoken, leaps, trills, is joyous, within me. Do you not hear a soft chanting?"

"Yes," he replied; "it sounds like the voice of Jesus and Margaret."

"How glad I am our little Margaret is to have her birthplace in song!" said Jane. "She feeds on melodies. Yet if I should die before her birth, will she die too? Tell me, Gottfried."

"I think her spirit will go with ours," he answered.

"Then we could nourish and mould the undeveloped, unformed spirit in heaven. And our other Margaret will be there to help us bring up the little Margaret. Will Jesus bless our child, as you say he blessed the children of olden times?"

"Yes," replied Gottfried. "He died for all, and lives to give all life."

"I shall not need to make her clothes?"

"You had better do that, Jane, we may both survive her birth."

Acting upon this hint, their private funds having become well nigh exhausted, she repaired to her father's house to procure some articles of her own, out of which suitable garment's might be prepared. By a back entrance she ascended to her old chamber, where, as the event should prove, Mr. Girardeau detecting her, drove her off. At this moment, as she retreated through the store, Nimrod, who in the mean time had succeeded to the deceased Samuel, saw her, as has been related in the previous chapter. Here, also, the two episodical branches of this memoir unite.

When Nimrod learned from Mr. Girardeau who the woman was, how she stood related to him, and what were her fortune and condition, we may naturally imagine his curiosity, always restive, always errant, would be more than usually aroused. A new object presented itself; he must pry into it. Having ascertained the place of Jane and Gottfried's residence, being out of an errand, he made bold to enter the house, and knock at the door.

"Ax your pardon, marm," he said, shuffling into the room, as Jane opened the door, and the sick man lay on the bed before him; "hope I don't intrude. I sarve at Master Girarder's, since Samuel's dead. I am the fellow what see you running out of the store like a duck arter a tumble-bug. What was you so skeered for? I wouldn't a hurt you any more than an old shoe. I guess the old gentleman ain't any better than he should be—"

"Young man!" said Jane, breaking in upon him, "whoever you are, we have no connection with Mr. Girardeau."

"Yes—marm," said Nimrod, who, nothing daunted, approached the bed. Gottfried rose a little, with his wan, beautiful face. Jane, paler if possible, and more beautiful, held her arm under his head, and her dark, loving eyes brimmed with tears, the nature of which Nimrod could not understand.

"I vum," said he, "what is the matter? If the Widder was here she could cure him in a wink. Won't your Dad let you go home? Won't he give you a limb to roost on! I tell you what it is, he's close as a mink in winter; he's hard as grubbing bushes. I don't guess he's so poor."

Jane, remembering her father's servants in Samuel, who was a perfect creature of his master, if at first she was annoyed by the familiarity of Nimrod or was suspicious of his motives, soon perceived that his manner was undisguised and rusticity sincere. She was led to question him as to himself and who he was. He gave her his real name, and that of his parents. In fact he became quite communicative, and rendered a full description of his family, their residence and mode of life. He was pleased with his visit, which he promised to repeat, and whenever he had a chance, he dropped in to see his new found friends. As our readers will have anticipated the result of this story of Gottfried Brückmann and Jane Girardeau, we shall hasten to its close. When Mr. Girardeau became apprised of the real situation of his daughter, he manifested deep disturbance of spirit. He addressed himself anew to Nimrod. "That girl," said he, "is a runaway, a spendthrift, a wanton. She is about to have a child, the fruit of her reckless, ruinous misconduct. That child may do me an injury, a great injury. The offspring of that viper may turn upon me with the malignity of the mother. That child must be watched. You know, Mr. Foxly, we are identified in interest. You know if I let you go, or you me, we both fall. That child must be watched. Do you understand?"

"That wa'nt in the bargain when I came to live with ye," replied Nimrod. "I must have a little more, a little of the ready."

Nothing could be more opportune for Nimrod. He was now at liberty to prosecute his visits to Jane and Gottfried at his leisure. Whatever money he obtained from Mr. Girardeau, eked out by his own scant purse, he applied to their necessities. He felt himself to be of more consequence than he had ever been before, and although exercising his function rather pragmatically, he made himself greatly useful. Brückmann grew more feeble; Jane approached the period of her child's birth.

"Nimrod," said she a few days before that event, "we are going to die."

"No, no," he rejoined. "He'll give up the ghost as sure as wild geese in cold weather. But you will come out as bright as a yaller bird in spring."

"We must die—I shall die," she continued, hardly noticing what he said, having become quite used to his manner. "We have loved, tenderly loved, if you know what that means."

"Yes—marm," replied Nimrod. "If I am a Ponder and you live in the city, you need'nt think we are as dull as millers that fly right into your links and never know whether they are singed or not. When I have been by uncle Bill Palmer's, that lives at the Ledge, as you go up to Dunwich, and seen his Rhody out there, jolly! she has gone right through me like an earwig; it sticks to me like a bobolink to a saplin in a wind. I an't afeered of the old Harry himself, but I say for't! I never dare speak to Rhody. But you great folks here don't care any thing about us, no more than Matty Gisborne and Bet Weeks down among the settlers."

"Yes I do care for you," said Jane; "you have been very kind to us. I know not what we should have done without you. But we are really going to die. It has been foretold that we should."

"O yes," said Nimrod, relapsing into a more thoughtful mood, "I remember. I heard a dog howl in the streets the other night, and I dreamed of seeing monkeys, and that is sartin death."

"You must bury us, Nimrod," continued Jane. "And you must promise one thing, to take care of our child. Its name is Margaret, you must call it by no other. You will contrive means to take it to your own home, the Pond. You are poor, you say, that is the greatest of blessings. Your house is apart from the world. Your little brother Chilion you think would love it as his own sister. Now promise us, Nimrod, that you will do all we desire."

Nimrod not only promised, but volunteered a declaration

having the full weight of an oath, that her wishes regarding the child should be studiously fulfilled. At this crisis they were also visited by a daughter of the clergyman who married them; she having become informed of their state, sought to minister to their needs. Brückmann died as he had presaged. "Farewell, Jane!" he said. "Yet not farewell, but, follow me. I kiss you for the night, and you shall see me in the morning. The sun fades, the stars glow, brighter worlds await us. We go to those who love us." Nimrod bent reverently over the dead form, that did perhaps what life itself could never have done, it made of the strong man a child, and tears gushed from his eyes. Jane knelt calmly, hopefully by his side, kissed his lips, and smoothed the bright curling locks of his hair. Nimrod, assisted by the clergyman before mentioned, and some of Brückmann's countrymen that remained in the city as servants, bakers, or scavengers, and could do little more for their old friend than bear him to his grave, saw him decently buried. The wife and daughter of the clergyman were with Jane at the period she had anticipated with so much interest. Her hour came, and as she had predicted, a girl, the "little Margaret," was born. She lingered on a few days, without much apparent suffering or anxiety, blessed her child, and melted away at last in the clouds of mortal vision. The child was taken in charge by those ladies who had kindly assisted at its birth.

Mr. Girardeau, who had exhibited ceaseless anxiety, as well as glimpses of some unnatural design, during these events, the progress of which he obliged Nimrod carefully to report, ordered the child to be brought to his house. His language was, "it must be put out of the way." It was a dark night; Mr. Girardeau, availing himself of a weakness of his servant, plentifully supplied him with liquor. He also threatened him, in case of disobedience, with a legal prosecution on the score of his smuggling connections. Nimrod, sufficiently in drink to make a rash promise, started for the child. But apprehensions of some dark or bloody deed came over him ; the recollection of his solemn vows to the mother of the child upbraided him ; the spectral shadows cast by the street-lamps startled him. He remembered the smuggling vessel which had made another trip, and was about to return. The child was delivered to him, and in place of going back to his master, he made directly for the sloop, which was even then on the point of sailing. The captain and crew, however serviceable they might be to Mr. Girardeau's interest, cherished little respect for his character, and Nimrod had no difficulty in enlisting their aid for his purposes. We need not follow him all the way to the Pond, or recite the methods he adopted to sustain and nourish the child. On his way up the river he found plenty of milk in the cabin. Leaving the vessel, he spent one night in the shanty of an Irishman, whose wife having a nursling at her side, cheerfully relinquished to Margaret one half of her supply. One night he slept with his charge in a barn. On the third evening he reached his home. The family were all abed ; his father and mother, however, were soon ready to welcome their son. Surprise was of course their first emotion when they saw what he had with him. He recounted the history of the child, and his purpose to have it adopted in the family. The course of his observations on the subject was such, as to allay whatever repugnance either of his parents may have felt to the project, and they became as ready to receive the little stranger as they might have been originally averse.

" Call up Hash and Chilion," said Pluck. " The child must be baptized to-night."

" Wait till to-morrow, do Dad," said Nimrod. " I guess

she needs something to wet her stomach more than her head."

"Fix her something, woman, can't wait."

His wife prepared a drink for the child, while Nimrod aroused his brothers. Chilion, then a boy, seven or eight years old, held a pine-torch that streamed and smoked through the room. Mistress Hart supported the child, while Nimrod and Hash stood sponsers. The old man called her Mary. "No, Dad," interposed Nimrod, "it must be Margaret."

"No! Mary," replied his father, "in honor of my esteemed wife. Besides, that's a Bible name, and we can't liquor up on Margaret. Yours is a good name, and you never will see cause to repent it; and there is Maharshalalhashbaz,—that I chose because it was the longest in the Bible; I wanted to show my reverence for the book by taking as much of it as I could; and Chilion's is a good one too; all Bible names in this family."

"I tell you no, Dad, she *must be called Margaret*," repeated Nimrod.

"Do call her Margaret," said Chilion.

"Well, well," replied Pluck, "we will put it to vote.—Three for Margaret, I shall call her Mary, and Hash goes for Peggy. We won't break heads about it, if we do we shan't the bottle. So here goes for Margaret and Mary."

The family, severally and collectively, laid themselves under strict injunctions to keep the history of the child a secret, and cherish it as their own. Mr. Hart and his little son Chilion were glad enough to receive it on its own account; Mistress Hart, if for no other reason, in consideration of the money Nimrod represented he would get from its grandfather, a reflection that prevailed with Hash also. The secluded position of the family rendered it possible indeed for children to be born and die without exciting observation. Their neighbor, the Widow Wright, was the only person from whom they had cause of apprehension. It was presumed however to be an easy matter to bring her into the arrangement of secrecy, which was accordingly done by an oath sealed with a small douceur. In behalf of the child were enlisted both the Widow's superstition and her avarice. What *might* befall her son Obed, then six or seven years of age, she knew not. So Margaret was only spoken of as a child of the Pond. When Obed asked his mother where the little baby came from, she said it dropped from an acorn-tree.

Such is the origin of Margaret, who a few months later has been phantasmagorically introduced to our readers.

We might add, in conclusion of this chapter, that Nimrod, the next year, made a visit to New York, and sought an interview with his old master. The disappointment, chagrin and displeasure of the latter were evidently great. Their conference was long and bitter. In the result, Nimrod declared in cant phrase that he would "blow" on the old gentleman, not only as a smuggler, but as a murderer, unless he would settle on the child a small annual sum, to be delivered at sight. To such a bond Mr. Girardeau was obliged to give his signature. He asked where the child was, but on this point Nimrod kept a rigid silence.

CHAPTER XIII.

RETURNS TO MARGARET, WHO ADVANCES IN CHILDHOOD AND KNOWLEDGE OF THE WORLD.

Military Trainings we have alluded to as a sort of New England holiday. Pluck, taking with him Margaret, Hash, Chilion and the dog, went down to the village at an early hour. The Green flowed with people, soldiers, men, women and children. Portions of the horse-sheds were converted into booths for the sale of liquors, fruits and bread ; wheelbarrows and carts were converted to the same use. An angle of the Meeting-house, Mr. Smith, the Tavern Keeper at No. 4, appropriated for his peculiar calling. Pluck engaged himself as tapster in one of the horse-sheds. Margaret, having orders not to go home, till her father returned at night, sat with Bull on the grass near the Meeting-house by the side of some other boys and girls, who all moved away when she approached. Tony's beat of the troop was the signal for the soldiers to assemble They were first marched to the front of the church, when prayer, as usual, was offered by Parson Welles, standing on the steps. "O Lord God," thus he prayed, "we thank thee that thou hast raised up a defence to Israel, whereby thou hast cut off the mighty men of valor, and the leaders and captains in the camp of the king of Assyria. We humbly beseech that thou wouldst send prosperity, that thou wouldst be an enemy to our enemies, and destroy all them that afflict our soul. Let the gates be lifted up, and the Lord, the Lord strong and mighty, the Lord mighty in battle, come in. And now, O God, we fall down upon our knees before thee, for and in behalf of thy cause, name, people and interest, that in this day are so deeply designed against by the serpent and his seed, and from this black cloud of tumult and confusion among the nations, wilt thou bring forth the accomplishment of those promises thy people are so earnestly looking after and waiting for?"

The old man was fervid and earnest. His massive white wig fluttered in the wind, his venerable form bent over his ivory-headed cane. Some of the people were moved to tears.

The soldiers were then drawn into a line for inspection. Their equipment presented hardly so uniform and symmetrical an aspect as appears in the militia of our day. There had been however a gradual improvement from the primitive array of Colonial times; when the troops were made up of pikemen, bowmen, and musketeers with match-locks. Miles Standish was dressed in a coat of mail, on his left arm he bore a target, in his right a rapier or broadsword, iron gloves shielded his hands, an iron helmet with a visor covered his head and face, his breast was plated with iron. In this Livingston Company many wore three-cornered hats, shad-bellied coats, shoe and knee buckles. Some retained the identical dress of the late war. The children who may read this memoir, and we hope there are many such, do not fancy that the Revolution was fought in cocked-hats and small-clothes!

Among the spectators, seated on the grass under the eaves of the Meeting-house, were several, whose wounds and infirmities contracted during the war, rendered them muster-free. There were six or eight of this description; one had lost a leg, another an arm, one had survived a shot through the groin, one had pined away on insults, blows, hunger and cold in the Jersey prison-ships, and bringing home his stark skeleton, became a town pauper. Another one, whose name was Alexis Robinson, having the side of his face shot away, and with one eye and ear losing a moiety of his senses, and failing besides in his earnings, the certificates of which he always carried, by the depreciation of the currency, was also provided for by the town. These severally had hobbled out to see the training.

To these must be added certain soldiers of an earlier date. Prominent among whom was lame Deacon Ramsdill, leaning with his left hand on a smooth crooked mountain-laurel cane, and having his right folded over his narrow wrinkled face, perpetually endeavoring to suppress a good-natured but somewhat undiaconal smile, a risible labitur et labetur, that spirted out like water between his fingers, and ran through the channels of his cheeks, all around his eyes, and even back to his ears. At the age of sixteen, in 1755 he was engaged in what is known as the expulsion of the Acadians, or French neutrals, from Nova Scotia ; in 1757 he was at the surrender of Fort William Henry ; 1759 found him with Gen. Wolfe at the battle on the Plains of Abraham, where he received a wound in his leg. There was also his brother Deacon, Hadlock, of a more Pythagorean temper, who was engaged in the Spanish war, and served under General Wentworth in the attack on Carthagena, 1740, and afterwards was in the defeat of General Braddock, 1755.

Nor would one forget to notice the children on this occasion, whose chief business consisted in buying ginger-bread, pitching coppers, watching the drill and following the steps of the soldiers ; or fail to be reminded of a difference in their habits between this and "good Old Colony times," when the Legislature conceiving " that the training up of youth to the art and practice of arms will be of great use; do therefore order that all youths within this jurisdiction, from ten years old to the age of sixteen years, shall be instructed by some one of the officers of the band, upon the usual training days, in the exercise of arms, as small guns, half pikes, bows and arrows."

Captain Hoag was an accomplished disciplinarian, esteemed such at least by his contemporaries. His hair was powdered, his coat faced with blue, on his hat glistened a large white cockade, his waist was ornamented with a scarlet sash, his shoulder rounded off with a silver epaulette, and silver lacings graced his yellow buck-skin breeches. But what more peculiarly distinguished him was the badge of the order of the Cincinnati, a gold medal with the spread eagle, and blue ribbon hanging from his coat buttons. "Attention! At this word," said he, giving instructions designed for the younger members of the company, "you must be silent, moving neither hand nor foot. To the left, dress! You will turn your heads briskly to the left, so as to bring your right eye in the direction of your waistcoat buttons. At the word Fire!" continued he, "you will pull the trigger briskly, then return to the priming position, the muzzle of your firelock directly in front, the left hand just forward of the feather-spring, seize the cock with the thumb and forefinger of the right hand." After the inspection and manual drill, the soldiers were marched and countermarched across the Green.

There came also to the training Master Elliman, who, exempt by his profession from arms, and rated always as a Tory, nevertheless made it a point to appear at these times, as it would seem to air his antipathies. If he encountered Pluck, well; but this morning he saw one whom he liked better, Margaret, sitting with her dog.

"How do you enjoy it?" said he.

"Very well," was the reply. "I love to see them."

"Sævit toto Mars impius orbe."

"I do not understand that."

"I know you do not. You will by and by."

"Chilion plays so on his fife, and Tony drums so well,—it is almost as good as dancing; only the girls and women don't go with them. See how they follow Chilion round just like the dancers! Why don't they dance? How slow they step!"

"It is not Chilion they follow," replied the Master, "it is that little laced android with a long knife in his hand, and a lackered bunch on his shoulder. But here are Deacons Ramsdill and Hadlock, ἄξιοῖ πρεσβῦτεροι ἐκκλησῖας τοῦ θεοῦ καὶ Αἰῦιγγστὸν and our broad-brimmed nay nay and yea yea android, Anthony Wharfield Salvete, Deacons; God bless thee, Friend Anthony. Miss Margaret Hart, Friend Anthony."

"How does thee; sister Margaret?" said the latter.

"A Pond gal!" poh'd Deacon Hadlock.

"What on arth is the Master doing with that little critter?" laughed Deacon Ramsdill. "Larnin' the young pup new tricks?"

"The dog that trots about will find a bone," quoth Deacon Hadlock.

"Qui vult cædere canem, facile invenit fustem," responded the Master.

Bull, whether that his name was used too freely, or from an old habit in the presence of strangers, began to growl.

"Lie still," said Margaret.

"There, you see the Scripture fulfilled. Soft words turn away wrath," remarked Deacon Ramsdill, with his right hand on his mouth striving in vain to curb his laughter.

"So Friend Anthony gets rid of the wars, and trainings, by his soft answers, I suppose," said the Master.

"Not of paying the fines," responded the Quaker. "Ruth and I were stripped of most we had, to support the troops."

"See how God has blessed you! What an army he is raising for our defence," exclaimed Deacon Hadlock, pointing to the soldiers.

"What is that little man, with a long knife, doing to the men?" asked Margaret.

"He is preparing them for war; he will prove a Joshua to us," said Deacon Hadlock, not so much however in reply to Margaret, as to illustrate sentiments which he feared did not sufficiently prevail with his friends.

"I ruther guess he's larnin' them bagonets and hatchets to make pretty free work with our legs," said Deacon Ramsdill, pressing down upon his cane.

"He is teaching the science of puppetry," said the Master.

"He is teaching them to break the commandments of Christ," said the Quaker.

"What is it for? what for!" exclaimed Margaret, starting up with some surprise.

"I can tell you all," said Deacon Hadlock. "It is, under God, the defence of our lives, liberties and fortunes."

"How many of our people were killed in the French war, and in the last war," said Deacon Ramsdill.

"How many of us were shut in the Jail yonder," said the Master.

"How many farms in this town were ruined," said the Quaker.

"What blunders are ye all making," answered Deacon Hadlock. "It is our enemies that we expect to kill."

"Who?" asked Margaret.

"Our enemies, I say."

"Who are our enemies?"

"Those that injure us."

"What, kill them!" said Margaret. "Now I wish Chilion would bring his violin and make them dance. They wouldn't kill one another then. Why don't he play Chorus Jig, and set them a dancing."

"Clear nater," said Deacon Ramsdill; "I make no doubt the gal feels just so."

"O, Brother Ramsdill," sighed Deacon Hadlock, "how can you! What are we coming to! I was informed you countenanced mixed dancing; that you told Bethia Weeks, a church member, there was no harm in it if she didn't carry it too far. Here you are encouraging that sinful amusement and opposing our military preparations! I do believe the Lord has forsaken us indeed."

"Behold your defenders, pro aris et focis," sneered the Master, directing attention to the soldiers. A difficulty had arisen. The Captain was seen running towards the rear of the company.

It will be remembered that Hash, the brother of Margaret, had a difference with Zenas Joy, a Breakneck at the Turkey Shoot. We would also state that Zenas was engaged to Delinda Hoag, a daughter of the Captain. On the parade this morning, Hash's conduct had been very unmannerly towards Zenas, so much so as to offend Captain Hoag, both officially and personally; and he changed Hash's place, transferring him to a platoon under command of Corporal Joseph Whiston, also a Breakneck. Hash could not brook this, and carried his resentment to the extent of striking his superior on the march; an offence that Joseph sought to punish by a blow in return. Obed, also, who was this day doing his first military duty, became somehow involved in the affray. The music ceased; order was lost. Several voices called for Deacon Hadlock to interfere in his capacity as Justice of the Peace. The soldiers speedily resolved themselves into a civil tribunal, and Hash and Obed were equitably tried and sentenced, the former to twenty-four hours' imprisonment in the Jail, and a fine of twenty shillings; the latter to twenty-nine lashes at the whipping-post.

The culprits were immediately taken to their respective dooms, followed by the populace. Margaret, not comprehending precisely the nature of events, lingered on the steps of the crowd. The screams of Obed aroused her, and she dashed through the press of people, as she would through a field of bushes, to the point whence they proceeded. A half dozen blows of the formidable cat had sufficed to fetch blood on the naked back of the youth. Margaret flew toward her suffering friend and folded her arms about him, as it were, in the way at once of pity and protection. The constable tried to wrench her off; she clung with an almost preternatural grasp. He threatened to lay the lash upon her. She told him he should not whip Obed. Judah Weeks, brother of Isabel, set up a cry "For shame!" Isabel herself, who was playing near by, began to utter a loud lament, all the children raised piteous moans, the older people became confused; in fine, Deacon Hadlock himself, hearing Obed's entreaties, consented to remit the balance of the penalty. Margaret walked through the people, who drew off on either side, her face and clothes dabbled with blood. She went with Isabel to the brook and washed; Isabel going into her house, which was near by, brought a towel to wipe her, and asked her to walk in and see her mother. Margaret said she must go back to her brother Hash.

The Jail yard, constructed of high posts, was close upon the street, and when Margaret returned she found boys and girls looking through the crevices; an example that she imitated. Deacon Ramsdill approaching, asked her if she wanted to go in; she replied that she did. After considerable parleying, the Deacon was able to obtain of the Jailer, Mr. Shooks, permission for her to enter, with Bull, whom it was not an easy matter to keep out. She found Hash in a small, dimly lighted cell, rolling and blubbering on the floor. She aroused him, and he took her in one arm, and held the head of the dog by the other, and seemed very much pleased to have them with him. She said she would stay all night, but he told her that would not be allowed. She saw another man in the cell, who, Hash whispered to her, was a murderer. This person sat in silence, muffled like an owl, in his black beard, tangled hair, begrimed face, and ragged clothes. She went to him, he took her in his lap, pressed her hard to his breast, and stroked her hair. She called Bull, and he patted the dog's head. He said he had a little boy about as old as she was, whom he had not seen for a long time, and never expected to see again. She gave him some gingerbread which she had in her pocket, and he munched it greedily. Hash offered him a quid of tobacco, whereat he seemed greatly delighted, and tears ran down his cheeks. Margaret said she would fetch him flowers the next time she came to the village. He thanked her and said he should be glad to see them, that he had not seen a flower for two years. The Jailor presently entered, and ordered Margaret to leave. She went to the Horse-sheds, where her father was selling liquors. Seating her on a cider barrel, he gave her more gingerbread and cheese, which she ate with a relish.

The day approached its close, and the soldiers drew up to ballot for officers, Captain Hoag's term of service having expired. In the result, Lieutenant Eliashib Tuck was chosen Captain, and all the subaltern officers advanced their respective grades, excepting Corporal Joseph Whiston, whose name, for some reason, disappeared from the canvass. Captain Tuck replied as follows: "Fellow-soldiers, I lack words to express my sense of the honor conferred upon me, as unexpected as it is undeserved. We live in a glorious era, one that eclipses all past time, and will be a model for future ages. The close of the eighteenth century is as sublime as its meridian was grand. It were an honor for a man to be born in this period, how much more so to be honored by it! My brave compatriots! military life is the path to distinction, and the means of usefulness. An immortal crown awaits the head of the hero! The Lion of Britain we have bound, and the Unicorn of France shall ere long bite the dust! Livingstonians! my blood is aroused, my ambition fired to be at the head of such a corps! Your fame has spread from Bunker Hill to Saratoga, from Genessee to King's Mountain. I will lead wherever you will follow, I will dare all dangers with your support."

Agreeably to custom, he then announced a treat. The company was marched to the Crown and Bowl, and dismissed. The citizens, old and young, thronged to the scene. Pluck, leaving Margaret and his tapstership, joined in the general exhilaration. Pails of toddy were brought from the bar-room. The men drank freely, gave huzzas, and sang patriotic songs. Ex-Corporal Whiston, however, and his particular friends, dignifiedly indignant, withdrew, and went to the store for their entertainment. The old men drank, and the young men; boys crept under the legs of the soldiers, and lifting the pails, tugged at the slops.

The sun went down, clouds gloomed in the sky, and

heavy vapors drifted over the town. Solomon Smith, son of the Tavern-keeper from No. 4, erected pine torches in his booth. Lights burst forth from wheelbarrows and carts throughout the Green. But an excessive use of alcoholic stimulants aggravates the ordinary symptoms of good cheer, and produces effects which the most considerate do not always foresee. Intoxication supervenes, accompanied by a paralysis of the physical, or an inflammation of the nervous, system. Captain Tuck was borne dead drunk by his reeling troops to the Tavern. Ex-Corporal Whiston with his friends sallied from the store well sprung, and encountering their enemies at all points, a medley of brawls ensued. The Horse-shed becoming scenes of varied disorder, Margaret was compelled to retreat.

It had begun to rain, the clouds emptying themselves in bulk as it might seem to animate and refreshen the people, but really to superadd a burthen on such as already had more than they could carry, and bury those who were fallen deeper in the soil. Margaret hurried she knew not where; Solomon Smith, leaving his own now deserted and useless stand, discovering her standing in the rain, kindly took her with him into the house to the kitchen; where was a parcel of persons, including boys and girls, some drying themselves by the fire, some waiting for the rain to hold up, others singing, laughing and drinking. Here also was Tony with his fiddle playing to a company of dancers; and Pluck, sitting on the hearth, with his full-orbed cabbage-head, swaying to and fro, beating time with his arms and legs, and balancing in one hand a mug of flip. "Ha! my little lady!" said he, catching Margaret with a bounce into his lap, and holding her near the fire, "won't you drink a little, now do drink a little. See how it creams; don't be snuffy, Molly, none of your mulligrubs. Here's blood now,

Obed's blood, on your pinafore. A brave deed that; you must take something. It's training day, and that don't come only four times a year. There's Beulah Ann, she loves it as well as a calf likes to be licked. Sweet pinkey-posy, it is as good for your wet clothes, as the Widder's horse-raddish for dropsy. Ha! ha!"

As he proffered the mug to Margaret's lips, Tony, reaching over with his fiddle-bow, struck it from his hand into the fire. The blue blaze whirred up the chimney and flashed into the room. There was a cry of fire, and Mr. Stillwater, summoning himself, lifted Pluck to his feet, and shoved him into the street. The old toper anticipating some such issue of the day, agreeably to custom, had taken Margaret with him to the village to be conducted home by her at night.

They ascended the West Street, crossed the pasture, and entered the woods. The clouds hung low, and their floating skirts seemed to be pierced and hetcheled by the trees. The rain had thinned into a fine close mist. The path, to inexperienced eyes, would have been absolutely indistinguishable. They had threaded it before in similar darkness. They came to the Brook, which, increased by the rain, flowed with a dismal sound; they groped along its banks, and arrived at the Tree Bridge. Pluck seemed terrified, and hesitated to cross. He sat down, then extended his length on the grass, and ere long fell asleep. Margaret would have been unwilling that her father should go over, and was not sorry to have him stop; though it was night, and rainy, and they were alone, and still a mile from home. The trees dripped on her head, the grass was wet underneath her, and her clothes were drenched. But of this she hardly thought; what she more feared was the ways of her father in his drunken sleep, his mysterious sufferings, his frenzied utterance, and spasmodic agitation.—

This, and for this she feared; she looked for it, and it came. She tried to quiet him, and as she rubbed his arm he said she was a dove feeding him with milk; and then he scratched and tore at his breast, which she soothed with her hand, hot and rough as it was; then he said he was boiling in the still, and Solomon Smith was holding the cap on; he shrieked and yelled till his roar exceeded that of the Brook. Then he began to laugh wildly. "Old Nick is turning the North Pole. There comes out of the sea a whale walking on his tail; Parson Welles has got astride of his gills with a riding stick, ha! ha! Ho! a star rolling on its five points! Grind away, old fellow. Round, round they go over the mountains, splash, splash across rivers. Can't you hear the pismires laugh! There's St. Paul with a cat-o'-nine-tails, and Deacon Hadlock going to take me to the whipping-post. I'll be poxed, if you do. Ho! Molly, Molly, help!" He leaped from the ground, Margaret clung to the skirt of his coat. Breaking from the arm that detained him, he cried, "The Tree Bridge," and ran towards that slippery structure, as if he could thereby escape his invisible pursuers.

Ere the child had time to exclaim against this rashness, or interpose any obstacle to the peril upon which the old man rushed, a plash in the water announced his fall, while the darkness and the swollen state of the stream appalled her with the feeling of his certain destruction. Then Margaret, for the first time in her life, experienced, what is often overwhelming in the onset and is not wont to sit lightly on the memory, *a sense of danger*.—What could be done? She hurried down the ravine, was enabled to seize an arm of the struggling man, and assist him to regain the bank. In silence, sickness and weariness, she toiled homewards; in darkest dead of night she went to her bed, when that good angel, sleep, came and comforted her.

CHAPTER XIV.

THE SABBATH.—MARGARET GOES TO MEETING FOR THE FIRST TIME.—HER DREAM OF JESUS.

It was a Sabbath morning, a June Sabbath morning, a June Sabbath morning in New England. The sun rose over a hushed, calm world, wrapt like a Madonna in prayer. It was The Day, as the Bible is The Book. It was an intersection of the natural course of time, a break in the customary order of events, and lay between, with its walls of Saturday and Sunday night on either side, like a chasm or a dyke, or a mystical apartment, whatever you would please liken it to. It was such a Sabbath to the people of Livingston as they used to have before steam, that arch Antinomian, "annihilated time and space," and railroads bridged over all our valleys. Its light, its air, its warmth, its sound, its sun, the shimmer of its dawn on the brass cock of the steeple, the look of the Meeting-house itself, all things, were not as on other days. And now when those old Sabbaths are almost gone, some latent indefinable impression of what they were comes over us, and wrenches us into awe, stillness and regret.

Margaret had never been to Meeting; the family did not go. If there were no other indisposing causes, Pluck himself expressly forbade the practice, and trained his children to very different habits and feelings. They did not work on the Sabbath, but idled and drank. Margaret had no quilling, or carding, or going after rum to do; she was wont to sally into the woods, clamber up the Head and tend her flowers; or Chilion played and she sang, he whittled trellises for her vines, mended her cages, sailed with her on the Pond. She heard the bell ring in the morning, she saw Obed and his mother go by to meeting, and she had sometimes wished to go too, but her father would never consent; so that the Sabbath, although not more than two miles off, was no more to her than is one half the world to the other half.

From the private record of Deacon Hadlock we take the following:—

State *vs.* Didymus Hart.

" Stafford, ss. Be it remembered, that on the nineteenth day of August, one thousand seven hundred and seventy-eight, Didymus Hart of Livingston, in the County of Stafford, shoemaker and laborer, is brought before me, Nathan Hadlock, Esq., a Justice of Peace for and within the aforesaid county, by Hopestill Cutts, Constable of Livingston aforesaid, by warrant issued by me, the said Justice, on the day aforesaid, against the said Didymus Hart, at Livingston aforesaid, on the twelfth day of May last, being the Lord's day, did walk, recreate and disport himself on the south side of the Pond lying in the West District, so called, of Livingston aforesaid; which is contrary to the law of this State made and provided in such cases, and against the peace of this State, all which is to the evil example of all others in like case offending.

"Wherefore," witnesses being heard, &c., " it doth appear to me, the said Justice, that the said Didymus Hart sit in the stocks for two hours."

Pluck was disposed of in the manner prescribed, very much to the entertainment of the boys, who spattered him with eggs, the disturbance and exasperation of his wife, who preferred that all inflictions her husband received should come from herself, and quite resented the interference of others, and his own chagrin and vexation ; especially as the informer in the case was Otis Joy, father of Zenas, a break-neck, whose friendship he did not value, and Cutts, the executive officer, was the village shoemaker, and no agreeable rival, and the Justice was Deacon Hadlock. By way of redress, he chose to keep from meeting entirely, and suffer none under his control to go.

But Chilion and Nimrod both urged that Margaret might attend church at least once in her life, and her father at length consented. This morning she heard the bell ring ; she saw Obed and his mother on a pillion behind him riding by ; the latter dressed in a small shining black satin bonnet, and gown of similar material, with a white inside handkerchief ; the former in sky-blue coat and ruffled sleeves, white neck-stock, white worsted vest, yellow buckskin breeches, wh'te stockings, and silver-plated buckles, which had all belonged to his father, whose form was both shorter and thicker than his son's, and whose garments it certainly showed great filial reverence in the young man to wear without essential alteration. Obed had an old look, his face was furrowed as well as freckled, and his mother to remedy this disproportion and graduate her son that consideration which naturally attached to his appearance, had adopted the practice of powdering his hair and gathering it in a sack behind ; and for his near sightedness, she provided him with a pair of broad horn-bowed bridge spectacles. The entire structure was capped by a large three-cornered hat. Whatever might have been the effect of Obed's recent whipping, there was nothing apparent. His mother, unlike Pluck, would not suffer any thing of that kind to disturb the good understanding she ever wished to retain with the people of Livingston.

But let us, if the reader is willing, anticipate these

persons a little, and descend to the Village. The people are assembling for Meeting; they come on all the four roads, and by numerous foot-paths, cross-lots, and through the woods. Many are on horses, more on foot, and a very few in wagons. The horses' heads are garnished with branches of spruce and birch, a defence against flies; most of the boys and some of the men are barefoot, divers of them in their shirt-sleeves, carrying their coats on their arms; some of the young ladies have sprigs of roses, pinks, sweet-williams, and larkspurs; others both old and young bring bunches of caraway, peppermint, and southern wood; some of the ladies who ride leap from their horses with the agility of cats, others make use of horse blocks that stand about the Green. You would perhaps particularly notice old Mr. Ravel and his wife from the North Part of the town, on horseback, the former straight as an arrow, the latter a little crooked, and both more than eighty years of age. For sixty years they have come in that way, a distance of seven miles; for sixty years, every Sabbath morning, have they heated their oven and put in an iron pot of beans and an earthen dish of Indian pudding, to bake in their absence, and be ready for dinner when they return. To meet exigencies of this nature, in the mean time, you will observe that Mistress Ravel, in common with many other women, has on her arm a large reddish calico bag filled with nut-cakes and cheese. You will also see coming down the West Street Mr. Adolphus Hadlock, nephew of the Deacon's, with his wife and six children, and Mr. Adolphus will contrive in some way or other to give you the names of all his children without your asking, even before he reaches the steps of the Meeting-house; Triandaphelda Ada, Cecilia Rebecca, Purintha Cappadocia, Aristophanes, Ethelbert, and a little boy he carries in his arms, Socrates;

and you will hear the young men and boys that are lolloping on the steps repeat these names as the parties to whom they belong severally arrive.

The sexton, Philip Davis, now strikes the second bell, and those who live immediately on the Green begin to turn out, and when he commences tolling, it is a sign Parson Welles has started from his house, which is in plain sight an hundred rods or so down the South road. There are Mr. Stillwater, the tavern-keeper, Esq. Weeks, Judge Morgridge, Mr. Gisborne, the joiner, Lawyer Beach, Dr. Spoor, and other villagers, with their families. Tony, the barber, with his powdered hair and scarlet coat, is conspicuous. There is Mom Dill, a negro servant of Parson Wells, once a slave, fat, tidy and serene. The Widow Luce, who lives near the Brook, passes on leading her little hunchback son Job; then you see the Parson and his wife accompanied by their daughter, Miss Amy.

This venerable couple have nearly attained the allotted age of man, and are verging towards that period which is described as one of labor and sorrow; yet on the whole they seem to be renewing their youth, their forms are but slightly bent, and the step of the old minister is firm and elastic. He is dressed in black, the only suit of the color in town—if we except that of the sexton, which is known to be an off-cast of the Parson's—kerseymere coat, silk breeches and stockings; he has on a three-cornered hat, a fleece-like wig, white bands and black silk gloves. His wife's dress is black satin, like that of the Widow Wright's. Finally, as it were composing part of the sacerdotal train, riding slowly and solemnly behind, appears the Widow Wright, who always contrives to arrive at the Parsonage just as the bell begins to toll. The Parson and his wife with dignity and gravity ascend the steps of the church, the crowd meekly opens to let them pass, then all enter and take their appropriate seats within the sacred precincts. The bell ceases tolling; the sexton hangs the bell-rope on a high peg where the boys cannot reach it, shuts the inner porch doors, goes to the outer door and hem's twice quite loud to the vacant air, and all is still.

This morning, in church, considerable sensation was created—no more indeed than usual on such occasions—by Deacon Pemrose, the clerk of the town, reading the banns of marriage between Zenas Joy and Delinda Hoag.—Leaving these people, let us go back to the Pond.

Brown Moll, with unpretending yet deep satisfaction in the good looks of the child, carefully dressed Margaret's hair,—which in tendency to curl resembled that of Gottfried Brückman, while in color it fell between the flaxen of her German and jet of her Gallic but all unknown lineage,—put on her white muslin tunic and pink skirt and red-bead moccasons. For hat, the little novice had nothing more suitable than the green rush.

Margaret started away with a dreamy sense of mystery attaching to the Meeting, like a snow storm by moonlight, and a lively feeling of childish curiosity. On the smooth in front of the house, her little white and yellow chickens were peeping and dodging under the low mallows with its bluish rose-colored flowers, the star-tipped hedge-mustard, and pink-tufted smart-weed, and picking off the blue and green flies that were sunning on the leaves; and they did not seem to mind her. Hash had taken Bull into the woods, and Chilion told her she would not need him. Dick, her squirrel, and Robin, were disposed to follow, but her mother called them back. A little yellow-poll, perched in the Butternut, whistled after her, "Whooee whee whee whee whittiteetee—as soon as I get this green caterpillar, I will go too." A rusty wren screamed out to her, "Os's's' chipper w' w' w' wow wow wow—O shame, Molly, I am going to rob an oriole's nest, I would'nt go to Meeting." She entered the Mowing ; a bobolink clung tiltering to the breezy tip of a white birch, and said, "Pee wuh' wuh' ch' tut, tut, tee tee wuh' wuh' wdle wdle pee wee a a wdle dee dee—now Molly here are red clover, yellow butter-cups, white daisies, and strawberries in the grass ; ecod! how the wind blows ! what a grand time we shall have, let us stay here to day." A grass-finch skippered to the top of a stump, and thrusting up its bill, cried out, "Chee chee chee up chip' chip' chipperway ouble wee—glad you are going, you'll get good to-day, don't stop, the bell is tolling." She thought of the murderer, snatched a large handful of flowers, and hurried on, driven forward as it were by a breeze of gladness in her own thoughts and of vernal aroma from the fields. She gathered the large bindweed, that lay on its back floating over the lot, like pond-lilies, with its red and white cups turned to the sun ; and also, the beautiful purple cran's bill, and blue-eyed grass. She came to the shadows of the woods that skirted the Mowing, where she got bunch-berries, and star-of-Bethlehem's. She entered a cool grassy recess in the forest, where were beds of purple twin-flower, yellow star-grass, blue-violets, and mosses growing together family-like, under the stately three-leaved ferns that overhung them like elm-trees, while above were the birches and walnuts. A black-cap k' d' chanked, k' d' chanked over her head, and a wood-thrush whoot whoot whooted, ting a ring tinged in earnest unison, "We are going to have a meeting here to-day, a little titmouse is coming to be christened, won't you stop?" But a woodpecker rapped and rattled over among the chestnuts, and on she went. She crossed the Tree-Bridge, and followed the brook that flowed with a winsome glee, and while she looked at the flies and spiders dancing on the dark water, she heard a little yellow-throated fly-catcher, mournfully saying. "Preeo, preea preeeeo preeeea—Pray, Margaret, you'll lose your soul if you don't;" and she saw a wood-pewee up among the branches, with her dark head bowed over plaintively singing, "P' p' ee ee ou wee, p' p' ee ee ou wee'—Jesus be true to you Margaret, I have lost my love, and my heart is sad, a blue angel come down from the skies, and fold us both in his soft feathers." Here she got the white-clustering baneberry, and little nodding buff cucumber root.

The Via Dolorosa became to Margaret to-day a via juncundissima, a very pleasant way. Through what some would consider rough woods and bleak pasture land, in a little sheep-track, crooked and sometimes steep, over her hung like a white cloud the wild thorn tree, large gold-dusted cymes of viburnums, rose-blooming lambkill, and other sorts, suggested all she knew, and more than she knew, of the Gardens of Princes. The feathery moss on the old rocks, dewy and glistering, was full of fairy feeling. A chorus of fly-catchers, as in ancient Greek worship, from their invisible gallery in the greenwood, responded one to another;—"Whee whoo whee, wee woo woo wee, whee whoo, whoo whoo wee—God bless the little Margaret! How glad we are she is going to Meeting at last. She shall have berries, nutcakes and good preaching. The little Isabel and Job Luce are there. How do you think she will like Miss Amy?"

Emerging in Dea. Hadlock's Pasture, she added to her stock red sorrel blossoms, pink azaleas, and sprigs of penny-royal. Then she sorted her collection, tying the different parcels with spears of grass. The Town was before her silent and motionless, save the neighing of horses and squads of dogs that trapsed to and fro on the Green. The sky was blue and tender; the clouds in white veils like nuns, worshipped in the sunbeams; the woods behind murmured their reverence; and birds sang psalms. All these sights, sounds, odors, suggestions, were not, possibly, distinguished by Margaret, in their sharp individuality, or realized in the bulk of their shade, sense and character. She had not learned to criticise, she only knew how to feel. A new indefinable sensation of joy and hope was deepened within her, and a single concentration of all best influences swelled her bosom. She took off her hat and pricked grass-heads and blue-bells in the band, and went on. The intangible presence of God was in her soul, the universal voice of Jesus called her forward. Besides she was about to penetrate the profoundly interesting anagogue of the Meeting, that for which every seventh day she had heard the bell so mysteriously ring, that to which Obed and his mother devoted so much gravity, awe, and costume, and that concerning which a whole life's prohibition had been upon her. Withal, she remembered the murderer, and directed her first steps to the Jail.

She tried to enter the Jail House, but Mr. Shooks drove her away. Then she searched along the fence till she found a crevice in the posts of which the enclosure was made, and through this, on the ground floor of the prison, within the very small aperture that served him for a window, she saw the grim face of the murderer, or a dim image of his face, like the shadow of a soul in the pit of the grave.

"I have brought the flowers," said she; "but they won't let me carry them to you."

"We know it," replied the imprisoned voice. "There

is no more world now, and flowers don't grow on it; it's hell, and beautiful things, and hearts to love you, are burnt up. There was blood spilt, and this is the afterwards."

"I will fasten a bunch in this hole," she said, "so you can see them."

"It is too late," rejoined the man. "I had a child like you, and she loved flowers—but I am to be hanged—I shall cry if you stay there, for I was a father—but that is gone, and there are no more Angels, else why should not my own child be one? Go home and kiss your father, if you have one, but don't let me know it."

She heard other voices and could see the shadows of faces looking from other cells, and hear voices where she could see no faces, and the Jail seemed to her to be full of strange human sounds, and there was a great clamoring for flowers.

"I will leave some in the fence for you to look at," she said, in rather vague answer to these requests.

Now the faithful guardian of the premises, overhearing the conversation, rushed in alarm from his rooms, and presented himself firmly in the midst of what seemed to be a conspiracy. "What piece of villany is this?" he exclaimed, snatching the flowers from the paling. "In communication with the prisoners!—on the Lord's day!" Flinging the objects of Margaret's ignorant partiality with violence to the ground, Mr. Shooks looked as if he was about to fall with equal spirit upon the child in person, and she fled into the street.

Climbing a horse-block, from which could be seen the upper cells of the Jail, she displayed her flowers in sight of the occupants, holding them up at arm's length. The wretched men answered by shouting and stamping. "If words wont do, we'll try what vartue there is in stones," observed the indignant jailor, and thereupon suiting the action to the word, the persevering man fairly pelted the offender away.

She turned towards the Meeting-house and entered the square, buttress-like, silent porch. Passing quietly through, she opened the door of what was to her a more mysterious presence, and paused at the foot of the broad aisle.

She saw the Minister, in his great wig and strange dress, perched in what looked like a high box; above hung the pyramidal sounding-board, and on a seat beneath were three persons in powdered hair, whom she recognized as the Deacons Hadlock, Ramsdill and Penrose. Through the balustrade that surrounded the high pews, she could see the heads of men and women; little children stood on the seats, clutching the rounds, and smiled at her. The Minister had given out a hymn, and Deacon Hadlock, rising, read the first line. Then, in the gallery over head, she heard the toot toot of Master Elliman on the pitch pipe, and his voice leading off, and she walked farther up the aisle to discover what was going on. A little toddling girl called out to her as she passed, and thrust out her hand as if she would catch at the flowers Margaret so conspicuously carried. The Sexton hearing the noise, came forward and led her back into the porch. Philip was not by nature a stern man, he let the boys play on the steps during the week, and the young men stand about the doors on the Sabbath. He wore a shredded wig, and black clothes, as we have said, and was getting old, and had taken care of the Meeting-house ever since it was built, and though opposed to all disturbance of the worship, he still spoke kindly to Margaret.

"What do you want?" he asked.

"I want to go to Meeting," she replied.

"Why don't you go?"

"I don't know how," she answered.

"I should think so, or you would not have brought all these posies. This is no day for light conduct."

"May'nt they go to Meeting too?"

"I see—" he added. "You are one of the Injins, and they don't know how to behave Sabber days. But I'm glad you have come. You don't know what a wicked thing it is to break the Sabbath."

"Mr. Shooks said I broke it when I went to give the murderer some flowers, and threw stones at me, and you say I break it now. Can't it be mended again?"

"You should'nt bring these flowers here."

"I saw the Widow and Obed bring some."

"Not so many. You've got such a heap!"

"I got a bigger bunch one day."

"Yes, yes, but these flowers are a dreadful wicked thing on the Lord's day."

"Then I guess I will go home. It an't wicked there."

"I don't want to hurt your feelings if you have had a bad bringing up. Be a good gal, keep still, and you may sit in that first pew along with me."

"I don't want to be shut up there."

"Then you may go softly up the stairs, and sit with th gals."

She ascended the stairs, which were within the body of the house, and in a pew at the head she saw Beulah Ann Orff, Grace Joy, and others that she had seen before; they laughed and snubbed their noses with their handkerchiefs, and she, as it were repelled by her own sex, turned away, and went to the other side of the gallery, occupied by the men. But here she encountered equal derision, and Zenas

Joy, a tithing man, moved by regard to his office and perhaps by a little petulance of feeling, undertook to lead her back to her appropriate place in the church. She resisted, and what might have been the result we know not, when Mom Dill, who was sitting in one corner with Tony, asked her in. So she sat with the negroes. Parson Welles had commenced his sermon. She could not understand what he said, and told Mom Dill she wanted to go out. She descended the stairs, moving softly in her moccasons, and turning up the side-aisle, proceeded along under the high pews till she came to the corner where she could see the minister. Here she stood gazing steadfastly at him. Deacon Hadlock motioned her to be gone. Deacon Ramsdill limped almost smiling towards her, took her by the arm, opened the pew where his wife sat, and shut her in. Mistress Ramsdill gave her caraway and dill, and received in return some of the childs pennyroyal and lamb-kill, and other flowers. The old lady used her best endeavors to keep Margaret quiet, and she remained earnestly watching the Preacher till the end of the service.

Noon-time of a Sunday in a New England country town used to be, and even now is, a social and re-unitive epoch of no small interest. Brothers, uncles, cousins, from the outskirts, accompanied their relatives to their homes on the green. A certain class of men and boys, with a meek look and an unconscious sort of gait, would be seen wending their way to the stoops of the tavern. Some sat the whole hour on the Meeting-house steps talking of good things in a quiet undertone, others strolled into the woods in the rear; several elderly men and women retired to what was called a "Noon House," a small building near the School-house, where they ate dinner and had a prayer; quite a number went to Deacon Penrose's. Of the latter, the Widow Wright.

Mistress Ramsdill, who lived a little off the Green, offered to take Margaret to her house, but the Widow interfered, saying it was too long a walk, and all that, and prevailed with Margaret to go with her. This going to Deacon Penrose's consisted in having a seat in his kitchen Sunday noons, and drinking of his nice cool water. Seats were brought into the room, the floor was duly sanded, the pewter in the dresser was bright and glistening. The Deacon's own family and his particular relations occupied the parlor. To this place came Mistress Whiston, and Old Mistress Whiston, Mistresses Joy and Orff, Breaknecks; Mistress Ravel, from the North Part of the town; Widows Brent and Tuck, from the Mill; Paulina and Mercy Whiston, and others. They ate nutcakes and cheese, snuffed snuff, talked of the weather, births, deaths, health, sickness, engagements, marriages, of friends at the Ohio, of Zenas and Delinda's publishment, and would have talked about Margaret, save that the Widow protected the child, assured them of her ignorance, and hoped she would learn better by and by. Mistress Whiston asked Margaret how she liked the Meeting. She replied that she liked to hear them sing. "Sing!" exclaimed Paulina Whiston. "I wish we could have some singing. I was up to Brandon last Sunday, and their music is enough sight better than ours; they have introduced the new way almost every where but here. We must drag on forty years behind the whole world."

"For my part," said Mistress Orff, "I don't want any change; our fathers got along in the good old way, and went to Heaven. The Quakers use notes and the Papists have their la sol me's, and Deacon Hadlock says it's a contrivance to bring all those pests into the land. Then it makes such a disturbance in the meetings; at Dunwich two of the best deacons could'nt stand it, and got up and went out; and Deacon Hadlock says he won't stay to hear the heathenish sounds. It's only your young upstarts, lewd and irregular people, and the like of that, that wants the new way."

"If our hearts was only right," said Mistress Tuck, "we should'nt want any books; and the next thing we shall know, they will have unconverted people singing."

"We have better leaders," rejoined Paulina, "than Deacon Hadlock and Master Elliman; their voices are old and cracked, and they drawl on, Sunday after Sunday, the same old tunes in the same old way."

"If we once begin to let in new things, there is no knowing where they will stop," replied Mistress Orff.

"Just so," said the Widow Tuck. "They begun with wagons and shays, and the horses wan't used to it, and got frightened at the noise, and run away; and our Eliashib came nigh spraining his ancle."

"I remember," said the elder Mistress Whiston, "when old Parson Bristead down in Raleigh, used thirty bushels of sand on his floors every year, and I don't believe Parson Welles uses five."

"Yes, yes," said her daughter-in-law, "great changes, and nobody can tell where it will end."

"When I was a gal," continued the senior lady, "they didn't think of washing but once a month—"

"And now washing days come round every Monday," added Paulina. "If you will let us have some respectable singing, I will agree to go back to the old plan of washing, Grandma. ha ha!"

"It's holy time, child," said her mother.

"I remember," said the Widow Brent, who was a little

deaf, "milking a cow a whole winter for half a yard of ribbin."

"I remember," said Mistress Ravel, "the Great Hog up in Dunwich, that hefted nigh twenty score."

"If you would go to the Pond to-day," said Margaret, "I guess Chilion would play you a better tune on his fiddle than they sing at the Meeting."

"Tush, Tush!" said the Widow Wright.

"There, there! You see what we are coming to;" said Mistress Orff. "Booly Ann, where was the Parson's text this forenoon?"

The Widow Wright assumed the charge of Margaret in the afernoon. The child kept quiet till the prayer, when the noise of the hinge-seats, or something else, seemed to disconcert her, and she told her protectress she wished to go home. The Widow replied there was to be a christening, and prevailed with her to stop, and lifted her on the seat, where she could witness the ceremony. The Minister descended from the pulpit, and Mr. Adolphus Hadlock carried forward the babe, enveloped in a long flowing blanket of white tabby silk, lined with white satin, and embroidered with ribbon of the same color. The Minister from a well-burnished font sprinkled water in the face of the child, and after the usual formula baptized it "Urania Bathsheba." Margaret was not alone in the number of causes that disturbed the serenity of the Meeting that day; there was an amount of mirth in the minds of the people at large, touching Mr. Adolphus Hadlock's children, which as a matter of course must spend itself on what seemed to be their annual reappearance at the altar.

Finally Mistress Ramsdill insisted on Margaret's remaining to the catechizing. Margaret at first demurred, but Deacon Ramsdill supported the request of his wife with one of his customary smiles, remarking that "catechising was as good arter the sermon to the children as greasing arter shearing, it would keep the ticks off," which, he said, "were very apt to fly from the old sheep to the lambs." The class, comprising most of the youths in town, was arranged in the broad aisle, the boys on one side, and the girls on the other, with the Minister in the pulpit at the head.

"What is the chief end of man?" was the first question; to which a little boy promptly and swiftly gave the appropriate answer—"How many persons are there in the Godhead?" "There are four persons in the Godhead—" began a boy, quite elated and confident. There was an instant murmur of dissent. The neophite, as it were challenged to make good his ground, answered not so much to the Minister as to his comrades. "There is God the Father, God the Son, God the Holy Ghost, and God Buonaparte—Tony Washington said the Master said so." This anti-Gallicism and incurable levity of the pedagogue wrought a singular mistake; but it was soon rectified, and the Catechism went on. "Wherein consists the sinfulness of that state wherein man fell?" "The sinfulness of that state wherein man fell, God having out of his mere good pleasure elected some to everlasting life, is the fault and corruption of the nature of every man that is naturally engendered in him, and deserveth God's wrath and damnation," was the rapid and disjointed answer. The question stumbling from one to another, was at length righted by Job Luce, the little hunchback. The voice of this child was low and plaintive, soft and clear, and he quite engaged Margaret's attention. There were signs of dissatisfaction on the faces of others, but his own was unruffled as a pebble in a brook. Shockingly deformed, the arms of the lad were long as an ape's, and he seemed almost to rest on his hands, while his shoulders rose high and steep above his head. "That's Job Luce," whispered Mistress Ramsdill to Margaret; "and if there ever was a Christian, I believe he is one, if he is crooked. Don't you see how he knows the Catechism; he has got the whole Bible eeny most by heart, and he is only three years old." Margaret forgot every thing else to look at a creature so unfortunate and so marvellous.

When the Catechism was over and the people left the church, she at once hastened to Job and took one of his hands; little Isabel Weeks too, sister-like, took his other hand, and these two girls walked on with the strange boy. Margaret stooped and looked into his eye, which he turned up to her, blue, mild, and timid, seeming to ask, "Who are you that cares for me?" In truth, Job was we will not say despised, but for the most part neglected. His mother was a poor widow, whose husband had been a shoemaker, and she got her living binding shoes. The old people treated her kindly, but rather wondered at her boy; and what was wonder in the parents degenerated into slight, jest, and sometimes scorn, in the children; so that Job numbered but few friends. Then he got his lessons so well the more indolent and duller boys were tempted to envy him.

"You didn't say the Catechism," said he to Margaret.

"No," she replied, "I don't know it; but I have a Bird Book and can say Mother Goose's Songs." Their conversation was suddenly interrupted by an exclamation and a sigh from Miss Amy and the Widow Luce, who were close behind.

"Woe, woe to a sinful mother!" was the language of the latter.

"Child, child!" cried the former, addressing herself to Margaret, "don't you like the Catechism?"

"I don't know it," replied Margaret.

"She isn't bad, if she is an Injin," interposed Isabel.

"Does she understand Whipporwill?" abstractedly asked Job.

"God's hand is heavily upon us! ' mournfully ejaculated the Widow.

"Can any thing be done?" anxiously asked Miss Amy.

They stopped. Miss Amy was moved to take Margaret by the hand, and with some ulterior object in view she detached the child from Job, and went with her up the West Street—the natural rout to the Pond.

"Did you never read the Primer?" she asked.

"No, Ma'am," was the reply.

"Have you never learned how many persons there are in the Godhead?"

"One of the little boys said there were four, the others that there were but three. I should love to see it."

"How dare you speak in that way of the Great Jehovah!"

"The great what?"

"The Great God, I mean."

"I thought it was a bird."

"Can it be there is such heathenism in our very midst!" said the lady to herself. Her interest in the state of Margaret was quickened, and she pushed her inquiry with most philanthropic assiduity.

"Do you never say your prayers?" she asked.

"No, Ma'am," replied Margaret. "I can say the Laplander's Ode and Mary's Dream."

"What do you do when you go to bed?"

"I go to sleep, Ma'am, and dream."

"In what darkness you must be at the Pond!"

"We see the Sun rise every morning, and the snow-drops don't open till it's light."

"I mean, my poor child, that I am afraid you are very wicked there."

"I try to be good, and Pa is good when he don't get rum at Deacon Penrose's; and Chilion is good; he was going to mend my flower bed to-day to keep the hogs out."

"What, break the Sabbath! Violate God's holy day! Your father was once punished in the Stocks for breaking the Sabbath. God will punish us all if we do so."

"Will it put our feet in the Stocks the same as they did father?"

"No, my child. He will punish us in the lake that burneth with fire and brimstone."

"What, the same as Chilion and Obed and I burnt up the bees?"

"Alas! alas!" sorrowed the lady.

"We were so bad," continued Margaret, "I thought I should cry."

"Deacon Penrose and the rest of us have often spoken of you at the Pond; and we have thought sometimes of going up to see you. In what a dreadful condition your father is!"

"Yes, Ma'am, sometimes. He rolls his eyes so, and groans, and shakes, and screams, and nobody can help him. I wish Deacon Penrose would come and see him, and I think he would not sell him any more rum."

"Poor little one!—don't you know any thing of the Great God who made you and me?"

"Did that make me? I am so glad to know. The little chickens come out of the shells, the beans grow in the pods, the dandelions spring up in the grass, and Obed said I came in an acorn, but the pigs and wild turkeys eat up the acorns, and I can't find one that has a little girl in it like me."

"Would you like to come down to Meeting again?"

"I don't know as I like the Meeting. It don't seem so good as the Turkey Shoot and Ball. Zenas Joy didn't hurt my arm there, and Beulah Ann Orff and Grace Joy talked with me at the Ball. To-day they only made faces at me, and the man at the door told me to throw away my flowers."

"How deceitful is the human heart, and desperately wicked!"

"Who is wicked?"

"We are all wicked."

"Are you wicked? then you do not love me, and I don't want you to go with me any farther."

"Ah! my dear child, we go astray speaking lies as soon as we be born."

"I never told a lie."

"The Bible says so—do not run away; let me talk with you a little more."

"I don't like wicked people."

"I wish to speak to you about Jesus Christ, do you know him?"

"No, Ma'am—Yes, Ma'am, I have heard Hash speak about it when he drinks rum."

"But did you not hear the Minister speak about him in the pulpit to-day?"

"Yes, Ma'am,—does he drink rum too?"

"No, no, child, he only drinks brandy and wine."

"I have heard Hash speak so when he only drank that."

"The Minister is not wicked like Hash,—he does not get drunk."

"Hash wouldn't be wicked if he didn't drink. I wish he could drink and not be wicked too."

"O, we are all wicked, Hash and the Minister, and you and I; we are all wicked, and I was going to tell you how Christ came to save wicked people."

"What will he do to Hash?"

"He will burn him in hell-fire, my child."

"Won't he burn the Minister too? I guess I shall not come to Meeting any more. You and the Minister and all the people here are wicked. Chilion is good, I will stay at home with him."

"The Minister is a holy man, a good man I mean, he is converted, he repents of his sins. I mean he is very sorry he is so wicked."

"Don't he keep a being wicked? You said he was wicked."

"Why, yes, he is wicked. We are all totally depraved. You do not understand. I fear I cannot make you see it as it is. My dear child, the eyes of the carnal mind are blind, and they cannot see. I must tell you, though it may make you feel bad, that young as you are, you are a mournful instance of the truth of Scripture. But I dare not speak smooth things to you. If you would read your Bible, and pray to God, your eyes would be opened so you could see. But I did want to tell you about Jesus Christ, who was both God and Man. He came and died for us. He suffered the cruel death of the cross. The Apostle John says, he came to take away the sins of the world. If you will believe in Christ he will save you. The Holy Spirit, that came once in the form of a dove, will again come, and cleanse your heart. You must have faith in the blood of Christ. You must take him as your Atoning Sacrifice. Are you willing to go to Christ, my child?"

"Yes, Ma'am, if he won't burn up Hash, and I want to go and see that little crooked boy too."

"It's wicked for children to see one another Sundays."

"I did see him at Meeting."

"I mean to meet and play and show picture-books, and that little boy is very apt to play; he catches grasshoppers, and goes down by the side of the brook, before sundown; —that is very bad."

"Are his eyes sore, like Obed's, sometimes, and the light hurts him?"

"It is God's day, and he won't let children play."

"He lets the grasshoppers play."

"But he will punish children."

"Won't he punish the grasshoppers too?"

"No."

"Well, I guess I am not afraid of God."

Miss Amy, whether that she thought she had done all she could for the child, or that Margaret seemed anxious to break company with her, or that she had reached a point in the road where she could conveniently leave her, at this instant turned off into Grove Street, and Margaret pursued her course homeward. She arrived at the water a little before sunset; she fed her chickens, her squirrel and robin; her own supper she made of strawberries and milk in her wooden bowl and spoon. She answered as she best could the inquiries and banterings of the family touching the novel adventures of the day. She might have been tired, but the evening air and the voices of the birds were inviting, and her own heart was full of life; and she took a stroll up the Indian's Head.

Along a tangled path, trod by sheep, more by herself, and somewhat by visitors to the Pond, she wound her way to the summit. This, as we have said, was nearly one hundred feet above the level of the water; on the top were the venerable trunk of the Hemlock before referred to, a small cluster of firs, a few spears of yellow orchard grass and brown sorrel, sparse tufts of harebells and buttercups, bunches of sweet-fern, and mosses growing on the rocks. From the south front projected a smooth shelving rock directly over the water, forming the brow of the so called Head. This elevation commanded points of extensive and varied interest; the Pond below, its dark waters dotted with green islands, its forest-skirted shore, the outlet, the dam, the deep and perpetual gurgle of the falling water. Beyond the dam was a broken congeries, the result of wild diluvial force; horrid gulfs, high rocky pinnacles, trees aslant, green dingles; to the west, the hills crept along by gentle acclivities, and swelling upwards, formed, to an untrained eye, the apparent boundaries of this nether world. On the north was a continuation of the ridge of mountains of which the Head itself seemed to be the close, proceeding indefinitely till they met and melted into the sky. On the north-west, buried like a cloud in the dimmest distance, appeared the round, bald, but soft and azure crown of Old Umkiddin. Beyond the Pond, on the south, was a forest, sweeping onwards to the heavens without break or bound. Turning to the east one beheld the River, its meadows, and portions of the village. In every direction, here and there, on side hills, in glades of the forest, among orchard-groves, appeared the roofs of houses and barns, dappling the scene, and reflecting in the middle of the day a gray, silvery light, like mica in granite. To this place Margaret ascended; hither had she often come before, and here in her future life she often came.

She went up early in the morning to behold the sun rise from the eastern hills, and to be wrapped in the fogs that flowed up from the River; at noon, to lie on the soft grass under the murmuring firs, and sleep the midtide sleep of all nature; or ponder with a childish curiosity on the mystery of the blue sky and the blue hills; or, with a childish dread, to brood over the deep dark waters that lay chasmed below her. She came up in the Fall to pick bramble berries and gather the leaves and crimson spires of the sumach for her mother to color with.

She now came up to see the sun go down. Directly on the right of the sunsetting was an apparent jog or break at the edge of the world, having on one side something like a cliff or sharp promontory, jutting towards the heavens, and overlooking what seemed like a calm clear sea beyond; within this depression lay the top of Umkiddin, before spoken of; here also, after a storm, appeared the first clear sky, and here at midday the white clouds, in long ranges of piles, were wont to repose like ships at anchor. Near at hand, she could see the roads leading to Dunwich and Brandon, winding, like unrolled ribbons, through the woods. There were also pastures covered with gray rocks that looked like sheep; the green woods in some places were intersected by fields of brown rye, or soft clover. On the whole, it was a verdant scene, Greenness, like a hollow ocean, spread itself out before her; the hills were green and the depths also; in the forest, the darkness, as the sun went down, seemed to form itself into caverns, grottoes, and strange fantastic shapes, out of solid greenness. In some instances she could see the tips of the trees glancing and frolicing in the light, while the greedy shadows were crawling up from their roots, as it were out of the ground to devour them. Deep in the woods the blackcap and thrush still whooted and clang unweariedly; she heard also the cawing of crows, and scream of the loon; the tinkle of bells, the lowing of cows, and bleating of sheep were distinctly audible. Her own

Robin, on the Butternut below, began his long, sweet, many-toned carol; the tree-toad chimed in with its loud trilling chirrup; and frogs, from all the waters around, crooled, chubbed and croaked. Swallows skimmered over her, and plunged into the depths below; swarms of flies in circular squadrons skirmished in the sunbeams before her eye; at her side, in the grass, crickets sung their lullabies to the departing day; a rich, fresh smell from the water, the woods, wild-flowers, grass-lots, floating up over the hill, regaled her senses. The surface of the Pond, as the sun declined, broke into gold-ripples, deepening gradually into carmine and vermilion; suspended between her eye and the horizon was a table-like form of illuminated mist, a bridge of visible sunbeams shored on pointed shining piers reaching to the ground.

Margaret sat, we say, attentive to all this; what were her feelings we know not now, we may know hereafter; and clouds that had spent the Sabbath in their own way, came with her to behold the sunsetting; some in long tapering bands, some in flocky rosettes, others in broad, many-folded collops. In that light they showed all colors, rose, pink, violet and crimson, and the sky in a large circumference about the sun weltered in ruddiness, while the opposite side of the heavens threw back a purple glow. There were clouds, to the eye of the child, like fishes; the horned-pout, with its pearly iridine breast and iron-brown back: floating after it was a shiner with its bright golden armory; she saw the blood-red fins of the yellow-perch, the long snout of the pickerel with its glancing black eye, and the gaudy tail of a trout. She beheld the sun sink half below the horizon, then all his round red face go down; and the light on the Pond withdraw, the bridge of light disappear, and the hollows grow darker and grimmer. A stronger and better defined glow streamed for a moment from the receding depths of light, and flashed through the atmosphere. The little rose-colored clouds melted away in their evening joy, and went to rest up in the dark unfathomable chambers of the heavens. The fishes swam away with that which had called them into being, and plunged down the cataract of light that falls over the other side of the earth; the broad massive clouds grew denser and more gloomy, and extended themselves, like huge-breasted lions couchant which the Master had told her about, to watch all night near the gate of the sun. She sat there alone with no eye but God's to look upon her; he alone saw her face, her expression, in that still, warm, golden sunsetting; she sat as if for her the sun had gone down, and the sky unloosed its glory; she sat mute and undisturbed, as if she were the child-queen of this great pageant of Nature.

While at the Pond the birds were closing their strains and Margaret was taking her parting look of the sky, in the village, at the same moment, broke forth the first song of the day, and was indulged the first unembarrassed vision. When the last shimmer of blue light vanished from the top of the mountain beyond the River, whither tenscore eyes were turned, there exploded the long twenty-four hours pent and swollen emotion of tenscore hearts and voices. "Sun's down!" sun's down!" was the first unrestrained voice the children had uttered since the previous afternoon. This rang out in every family and echoed from house to house. The spell was broken, the tether cut, doors and gates flew open, and out the children dashed into the streets, to breathe a fresh feeling, clutch at the tantalizing and fast receding enjoyment, and give a minute's free play to hands, feet and tongues. An avalanche of exuberant life seemed to have fallen from the glacier summits of the Sabbath, and scattered itself over the Green. The boys leaped and whooped towards the Meeting-house, flung their hats into the air, chased one another in a sort of stampede, and called for games with all possible vociferation.

Little Job Luce alone seems to have no share in the general revel. He has been sitting by the Brook under a willow, and as the boys come trooping by, he shrinks into the house; his mother holds him a while in her lap at the window, when he, as the grasshoppers have already done, goes to bed.

The villagers, husbands and wives, grave and venerable men, beaux and sweethearts, appear in the streets, walk up the different roads, and visit from house to house.

The Indian's Head meanwhile is folded in shadows and silence, and Margaret is hushed as the sky above her; the cool fresh evening wind blows upon her, thrills through her brown curls and passes on. Her mother appeared on the top of the hill, and without words or noise sat down beside her. She folded her arm about Margaret's neck, and with one hand grasped that of the child, and with the other dallied with the locks of her hair;—but abstractedly, and with her eye wandering over the misty expanse. Her own grizzled hair was swept by the wind, and her bared swarthy bosom seemed to drink in life from the twilight world. In calm sternness, in mute brownness she sat, and apparently thoughtful, and as it were unconsciously she pressed Margaret hard to her breast. Was it an old memory, some old hope, some recollection of her own childhood, some revival of her own mother's image?—was it some feeling of despair, some selfish calculation, a dim glimpse into eternity, an impulse of repenting sin, a visitation of God's spirit?—was it a moment of unavowed tenderness?

Presently Chilion came up with his viol, and going to the projecting rock, sat with his feet dangling over the precipice. Margaret withdrawing from her mother went to her brother, leaned on his shoulder, and looked down into the mysterious depth below. Her brother began to play, and as if he had imbibed the dizziness, dread and profundity of that abyss, he seemed to play with a similar impulse, and she shuddered and started; then relieving the impression, he played the soft, starry, eternal repose of the heavens, and chased away that abyss-music from her soul. Her father, too, joined them, his red face glistening even in the shadows; he had with him a flask of rum which he drank; he laughed, too, and repeated many passages of the Bible, and imitated the tones, expression and manners of all the religious persons whom Margaret had seen in the village; then making a pappoose of her, he carried her down to the house.

That night Margaret dreamed a dream, and in this wise dreamed she. She was in a forest, and the sun was going down among the trees. Its round red disk changed to yellow, as she looked, and then to white; then it seemed to advance towards her, and the woods became magically luminous. She beheld her old familiar birds flying among the branches with a singularly lustrous plumage, the wild-flowers glowed under her feet, and the shrubbery was all a-flame. The ball of light come forward to a knoll about a dozen rods before her, and stopped. A gradual metamorphosis was seen to go on to it, till at last it came out in the form of a man, like a marble statue, dressed not as Margaret had been accustomed to see, but in a simple robe that descended to his feet, and leaning upon a milk-white cross. Near this appeared another form of a man, clothed in a similar manner, but smaller in size, and perched on his hand was a milk-white dove. Margaret looked at these men, or forms of men, in silent wonder. Presently she saw a suffusion and outflowing of animal life in them. The face of the first was pale but very fair, and a hidden under-tinge of color seemed to show through an almost transparent skin, as she had seen the blush of the white goosefoot shining through a dew drop. In the preternatural light that filled the place, Margaret saw that his eyes were dark blue, and his hair, parted on the crown, flowed in dark-brown curls down his neck. The appearance of the other was similar, only the glow on his cheeks seemed to be more superficial, and his look was more youthful. The cross on which the elder leaned, Margaret now saw set in the ground, where it grew like a tree, budded and bore green leaves and white flowers, and the milk-white dove, becoming also endowed with life, flew and lit upon the top of it. She then saw the younger of the two men pick flowers from the blooming cross-tree, and give them to the other, who seemed pleased with their beauty and fragrance. She found herself moving towards these two persons who had so singularly appeared to her, and when she saw one of them pick off the flowers, she was secretly impelled to do the same. So she gathered quite a bunch of calico bush, Solomon's seal, lambkill and others similar to those she found in the woods on her way to the Meeting, which she tied with a grass string. Then she got a parcel of checkerberries. All at once the milk-white dove flew from the green cross-tree and alighted upon her shoulder, thus seeming to establish a communication between herself and these two persons, and as she moved on, all the birds in the woods, the same as she had heard in the morning, sung out right merrily. When she stopped, they ceased to sing, and when she started, they began again. As she was going on, suddenly issuing from behind a tree, appeared to her in her dream the same lady who had talked with her after meeting, Miss Amy.

"Where are you going?" said the lady.

"I am going to see those men, and give that beautiful one those flowers and berries."

"That is Jesus Christ that I told you about this afternoon, and the other is the Apostle John," rejoined the lady.

"Is it?" queried Margaret, "then I think he won't want my flowers."

"He is God, the second person in the Godhead. He does not want flowers. He wants you to believe in him; you must have faith in that cross."

"I was going to carry him flowers, I saw him smell of some. He looks as if he would love me."

"Love you?" rejoined the lady. "What does the Creed say? That you deserve everlasting destruction."

While they were talking, the birds ceased to sing, and the dove leaving Margaret's shoulder flew back to the cross. She started impulsively and said, "I will go." As she proceeded slowly along, in the shifting and multiform phenomena of the dream, Deacon Hadlock stood before her, and asked where she was going, to whom she made the same reply as before.

"You cannot go," said he, "unless you are effectually called. You are wholly disabled by reason of sin."

"It is only a little ways," replied she, "and I went clear down to the village to-day alone. He looks as if he wanted me to come."

"Yes," rejoined the Deacon, "if you were in a right frame of mind, if you were duly humbled. You are vain, proud, deceitful, selfish and wholly depraved."

"I guess I am not."

"Even there you show the blindness of the carnal mind."

"He is beckoning to me," cried Margaret, with childish earnestness.

"If he should appear to you as he truly is, a just God, who hates sin, and should gird on his sword, then your rebellious heart would show itself, then you would hate him."

While Deacon Hadlock detained Margaret, the Widow Luce went by leading her crooked boy Job, also Mistress Hatch and her little boy Isaiah, and Helen Weeks with her brother and sister Judah and Isabel, and several elderly people.

"He does'nt hang on the cross as he does in the Primer," said Isaiah.

"Blessed Savior! by faith I behold thee!" exclaimed Mistress Palmer, coming through the woods.

"I thought he was coming to judgment, in clouds and flaming fire, taking vengaance on them that know not God," said the Camp-Preacher looking from behind a tree.

John the disciple and companion of Jesus was now seen approaching. "Welcome to Jesus!" he said, as he came near to the people. "The good shepherd welcomes his flock! as saith the old Prophet, 'He will take the lambs in his bosom, and gently lead those that are with young.' He is the Eternal Life now manifested unto you; come to him that he may give you some of his life; he is the truth, he will impart to you that truth; approach him that his own divine image may be reflected in you; love him, and so become possessed of his spirit." The crowd drew back as the holy Apostle approached. Children snuggled to their parents, and the elderly people seemed disconcerted. "Christ bids me say," continued the Apostle, "Suffer the little children to come unto me, for of such is the kingdom of heaven."

"I know not how many of us may be included in this invitation," said Deacon Hadlock, as the senior officer of the church, and more prominent man, speaking on behalf of the company.

"Whosoever thirsts," replied the Apostle, "let him come. Whoever would have the true life, like a well of water springing up in his soul, let him come to the living source."

"It is to be hoped that some of us have been made worthy partakers of the efficacy of Christ's death," said Deacon Penrose.

"Whosoever doeth not righteousness," rejoined the Apostle, "is not of God, neither he that loveth not his brother; every one that loveth is born of God, and knoweth God."

"I want he should take me in his arms and bless me, as he did the little children in the Bible," said Isabel Weeks to her sister.

"He looks so beautiful and good," said Helen, "I should rejoice to go near him. It seems as if my heart had for a great while longed to meet such gentleness and purity."

"Alas!" exclaimed Deacon Hadlock, "that you should apply again that unction to your lips! You think your natural amiability will commend you to Christ. You believe there is something good in your nature,—When," added he, turning to the Apostle, "will this young woman see herself as she is, feel her own sinfulness, her utter helplessness by nature, and throw herself on the mere mercy of God?"

"Hold!" said the Apostle. "She is in the way of salvation. Her natural amiability is pleasing to Christ. He was amiable in his youth before God and man. No human being is sinful by nature. If she have deep love in her soul, that will remove all traces of the carnal mind. Her love, I see it now, flows out to Jesus, and his love ever flows out to her, and all the children of men, and in this union of feeling and spirit will she become perfect in holiness."

By this time, little Job Luce, as it seemed in the dream, forgotten and neglected by the crowd, slipping away unobserved and creeping through the bushes and trees, had gone round and come out near the cross, under which he stood, and began playing with the Dove that offered itself very familiarly to him. The little crumpled boy appeared to be cured of his deformity, he walked erect, the hump had fallen from his back, and his hands no longer touched the ground.

Jesus himself was now seen to be drawing near. The tree-cross, green and flowering, moved along with him; the birds in the woods renewed their song, and even the milk-white dove flew from tree to tree, as it were to give good cheer to the timid little birds. Some of the people retreated and stood afar off in the shade of the forest, others clustered about Deacon Hadlock.

"Behold him!" outspoke the Apostle John, "the fairest among the sons of men; our elder Brother; he took upon himself our nature, and is not ashamed to call us brethren. He hath loved us, and given himself for us, as the good Paul said, an offering and a sacrifice to God for a sweet smelling savor."

The voice of Jesus himself was heard at last sounding heavenly sweet and tenderly free among the bewildered people. "Come unto me all ye that labor and are heavy laden, and I will give you rest. Learn of me, for I am meek and lowly of heart." "The bruised reed he will not break," added John, "nor quench the smoking flax."

"I am not come to condemn you," continued the voice of Jesus, "but that by me you may be saved. I give myself for your life. Through my holiness ye shall sin no more."

"We will go to him!" exclaimed Helen Weeks earnestly. "Come Isabel, come Margaret."

These three interlocked, Margaret still retaining her berries and flowers, the kind Apostle led forward, and Jesus smiled upon them as they approached, and took each of them by the hand, and spake comforting and assuring words to them, and they looked with a reverential pleasure into his face. Margaret, who from her own ignorance of the person she addressed felt less fear of him than the others, was the first to speak. "Do you love flowers?" said she, at the same time extending the bunch she had in her hand. Christ took them, and replied, "God bless you, my dear child." "Can he bless and love me?" said Helen, addressing herself directly to Jesus, but adopting the customary third person. "I love those that love me," he replied. "Keep your heart pure, for out of it are the issues of life, and I and the Father will come and dwell with you."

"Can he have mercy on a poor sinner like me?" asked Mistress Palmer.

"I forgive you, Daughter," he answered; "Go and sin no more."

"Are you God?" asked Margaret.

"I am not God. But love me, and you will love God," he said.

"There is some mistake here," observed Deacon Hadlock, as if he was afraid Christ had not fully explained himself.

"There is no mistake," interposed the Apostle.

"But are we not saved by the Atoning Sacrifice, and can that be made except by an infinite being, and is not that being God?" added the Deacon.

"We are saved by a divine union with God and Christ. He that dwelleth in love dwelleth in God and God in him. This inter-dwelling is our salvation, and this is the Atonement."

"That's nater," said Deacon Ramsdill, "I understand that. I am afeered some of us are resting upon a sandy foundation."

"I was a poor sinner," continued the Apostle, "till I came into this oneness with Christ. I feel safe and happy now, my soul is elevated and purified. To be with him is like being with God; to possess his spirit is to bear the virtues of heaven; to be formed in his image is the blessed privilege of humanity. To effect such a change is the object for which he came into the world, and that which I have seen and heard, and handled and enjoyed, I declare unto you, that you, beloved friends, may have fellowship with me; and truly my fellowship is with the Father, and with his Son Jesus Christ."

"We are emptied of all self-righteousness," said Deacon Hadlock, "we are altogether become filthy."

"Have you no love, joy, peace, long-suffering, goodness, faith?" asked the Apostle.

"Alas, none," replied the Deacon.

"Say not so, a single look of his will pierce you through and through."

"What the gentleman says may be true," interposed Deacon Penrose; "but I think it highly inexpedient to speak of these things. We might adjourn, a few of us, to my counting-room, or to the Parson's study, and confer upon the matter; but to talk in this way before all the people is the worst policy that could have been adopted." So saying he disappeared.

"Look at these children," continued St. John, "the very flowers and berries they bring are the affectionate tribute of their hearts to the Infinite Goodness and Divine Beauty that appear in Christ; it is the outflowing of a pure love; it is the earnest and foreshadowing of the salvation that has already begun in their souls. That young lady's yearning after the love of Jesus is a sign that the Regeneration has commenced within her, and by it a communication is opened between her soul and his, which is the Atonement, and so also she becomes united to God, who is manifested and resident in Christ."

"What have we been about all our lives, that we know not so much of the Gospel as these children!" exclaimed Deacon Hadlock mournfully and yet resistingly. Whereupon it came to pass that the crowd withdrew or melted away like a mist, and Margaret, Helen, Isabel, Judah, and Job Luce, were left alone with Jesus and John. Helen fell at the feet of Jesus, and overpowered by emotion wept with a calm deep weeping; Margaret looked into his face, and tears came into her eyes also.

"Will you forgive me, Job," said Judah to the little boy, "for all that I have done to you?"

"I will," replied Job.

"Be good children and love one another," said Jesus to them, and the two boys disappeared.

"Weep not, child of my love," said he to Helen, "confide in me, dwell near my heart, obey the Gospel; I will be the life of your life, the wellspring of your soul, and in purity shall Heaven be revealed in you. The little Isabel, she shall be blest too, I will carry the lamb in my bosom." When he had said this, they two vanished from the dream.

"You ask me who is God, child," said he turning to Margaret, who now alone remained; "God is Love. Be pure in heart, and you shall see God. Love much, and he shall be manifest to you. Your flowers are fair, your spirit is fairer; I am well pleased with their fragrance, the breath of your love is sweeter to me.—Margaret!" he continued, "to you it shall be given to know the mysteries of Heaven. But the end is not yet. Man shall rise against his fellow; and many shall perish. The Church has fallen. The Eve of Religion has again eaten the forbidden fruit. You shall be a co-worker with me in its second redemption. I speak to you in parables, you understand not. You shall understand at another day. You are young, but you may advance in knowledge and goodness. You must be tempted, blessed if you can endure temptation. Be patient and earnest, hopeful and loving. I too was a child like you, and it is that you must be a child like me. Through the morning shadows of childhood you shall pass to the perfect day. I unconsciously grew in favor with God and man, so shall you. This Cross is the burden of life, which all must bear. Bear it well, and it shall bring forth flowers and fruit to you. This Dove stands for the innocency and virtue, strength and support, that flow from God to all. In a dream have all these things passed before you. Forget not your dream. There is much evil in the world, sin not. You must be afflicted, faint not. Let me kiss you, my sweet child."

Thus spake Jesus, and the dream again changed. The two persons were seen to return to marble-like forms, and these forms became a round ball of light, which, receding through the forest, stood on the distant mountains like the setting sun, and Margaret awoke. The morning light streamed into her chamber ; from her window she saw the golden sun coming up over the dark woods, and the birds were pealing their songs through the amber air.

The child went down with bright feelings, light-hearted and free ; she brought water from the cistern for her mother to wash, spread the clothes on the bushes, and scared the birds from yarn that was hung out to dry.

CHAPTER XV.

MARGARET PASSES A NIGHT AT THE STILL, AND SOLOMON SMITH MAKES HER USEFUL.

It will be remembered that Hash, the brother of Margaret, at the Spring training, was punished not only by imprisonment, but also with an inconsiderable fine, for disorderly behavior on that occasion. Not being himself possessed of the money, he had recourse to the Smiths at No. 4, to whom he pledged his oxen for the necessary sum. To acquit himself in that quarter, he engaged his services as night-warden at the Still. In addition—for this seemed to be a point especially insisted upon—he promised that Margaret should accompany him in that duty.

The "Still," or Distillery, was a smutty, clouted, suspicious looking building, down in a hollow by Mill Brook. It rose a single story on one side and two on the other, into the former of which the barrels of cider were rolled, and emptied into the cauldron below. The latter was the chief scene of operation; here were the furnace; the boiler with its *cap* for collecting the vapor and conveying it into the worm-pipe or condenser; the *refrigerator*, an immense cask, holding the worm, and supplied with fresh water by long wooden troughs from the Brook above; and the *receiver*, a barrel, into which the condensed vapor of the cider, now having assumed the form called spirits, issuing from the worm, fell drop by drop.

Here at nightfall were wont to assemble the people of the neighborhood, including even some young females.

Hither came Margaret with Hash and Bull. A pine torch blazed from the bunghole of a barrel. Boys were crouched on the earth playing mumble-the-peg. Old Isaac Tapley, with both hands in his waistband, leaned on the boiler critically quaffing jets of steam that a lucky leak afforded. Little Isaiah Hatch would desperately steal on his finger's end a drop that fell from the worm. The neighbors were kind, and seemed to vie with one another who should be most useful, helping Solomon roll up the barrels, tier on tier, bring in fuel, and keep the fire in good countenance.

Damaris Smith politely offered to instruct Margaret in the game of Fox and Geese, which they played sitting on a bench with little hollows and lines branded in it.

At length the nine o'clock bell was heard from the village, a tone mellowed by the distance and the woods, and which breaking in upon many a scene of idleness, dissipation, domestic quiet, or friendly visit, admonished the gay of vanity, the devout of prayer, and all of bedtime. The neighbors left, and presently the head of the establishment retired also, leaving Margaret and Hash to their night's work, that of tending the fire. It was not long before Hash, whom Solomon had been treating with singular generosity, exhibited signs of intoxication, and in a few minutes fell senseless to the ground. Then was Margaret left alone with a dead-drunk brother, a roaring furnace, a hot and hissing cauldron, barrels of detestable drink, grotesque and frightful shadows leaping on the beams; while through holes in the floor above, from the dark and lonely upper room, the reflected light seemed to grin at her like a demon of Despair. When the fire burnt low, she replenished it with dry hemlock, which snapped like the report of subterranean musketry; while the sparks pouring out like hail and falling on her brother's face, she was obliged to shield it with boards. The gurgling of the water, as it flowed in and out from the vat, would have been music to her ears, if she were free to enjoy it; but it was her own sweet Pond contributing to the wicked business of rum-making;—and so too was she. Would she finish her work, and flow away as uncontaminated?

Her father had never troubled her with ghost-stories, and she was not inclined to yield to unreal alarms. The night was dark and chilly. She could see nothing out doors but great tremulous masses—masses of shadow, and hear nothing save the Brook, which sounded as if it ran somewhere very deep under ground. Yet it was quite refreshing to turn from the hot furnace and fetid atmosphere of the place to the cool and pure door-way, even if it was dark all round and she seemed to be at the bottom of an infinite loneliness. Her good angel, the dog, followed her steps wherever she went; and once he looked so in her face, as if there was a tear of sympathy in his eye: what, indeed, she had done before in her life,—she put her arms about his neck, and wept. She did not complain, or fear, or feel any wrong or loss, but she wept irresistibly because her dog loved her; and then she continued to weep as it were mechanically because there was nothing to occupy her deep sensitive faculties, and her tears alone remained to flow out; and so too she fell to laughing, and laughed almost wildly and incoherently; then chills crept over her, partly from the increasing and overpowering coldness of the air, and partly from an irrepressible nature which must always feel cold if it be not deeply and warmly loved.

She then went and sat on the bench before the fire, and Bull crouched right in front of her and seemed to be keeping watch over her countenace; and she fell to gazing into his eyes; and as she looked the eyes appeared to swell till they became big as saucers, and the circle spread more and more till it was like a great sheet of water. She saw in the water, purple waves, like sunset, and moonlight doings in the shape of golden fish, fiery lizards, and little young lightnings at play, such as she had often seen in the Pond. She seemed to herself to be going into the water, and down and down she went till she came to a hollow place at the bottom, where she stood as it were on a plain.

Here she saw a large silver cauldron over a fire,—something like the arrangement her brothers adopted for boiling maple sap,—and her first impulse was to go to the fire and dry her clothes. Refore she could reach it, there passed her three blooming and fairy-like girls, the like of whom she had never seen. One of them ran and cast on the fire an armful of rosebushes, bright autumnal leaves, aromatic dead ferns, and white cotton grass, which made quite a blaze. Another one collected wild flowers that were seen growing every where, and threw into the cauldron eyebrights, azaleas, rhodoras, and many more. The third girl stood by the vessel and stirred it with a long silver ladle.

These persons did not speak to Margaret, nor she to them. Events passed quietly, though every thing was full of interest. The girls kept at work; they caught the wriggling moonbeams and threw them into the pot; they skimmed off the purple twilight to add to the ingredients; turning a faucet at the end of a silver pipe connecting with the blue sky, they set that running in; one had a mortar in which she pounded sweet-scented herbs, as chamomile and marjoram, for seasoning; two or three rainbows were picked up and thrown in.

After it was sufficiently boiled, they began to dip out this singular compound and pour it on the ground. The liquor congealed as it fell, and the mass increased in an opal-like human form. As they continued to discharge the contents of the vessel, feet were formed, and legs, breast, arms, and the shape of a head. One poured on another ladle full, and beautiful eyes appeared; a second ladle produced a delicate lovely color in the face; another covered the head and neck with long, dark, curling hair. When the Form, which was that of a woman, was complete, they wove with their fingers out of the light a sort of drapery, which they threw over it. Then one began to sing, and another to play on a harp; while the third led down from the skies the brilliant Planet Venus, by a bridle of blue taste tied to one of its rays, and fastened it to a spear of grass to keep it from running off. While the two first were singing and playing, the Spirit of Life came into the Form, filling it with soul, and it stood before them a perfect human being. The three girls seemed greatly delighted with the beautiful lady they had created, and were even transported to such a degree as if they would worship her. The Beauty, for such the new-formed woman might worthily be called, did not however long consent to receive the adulation of the others, but took pains to demonstrate her equality with them in sundry pleasing ways, and the four disported together on the green grass; then they all went to bathe in a stream of clear water that opened near by. After this the Beauty was seated on the brilliant Planet Venus, which was unhitched, and seemed very eager to be off.

Now Margaret had not been able to communicate with what was going on; but wishing to do something, and thinking she ought first to dry her clothes before appearing before such nice people, she went to the fire, when lo! her dress was not wet, for it instantly took fire, and blazed right up, and spread a bright iridine-like illumination all about her. Then such joy as these wonderful creatures showed when they saw the little Margaret all a-fire was never seen; and so beautifully flaming! and they all seemed to be in flame-land and in flame-feeling. The steed, if such it might be called, the evening star, could stand it no longer, it leaped away with its fair rider, and these lovely creations of a dream vanished into the most beautiful light that ever was.

The growling of the dog waked Margaret, and she found she had been dreaming; and that with her head pillowed on the neck of her dumb protector.

The cur had no bad motive in disturbing the fancies of his little mistress ;—like a wise mentor, he wished to call her attention to impending realities. Somebody was about the Still. Somebody's footsteps could be heard in the thick midnight without, and somebody's head was presently seen looking in at the door. If it had been one of the beautiful girl's of the dream, we guess Bull would not have growled as he did, for he was a very partial and discriminating dog, and always liked every one that Margaret liked; therefore she was a little frightened when he growled so strong, and one might almost say she snuggled down in the dog's lap, so closely did she cling to him.

But this strange Somebody at the door spoke, and then Margaret knew who it was—that it was Solomon Smith—and he spoke very kindly. Crossing the threshold, he looked as if he was more afraid of being hurt, than of hurting. He seated himself rather timidly on an end of the bench, and edged towards her. One might see that this fellow was very much pleased to find Hash so sound asleep, and that he had no intention of waking him. He spoke under his breath, and commended the child for minding the fire so well, and asked her if she wouldn't have some toddy, which she refused.

"You are a curis creeter," he continued, "and an't no moon-calf nuther. You know at the trainin', guess as how I found you out in the rain, and took you into the Tavern, and you might have staid there all night for all any body else lookin' arter you. Now you won't begrutch me a favor will you, Peggy? Can you tell what makes the likker come out of that are pipe?"

"I can't," she replied. "I wish it didn't."

"What makes dogs howl when you die?"

"I don't know. I think Bull would, if I should die."

"Didn't you know you could catch a thief by putting a rooster under a kittle? It'll crow as soon as the rascal touches it, guess as how."

"I didn't know that."

"You found the water up to Mr. Palmer's, didn't you, Peggy?" he inquired in an increasingly low and earnest manner.

"The boys found it."

"You carried the stick, and Nimrod said you found it, and so did Rhody and the Widder."

"Did they say so?"

"Now I want you should tell me if you ever found a four-leaf clover? Speak low; walls have ears."

"Yes," she answered, "twenty in the Mowing."

"Did you ever kill a cricket?"

"They sing so pretty, I couldn't kill one."

"That's you. I wouldn't kill one. It's dum bad. Do you put a Bible under your pillow when you go to bed?"

"What, such as Miss Amy told me about? She says the Bible makes people all wicked; and Pa's Bible makes us wicked too. I don't like Bibles."

"Little coot! Don't you know the Bible is the best book in the world. I always sleep with one, guess as how. Let me see your finger nails. Is there any black spots on them?"

"When they are dirty, and I dig roots for Obed."

"Now keep shy, Peggy, I want to tell you something. I have had a dream."

"Do you dream too?"

"I have had a dream three nights a runnin'. I can't tell you all about it now. But look here, Peg, Hash owes us, and he'll have to lose his oxen if the money is'nt paid dum soon. He drinks more than his work comes to, but if you are willing to do what I want you to, I'll let him off."

"What shall I do?" asked Margaret, with a slight twinge of uncertainty and distress.

"I want you to go up with me to-night, to the Fortune-teller's, Joyce Dooly's."

To this proposal, the young man, after considerable coaxing and threatening, succeeded in gaining Margaret's consent; promising that he would release Hash altogether from his obligations, if she would do as he wished.

In a few minutes a horse was at the door, and taking Margaret behind, with the dog of course as sort of king's guard, Solomon rode off, plunging as it were into bottomless night and interminable woods. Up the Brandon road half a mile or so, they dismounted and struck into a thicket. Margaret had to hold by the skirt of Solomon's coat, while he felt his way before. They espied at length a light, and entered a door. In a small, low, ragged room, in what sort of a house or place it was impossible for Margaret to tell, she saw an old woman with a dish of coals and two tallow candles burning before her on a table, both of which she seemed to be intently watching. She was evidently prepared for the visit, and showed by her manner that she had been waiting their arrival. Joyce Dooly, the Fortune-teller, was of course old, with a peaked and shrivelled face, and black and sharp eye.—Why should not a fortune-teller be young and pretty?—Her dress withal was fantastic as her art. She muttered and peeped, as the Bible says, like a wizard.

Five cats darted from chairs and the chimney side, when the dog entered, hissing and spitting, and all raised their backs together in one corner of the room. This movement seemed to disturb the magician for a moment, but observing it more attentively she became quiet, as if all was right.

Her immediate business was with Margaret, whom, after settling certain preliminaries with the coals of fire, the candle wicks, the cats, some cards and astrological tracts that lay on the table, but which we need not describe, she proceeded to examine.

"In what month were you born?" asked the Fortune-teller.

"I don't know," replied Margaret.

"What, how!" exclaimed the old woman, in a tone of surprise and rebuke. "Why have you brought the little one here? Nativity is the most important. In what house, Aquarius, Cancer, or Mercury,—we know nothing about it. Was Jupiter in the ascendant? The Moon in aspect to what? How can we tell?"

"I don't care for your riggledorums," retorted Solomon, with suppressed impatience. "Will she answer my purpose? You have got your money to find out that, and that is all I want to know."

"Hold, Solomon!" she said with an overawing sternness. "The cats are against you. Keep still. Here, child, let me look at you. Curled hair," so she went on, "denoteth heat and drought; brown, fairness, justice, freedom and liberality. Your signs are contradictory, child. Venus *must* have been in square signs, when you were born. Do you never have any trouble?"

"Sometimes," she replied, "when Deacon Penrose and Mr. Smith sell rum to Pa and Hash."

"Take note, Solomon," so the woman admonished the fellow, "she refers her troubles to you. She prognosticates disaster, sorrow and death. You had better let her alone."

Solomon became inwardly greatly excited, but he strove to control himself, and whispered something in the ears of the woman, who turned again to the child.

"Lips," she continued, "fairly set and well colored argue fidelity, and a person given to all virtue; brow high and smooth, signifieth a sincere friend and liberal benefactress; small ears, a good understanding; neck comely and smooth, a good genius; brown eyes, clear and shining, ingenuity, nobility and probity. Let me see you laugh. Teeth white and even, argue sweetness and reverence; dimples, persuasion and command; hand, soft and clear, hath discretion, service, delight in learning, peace-loving; palm D in mount of the Moon,—ha! ha! do you want to know, child! many and dutiful and fair children,—would you like to have children?"

"Yes, Ma'am," replied Margaret.

The old lady seemed to be wandering, and becoming quite absorbed in the characteristics and tokens of the child, she gave renewed uneasiness to Solomon, who expressed his feelings in a loud and somewhat menacing tone.

"Rest thee, young man!" she replied, "thy fortune is wrapt in that of the child. The hour cometh. Your significator must apply to a sextile of Mercury and Venus. I see a coffin in the wick of this candle. Scare the cats, let me see them jump once more. Now is your moment, depart."

Whatever might be the meaning of this visit and this singular mummery to Margaret, Solomon, it appeared, had accomplished his object, and was ready to leave. Retracing their steps through the darkness and wood, they came back to the Still. Margaret would have gone in to her brother, but Solomon declared he had something more for her to do, and insisted that she should go a little farther with him. They went up the road leading to the Pond, and arriving at a growth of trees known as the Pines, Solomon hitched his horse, and led Margaret once more into the depths of the forest. Reaching a spot which he seemed previously to have in his mind, he put a hazel-twig into the child's hand, and bade her go about among the trees in the same manner as she did at Mr. Palmer's at the Ledge. She was not long in announcing the movement of the stick, and the young man identified the magic spot as well as he could in the darkness, by piling a heap of stones over it. She asked him what it was for, but he declined telling; and what he would not do, we must, since in the sequel the whole affair came out.

This young Smith had a dream, three nights successively, of gold hid in the Pines. He could not ascertain the precise locality, and sundry private canvassings of the earth with a spade had hitherto been fruitless. Hence his anxiety to secure the services of Margaret, whose success on a former occasion with the divining rod he had been apprized of; hence also his visit to Joyce Dooly, the Fortune-teller, for the purpose of fortifying himself more completely in his undertaking.

Once more in this night of wanderings and mystery was Margaret conducted to the Still. Nor did morning dawn until Solomon had time to dispose of his horse in the stable, and himself in bed, before any of his family were stirring. Margaret found Hash yet in his sleep, the fire decayed, and the Still dark, cold, and dismal as the morning after a debauch. She rekindled the fire, sufficiently at least for her own comfort, and lying down before it, sheltering herself in what never failed either in kindness or support, the arms of her dog, fell fast asleep.

CHAPTER XVI.

MARGARET INQUIRES AFTER THE INFINITE; AND CANNOT MAKE HER WAY OUT OF THE FINITE.—HER PROGRESS QUITE EXCITING.

"WHAT is God?" said Margaret one morning to the Master, who in his perambulations encountered her just as she was driving the cow to pasture, and helped her put up the bars; both of them standing under a large oak that shaded the spot.

"God, God—" replied he, drawing back a little, and thrusting his golden-headed cane under his arm, and blowing his nose with his red bandanna handkerchief. "You shut your cow in the pasture to eat grass, don't you, mea discipula?" added he, returning the handkerchief to his pocket, and planting himself once more upon his cane.

"Yes," she replied.

"What if she should try to get out?"

"We put pegs in the bars."

"Pegs in the bars! ahem. Suppose she should stop eating, and leaning her neck across the bars, cry out, 'O you, Mater hominum bovumque! who are you? Why do you wear a pinafore?' In other words, should ask after you, her little mistress; what would you think of that, hey?"

"I don't know what I should," replied Margaret, "it would be so odd."

"Cows," rejoined the Master, "had better eat the grass, drink the water, lie in the shade, and stand quietly to be milked, asking no questions."

"But do, sir," she continued, "tell me what God is."

The Master folded back both his ruffle cuffs, lifted his golden-headed cane into the air, and cleared at a sudden bound the road-side ditch, leaping with such force his large shovel hat fell into the water. Margaret picked up the unfortunate article, and wiping it very carefully on her apron returned it to its owner, a circumstance that seemed to recall the bewildered man to the thread of the child's feelings. And he replied to her, saying,—

"Felix qui potuit rerum cognoscere causas. God, child, is Tetragrammative, a Four-wordity; in the Hebrew רדדח, the Assyrian Adad, the Egyptian Amon, the Persian Syre, the Greek Θεος, Latin Deüs, German Gott, French Dieu; *Τὸν πταρμον Θεον ηγουμεθα*, says Aristotle; 'God is the Divine Being,' says Bailey; 'Jupiter Divum Pater,' says Virgil."

"Christ the Beautiful One, I saw in my dream, said if I loved I should know God," replied Margaret.

"Verily, as saith the holy Apostle, God is Love."

"Did Love make me?"

"Mundum fecit Amor; or as Jamblicus has it, 'God produced matter by separating materiality from essentiality,' or as Thomas writes, 'Creation is extension produced by the Divine power.'"

"Is God Latin?"

"He is in Latin. Deus is Latin for God."

"I don't know any thing about it. I had a good deal rather go to Obed's.—His mother wants to see you; she told me to ask you to call there, the next time you came to the Pond."

"I thought she did not like me."

"She wants to see you very much."

"I hope she has no designs upon me?"

"I don't know.—It is something she wants."

"She does'nt contrive to marry me?"

"I guess that is it. Hash said Miss Amy was going to marry you."

"What, both? You are a ninny. You never heard of the Knights of the Forked Order. There is the old song,—

'Why, my good father, what should you do with a wife?
Would you be crested? Will you needs thrust your head
In one of Vulcan's helmets? Will you perforce
Wear a city cap, and a court feather?'

Malum est mulier, women are an evil."

Thus talking, they approached the Widow's. To the road up which they went, the Master gave the name Via Salutaris, the stile by which they crossed the stump-fence into the herb-garden or front yard, he called Porta Salutaris, as the Leech herself he had already honored by the title of Diva Salus.

"The child said you wanted me," outspoke the Master, as he entered the house, in a tone that savored both of irritated dignity and sarcastic inquisitiveness.

"Please ma'am," interposed Margaret, both to explain and appease, "he says he won't marry you."

"Mehercule! What are you about, my little Beadswoman?" exclaimed he, endeavoring to silence the child. "In what way, capacity, office, character, can I do you service, Mistress Wright?"

"Gummy!" retorted the woman. "He has been a talkin' about me, and a runnin' of me down. I wouldn't stoop so much as teu pick him up. I wouldn't crack my finger jints for him."

"He didn't mean you," replied Margaret. "He said women were an evil."

"Not widows, child," added the Master.

"Yes," said the woman, "we are evil, but not evils, I trust. No offence, I hope, sir," she added, softening her cadence.

"None in the world," answered the Master. "A widow the good Fuller enumerates in his Holy State."

"They would try teu make us think we are sutthin when we are nothin, as the Parson says," she sighed.

"She is one, as that old writer observes, whose head hath been cut off, yet she liveth, and hath the second part of virginity!"

"The Lord be praised," said the woman, looking meek, and wiping the edge of the table with a corner of her apron; "I do survive as good a husband as ever woman had."

"Her grief for her husband," continues the worthy to whom I refer, "though real, is moderate."

"I am a widder," she answered, "and know what widders feel, and can speak from experience."

"She loveth to look on the picture of her husband, in the children he hath left her, as adds our reverend Author," subjoined the Master, turning his eye towards Obed, who stood in the door, tugging at the waistband of his breeches.

The manner of the Master was too pointed not to be felt, and when he had succeeded in smarting the good woman's sensibilities, his object was attained. But she, on the other hand, had the faculty, by a smile that was peculiar to her, of disguising her emotions, and always contrived to cover up any sense of humiliation with airs of victory. These two persons, as we have formerly remarked, did not like each other very well, and in whatever respects they stood mutually beholden, it was the object of each to make it appear that favors were given without grace, and received without gratitude. We will not follow their diplomatic banterings, but join them when they have concluded to go peaceably about their business. The Widow had invented a new medicine that would cure a variety of diseases. But she wanted a scientific name for it, and also the scientific names of its several virtues. Her own vocabulary would afford an abundance of common appellations, but her purposes aspired to something higher, and the Master's aid was brought in requisition. The Leech sat by a table, holding a pen, with a pewter inkstand and some scraps of dingy paper before her, and endeavored to avail herself of every suggestion of the Master's by committing it to writing.

"Widder or woman," said she, "I knows what I knows, and I know what is in this ere medicine, how many yarbs, and how I gathered 'em, and how I dried 'em, and how they are pounded and mixed, and I cal'late there is a vartue in every drop of it. It'll kill fevers, dry up sores, stop rumatiz, drive out rattlesnake's bite, kill worms—there an't a disorder you can mention that won't knock under to't."

"Except one."

"What is that?"

"Cacoethes Feminarum."

"Up-a-daisy! What a real soundin' one! Bile me up for soap, if that an't a pealer," exclaimed the delighted woman, giving a kind of chuckling grin both to the Master and Margaret. "Deu tell us what it is?" she added. "Is it round hereabouts much? Has any died on't?"

"I know," said Margaret, "it is something about women. Femina is Latin for woman."

"O, forever! I dussay," rejoined the Widow, "it's some perlite matter, and he would'nt like to speak it out before a body. How vallible is sientifikals and larnin'! Prehaps he'd tell what brings it.—Lor me, what a booby I be teu ask. My skull for a trencher, if I can't cure it, if it's as bad as the itch itself."

"Humors—" said the Master.

"Humors! Humors in wimmin—now don't say no more. I knew 'twas some perlite matter. But I can cure it, only if I had the name,—a name that has the sientifikals and larnin' in't. There was four cases to Snake Hill, and I got two, and should have got the whole, bein' Dr. Spoor hadn't a come in, with his larnin' words, and that took. They'll all go teu the dogs if it wasn't for a little schoolin'. If he would only be so kind as to give a poor woman a name for her medicine—but I won't beg, no I won't."

"Nominis stat umbra," said the Master slowly and solemnly, while with assumed gravity and inward impatience he had been listening to the balderdash of the woman.

"Is that it?" asked she hastily.

"Verily," he replied, "Nominis stat umbra."

"Nommernisstortumbug," said the Leech. "Why now, I vum, I could a thought of that myself. Obed here, see how easy 'tis, Nommernisstortumbug, remember, Obed, and you'll be as larnt as Miss Molly. Git Molly some honey, prehaps the Master would like teu tas't on't.—Dr. Spoor may hang his saddle-bags in his garret. There's Deacon Penrose's gally pots and spattles, and Nigger Tony's prinked up Patents, I an't afeered of none of 'em, no, nor of old Death himself. He daren't show his white jaws where I am. A box of Nommernisstortumbug would give the saucy rascal an ague fit, and he'd be glad teu put on some skin and flesh, and dress up like a man, and not be round skeerin' people so with his old bones. There's Parkin's Pints has been makin' a great pudder over to England, but they an't knee high to a toad to't. The thing of it is, people has got teu be so pesky proud and perlite, they won't look at a cure unless it's a dreadful perlite one. They'd all die every one on 'em, before they'd touch the

Widder's stuff, as they call it; but the Nommernisstortumbug they'll swallow box and all, and git well teu, ha, ha! I knows what I knows, I've seen how the cat has been jumpin'. The ministers try to save their souls, and have to preach sich things as 'll take; I mean to save their bodies, and I must fix it so it 'll take;—I han't a grain of interest in the matter, not I. As soon as Obed gits a leetle older, I mean teu send him teu Kidderminster, and Hartford, and Boston, and all about the country, with my medicines, and there won't be a spice of disease left. The Pints is a pound sterling, and I shall put my Nommernisstortumbug right up, and when you ax a good round price, it means a good round cure, and folks that is any body knows it."

The Master, secretly amused at the Widow's complacency, was not disposed to interrupt her, at least so long as he ate of her clear white honey, which Obed supplied in liberal quantities, and of which he was thoroughly fond. Nay, he went farther, and at her request wrote down for her in scientific terms the several and various properties of her nostrum, which she described to him. The lady's bad feelings towards the Master were likewise so melted down in the thought of her good fortune as for the moment to throw her off her guard, and she forgot her usual self-possessed spitefulness. Their interview was in fair progress towards an amicable termination, when the Master happened to say he wanted Margaret to do a service for him that day. But the Widow meanwhile had been concocting plans of her own that included the aid of the child. Difficulties broke out anew, there were taunts on the one side and objurgations on the other. How far the matter may have been carried we know not, when Margaret took the decision into her own hands by running off and escaping into the street. Both started for her, and came to the stile at the same moment. Between the narrow and tangled roots of which the fence was made they were both wedged, and as it were locked in a common embrace. It was a sorry sight to behold. They might have torn each other's eyes out. Obed seized an arm of his mother to withdraw her on one side, and Margaret sought to perform a like office for the Master on the other. But the Widow had no notion of being extricated. Obed shed tears of filial alarm. Margaret shouted with untamed glee. The parties, finding escape and victory alike impossible, had to beat a truce.

It was agreed Margaret should be at the service of the Master that day, and assist the Widow some other.

Her old teacher sometimes employed his little pupil to scour the woods in search of wild flowers, a pursuit for which she was fitted both by her own lightness of heart and foot, and a familiar acquaintance with the region. He instructed her to preserve specimens of almost all kinds she encountered, in the expectation, partly, of discovering some new variety. He furnished her with a tin box to keep the flowers fresh and sound. Providing herself with a lunch of bread and cheese, she took a familiar route through the Mowing into the rich birch and walnut woods lying towards the village. Bull having gone off with Hash in the morning, she was obliged to do without the usual companion of her rambles.

The sun shone warm and inviting, and the air felt soft and exhilarating. The olive-backs trolled and chanted among the trees, and in the shadowy green boughs innumerable and invisible creepers and warblers sang out a sweet welcome wherever her footstep was heard. She found varieties of fungus, yellow, scarlet, and blood-colored, which she tore from the sides of trees, from stumps and rails. She gathered the wild columbine, snakeroot, red cohosh, purple bush-trefoil, flaxbell-flower, the beautiful purple orchis, and dodder, that gay yellow-liveried parasite; and other flowers, now so well known and readily distinguished by every lover of Nature, but which, at the period of our Memoir, had not been fully arranged in the New England Flora.

Turning to the right, or towards South, she came to a spot of almost solid rocks, through the hard chinks and seams of which great trees had bored their way up, to spread their trunks and branches in the light and air. This place was set down in the vocabulary of the district as the Maples, or Sugar Camp, from its growth of sugar maple-trees. Over these stones she stepped as on a pavement, or leaped from one to another as one does on the foam-crags at Nahant. In the dark crevices she found bright green bunches of the devil's ear-seed and the curious mushroom-like tobacco-pipe; all about her, on the rocks, the bright green polypods and maiden's hair waved in silent feathery harmony with the round dots of quavering sunlight, that descended through the trees—little daughters of the sun dallying with these children of the earth, and like spiders, spinning a thin beautiful tissue about them, which was destroyed every night and patiently renewed every morning. Here also she found beds of shining white, and rose-colored crystal quartz stones, all draped and ruffled with green moss. On the flat top of a large bowlder, she saw growing a parcel of small polypods in a circle, like a crown on a king's head. Up this she climbed, and sitting among the ferns, she sang snatches from old songs she had learned:—

"There were three jovial Welchmen
As I have heard them say,
And they would go a-hunting
Upon St. David's Day."

Sorting out the fairest of the fronds, she still sung,—

"Robin and Richard were two pretty men,
They laid in bed till the clock struck ten;
Then up starts Robin, and looks at the sky,
O, Brother Richard, the sun's very high,"—

and down she leaped. A humming-bird that she had seen, or fancied she saw, early in the morning at her scarlet bean flowers, shot by like an arrow. She would follow it. On she went till she found its nest in a tree, and climbing a rock and bending down the branch, she could look into it. In a pretty cradle of moss lined with mullein down lay two baby eggs. But the watchful parents did not know who it was that was looking in upon them, and seemed afraid she would hurt the eggs. She would'nt for the world. They ruffled their golden-green and pretty tabby feathers at her, and almost flew into her eyes. She saw how mistaken they were, and took off her hat that they might see her face and curly hair, and that it was really the little Margaret whom they had seen at Pluck's. When she did this, and spoke to them, the excited creatures saw at once how it was, and seemed to be mightily ashamed of themselves, especially when they remembered how often they had got honey out of the flowers she kept growing for them. One of them leaped into the nest where she sat looking at Margaret, as much as to say, "I'm glad you called;" the other hummed a pleasant little song to her, flying about her head.

Leaving the birds, she crossed the road and entered the Pines, where Solomon Smith took her a few nights before. Here under the trees she found a crowd of persons, men and women, boys and girls, who seemed bent on some mysterious thing, which they pursued with an unwonted stillness. Among them was a man, whom she knew to be

Zenas Joy, pacing to and fro with a drawn sword, and preventing the approach of spectators.

Let us explain, what Margaret herself did not know, though vitally connected with the whole affair, that through the hocus pocus of the Fortune-teller and divination of the child, young Smith of No. 4 had discovered what he supposed to be a deposit of gold.

Having canvassed the ground privately to none effect, he was obliged to communicate the secret while he invoked the aid of his neighbors.

Several men had been digging now for a week, day and night. They had excavated the ground to the depth of nearly thirty feet. A prodigious heap of earth and stones had been cast up, and great trees undermined. When Margaret approached near enough to look in, she saw the men, noiseless and earnest, at work with might and main. Among them were her brother Hash, and others, whom she knew to be No. 4's and Breaknecks. It was a received notion of the times that if any spoke during the operation the charm was destroyed, hence the palpitating silence Margaret observed, and for this purpose also a sentry had been appointed to keep order among the people.

Margaret seeing Hash, was inconsiderate enough to speak to him and ask where Bull was. For this, Zenas Joy, since words were out of the question, administered a corporeal admonition with his sword flatlong, and Damaris Smith, with other girls, seconding his endeavors, fairly drubbed the child from the place. She went off, singing as she went,—

"Little General Monk
Sat upon a trunk
Eating a crust of bread;

There fell a hot coal
And burnt in his clothes a hole,
  Now little General Monk is dead ;—
Keep always from the fire,
Keep always from the fire "

She had not gone far when Bull, who had been asleep under a rock, awakened by the familiar voice of his mistress, came leaping out to her, and went with her.

In the Pines she gathered such flowers as for the most part are proper to that description of soil ;—the sleepy catchfly that is wide awake nights, pennyroyal with its purple whorls, yellow bent spikes of the gromwell, the sweet-scented pettymorrel, the painted cup with its scarlet-tipped bractes, peach-perfumed waxen ladies' tresses, nodding purple gay feather ; she climbed after the hairy honeysuckle, and the pretty purple ground-nut, which, despising its name, overmounts the tallest shrubs. She encountered in her way a "clearing," now grown up to elecampane and wild lettuce. She forced herself through a thicket of brakes, blackberries and thistles, and clambered upon a fence, where she sat to look at the tall lettuces that shot up like trees above the other weeds. The seeds disengaging themselves from the lofty capsule and spreading out their innumerable long white filaments, but still hovering about the parent stalk, gave the plant an appearance as if it had instantaneously put forth in huge gossamer inflorescence. Then a slight agitation of wind would disperse these flowers or egrets and send them flying through the air, like globes of silver light, or little burred fairies, some of them vanishing in the white atmosphere, others brought into stronger relief as they floated towards the green woods beyond. Descending towards the Brook, she gathered the beautiful yellow droops of the barberry-bush and flowers of the sweetbriar. She came to the stream, Mill Brook, that flowed out from her Pond, where grew the virgin's bower or traveller's joy, bedstraw, the nighshades, the beautiful cardinal flower or eye-bright just budding, and side-saddle flowers.

On the grassy bank, with the water running at her feet, she sat down and prepared for dinner; which consisted of bread and cheese, and boxberries. She kneeled on a stone and drank from the swift sparkling waters. It was now past noon; her box was full, and quite heavy enough for one so young to carry, and she might have returned home. The woods beyond, or to the west of the Brook, were close and dark; hardly did the sun strike through them, but the birds were noisy there, and she must perforce enter them, as a cavern, and walk on the smooth leaf-strewed floor. The ground sloped up, then rounded over into a broad interval below, down into which she went. Here a giant forest extended itself interminably, and she seemed to have come into a new world of nature. Huge old trees looked as if they grew up to the skies. Birds that she had never seen before, or heard so near at hand, hooted and screamed among the branches. A dark falcon pierced the air like an arrow, in pursuit of a partridge, just before her eyes. An eagle stood out against the sky on the blasted peak of a great oak; a hen-harrier bore in his talons a chicken to his young; large owls in hooded velvety sweep flew by her; squirrels chattered and scolded one another; large snake-headed wild turkeys strutted and gobbled in the underbrush; a wildcat sprang across her path, and she clung closer to her dog.

Here beneath a large pine she stopped to rest; the birds fluttered, rioted and shrieked in strange confusion, and she entertained herself watching their motion and noise. The low and softened notes of distant thunder she heard, and felt no alarm; or she may have taken it for the drum-like sound of partridges that so nearly resemble thunder, and which she had often heard, and thought no more of the matter. Had she been on the tops of the trees where the birds were, she would have seen a storm gathering, cloud engendering cloud, peaks swelling into mountains, the entire mass sagging with darkness, and dilating in horror. The air seemed to hold in its breath, and in the hushed silence she sat, looking at the rabbits and woodchucks that scampered across the dry leaves, and dived into their burrows. She broke into a loud laugh when a small brown-snouted marten gave vigorous chase to the bolt-upright, bushy, black-tipped tail of a red fox, up a tree, and clapped her hands and stamped her feet, to cheer the little creature on. She sung out, in gayest participation of the scene, a Mother Goose Melody, in a Latin version the Master had given her :—

"Hei didulum! atque iterum didulum! felisque fidesque,
Vacca super lunæ cornua prosiluit:
Nescio qua catulus risit dulcedine ludi;
Abstulit et turpi cochleare fuga."

While she was singing, hailstones bounded at her feet, and the wind shook the tops of the trees. Suddenly it grew dark; then, in the twinkling of an eye, the storm broke over her,—howling, crashing, dizzying it came. The whole forest seemed to have given way—to have been felled by the stroke of some Demiurgic Fury, or to have prostrated itself as the Almighty passed by. The great pine, at the root of which she was sitting, was broken off just above her head, and blown to the ground; and by its fall, enclosing her in an impenetrable sconce, under which alone in the general wreck could her life have been preserved.

A whirlwind or tornado, such as sometimes visits New England, had befallen the region. It leaped like a maniac from the skies, and with a breadth of some twenty rods and and an extent of four or five miles, swept every thing in its course; the forest was mown down before it, orchard-trees were torn up by the roots, large rocks unearthed, chimneys dashed to the ground, roofs of houses whirled into the air, fences scattered, cows lifted from their feet, sheep killed, the strongest fabrics of man and nature driven about like stubble. In bush and settlement, upland and interval, was its havoc alike fearful.

When Margaret recovered from the alarm of the moment, her first impulse was to call for the dog;—but he, already at a distance whither the eagerness of chase had carried him, overtaken by the devastation of the storm, loosing all sense of duty, wounded and frightened, fled away. She herself was covered with leaves, bark, hailstones and sand; blood flowed from her arm, and one of her legs was bruised. A stick had penetrated her box of flowers and pinned it to the earth. The sun came out as the storm went by; but above her the trees with their branches piled one upon another; what indeed had been her salvation, now roofed her in solitude and darkness.

Making essays at self-deliverance, she found every outlet closed or distorted. Trees cemented with shrubs overlaid her path, while deep chasms formed by upturned roots opened beneath her. When at last she reached the edge of the ruins and stood in the open woods, she knew not where she was or in what direction lay her home. No cart-tracks or cow-paths, no spots or blazes on the trees were to be seen. The sun was setting, but its light was hidden by the still interminable foliage. Every step led her deeper into the wood and farther from the Pond. She mounted knolls, but could discern nothing; she crossed brooks and explored ravines, to no purpose.

Despairing, exhausted, her sores actively painful, she sank down under the projecting edge of a large rock. She had not been sitting long when she saw approaching the same place a large, shaggy, black bear, with three cubs. The bear looked at Margaret and Margaret looked at the bear. "It is very strange," the old bear seemed to say; the little bears frisked about as if they thought it was funny to see a little two-legged child in their bed. Margaret sat very still and said nothing, only she wished she could tell the bears how tired she was, and hoped they would'nt take offence at her being there. The big bear came close to her, and, as bears are wont to do, smelt of her hand, and even licked the blood that flowed from her arm; and Margaret went so far as to stroke the long brown nose of the bear, and was no more afraid than if it had been her own Bull. The motherly beast seemed to be thinking, "How bad I should feel if it had been one of the cubs that was hurt!" Then she lay on the ground, and the little bears knew supper was ready. Now the old bear saw that Margaret was tired and bruised, and must have felt that she was hungry also, for she gave a sort of wink with her eyes that seemed to say, "Won't you take a seat at our table, too? It is the best I can set, for, as you see, I hav'nt any hands, and we can't use spoons." It would have been ungrateful in Margaret not to accept so kind an invitation. Finally the good dam and her young and Margaret all cuddled down together, and were soon asleep; only one of the little bears could not get to sleep so easy for thinking what a strange bedfellow he had, and he got up two or three times just to look at the child.

Meanwhile the rumor of the tornado had reached the

Pond, and the family were not a little excited. Hash had not returned; after finishing his bout in the Pines he went with his comrades to see the results of the wind at No. 4, and have a drunken carouse. The Widow and her son came down both to seek news of the storm, and inflame the impression of its terror. The ruddy and wanton face of Pluck became pale and thoughtful. The dry and dark features of his wife were even lighted up with alarm. Chilion, who had been to the village, when he learned the absence of his sister, seemed smitten by some violent internal blow. He paced to and fro in front of the house, listening to every sound, and starting at every leaf. The intercourse of the family, if not positively rude and rough, ordinarily affected a degree of lightness and triviality, and unaccustomed to the expression of deeper sentiments, if they had any, now in the moment of their calamity they said but little. Yet they watched one another's looks and slightest words with an attention and reverence which showed how strongly interested they were in one another's feelings, as well as in the common object of their thoughts. They watched and waited and waited and watched, uncertain what course the child had taken, not knowing where to go for her, and hoping each successive instant she might appear from some quarter of the woods.

It was now near sunset. Obed was despatched in the direction of the dam at the north end of the Pond ; Pluck went over into the Maples ; Chilion, seizing the tin dinner-horn, ran to the top of Indian's Head, and blew a loud blast. No response came from the far glimmering, passionate sound but its own empty echo. Descending, he beheld Bull returning alone, lame and bloody. The dog was at once questioned, and as if convicted of weakness and infidelity to his mistress, or with that native instinct which is proper to the animal, he pulled at Chilion's trousers and made as if he would have him follow him.

Chilion seized the hint, and went rapidly where his guide would lead. Soon striking the track of the child, the dog conducted the way along which Margaret had gone in the morning. They reached the gold-digging, where deluded men, under the light of pine-knots, sweltered in silence. They crossed the Brook and entered the thick woods. It was now night and dark, but Chilion was familiar with every part of the forest, and had often traversed it in the night. They followed the footsteps of the child till they came to the line of the storm. Here prostrate trees, upturned roots, vines and brush, knitted and riven together, broke the scent and checked advance.—The dog himself was baffled. He ran alongside the ruins, tried every avenue, wound himself in among the compressed and perplexed fissures of the mass, but failing to recover the path, he returned to his master, and set up a loud howl. What could Chilion do? He called his sister's name at the top of his voice, he rung out the farthest reaching alarm-cry. He then repeated the attempt of his dog to gain an entrance. He crept under trunks of trees, tore a passage through brambles, and seemed almost to gnaw his way as he crawled along the encumbered earth. At intervals he gasped,—"She's dead, she's dead, she's crushed under a tree." Such was the dreadful reflection that began to tide in upon his heart, and form itself in distincter imagery to his thoughts. With renewed energy he explored with his fingers every vacant spot, trembling indeed lest he should encounter the dead and mangled form. A large limb, broken off in the storm, which he was endeavoring to remove, fell upon his foot, bruising the flesh, and nearly severing the cords; but of this he took no notice. In uttermost despair he exclaimed, "She *is* dead, she *is* dead!" He, the moody and the silent, gave utterance to the wildest language of distress. That deaf and dismal darkness was pierced with an unwonted cry. "O, my sister! my dear, dear sister, sweet Margery, dead, dead!" He fell with his face to the earth, his spirit writhed as with some most exquisite torture; from his stimulated frame dropped hot sweat. "O Jesus, her Beautiful One, how couldst thou let the good Margery die so? My music shall die, my hopes shall die, all things die; sweet sister Margery, your poor brother Chilion will die too." His frenzy seemed to assume the majesty of inspiration, as in simplicity of earnest love he gave vent to his emotions.

Pain and weariness, along with the want of success, served to divest him of the idea of finding her that night. Extricating himself from the forest-wreck, yet as it were plunging into deeper despair, he returned home. His father and mother were still up, restless and anxious. His foot was immediately dressed and bandaged, and Chilion was obliged to be laid in his parents' bed. Obed was also there, strongly moved by an unaffected solicitude, who, as soon as it was light, was sent to the village to have the bell rung and the town alarmed; Pluck himself immediately went down to No. 4. In the course of two or three hours the entire population of Livingston received the exciting and piteous intelligence of "A child lost in the woods, and supposed to have perished in the storm!" At No. 4, Hash was aroused from his boosy stupor to something like fraternal activity, and the four families composing the hamlet started for the scene of the disaster. The village was deeply and extensively moved. Philip Davis, the sexton, flew to the Meeting-house and rang a loud and long fire-alarm. The people flocked about Obed to learn the news, and hurried away to render succor.

The Master, who was on his way to the barber's, hearing of the sad probability respecting his little pupil, was like one beside himself; perfectly bemazed, he made three complete circles in the road, drew out his red bandanna handkerchief, poised his golden-headed cane in the air, then leaped forward, like a hound upon its prey, run down the South Street, and disappeared at full speed up the Brandon road. Judge Morgridge and his black man Cæsar rode off in a swift gallop, on two horses. Men with ox-carts, going into the Meadows, threw out their scythes, rakes, pitchforks, or whatever they had, wheeled about, took in a load of old men, women and children, and drove for No. 4. Deacon Penrose shut up his store, Tony his shop; Mr. Gisborne the joiner, and Mr. Cutts the shoemaker, left their benches. Lawyer Beach, Esq. Weeks and Dr. Spoor started off with axes and billhooks. Boys seized tin dinner-horns and ran. There surged up the Brandon road, like a sea, a great multitude of people. The Pottles and Dunlaps, from Snake Hill and Five-mile-lot, came down on foaming horses. A messenger had been posted to Breakneck, and those families, the Joys, Whistons and Orffs, turned out. Of all persons engaged in the hunt, were absent the two most interested in it, Chilion and Bull, whose wounded and stiffened limbs rendered it impossible for them to leave the house. Dr. Spoor rode up to see Chilion, and little Isabel Weeks and her sister Helen brought him cordials and salves. It was his irrepressible conviction that Margaret was dead, and he was slow to be comforted.

Successively, as the several parties arrived at the spot

in the woods where Chilion had gone the night before, they set themselves at work clearing away the trees. It was the universal impression that the child lay buried somewhere under the windfall. Capt. Eliashib Tuck and Anthony Wharfield, the Quaker, took the superintendence of operations. The melancholy silence of the workmen singularly contrasted with the vehemence of their action. The forest resounded with the blows of axes and the crashing of limbs. Broad openings were made in the compact mass. Little boys crept under the close-welded vines prying about in anticipation of the men. Beulah Ann Orff and Grace Joy helped one another bear the heavy branches. Abel Wilcox and Martha Madeline Gisborne lifted large billets of wood. Deacon Penrose executed lustily with a billhook. Pluck, Shooks the Jailor, Lawyer Beach and Sibyl Radney, rolled over a great tree, roots and all, while Judge Morgridge and Isaac Tapley stood ready to dig into the mound of earth and stones, which the roots had formed in their sudden uprise. Zenas Joy and Seth Penrose rode off to get refreshments. The Master alternately worked with the others and sat on a stump, covering his eyes with his hands, foreboding each moment some dreadful sight. In the midst of all, kneeling on the damp leaves in the open wood, might be heard the voice of the Camp-preacher, in loud and importunate prayer, beseeching the Most High for the life of the child, and for submission to a dreadful peradventure.

To return to Margaret. The night had passed quietly, and she awoke refreshed, though stiffened in every joint She tried, but could not walk. She cried for help, but she had wandered far from any neighborhood and beyond the ordinary haunts of men. Dreary feelings and oppressive thoughts came over her, and tears flowed freely, which the tender-hearted bear wiped away with her tongue. Then the three little bears began to play with their dam, one climbed up her back, another hugged her fore leg, and the third made as if it would tweak her nose, and the one upon her back bandied paws with the one that was hugging the leg, like kittens; and Margaret was forced to be amused despite herself. Then she fell to singing, and as she sang, the animals seemed to be moved thereby, and the old bear and the three little bears seated themselves on their haunches all in a row before her, to hear her; and they were so much pleased with the performance that neither of them spoke a word during the whole of it.

Where the people were at work, they canvassed a pretty large area. One of the boys, Isaiah Hatch, who was burrowing mole-like under the ruins, raised an exclamation that brought several to the spot. He had discovered the flower-box, which was at once recognized as having been carried by the child. The little utensil, battened and perforated, was borne to the Master, who clutched it with a mixed and confused utterance of pleasure, apprehension and regret. The conjecture arose that she might have escaped from the storm, and while a few remained and continued the search, it was agreed that the main body should distribute themselves in squads and scour the forest and region round about. They took horns wherewith to betoken success, if success should attend them.

Margaret, who, as the hours wore away, could no more than resign herself to passing events, was startled from her reveries by the rustling of footsteps and the sound of a human voice. At the same instant she saw the Master running precipitously across the woods, and crying out, "Ursa major! Ursæ minores! Great Bear! Little Bears! O!" The man's arms were aloft, his hat and wig had fallen, the flaps of his coat were torn in the underbrush, his tall form like a stone down a precipice seemed to rebound from stump to puddle and puddle to stump. Close at his heels was the bear with her young, running with similar velocity, but more afraid of *her* pursuers than the Master was of her, and whose track she pursued only for the instant that it happened to identify itself with the direct course to her lair, whither she betook herself, while the Master, making a desperate effort to dodge the fury of the animal, flung himself into the arms of a tree.

At the same moment men and boys appeared storming and rattling through the brush, with uplifted axes, clubs and stones, in hue and cry after the bear, whom happening to alight upon, they had given chase to, and driven to her retreat. Their shouts after the beast were changed into exclamations of a very different character when they beheld the child. They sprang forward to Margaret, caught her in their arms, and asked her a thousand questions. The horns were blown, and presently there came up from hill and hommoc, wood and bosket, rock and dingle, all around, an answering volley. A loud trine reciprocating blast conveyed the glad intelligence wherever there were those interested to hear it. The Master at length ventured forward. What were his emotions or his manners at finding the lost one alive, we will not detail. To show feeling before folks mortified him greatly; the received mode of expression he did not follow; nor were his contradictions executed by any rule that would enable us to describe them. "We have found the child, let us now kill the bear," became the cry;—the animal in the mean time having slunk, trembling to the death, under the low eaves of her den.

"Never, never!" was the vehement expostulation of

Margaret, as she recounted the passages between herself and the animal.

"Wal," said the boys, "if she has been so good to the gal, we won't touch her."

It was a question how the child should be got home. Some proposed carrying her in their arms, but the general voice suggested a litter, which, of poles and green boughs, was quickly made, and borne by four men. The hat and wig of the Master were replaced, and his tattered garments mended by the women, who, leaving their homes in haste, carried away scissors, thread and needle in their pockets. Their best course to the Pond was through Breakneck, and so down the Brandon road by No. 4. A fearful gorge, terminating, however, in a rich bottom, gave the name Breakneck to what was in reality a pleasant neighborhood, consisting of the three families before mentioned, the Orffs, Joys and Whistons, who were all substantial farmers. Joseph Whiston led the way to his father's. Margaret was carried into the house, where Mistress Whiston and other ladies examined and dressed her wounds, and had some toast made for her, and a cup of tea, adding also quince preserves. While Margaret was resting, the young men busied themselves in putting together a more convenient carriage than the litter, and Beulah Ann Orff brought thick comfortables to cover it with, and pillows and bolsters to put under the child's head. On this Margaret was placed, and born off on the shoulders of the young men. For the Master a horse was kindly provided. Again they started; the boys whooping, capering, and sounding their horns. Passing the side-path that led to Joyce Dooly, the Fortune-teller's, there, at the entrance of the woods, on a high rock stood the mysterious woman herself, holding by strings her five cats.

At sight of her the people were silent. She enacted sundry grimaces, uttered mumming sentences, declared she foresaw the day previous the loss and recovery of the child, pronounced over her some mystic congratulations, waved her hand and departed, and the people renewed their shouts. Over fences, through the woods, up from ravines, came others who had been hunting in different directions, and when the party reached No. 4, its number was swelled to more than a hundred. Here they found another large collection of people, some of whom had arrived at a later hour from the village, and others were just returned from the search. Here also were desolating marks of the storm, in roofs, chimneys, windows, trees, fences, fields. Deacon Ramsdill, lame as he was, and his wife, had walked from their home beyond the Green. Parson Welles and the Preacher were engaged in familiar conversation,—the first time they had ever spoken together. "The Lord be praised!" ejaculated the Preacher. "We see the Scripture fulfilled," said the Parson. "There is more joy over one that is brought back, than over the ninety and nine that went not astray." "Amen," responded the Preacher.

"You came pretty nigh having considerable of a tough sort of a time, didn't you, dear?" said Deacon Ramsdill, advancing and shaking Margaret's hand; "but like-to never killed but one man and he died a laughin'. It'll do you good; it is the best thing in the world for calves to lie out of nights when the dew is on."

"Our best hog was killed in the pen," said Mistress Gubtail; "but here's some salve, if it'll be of any sarvice to the child."

"Salve!" retorted the Widow Wright, indignantly, and elbowing her way through the crowd. "*Here's* the Nommernisstortumbug, none of your twaddle, the gennewine tippee, caustic and expectorant, good for bruises and ails in the vitals."

"I've got some plums that Siah picked under the tree that blowed down," said Mistress Hatch; "I guess the gal would like them, and if any body else wants to eat, they are welcome, if they are all we've got."

"Bring um along, Dorothy," said Mistress Tapley to her little daughter. "A platter of nutcakes. The chimbly tumbled in while I was frying, and they are a little sutty, but if the gal is hungry they'll eat well."

Provisions of a different description were furnished from the Tavern, of which the multitude partook freely. People from the village also sent up quantities of fruit and cakes. But they could not tarry, they must hasten to the child's home. They went up the hill, Margaret on the shoulders of the young men, escorted, as it would seem, by half the town, all wild with joy. Pluck was in transports; Obed laughed and cried together; Hash was so much delighted that he drank himself nearly drunk at the Tavern. When they came in sight of the house, a new flourish of the horn was made, three cheers given, hats and green twigs swung. Chilion, whom the good news had already reached, was seated in a chair outside the door; Bull, unable to move, lay on the grass, wagging his tail with joy; Brown Moll took to spinning flax as hard as she could spin and smoking, to keep her sensations down; the little Isabel did not know what to do, she was so glad.

Margaret was conveyed to her mother's bed. Dr. Spoor examined her wounds and pronounced them not serious, and all the women did and said the same thing. Parson Welles suggested to the Preacher the opportuneness of a prayer of thanksgiving, which the latter offered in a becoming manner. A general collation was had in which the family, who had tasted of nothing since the noon before, were made glad participants. Chilion, to express his own transport, or to embody and respond to the delight of the people, called for his violin. He wrought that effect with his instrument, in which he took evident pleasure, moving the parties in a kind of subservient unison, and gliding into a familiar reel he soon had them dancing. On the grass before the house, old and young, grave and gay, they all danced together. Parson Welles, the Preacher and Deacon Hadlock, looked on smilingly. Deacon Ramsdill's wife declaring Margaret *must* see what was going on, had her taken from the bed, and held her in her lap on the door-sill. There had been clouds over the sun all day, and mists in the atmosphere, and much dark feeling in all minds, nor did the sun yet appear, only below it, while it was now about an hour high, along the horizon, cleared away a long narrow strip of sky flushing with golden light. Above the people's heads still hung gray clouds, about them were green woods, underneath them the green grass, and within them were bright joyous sensations, while through all things streamed this soft-colored light, and every thing became a sort of pavonine transparency, and the good folks' faces glowed with magical lustre, and their hearts beat with a kind of new-birth enthusiasm. Deacon Hadlock, stirred irresistibly, gave out, as for years he had been accustomed to do in Church, the lines of the Doxology,—

> "To God the Father, Son,
> And Spirit, glory be,
> As 'twas, and is, and shall be so
> To all eternity."

Chilion giving the pitch, and leading off on the violin as he alone could, they sung as they felt. When they were about breaking up, Deacon Ramsdill said, "Shan't we have a collection? We have had pretty nice times, but strippins arter all is the best milk, and I guess they'll like it as well as any thing now. We shall have to feather this creeter's nest, or the bird will be off agin. Here's my hat if some of these lads will pass it round."

A contribution was made, and thus the night of the morning became a morning at night to the Pond and the people of Livingston.

CHAPTER XVII.

WINTER.

It is the middle of winter, and is snowing, and has been all night, with a strong north-east wind. Let us take a moment when the storm intermits, and look in at Margaret's and see how they do. But we cannot approach the place by any ordinary locomotion; the roads, lanes and by-paths are blocked up; no horse or ox could make his way through this great Sahara of snow. If we are disposed to adopt the means of conveyance formerly so much in vogue, whether snowshoes or magic, we may possibly get there. The house or hut is half sunk in the general accumulation, as if it had foundered and was going to the bottom; the face of the Pond is smooth, white and stiff as death; the oxen and the cow in the barnyard, in their storm-fleeces, look like a new variety of sheep. All is silence and lifelessness, and if you please to say, desolation. Hens there are none, nor turkeys, nor ducks, nor birds, nor Bull, nor Margaret. If you see any signs of a human being, it is the dark form of Hash, mounted on snowshoes, going from the house to the barn. Yet there are, what by a kind of provincial misnomer is called the black growth, pines and firs, green as in summer, some flanking the hill behind, looking like the real snowballs, blossoming in mid-winter, and nodding with large white flowers. But there is one token of life, the smoke of the stunt gray chimney, which, if you regard it as one, resembles a large, elongated, transparent balloon; or if you look at it by piecemeal, it is a beautiful current of bluish-white vapor, flowing upward unendingly; and prettily is it striped and particolored, as it passes successively the green trees, bare rocks, and white crown of Indian's Head; nor does its interest cease, even when it disappears among the clouds. Some would dwell a good while on that smoke, and see in it many outshows and denotements of spiritualities; others would say, the house is buried so deep it must come from the hot, mischief-hatching heart of the earth; others still would fancy the whole region to be in its winding-sheet, and that if they looked into the house they would behold the dead faces of their friends. Our own notion is that that smoke is a quiet, domestic affair, that it even has the flavor of some sociable cookery, and is legitimately issued from a grateful and pleasant fire; and that if we should go into the house we should find the family as usual there; a suggestion which, as the storm begins to renew itself, we shall do well to take the opportunity to verify.

Flourishing in the midst of snowbanks, unmoved amid the fiercest onsets of the storm, comfortable in the extremity of winter, the family are all gathered in the kitchen, and occupied as may be. In the cavernous fireplace burns a great fire, composed of a huge green backlog and forestick, and a high cob-work of crooked and knotty refuse wood. The flame is as bright and golden as in Windsor Palace, or Fifth Avenue, New York. The smoke goes off out-doors with no more hesitancy than if it was summer time. The wood sings, the sap drops on the hot coals, and explodes as if it was Independence Day. Great red coals roll out on the hearth, sparkle a semibrief, lose their grosser substance, indicate a more ethereal essence in prototypal forms of white, down-like cinders, and then dissolve into brown ashes.

To a stranger the room has a sombre aspect, rather

heightened than relieved by the light of the fire burning so brightly at midday. The only connection with the external world is by a rude aperture through the sides of the building;—yet when the outer light is so obscured by a storm, the bright fire within must any where be pleasant. In one corner of the room is Pluck, in a red flannel shirt and leather apron, at work on his kit mending shoes; with long and patient vibration and equipoise he draws the threads, and interludes the strokes with snatches of songs, banter and laughter. The apartment seems converted into a workshop, for next the shoemaker stands the shingle-maker, Hash, who with froe in one hand and mallet in the other, by dint of smart percussion, is endeavoring to rive a three-cornered billet of hemlock. In the centre sits Brown Moll, with bristling and grizzly hair, and her inseparable pipe, winding yarn from a swift. Nearer the fire are Chilion and Margaret; the latter with the Orbis Pictus, or World Displayed, a book of Latin and English, adorned with cuts, which the Master lent her; the former with his violin, endeavoring to describe the notes in Dr. Byle's Collection of Sacred Music, also a loan of the Master's, and at intervals trailing on the lead of his father in some popular air. We shall also see that one of Chilion's feet is raised on a stool, bandaged, and apparently disabled. Bull, the dog, lies rounded on the hearth, his nose between his paws, fast asleep. Dick, the gray squirrel, sits swinging listlessly in his wire wheel, like a duck on a wave. Robin, the bird, in its cage, shrugs and folds itself into its feathers, as if it were night. Over the fireplace, on the rough stones of the chimney, which day and night through all the long winter now cease to be warm, are Margaret's flowers; a blood-root in the marble pot Rufus Palmer gave her, and in wooden moss-covered boxes, pinks, violets and buttercups, green and flowering. Here, also, as a sort of mantletree ornament, sits the marble kitten that Rufus made, under a cedar twig. At one end of the crane, in the vacant side of the fireplace, hang rings of pumpkin rinds drying for beer. On the walls, in addition to what was there last summer, are strings of dried apples. There is also a draw-horse, on which Hash smooths and squares his shingles; and a pile of fresh, sweet-scented white shavings and splinters. Through the yawns of the back-door and sundry rents in the logs of the house filter in, unweariedly, fine particles of snow, and thus along the sides of the rooms rise little cone-shaped, marble-like pilasters.

Within doors is a mixed noise of miscellaneous operations; without is the rushing of the storm. Pluck snip-snaps with his wife, cracks on Hash, shows his white teeth to Margaret; Chilion asks his sister to sing; Hash orders her to bring a coal to light his pipe; her mother gets her to pick a snarl out of the yarn. She climbs upon a stool and looks out of the window. The scene is obscured by the storm; the thick driving flakes throw a brownish mizzly shade over all things, air, trees, hills, and every avenue the eye has been wont to traverse. The light tufts hiss like arrows as they shoot by. The leafless butternut, whereon the whippoorwill used to sing, and the yellow warbler make its nest, sprawls its naked arms, and moans pitifully in the blast; the snow that for a moment is amassed upon it, falls to the ground like a harvest of alabaster fruit. The peach-tree, that bears Margaret's own name, and is of her own age, seems to be drowning in the snow. Water drops from the eaves, occasioned by the snow melting about the chimney.

"I should'nt wonder if we had a snow-storm, before it's over, Molly," said Pluck, strapping his knife on the edge of the kit.

"And you are getting ready for it, fast," rejoined his wife. "I should be thankful for those shoes any time before next July. I can't step out without wetting my feet."

"Wetting is not not so bad after all," answered Pluck. "For my part I keep too dry.—Who did the Master tell you was the god of shoemakers?" he asked, addressing Margaret.

"St. Crispin," replied the child.

"Guess I'll pay him a little attention," said the man, going to the rum bottle that stood by the chimney. "I feel some interest in these things, and I think I have some reason to indulge a hope that I am among the elect."

"He wouldn't own you," said his wife, tartly.

"Why, dear?"

"Because you are not a man; you are not the thrum of one. Scrape you all up, and we shouldn't get lint enough to put on Chilion's foot."

"Look at that," said her husband, exposing his bare arm, flabby and swollen; "what do you think now?"

"Mutton fat! Try you out, run you into cakes, make a present of you to your divinity to grease his boots with. The fire is getting low, Meg; can't you bring in some wood?"

"You are a *woman* really!" retorted Pluck, "to send the child out in such a storm, when it would take three men to hold one's head on."

"Ha, ha!" laughed out his spouse. "You must have stitched your own on; I don't wonder you are afraid.—That is the way you lost your ear trying to hold on your head in a storm, ha ha!"

"Well," rejoined Pluck, "you think you are equal to three men in wit, learning, providing, don't you?"

"Mayhaps so."

"And weaving, spinning, coloring, reeling, twisting, cooking, clinching, henpecking?—I guess you are. Can you tell, dearest Maria, what is Latin for the Widow's Obed's red hair?"

"I can for the maggot that makes powder-post of our whole family, Didymus Hart."

Pluck laughed, and staggered towards his bench.

"I knew we should have a storm," said his wife, "after such a cold spell; I saw a Bull's Eye towards night; my corns have been pricking more than usual; a flight of snow-birds went by day before yesterday. And it won't hold up till after the full, and that's to-night."

"I thought as much too," answered Pluck. "Bottle has emptied fast, glums been growing darker in the face, windle spun faster, cold potatoes for dinner, hot tongue for supper.'

"You *shall* fetch the wood, Meg, or I'll warm your back with a shingle," said her mother, flinging out a threat which she had no intention of executing. "Hash is good for something, that he is."

"Yes, Maharshalalhashbaz, my second born," interjected Pluck, "sell your shingles to the women; they'll give you more than Deacon Penrose; it is such a nice thing for heating a family with. We shan't need any more roofs to our houses—always excepting, of course, your dear and much-honored mother, who is a warming-pan in herself, good as a Bath Stove."

Hash, spurred on by this double shot, plied his mallet the harder, and declared with an oath that *he* would not get the wood, they might freeze first; adding that he hauled and cut it, and that was his part.

Chilion whispered to his sister and she went out for the purpose in question. It was not excessively cold, since the weather moderated as the storm increased, and she might have taken some interest in that tempestuous outer world. The wind blazed and racketed through the narrow space between the house and the hill. The flakes shaded and mottled the sky, and fell twirling, pitching, skimble-scamble, and anon, slowly and more regularly, as in a minuet; and as they came nearer the ground, they were caught up by the current, and borne in a horizontal line, like long, quick spun, silver threads, afar across the landscape. There was but little snow in the shed, although entirely open on the south side; the storm seeming to devote itself to building up a drift in front. This drift had now reached a height of seven or eight feet. It sloped up like the roof of a pyramid, and on the top was an appendage like a horn, or a plume, or a marble *jet d'eau*, or a frozen flame of fire; and the elements in all their violence, the eddies that veered about the corner of the house, the occasional side blasts, still dallied, and stopped to mould it and finish it; and it became thinner, and more tapering and spiral; each singular flake adjusting itself to the very tip, with instinctive nicety; till at last it broke off by its own weight—then a new one went on to be formed. Under this drift lay the wood Margaret was after, and she hesitated to demolish the pretty structure. The cistern was overrun with ice; the water fell from the spout in an ice tube, the half barrel was rimmed about with a broad round moulding of similar stuff, and where the water flowed off, it had formed a solid wavy cascade, and under the cold snows the clear cold water could be heard babbling and singing as if it no whit cared for the weather. From the corner of the house the snow fretted and spirted in continuous shower. A flock of snowbirds suddenly flashed before the eyes of the child, borne on by the wind; they endeavored to tack about, and run in under the lee of the shed, but the remorseles elements drifted them on, and they were apparently dashed against the woods beyond. Seeing one of the little creatures drop, Margaret darted out through the snow, caught the luckless or lucky wanderer, and amid the butting winds, sharp rack, and smothering sheets of spray, carried it into the house. In her Book of Birds, she found it to be a snow-bunting; that it was hatched in a nest of reindeer's hair near the North Pole, that it had sported among eternal solitudes of rocks and ice, and come thousands of miles. It was purely white, while others of the species are rendered in darker shades. She put it in the cage with Robin, who received the travelled stranger with due respect.

Night came on and Margaret went to bed. The wind puffed, hissed, whistled, shrieked, thundered, sighed, howled by turns. The house jarred and creaked, her bed rocked under her, loose boards on the roof clappered and rattled snow pelted the window-shutter. In such a din and tustle of the elements lay the child. She had no sister to nestle with her, and snug her up; no gentle mother to fold the sheets about her neck, and tuck in the bed; no watchful father to come with a light, and see that all was safe.

In the fearfulness of that night, she sung or said to herself some words of the Master's, which he however must have given her for a different purpose—for of needs must a stark child's nature in such a crisis appeal to something above and superior to itself, and she had taken a floating impression that the Higher Agencies, whatever they might be, existed in Latin:—

"O sanctissima, O purissima,
Dulcis Virgo Maria,
Mater amata, intemerata!
Ora, ora, pro nobis!"

As she slept amid the passion of the storm, softly did the snow from the roof distil upon her feet, and sweetly did dreams from heaven descend into her soul. In her dream she was walking in a large, high, self-illuminated hall, with flowers, statues and columns on either side. Above, it seemed to vanish into a sort of opaline-colored invisibility. The statues, of clear white marble, large as life, and the flowers in marble vases, alternated with each other between the columns, whose ornamented capitals merged in the shadows above. There was no distinct articulate voice, but a low murmuring of the air, or sort of musical pulsation, that filled the place. The statues seemed to be for the most part marble embodiments of pictures she had seen in the Master's books. There were the Venus de Medicis; Diana, with her golden bow; Ceres, with poppies and ears of corn; Humanity, "with sweet and lovely countenance;" Temperance, pouring water from a pitcher; Diligence, with a sickle and sheaf; Peace, and her crown of olives; Truth, with "her looks serene, pleasant, courteous, cheerful, and yet modest." The flowers were such as she had sometimes seen about houses in the village, but of rare size and beauty;—cactuses, dahlias, carnations, large pink hydrangeas, white japonicas, calla lilies, and others. Their shadows waved on the white walls, and it seemed to her as if the music she heard issued from their cups.

Sauntering along she came to a marble arch, or door-way, handsomely sculptured, and supported on caryatides. This opened to a large rotunda, where she saw nine beautiful female figures swimming in a circle in the air. These strewed on her as she passed leaves and flowers of amaranth, angelica, myrtle, white jasmin, white poppy, and eglantine; and spun round and round silently as swallows. By a similar arch, she went into another rotunda, where was a marble monument or sarcophagus, from which two marble children with wings were represented as rising, and above them fluttered two iris-colored butterflies. Through another door-way she entered a larger space opening to the heavens. In this she saw a woman, the same woman she had before seen in her dreams, with long black hair, and a pale beautiful face, who stood silently pointing to a figure far off on the rose-colored clouds. This figure was Christ, whom she recognized. Near him, on the round top of a purple cloud, having the blue distant sky for a background, was the milk-white Cross, twined with evergreens; about it, hand in hand, she saw moving as in a distance four beautiful female figures, clothed in white robes. These she remembered as the ones she saw in her dream at the Still, and she now knew them to be Faith, Hope, Love, and their sister, who was yet of their own creation, Beauty. Then in her dream she returned, and at the door where she entered this mysterious place she found a large green bull-frog, with great goggle eyes, having a pond-lily saddled to his back. Seating herself in the cup, she held on by the golden pistils as the pommel of a saddle, and the frog leaped with her clear into the next morning, in her own little dark chamber.

When she awoke the wind and noise without had ceased. A perfect cone of pure white snow lay piled up over her feet, and she attributed her dream partly to that. She opened the window-shutter; it was even then snowing in large, quiet, moist flakes, which showed that the storm was nearly at an end; and in the east, near the sunrising, she saw the clouds bundling up, ready to go away. She descended to the kitchen, where a dim, dreary light entered from the window. Chilion, who, unable to go up the ladder to his chamber, had a bunk of pelts of wild beasts near the fire, still lay there. Under a bank of ashes and cinders, smoked and sweltered the remains of the great backlog.

Pluck opened the ashes and drew forward the charred stick, which cracked and crumbled into large deep crimson, fine-grained, glowing coals, throwing a ruddy glare over the room. He dug a trench for the new log, deep as if he were laying a cellar wall.

After breakfast Margaret opened the front door to look out. Here rose a straight and sheer breastwork of snow, five feet or more in height, nicely scarfing the door and lintels. Pluck could just see over it, but for this purpose Margaret was obliged to use a chair. The old gentleman, in a fit of we shall not say uncommon good feeling, declared he would dig through it. So seizing a shovel he went by the back door to the front of the house, at a spot where the whiffling winds had left the earth nearly bare, and commenced his subnivean work. Margaret, standing in the chair, saw him disappear under the snow, which he threw behind him like a rabbit. She awaited in great excitement his reappearance under the drift, hallooed to him, and threatened to set the dog on him as a thief. Pluck made some gruff unusual sound, beat the earth with his shovel; the dog bow wow'd at the snow; Margaret laughed. Soon this mole of a man poked his shovel through, and straightway followed with himself, all in a sweat, and the snow melting like wax from his hot, red face. Thus was opened a snow-tunnel, as good to Margaret as the Thames, two or three rods long, and three or four feet high, and through it she went.

The storm had died away; the sun was struggling through the clouds as if itself in search of warmth from what looked like the hot, glowing face of the earth; there were blue breaks in the sky overhead; and far off, above the frigid western hills, lay violet-fringed cloud-drifts. A bank of snow, reaching in some places quite to the eaves of the house, buried many feet deep the mallows, dandelions, rosebushes and hencoops.

The chestnuts shone in the new radiance with their polished, shivering, cragged limbs, a spectacle both to pity and admire. The evergreens drooped under their burdens like full-blown sunflowers. The dark, leafless spray of the beeches looked like bold delicate netting or linear embroidery on the blue sky, or as if the trees, interrupted in their usual method of growth, were taking root in midwinter up among the warm transparent heavens.

Pluck sported with Margaret, throwing great armfuls of snow that burst and scattered over her like rocks of down, then suffering himself to be fired at in turn. He set her astride the dog, who romped and flounced, and pitched her into a drift whence her father drew her by her ankles. As he was going in through the tunnel, a pile of snow that lay on the roof of the house fell and broke the frail arch, burying the old man in chilly ruins. He gasped, floundered, and thrust up his arms through the superincumbent mass, like a drowning man. Margaret leaped with laughter, and Brown Moll herself coming to the door was so moved by the drollery of the scene as to be obliged to withdraw her pipe to laugh also. Bull was ordered to the rescue, who, doing the best he could under the circumstances, wallowing belly-deep in the snow, seized the woollen shirt-sleeve of his master, and tugged at it, till he raised its owner's head to the surface. Pluck, unmoved in humor by the coolness of the drench, stood sunk to his chin in the snow, and laughed as heartily as any of them, his shining bald pate and whelky red face streaming with moisture and shaking with merriment. At length both father and child got into the house and dried themselves by the fire.

Chilion demanded attention; his foot pained him; it grew swollen and inflamed. Margaret bathed and poulticed it, she held it in her lap and soothed it with her hand. A preparation of the Widow's was suggested. Hash would not go for it, Pluck and his wife could not, and Margaret must go. Bull could not go with her, and she must go alone. She was equipped with a warm hood, martin-skin tippet, and a pair of snowshoes. She mounted the high, white, fuffy plain and went on with a soft, yielding, yet light step, almost as noiseless as if she were walking the clouds. There was no guide but the trees; ditches by the way-side, knolls, stones, were all a uniform level. She saw a slightly-raised mound, indicating a large rock she clambered over in summer. Black spikes and seed-heads of dead golden rods and mullens dotted the way. Here was a grape vine that seemed to have had a skirmish with the storm and both to have conquered, for the vine was crushed, and the snow lay in tatters upon it. About the trunk of some of the large trees was a hollow pit reaching quite to the ground, where the snow had waltzed round and round till it grew tired, and left. Wherever there was a fence, thither had the storm betaken itself, and planted alongside mountain-like embankments, impenetrable dikes, and inaccessible bluffs.

Entering thicker woods Margaret saw the deep, unalloyed beauty of the season; the large moist flakes that fell in the morning had furred and mossed every limb and twig, each minute process and filament, each aglet and thread, as if the pure spirits of the air had undertaken to frost the trees for the marriage festival of their Prince. The slender white birches, with silver bark and ebon boughs, that grew along the path, were bent over; their arms met intertwiningly; and thus was formed a perfect arch, voluptuous, dream-like, glittering, under which she went. All was silent as the moon; there was no sound of birds, or cows, sheep, dinner-horns, axes or wind. There was no life, but only this white, shining, still-life wrought in boreal ivory. No life? From the dusky woods darted out those birds that bide a New England winter; dove-colored nuthatches quank quanked among the hemlocks; a whole troop of titmice and woodpeckers came bustling and whirring across the way, shaking a shower of fine tiny raylets of snow on the child's head; she saw the graceful snowbirds, our common bird, with ivory bill, slate-colored back and white breast, perched on the top of the mulleins and picking out the seeds. Above all, far above the forest and the snow-capped hills, caw cawed the great black crow. All at once, too, darted up from the middle of a snowdrift by the side of the road a little red squirrel, who sat bolt upright on his hind legs, gravely folded his paws and surveyed her for a moment, as much as to say, "How do you do?" then in a trice, with a squeak, he dove back into his hole.

Approaching the Widow's, she crossed the Porta Salutaris and all the scrawls of the stump fence, without touching them, on a mound of snow that extended across the garden, half covering the side of the house, wholly hiding Obed's savory beds, and nearly enveloping the beehive, where, on the pardoxical idea that snow keeps out cold, the bees must have been cozy and warm. Reaching the door, she stooped to find the handle, but Obed, who espied her coming, was already on the spot, and handed her down from the drift as he would from the back of a horse. The Goddess of the Temple very cordially received her in her adytum, that is to say, the kitchen.

What with the deep snowbanks without, the great fire within, and the deft and accurate habits of the lady of the house, every thing was neat, snug and comfortable as heart could wish. A kettle over the fire simmered like the livelong singing of crickets in a bed of brakes in summer time, and there was a pleasant garden perfume from numerous herbs dispersed through the room.

The Widow asked her son to read sundry scraps of writing she had, for Margaret's particular edification. "You see," she said, "he's as smart and perlite as any on um. His nat'ral parts is equal to the Master's, and he only needs a little eddecation teu be a great man. There's a good deal in the way of bringing children up Peggy; you'll know when you have been a mother as long as I have. How much have I sold, think, sen the Master was here? Nigh forty boxes."

After having sufficiently enlightened Margaret in these matters, she promised her the salve of which she was in quest, provided she would help Obed a while in pasting labels on the boxes. These she had sent to Kidderminster to be printed, black tvpe on a red ground.

When Margaret left for home, the sun had gone down, and the moon rose full, to run its high circuit in these winter heavens. The snow that had melted on the trees during the day, as the cool air of evening came on, descended in long wavy icicles from the branches, and the woods in their entire perspective were tricked with these pendants. It was magic land to the child, almost as beautiful as her dream, and she looked for welcome faces up among the glittering trees, and far off in the white clouds. It was still as her dream, too, and her own voice as she went singing along, echoing in the dark forest, was all she could hear. The moon tinged the icicles with a bright silver lustre, and the same pure radiancy was reflected from the snow. Anon she fell into shade of the Moon on her left; while at her right, through the dark boughs of the evergreens, she saw the planet Venus, large and brilliant, just setting on the verge of the horizon in the impearled pathway of the sun. She thought of her other dream at the Still, of Beauty, fair sister of three fair sisters, and she might have gone off in waking dreams among the fantasies of real existence, when she was drawn back by the recollection of her brother, to whose assistance she hastened. It was very cold, her breath showed like smoke in the clear atmosphere, and the dew from her mouth froze on her tippet. All at once there was a glare of red light about her, the silver icicles were transformed to rubies, and the snowfields seemed to bloom with glowing sorrel flowers. It was the Northern Lights that shot up their shafts, snapped their sheets, unfurled their flaming penons, and poured their rich crimson dies upon the enamelled earth. She thought the Winter and the World were beautiful, her way became more bright, and she hurried on to Chilion;—for whom, day by day, hour by hour, she labored and watched, assiduously, tenderly; till his foot mended apace, though it never got entirely well.

One morning Obed called for Margaret to go with him to the village. There had been a rain the day before, followed by a cold night, and the fields were glazed with a smooth hard crust. They both took sleds, Margaret her blue-painted Humming Bird, which she received as a Thanksgiving present a while before. Obed had on a bright red knit woollen cap, that came down over his ears, and fitted close to his head, having a spiral top surmounted with a tassel.

It was a clear day, and the sun and the earth seemed to be striving together which should shine with the greatest strength; and they served as mirrors respectively in which to set off one another's charms. As Margaret and Obed went on, the light seemed to blow and glow through the forest like a blacksmith's forge, and the traveller would almost be afraid of encountering fiery flames if he went on. Now riding down pitches, now dragging their sleds up acclivities, they emerged so far from the woods as to overlook the village and open country beyond. A steam-like vapor arose from the frozen River, diffused itself through the atmosphere, and hung like a blue thin veil over the snowy summit of the Mountain. A long band of white mackerel-back clouds garnished the sky. They came at length to Deacon Hadlock's Pasture. Here the scattered trees were all foaming with ice, and the rain having candied them over, trunk and branch, they shone like so many great candelebras; and the surface of the lot, in all its extent, burnt and glared in the singeing sunbeams. Here also they encountered a troop of boys and girls coasting. Some were coming up the hill, goring and scranching the crust with their iron corks, others wheeling about and skimmering away through the bright air, the ups and downs forming a perfect line of revolution. Margaret and Obed, joining the current, mounted their sleds, and scudded away down the glassy slope, with a rapidity that would almost take one's breath away.

At the bottom of the Pasture, surmounting the fence, was a high envelope of snow; over which some of the sleds passed into the road beyond, some came to top and halted, some with a graceful recurve turned off aslant, while others with less momentum going up half way ran backwards, and haply striking an obstruction, reared, and threw their riders heels over head. Margaret elevated in feeling, and supported withal by a very spirited sled, rushed into the thickest of the sport, dashed down the hill, made a graceful return on this terrace and mingled with the moiling merry-hearted ups. There were trees scattered through the lot, and small rocks just rounded off with snow, and larger ones with a pitch in front, and diversities of soil that gave a wavy huckle-backed character to the entire field. The boys wore steeple-crowned caps like Obed's; the girls were dressed both in short and long gowns. Their sleds were adorned with brave and emulous names,—Washington, Napoleon, Spitfire, Racer, Swallow. The downs whooped by, curvetting among the trees, leaping from rocks, jouncing over hollows. They took it in all ways, astride, kneeling, breast-wise, haunch-wise. It was a youthful, exhilarating, cock-brained winter, New England dytharimb.

"This is music," said one boy.

"Something of the broomstick order—a fellow gets thwacked most to death," replied a second.

"There goes Judah Weeks, his trotters are getting up in the world," cried a third.

"Old Had is hard upon him," rejoined the second speaker.

"He always is upon the boys, but we get some fun out of him, don't we?" added the first.

"Spitfire is as skittish as the Deacon's sorrel colt; Jude might have known he would have got cast," interposed the third.

"I declare, how they ache," said Judah, blowing his red snow-dripping fingers, as he joined the ups.

"Clear the coop!" cried all hands, "here comes a straddle-bug." But the rider, it happened to be Obed, losing his balance, his sled bolted, raking and hackling the crust, and scattering the glittering dust on every side, while the luckless lad himself tumbled headlong to the ground.

"Hurt, Obed?" asked Margaret.

"No," replied the youth, trying to appear brave.

"Does your Marm know you are out?" asked one of the large boys.

"She said I might come!"

"Do you know what will cure cold fingers?" said Judah.

"Take garlic and saffron blows, and bile um an hour and drink it just as you are gittin' into bed, and it'll cure any cold that ever was, Marm says," replied Obed.

"There go Washington and Napoleon!" cried several voices; "Old Bony'll beat as true as guns; she's all-fired swift."

"Peggy's Hummin' Bird'll beat any thing," said Obed. "She'll go like nutcakes," an allusion he was in the habit of making, founded on a favorite dish his mother cooked for him every Saturday night.

"Guess Racer'll give her a try, or any thing there is on the ground," answered one of the larger boys, Seth Penrose, son of the Deacon's. "Pox me! if these Injins put their tricks on me as they do on daddy."

"Sh'! sh'! Seth," whispered Judah, "you didn't talk so when you was digging her out of the woods. We don't have such a time as this every day. Let us make the best of it."

"Ho ho, hoop ho!" rang along the ranks as they reached the top of the hill. Something was in prospect. Below were seen two collections of boys, each hauling with might and main at an outlandish structure. "A race! a race!"

"Hoora for the Old Confederation!" shouted some, "Hoora for the Federal Constitution!" echoed others, as the objects of their attention drew near. These were rude sapling runners, surmounted by crockery crates.

The boys, in whom the strong political feeling of the time could not well fail to develop itself, had planned an adventure, and were about to test and signalize their respective merits and capabilities by a race in which grotesqueness and temerity, more than anything else, seemed to be the combatants. Their ark-like chariots being duly disposed, were soon filled, some of the boys sitting in front to steer, while others performed like office behind. They started off in high spirits and amidst a general enthusiasm. They skewed, brustled and bumped along, the crates wabbled and warped from side to side, the riders screamed, cross-bit, frumped and hooted at each other; they lost control of their crazy vehicles, their bows struck and parted with a violent rebound; one went giddying round and round, fraying and sputtering the snow, and dashed against a tree; the other whirling into the same line was plunged headlong into the first. It was a new style of salmagundi; some of the boys were doused into each other, some were jolled against the tree, some sent grabbling on their faces down the hill; here one was plumped smack on the ice, there another, after being sufficiently whisked and shaken, was left standing. There was a shout from the top of the hill, and a smothered response from below, then a clearer shout, and at last a full-toned hoora. None were seriously hurt; who was ever hurt sliding down hill? Yet what with their lumbering gear staved to atoms, splinters, nails, and the violence of the concussion, it was a wonder some were not killed.

The call was now for a single race. Twenty or more of

the sleds were drawn into a line, Margaret's and Obed's among the rest. The fence at the foot of the Pasture was the ordinary terminus of their slides; but they sometimes went farther than this. Crossing Grove Street, and an orchard in the neighborhood, they could even reach the Green;—to gain, by methods unimpeachable, the farthest point on which was the stake, and comprised a distance of nearly half a mile. The girls sat with their skirts trussed about their ankles, and the boys took postures as they liked best. The signal was made, and they flushed away. Falling into all sorts of order, some went crankling and sheering, some described somersets, others were knocked sternforemost; but on, on, they flew, skittering, bowling, sluice-like, mad-like; Margaret glided over the mounds, she leaped the hollows, going on with a ricochet motion, pulsating from swell to swell, humming, whizzing, the fine grail glancing in her eyes and fuzzing her face; her hood fell back over her shoulders, her hair streamed bandrols in the wind; she reined her sled-rope as if it had been the snaffle of a high-spirited horse: she passed the first fence, and the second—others were near her—some lodged on the fences, some dropped in the street. Three or four sleds were in full chase through the orchard, they gained the Green, where momentum exhausted itself. Margaret was evidently foremost and farthest.

"She hitched," said Seth Penrose, somewhat angrily.

"I didn't," said Margaret, somewhat excited.

"She didn't hitch," observed little Job Luce, who had been hovering about the hill all the morning watching the sport, and now crept to the Green to see them come in.

"I thought Spitfire was up to anything," out spoke Judah Weeks, jumping from his snow-bespattered sled; "but she is beat."

Margaret had indeed won the race, and that without a miracle. Chilion, her mechanical genie, had constructed her sled in the best manner of the best materials, and shod it with steel. In her earliest years he inured her to the weather, hauled her on the snows before she could walk, made her coast as soon as she could sit a sled, graduated her starting points up Indian's Head, so that she became equal to any roughness or steepness, and could accomplish all possible distances.

"Who beat? who beat?" asked a score of breathless voices rushing to the spot.

"Little Molly Hart," roundly answered Judah.

"The wicked Injin didn't beat nuther," rejoined Seth.

"She did beat teu," interposed Obed. "I know she did."

"How do you know she did, Granny?" thundered Seth.

"'Cause Hummin' Bird can beat any thing, and I know she did," replied Obed.

"You are done for," said one or another to Seth.

"I an't done for—she hitched," persisted the sturdy rival.

"I guess she didn't hitch," argued little Isabel Weeks, "'cause Ma says good children don't cheat; and she is good, 'cause Ma says good children helps their ma's, and she helps her ma."

"I *know* she didn't," repeated Job, "'cause I was here and saw it."

"Bawh! Ramshorn!" blurted the indignant Seth, thrashing about and by a side-trick knocking Job on the hard crust.

"He must pick him up; he's a poor lame boy," said Isabel; "Jude, take hold of his feet."

"I'll help you," said Margaret.

"Don't touch him!" exclaimed Obed, addressing Margaret. "He's—he's—he'll kill ye, he'll pizen ye, he'll give ye the itch. He's a ghost."

"He won't hurt you," replied Isabel, "its only little Job Luce with a crook in his back, Ma says; and it's handy to lift by. Up with him."

They placed the unfortunate lad on Margaret's sled, and the two girls drew him to his mother's. They went on the crust, with the road two or three feet below them, straight and narrow, fluted through the solid plane of the snow. They passed sleighs or cutters that were what we should now call large and heavy, with high square backs like a settle, and low square foot-boards, and looking naked and cold, without buffalo, bearskin or blanket. They carried Job into the house and deposited him in a low chair by the fire. Mistress Luce, a wan, care-worn, ailing looking woman, yet having a gentle and placid tone of voice, was binding shoes. The bright sunlight streamed into the room, quite paling and quenching flames and coals in the fireplace. A picture hung on the walls, an embroidery, floss on white satin, representing a woman leaning mourningly on an urn, and a willow drooping over her. The woman did not appear to be at all excited by her boy's misfortune, only the breeze of her prevailing sorrow, that sometimes lulled, seemed to blow up afresh a little, as she resumed her seat after attending to his wants.

"He gets worse and worse," she sighed,—"we did all we could."

"Won't he grow straight and stout?" asked Margaret.

"Alas!" she answered, "a whippoorwill sung on the willow over the brook four nights before he was born;—we had him drawn through a split tree, but he never got better."

"Whippoorwills sing every night most at the Pond in the summer," said Margaret.

"I have heard them a great many times," added Isabel. "Ma says they won't hurt us if we are only good."

"I know, I know," responded the woman, with a quick shuddering start.

"Ma says that they only hurt wicked people," continued Isabel.

"I always knew it was a judgment on account of my sins."

"What have you done?" asked Margaret anxiously.

"I cannot tell," answered the Widow, "only I am a great sinner; if you could hear the Parson preach you would think so too. I just read in my Bible what God says, 'Because you have sinned against the Lord, this is come upon you.'"

"I saw Job at the Meeting one day," said Margaret; "he recited the catechism so well. Do you know what it meant?" she continued, turning to the boy.

"If I do not, Mammy does," replied the latter. "But I know the whippoorwill's song."

"Do you?" asked Margaret; "can you say it?"

"No, only I hear it every night."

"In the winter time?"

"Yes, after I go to bed."

"Do you have dreams?"

"I don't know what it is," replied the boy, "only I hear whippoorwill. It sings in the willow over the urn, and sings in here," he said, pointing to his breast. "I shall die of whippoorwill."

"O Father in heaven!" groaned the mother bitterly, yet with an air of resignation, "it is just."

"It sings," added the boy, "in the moonshine, I hear it

in the brook in the summer, and among the flowers, and the grasshoppers sing it to me when the sun goes down, and it sings in the Bible. I shall die of whippoorwill."

"How he talks!" said Isabel. "I guess Ma wouldn't like to have me stay, only Job *is* a good boy, he says his prayers every night, and don't kill the little birds, like the other boys, and Ma says he will go to heaven when he dies. I wish they wouldn't tease him so."

A horn was heard, and Isabel said it was her dinner time, and Margaret must go with her.

"Good-by, Job," said Margaret, "in the summer I will come and see you again, and you must come up to the Pond, I will show you my bird-book, and you shall sail on the water."

Esquire Weeks, who lived nearly opposite the Widow Luce's, was an extensive farmer. Mistress Weeks was the mother of fourteen children, all born within less than twice that number of years, and living and cherished under the same roof.

"A new one to dinner, hey, Miss Bell?" said her mother. "So, so; just as your Pa always said, one more wouldn't make any difference. Take your places—I don't know how to cut the pudding downwise, crosswise—one, two, three, four, five, six, seven, eight, nine, ten, eleven. Eleven, where are they all? Don't I count straight?"

"John, Nahum, and the men have gone into the woods, Ma," said Bethia.

"I am sure I had fifteen plates put on," remarked the mother.

"Washington hurt his hand, and Dolly you said wasn't old enough to come yet," said Bethia.

"I like to have forgotten the dear innocent," answered the mother, laughing. "I don't remember any thing since we had so many children. Lay to——"

"Mabel hasn't a piece," observed Helen.

"Can't I get it right?" said the mother. "Girls I tell you all, study arithmetic. If I had known what a family I was going to bring up, I should have learnt mine better. Arithmetic is the best thing in a family, next to the Bible."

"And a good husband," interposed Esq. Weeks.

His wife laughed assent. "But," she added, "I recommend to my children to take up arithmetic, numeration, addition, subtraction, division and all the compounds, practice, tare and trett, loss and gain.—You've come all the way from the Pond, Miss Margery. How is your Ma'am? I really forgot to ask. It's pretty cold weather, good deal of snow, comes all in a bunch, just like children. And you liked to have been killed in the tornado? If it had been our little Belle how we should have felt."

"And me too?" asked the little Mabel.

"Yes, you too, can't spare any of you. Only be good children, be good children, eat all you want."

After dinner Margaret said she would go and see Master Elliman, and Isabel went with her. At the Widow Small's, the Master's boarding house, they were told he was over the way, at the Parson's; whither they directed their steps. The house of Parson Welles stood on the corner, as you turned from South Street up the Brandon, or No. 4, road. Isabel leading the way, they entered without knocking, and made directly for the Parson's study. The Parson and the Master were sitting over the fire, with their backs towards the door, smoking pipes with very long tails, and engaged in earnest conversation, so much so that the Master only nodded to the girls, and the Parson, who was a little deaf, did not notice them at all. Isabel held her breath, and made a low courtesy to the Parson's back, while Margaret stood motionless, and casting curious glances about the room. The Parson, whose hair was shaved close to his head, wore a red velvet cap, and had on in place of his public suit of black, a long, bluish brown linen dressing-gown, which his wife had probably wove for him at some by-gone period. The room had small windows, was wainscotted and painted a dark green, and rendered still darker by tobacco smoke. There was a bookshelf on the wall, and small portraits in black frames similar to those Margaret saw at the Master's; the sand on the floor was streaked in whimsical figures, and on a black stout legged table lay paper, ink, and some manuscript sermons of a size we should now call diminutive, not bigger than this book.

"Touching objections, Master Elliman," continued the Parson, laying his pipe on his hand, "fourteenthly, it is calumniously asserted by the opposers of divine truth that on this hypothesis God made men to damn them; but we say God decreed to make man, and made him neither to damn him nor to save him, but for his own glory, which end is answered in them some way or another."

"Whether they are damned or not?" answered the Master.

"Yes," said the Parson, "inasmuch as that is not the thing considered, but rather the executing of his own decrees, and the expression of his proper sovereignty, who will be glorified in all things. The real question is, whether man was considered in the mind of God, as fallen or unfallen, as to be created or creatable, or as created but not fallen. But the idea of things in the divine Mind is not as in ours. God understands all things *per genesin*, we understand them *per analysin*. Hence going back into the divine Mind, *a borigine*, we first seek the *status quo* of the idea. In that idea came up a vast number of individuals of the human specie as creatable, some as fallen, others as unfallen. He did not create them to cause them to fall——"

"But he made them fall that they might be created——"

"Now this idea considered as an active volition is God's decree, and this decree going into effect creates man on the earth; some predestined to everlasting life, some to everlasting death. And here the Universalists do greatly err, not perceiving that God is equally glorified in the damnation as the salvation of his creatures: so, St. Paul to the Romans, ix. 17, 18, 19. My pipe is out, and we must apply to King Solomon to help us in this matter."

"Yea, verily," responded the Master.

This King Solomon, we should explain, was a large silver snuff-box, with a mother-of-pearl lid, on which was carved the interview of the Queen of Sheba and the aforementioned king, a utensil that Parson Welles carried in his deep waistcoat pocket, and the contents of which he and the Master partook freely in the intervals of smoking.

"Why should man reply against God?" pursued the Parson.

"A very unreasonable thing indeed," quoth the attentive auditor.

"The riches of God's mercy do alone save us from the infernal designs of reprobate men. Those who oppose the divine decrees would soon have Satan in our midst—as truly whom do I now behold?"

The worthy minister surely did not mean to call Margaret the Evil One,—yet this exclamation, coupled as it was with a startled recognition of the face and sudden sense of the presence of the child, seemed to imply as much.

But the affectionate pedagogue, quick to notice and to arrest any insinuation of this sort, with a quiet adroitness, instantly brought Margaret to the Parson's knee, and formally introduced her.

"I understand," answered the venerable man. "Of the Hart family in Lichfield; I knew her grandfather well. He was an able defender of the truth."

"She is from the Pond, sir," added the Master. "Didymus Hart, alias Pluck's daughter."

"Indeed! of the Ishmaelitish race," responded the Parson, laughing. "If she could be baptized and jine the catechizing class; appinted means whereby the Atonement is made efficacious. Isabel," he continued, addressing the companion of Margaret, "you are sprung of a godly ancestry, and the blood of many holy persons runs in your veins. See that ye despise not the Divine goodness."

The Master took Margaret about the room, and showed her the books and pictures. Of the former were the writings of the most distinguished Divines on both Continents; there were "Prey taken from the Strong, or an Account of a Recovery from the Dangerous Errors of Quakerism;" "Thatcher's Sermons on "the Eternal Punishment of the Finally Impenitent;" "An Arrow against Profane and Promiscuous Dancing, drawn out of the Quiver of the Scriptures;" "Owen on Sin;" "Randolph's Revision of Socinian Arguments;" &c., &c. The latter were chiefly faces of the old clergy; in large wigs, long flowing curls, skull-caps, some with moustaches and imperials, all in bands and robes.

Parson Welles was the contemporary of Bellamy, Chauncey, Langdon, Cooper, Byles, Hopkins, West, Styles and others; with some of whom he was on terms of familiar acquaintance. He was a pupil of Edwards, and afterwards the friend and correspondent of that divine. Whitefield and his labors, the latter especially, he never brooked, and would not suffer him to preach in Livingston.

The Master presently retired with Margaret to his rooms, where she accomplished her errand, that of getting his advice respecting something she was studying, and where he also gave her some books. Parting with her little friend, Isabel, she went back to the Green for Obed, and returned home ;—where for the present we leave her.

PART II.

YOUTH.

PART II.

CHAPTER I.

SPRING.—ROSE.—MARGARET KEEPS SCHOOL.—SUNDRY MATTERS.—MR. ANONYMOUS.

This Part commences with an omission of five or six years, the particulars of which one familiar with life at the Pond will be at no loss to supply. Margaret has pursued the tenor of her way, even or uneven, as the case may be; assisting her mother, entertaining her father, the companion of Chilion, and the pupil of the Master. If variety in unity be the right condition of things, then her life has been quite philosophical. She has made considerable progress in her studies, pursued for the most part in a line suggested by the peculiarities of her instructor.

It is spring; Hash is about beginning his annual labor of making maple sugar and burning coal; Margaret has promised him her aid, and then she is to have her own time. She carries the alder spouts to the Maples, rights the troughs that have been lying overturned under the trees, and kindles a fire beneath the large iron kettle that hangs from a pole supported between two rocks. Wreathing the trailing arbutus in her hair and making a baldric of the ground-laurel, with a wooden yoke stretched across her shoulders she carries two pails full of sap from the trees to the boiler. With a stick having a bit of pork on the end, she graduates the walloping sirup when it is likely to overflow, while her brother brings more sap from the remote and less accessible part of the camp. The neighbors, boys and girls, come in at the "sugaring off;" the "wax" is freely distributed to be cooled on lumps of snow or the axe-head; some toss it about in long, flexile, fantastic lines, some get their mouths burnt, all are merry. Her mother "stirs it off," and a due quantity of the "quick" and "alive" crystal sweet is the result, a moiety of which is destined to the Smiths, at No. 4, in consideration for the use of the lot, and another portion to Deacon Penrose's for other well-known objects.

The coal-pit, lying farther up the road, on the Via Salutaris, next demanded attention. She helped clear off the rubbish, and remove the sod to make a foundation for the kiln and prevent the fire spreading. She lent a hand also in stacking the wood, covering the pile with turf, and constructing a lodge of green boughs, where her brother would stay during the night; one whole night she herself watched with him. Then she raked up the chips about the house, and with a twig broom swept the dirt from the new-springing grass; she hoed out the gutter where the water ran from the cistern, and washed and aired her own little chamber. The cackling of the hens drew her in search of their eggs in the manger and over the hay-mow in the barn. So four or five weeks pass away, and her own play-spell comes, if, indeed, her whole life were not a play-spell.

She would replenish her flower-bed, and goes into the woods to gather rare plants. She has books of natural history with which the Master kept her supplied. The forests at their first leafing and infloresence present an incipient autumual appearance, in the variety of colors and marked divisions of the trees, but the whole effect is thinned, and softened. The distant hills have a yellowish gray, merging into a dim silver look, and might be taken for high fields of grass in a bright dewy morning. She turned over logs and stones, and let loose to the light and air tribes of caterpillars, beetles and lizzards, that had harbored there all winter. The ants open their own habitations by demolishing the roof, which they convert into a redoubt; and she watched them coming up from their dark troglodital abodes bringing the fine grit in their teeth, and stepped with a kind caution among these groups of dumb, moneyless, industrious Associationists. Toads, piebald, chunk-shaped, shrugged and wallowed up from their torpid beds, and winked their big eyes at her.

The birds are going on with their grand opera, and she and the sun, who is just raising his eye glass above the trees, are the sole unoccupied spectators. Her father perhaps has some interest in the scene; he sits in the front door, pipe in mouth, the smoke rolling over his ruddy pate and muffling his blear eyes, but he contrives to laugh lustily, and his flabby dimensions shake like a bowl of jelly. She has caught a harry-long-legs and holds it by one of its shanks, while she very soberly inspects the book before her, to find out more about it than it is disposed to tell of itself.

Chilion used to love to go into the woods with her and point out the different birds, gather rare flowers, and discover green knolls and charming frescoes where she could sit. But he is lame now, and cannot walk far, having never recovered from the injury he received some years before, searching for her in the windfall. Besides, he never said much, and what value he put upon things that interested her, she could never precisely understand. He is engaged withal thwacking with his axe a long white ash stick, the successive layers of which being loosened, he tears off to make baskets with, which has become almost his sole employment. So she enjoys the world quite alone, and not the less for that, since she has always done so.

The place flows with birds, and they flow with song; robins, wrens, song-sparrows, thrushes, cat-birds, cow-buntings, goldfinches, indigo birds, swallows, martens; loons and bitterns on the water; and deep in the forest olive-backs, veeries, oven-birds, to say nothing of a huge turkey gobbling in the road, a rooster crowing on the fence, and ducks quacking in the ditches. A varied note breaks upon her, which if she is able to distinguish, she can do better perhaps than some of our readers, who will hardly thank us for giving names to what after all is very perceptible to the practised ear; twittering, chirping, warbling, squeaking, screaming, shrieking, cawing, cackling, humming, cooing, chattering, piping, whistling, mewing, hissing, trilling, yelping.

Chilion is passionately attached to music in his own way, is master even of some of its technicalities, and Margaret in this matter is his pupil; and it requires no great effort for her to discern a general hallelujah in this sylvan concert; affetuoso, con dolce and con furia are agreeably intermingled; nor are there wanting those besides herself to encore the strain. She is no Priapus to drive the birds away; but as if she were a bramble-net, their notes are caught in her ears, even if their feet are not seized by her fingers as they winnow the air, wheel, dive and dally about her. They frisk in the trees, pursue one another across the lots, start fugues in a double sense, compete with their rivals, clamor for their mates, sing amatory and convivial ditties, and describe more ridottoes than the Italians.

Could we suppose sounds to be represented by ribbons

of different colors, and the fair spirit of music to sit in the air some hundred feet from the ground, having in her hand a knot of lutestrings of a hundred hues, blue, pink, white, gold, silver, and every intermediate and combined shade and lustre, and let them play out in the sun and wind, their twisting, streaming, snapping, giddying, glancing, forking, would be a fair symbol of the voices of the birds in the ear of Margaret on this warm sunny spring morning.

Howbeit, the profusion of Nature offers other things to her attention besides the birds; or rather we should say the good Mother of all gives these beautiful voices wherewith to purify the sensibilities of her children and animate them in their several pursuits. Thus enlivened and impelled, Margaret entered other departments of observation.

Shod with stout shoes, armed with a constitution inured to all forces and mixtures of the elements, supported by a resolution that neither snakes, bears, or a man could easily abash, she penetrated a wet sedgy spot near the margin of the Pond, where she found clusters of tall osmunds, straight as an arrow, with white downy stems and black seed-leaves, curling gracefully at the top in the form of a Corinthian capital, and shining pearl-like in the sun with their dew-spangled chaffy crowns; the little polypods with green, feathery, carrot-shaped fronds, penetrating the solid dry heaps of their decayed ancestry; and horsetails with storied ruffs of supple spines: farther along were the fleecy buds of the mouse-ear, bringing beautiful cloud-life from the dank leaden earth; young mulleins, velvety, white, tender, fit to ornament the gardens of Queen Mab; and buttercup-sprouts with dense green leaves, waxen and glistening: in the edge of the woods she gathered straw-colored, pendulous flowers of the chaste bell-wort; liver-leaves, with cups full of snow-capped threads; mosses, with slender scarlet-tipped stems, some with brown cups like acorns, others with crimson flowers ; there were also innumerable germs of golden rod, blue vervain, and other flowers, which at a later season should fill the hedges and enliven the roads.

In the woods a solitary white birch, bedizened with long yellow, black-spotted flowers, pulsating in the wind, and having a scarlet tanager sitting in its thin sunny boughs, attracted her eye by its own gentle beauty ; in the grass stood hundreds of snowdrops, like a bevy of girls in white bonnets trooping through a meadow ; quantities of the slender, pink flowering wintergreen grew among the white dogweed ; and the twin-flower interlaced the partridge berry. Within the forest was a broad opening, where she loved to walk, and which at this time disclosed in high perfection the beautiful verdure of spring. Here were white oaks with minute white flowers, red oaks with bright red flowers, red maples with still redder flowers, rock maples with salmon-colored leaves, as it were birds fluttering on one foot, or little pirouetting sylphs; a growth of white birches spread itself before a sombre grove of pines, like a pea-green veil. The path was strewn with old claret boxberries, gray mosses, brown leaves, freaked with fresh green shoots ; and what with the flowers of the trees illumined by the sun on either side, one could imagine her walking an antique hall with tesseleated floor and particolored gay hangings. This opening sloped to the shore of the Pond, where under another clump of white birches she sat down. The shadows of the trees refreshingly invested her, the waves struck musically upon the rocks, and in the clear air, her own thoughts sped like a breath away ; the vivacity of the birds was qualified by the advance of the day, and while she had been delighted at first with what she saw, all things now subsided into harmony with what she felt. She hummed herself in low song, which as it had not rhyme, and perhaps not reason, we will not transcribe.

Some new tide of sensation bore her off, and she went up the Via Salutaris to the brook Cedron. This she threaded as far as the Tree-Bridge; golden blossoms of the alder and willow overhung the dark stream; she passed thickets of wild cherries in full snowy bloom; yellow adder's tongue diversified green cowslips, pink columbines festooned the gray rocks, red newts were sunning themselves on the pebbles of the brook; she saw a veery building its nest in a branch so low its young could be cradled in the music of the stream; green, lank frogs sprang from her feet into the swift eddies, and thrust up their heads on the other side, like their cousins, the toads, to look at her; clear water oozed from the slushy banks.

Crossing from the Via Dolorosa, through the Maples, she came to rocks that abutted the south-east boundary line of the elevated plain on which lay the basin of the Pond. Descending this, on the slope below, were evergreens; hereabouts also she discovered the splendid dogwood, and the pretty saxifrage.

But a circumstance occurred that quite diverted her from these things. She heard a sound issuing from the shady side of a young pine, like that of a woman singing or murmuring to itself. Stealing to the tree, through the boughs, she beheld a young lady of nearly her own age reclined on the dry leaves, whiling herself in rending to shreds the bright crimson flowers of the red-bud or Judas tree, and uttering plaintive broken sounds. This unknown person was delicately fair, with a fine profile, and long locks of golden hair trailing upon her neck; her hand was snowy white, and fingers transparently thin. She wore a white red-sprigged poplin, a small blue bonnet lay at her side, and a brocaded camlet-hair shawl falling from her shoulders discovered a bust of exquisite proportions. Her complexion was white, almost too white for nature or health, and her whole aspect betokened the subsidence and withdrawal of proper youthful vigor. Margaret, quite spellbound, gazed in silence. The young lady laughed as she scattered the flowers, and there was a marvellous beauty in her smile, melancholy though it seemed to be ; and even to Margaret's eye, who was not an adept in such matters, it rayed out like the shimmer of a cardinal bird in a dark wood. Margaret thought of the Pale Lady of her dreams, and that she had suddenly dropped from the skies. She saw the young lady press her thin fingers to her eyes as if she wept, then she smiled again, and that smile penetrated Margaret's heart, and she advanced from her ambuscade, but spider-like, as if she were about to catch some fragile vision of the fancy. The young lady sprang up at the noise and ran. Margaret pursued, and with her familiarity with the woods and fleetness of foot, she gained upon the other, who turned and said rather abruptly, "Why do you follow me ?"

"Why do you run ?" answered Margaret. "I would not hurt you ; let me hear your voice—let me take your hand," she continued. Her tone was kind, her manner innocent, and the young lady seemed so far won as to be willing to parley.

She rejoined, "I sought this spot to be away from the faces of all."

"How strange !" ejaculated Margaret. "Where is your home ? Are you from the village ?"

"I have no home, but you are Molly Hart, whom they have told me about."

"I am Molly Hart; but say who are you, and what is your name?"

"Those are questions I cannot answer."

"You look very unhappy."

"Were you ever unhappy?" asked the stranger.

"Not much," replied Margaret, "I have always been happy, I think."

"You seem to be fond of flowers," said the young lady.

"Are not you?"—

"I used to be;—I was going to say," she added, "I will help you carry your basket, and look for flowers with you; only you must not ask me any questions."

"Then I shall want to," said Margaret.

"But you must not," insisted the young lady.

"Very well," replied Margaret, "you will be another flower and bird to me, and equally unknown with all the rest; nor will you give me less pleasure for that you are unknown, since every thing else is."

"Then I shall like you very much, if you will consent to my being unknown; and perhaps in that way we can contrive to amuse one another."

They ascended the bluff, and returned through the woods together.

"Have you found the snapdragon, that recoils when it is touched?" asked the stranger.

"That does not come out in the spring," said Margaret. "But here are berries of the witch-hazel that blossomed last fall."

"And under our feet are withered dead leaves," rejoined the young lady.

"But they shone in vigorous starry brilliancy, after the frosts pinched them," said Margaret.

"Here is the morning glory," said the young lady, as they entered the Mowing, "that lasts but one hour."

This female, as we have said, evinced great waste of strength; hervoice was reduced in a corresponding degree, though it was sweet and clear as her face was beautiful; and there was something in her tone and manner of allusion that signified a secret unexpressed state of being which Margaret could not fail to remark, however far she might be removed from its proper comprehension; and her replies took the turn of one in whose breast, intuitively, will float veiled images and be reflected therefrom indistinct recognizances of latent deep realities in the breast of another.

"Look at this blue flag," she said; "our neighbor, a wise simpler, declares it will cure a host of diseases."

"The stargrass there," replied the other, "hides itself in the rank verdure, and only asks to be."

"The strawberry is very modest too, but its delicious fruit is for you and me, and every body. Shall I never see you again?" inquired Margaret emphatically. "Will you go away as suddenly as you came? Will you not *speak* to me? Have the naturalists given no account of such a one as you? You say you have no home—do you live under the trees? Where did you get that shawl and bonnet? No name? No genus, no species? Come into the house and let Chilion play to you."

"You have seen the pond lily," was the reply, playful but sad, "that closes its cup at night, and sinks into the water."

"It springs up the next morning blooming as ever," said Margaret. "Besides, if only one had appeared in my lifetime, I should be tempted to plunge in after it, come what might. You are very 'anagogical,' as my Master says, strange and mysterious I mean, like a good many other things. You remind me of a pale beautiful lady I have seen in my dreams, only her hair is black."

"The blood-root," replied the imperturbable unknown, "when it is broken loses its red juice."

"In truth!" exclaimed Margaret. "Yet it is a very pretty flower. I have a whole one just flowering in my bed. Do go and see it. You love flowers, and I do too, and perhaps they will talk you more to me."

The young lady shook her head, "I cannot go now. I am at the Widow Wright's; but do not follow me. You are very happy, you say, and you have no need of me; you are quite busy too, and I would not call you away."

"Do give me a name," urged Margaret, "some point that I can seize hold upon you by, be it ever so small. I am sure I shall dream about you."

"Since you like flowers," answered the young lady, "you may call me Rose, but one without color, a white one."

So they separated, and Margaret went to her house. From the stock of plants she had gathered, she transferred to her beds a spring-beauty, a rhodora, and winter-green, to grow by the side of sweet brier, cardinal flowers, and others. Chilion brought out a neatly made box in which he wished her to set a venus-shoe or ladies-slipper.

It was not singular that Margaret should desire again to see the strange young lady, who was called Rose, nor was she at loss for opportunities to do so. She pursued her sedulously, and even prevailed with her to come to her father's The spirit of Pluck seemed to rally this sad being, and Chilion's music penetrated and charmed her soul, albeit it failed to reveal the secret of her thoughts. It was of different kind from any that she had heard before; it operated as a simple melodious incantation, and did not, as music sometimes does, arouse feelings only to tantalize and distress them. Chilion played in a wild untutored way, catching his ideas from his own simple thoughts, and from what of nature was comprised above and below the horizon of the Pond, and this pleased her. Margaret, sensitively alive to whatever pertained to the due understanding of Rose, sometimes gave her brother a hint at which he played; but there was developed so plain an uneasiness within the concealed breast of the stranger, that both were fain to forbear.

Rose came frequently to Pluck's ; she loved to be with Margaret and Chilion ; even the sullen disposition of Hash she evinced a facility for softening by her playful repartees and beautiful smiles. She gained the favor of Brown Moll by assisting Margaret, who rising in domestic as well as natural science, had become equal to carding and spinning. The dog too was not insensible to her tatractions, but with an enlargement of heart not always found in the superior races, while he fell off no whit in his original attachments, he recognized her as a new lady-love, obeyed her voice, followed her steps, wagged his tail at her smiles, and leaped forwards to meet her as readily as he did Margaret. Nothing could have been more diverting than to see Brown Moll weaving, Margaret spinning, Rose carding, and Pluck reduced to Margaret's childhood estate, occupying her little stool, quilling ; a sight often seen.

Rose and Margaret walked in the woods, sailed on the Pond, and sometimes read together. Now also the peculiarities of Rose appeared. She would absent herself from Pluck's and Margaret whole days ; she would stay at the Widow's, between whom and herself some relationship was claimed, and work silently with Obed in his herb-beds, despite the most urgent solicitations of Margaret; she resorted alone to the thickest parts of the forest. No questionings, no attentions, no generosity were adequate to dislodge the secret that evidently labored in her breast, or a part of which she may have been. The Widow, and Obed, who took his cue from his mother, would answer nothing for her; save that the latter called her his cousin. At times she was cheerful, talkative, vivacious, even to exuberance; in the same moment she would relapse into a thoughtful and preoccupied state; not unfrequently she wept. Margaret learned to acquiesce in these diversities, at whatever expense of baffled solicitude. She was delighted with the gushes of Rose's sprightliness, she was overawed by her hidden pain, as by some great mystery of nature, which nevertheless she sometimes essayed critically to explore, sometimes humanely to compose; but the subject only reminded her of her ignorance, though meanwhile it haunted her with new and indefinable sensations of tenderness and reflective philanthropy.

In the latter part of May the Master appeared at the Pond, his thin gray face agreeably illumined by the pleasing intelligence he bore, this, that he had negotiated the Village School for Margaret. However Margaret might have regarded this proposal, there was one consideration that prevailed with her to accept it,—the pecuniary embarrassment of the family. Pluck's whole estate was under mortgage to Mr. Smith of No. 4, the original proprietor, and retained indeed from year to year with a diminishing prospect of redemption. That gentleman in fact threatened an ejectment, and if relief were not soon afforded, dismemberment and homelessness might at any moment become their lot.

Pursuant to orders, the next day Margaret paid a visit to Master Elliman's to receive such instructions as he felt bound to communicate relative to her new duties. He gave her to understand that there existed an opposition in the minds of some of the people to her having the School, but that he had secured the appointment through Parson Welles, whom he persuaded to his views. He next advised her as to the books to be used. He said the children would read daily in the Psalter, recite every Saturday morning from the Primer, and as to the Spelling Book, the only remaining channel of elementary instruction, he intimated there was a question. He informed her that he learnt from Fenning's Universal, which was afterwards supplanted by the New England, that many of the people were clamorous for a change, which had been effected in most of the towns; that one wanted Perry's Only Sure Guide, another Dilworth, a third Webster's First Part; and that he and Deacon Hadlock, who agreed in little else, had hitherto been united in resisting scholastic innovations, but the time was come when he supposed a concession must be made to the wishes of the public.

"Compare," said he, "the First Part, and the deific Universal. Look at the pictures even. Young Noah, who propounds to us his visage in the frontispiece of his book, has doffed, you see, the wig, and is frizzed, much to the alarm of your good friend Tony, who declares the introduction of said book will ruin him. Those super-auricular capillary appendages, hardened with pomatum, to what shall we liken them, or with what similitude shall we set them forth? They are like the eaves of a Chinese temple; or in the vernacular of your brother Nimrod, they are like a sheep's tail; yea, verily. But by a paradox, *id est*, by digressing and returning, we will keep in the straight track. The Deacon, the Parson and the Master, a megalosplanchnotical triad, have recommended Hale's Spelling Book.

Enoch was a pupil of mine, and though grown sanctiloquent of late, he always knew how to say the right thing, as his book abundantly teaches. Webster, moreover, advertises us that & is no letter; the goal of every breathless, whip-fearing, abcdarian's valorous strife, the high-sounding Amperzand, no letter! Mehercule! You apocopate that from the aphabet, and Deacon Hadlock will apocopate you from the School; yea, verily. It really signifies *and per se*, that for your private edification, Mistress Margaret. Moreover Perry makes twenty-six vowel sounds, Hale only sixteen; Webster enumerates nine vowels, Hale five; Hale preponderates in merit by reduction in number. Too many words, Margaret, too many words among men. The fewer vocals the better, as you will certainly know when you have the children to instruct. In spelling, let the consonant be suffixed to the last vowel thus, g-i v-e-n, not, g-i-v e-n, as they do in this degenerate age. It is revolutionary and monstrous. Hand me my pipe, I shall get angry. And, memor sis, mea discipula, vox populi, vox dei. You have asked me who God is; you will probably arrive at that understanding as soon as you desire. "Here," he continued, presenting a heavy ebony ruler, "is what serves to keep up the flammula vitalis in the simulacra hominum. You will find it a good Anamnetic in the School, and useful in cases of the Iliac Passion, the young androids are subject to. Let not the words of Martial be fulfilled in you,

'Ferule tristis, sceptra pædagogorum ceasant!'

The best Master I wot of is the Swabian who gave his scholars 911,000 canings, with standing on peas, and wearing the fool's cap in proportion. With my most pious endeavors, I could never exceed more than ten castigations per diem, one at each turn of the glass; and that in thirty yeras that I have borne the Solomonic function, amounts only to about sixty thousand; Jove forgive me! Here also is a clepsydra, yclept an hour-glass, for you, and this is the Fool's Cap, which it is hardly needful to put on in a world like this, but the Committee will be pleased to see it worn. Lupus pilum mutat, non mentem."

"Your friend Fenning," interrupted Margaret, "I see, writes thus in his preface: 'I must take the freedom to say, that I am sensible a Rod, a Cane, or Ferula, are of little signification; for I have experienced in regard to Learning itself, Infants may be cheated into it, and the more grown-up yôuth won by good nature.'"

"I don't wonder," replied the Master, "that Deacon Hadlock is confounded at the times, when the scholar presumes to arraign his tutor! My friend Fenning, peace to his shades! had a weak side, nor could all the divine Widow's embrocations cure him; I mean he was tainted with heresy; he denied the plenary inspiration of the Bible; not your father's, for of that there can be no doubt; but that wherein King Solomon appears—and this reminds you of the Parson's snuff, which is truly after a godly sort, kept in godly pockets, and is efficacious in the illuminating of the understanding of the saints—but of these things I do not discourse. It is somewhere said, 'Spare the rod and spoil the child;' this truth carefully concealed in the holy mysteries, my Friend Fenning most unbecomingly dared to question. But you are not through with your anagogics yet! You never saw a Mumming, or Punch and Judy? Nay, verily!"

While they were conversing, Deacon Ramsdill halted into the room, with one of those smiles, which, if it ever preceded him as a shadow, still was the promise of something kind and good-natured thereafter. "I heerd what the gal was about," said he, "and I thought I would try and give her a lift. I am abroad a good deal, and my woman is getting old and rather lonesome-like; and we made up our minds if Miss Margery would come and stay with us she should have her board and welcome. Hester Penrose, that kept the School last summer, got her lodgings free at the Deacon's, and we thought we could do as much for another. Don't know how you will like us, but we have found that swine that run at large in the woods make the sweetest pork, and we are willing to give you a try. What on earth are you going to do with that are piece of board?"

"If I understand the Master," replied Margaret, "he intends that I shall fence in the scholars with it."

"There, now," responded the Deacon. "I tell you children have nater, and you can't help it, no more than you can being a cripple when your hamstrings are cut. When they first come to school they are just like sheep, you put them into a new pasture and they run all over it up and down, shy round the fence, try to break out, and they won't touch a sprig of grass though they are hungry as bears. You send the youngsters of an arrant, and they climb all the rocks, throw stones at the horse-sheds, chase the geese, and stop and talk with all the boys and gals in the way, and more than as likely as not forget what they have gone upon. We old folk must keep patience, and remember we did just so once. It's sheer nater and there's no stoppin' on't, no more than a rooster's crowing a Sabber-day. Blotches are apt to come out in hot weather, and you may find the scholars a little *tar*bulent, particularly about dog-days; but nater must have its course. Don't keep them too tight. When the tea-kettle biles too hard, my woman has to take the cover off. 'Twon't do to press it down, it's agin nater, you see.—But, Molly, or Mistress Margaret, as we shall have to call you, for want of a nail the shoe is lost, as Poor Richard says; you must mind little things, and see that matters don't come to loose ends before you know it. Pull up the weeds and then throw down some brush for the cucumbers to fasten to; it's nateral, and they don't get snarled among themselves. But you understand how to work a garden; well, it's all nater alike. Ha, ha!"

This language, the Master, who perhaps on the principle that extremes meet, or what is more likely, that the simple, hearty pleasantry of the Deacon was always boon company to his own laughing humor, ever maintained friendly relations with the latter gentleman—this language, we say, the Master suffered to pass without animadversion or rejoinder.

Margaret, thus turned adrift to her own reflections by the pointed opposition of her friends, thanked them both for their magnanimous interest in her behalf, took the books and other pædagogical ensigns, and returned to the Pond. Early the succeeding Monday she reported herself at the School-house, took her seat behind the big desk, and opened with her scholars, who filed in after her, each one making his bow or her courtesy as they entered the door; and all with clean bright faces and bare feet. The boys took their places one side of the room, and the girls the other. They reckoned about twenty, and were all under twelve years of age, comprising the buds of the village population. Among them was little Job Luce, who, recompensed for deformity of body in vivacity of mind, and combining withal certain singularities of sentiment, could not fail to recommend himself to the favorable attention of his Mistress, however he stood reputed with the world at large.

She classed her scholars, heard their a's, ab's, acorns,

and abandonments, gave them their outs, rapped with the ferule on the window to call them in—the only application she made of the instrument in question—turned her glass every half hour, enjoyed the intermission at noon, and at night, if like most teachers, was as glad as her scholars to be dismissed. Her dinner this first day, which she brought from home, she ate at the School-house; a practice which she not unfrequently adopted, since Deacon Ramsdill's, where she had her quarters, was some distance from the Green,—and in this she was joined by many of her scholars; and she spent the hour cultivating their acquaintance, remarking their manifold, novel and diverse evolutions, moral and physical, and contributing to their pastime,—she never commanded the intimacy of children before. The Deacon's became in fact no more than her nominal abode, since there were others in the village who regarded her with kindness.

Isabel Weeks, whom she had occasionally encountered, and who even visited her at the Pond, was her stanch friend. Of Isabel we might say many things, and on Margaret's account, some amplification perhaps were demanded; but agreeably to the well used maxim, that times of peace furnish few topics for the historian, we follow all precedents, and forbear. Isabel was emphatically a time of peace, she had no contentions, intrigues, or revolutions. She was so quiet and unobtrusive, she would be set down for an ordinary character. She was just as commonplace and unnoticed as the sun is. She had no veiled secret like Rose, to tantalize expectation and stimulate curiosity; she was transparent as the air, and like that element, was full of refreshment and health, sweet odors and pleasant sounds. She had always been indulgent of Margaret and of the people at the Pond, from her childhood; and perhaps, if we ascribe to her a portion of that self-love of which so few are deprived, she found she lost nothing in continuing this friendship, which indeed had cost her something with her neighbors. She sometimes staid at the Widow Small's, where the Master kept her late in the evening employed in a manner that gave him the greatest possible gratification, playing backgammon. One day of the first week, at the close of the School, following her scholars from the house, who broke forth in noise, freedom and joy, the boys betaking themselves to their several diversions, snapping the whip, skinning the cat, racing round the Meeting-house, or what not, she found herself engaged with a group of girls, saying,—

" Intery, mintery, cutery-corn,
Apple seed, and apple thorn;
Wine, brier, limber-lock,
Five geese in a flock,
Sit and sing by a spring,
O—U—T and in again."

"It's the Ma'am's, it's the Ma'am's!" shouted the girls, "she must stand;" and stand she did, blinded her eyes, counted a hundred, went in search of the hiders, anticipated their return, and in fine went through a regular game of "Touch Goal," with the ardor and precision of her pupils.

Saturday forenoon she omitted the customary lesson in the Primer, and on her return home deliberately reported what she had done to the Master, dropping something at the same time about not understanding the book. "Understand the Primer!" retorted her supervisor with considerable vehemence. "What most people dread, I am fain to confess I love, lunacy, to be out of one's head. Didn't you know that you must be out of your head when you undertook the School. Are not all teachers, preachers, speakers, out of their head? What do they know or pretend to know of what they froth and jabber about! Ugh! Eidepol! Is it not all a puppet-show, and each of us a wheel-grinder? Are not Patriots cap wearers and Priests mummers? Wag your mouth and blink your eyes like most genuine pasteboard when you come out into the world among folk. Not teach the Creed hey? That is the finest part of the whole. You would banish Harlequin from the play, like some other good moral people! Go to, go to, you little prude! Lie out in the moon this and to-morrow night, and you will be ready to begin your work again Monday, like any good saint."

With these condolences and ministrations, she continued her way to the Pond, where she proposed to spend the Sabbath. Rose came to see her, to whom she recounted the passages of the week, new and reflective, painful and pleasing. Pluck nearly split with laughter at what she related of the Master and the Primer, whereby also Rose was similarly affected, yet not so naturally as the old man, but like one startled from a dream, or in whom an imprisoned phantasmal voice breaks out wild and derisory.

"The bell tolls; who is dead?" asked Brown Moll, as they were sitting in the doorway about sunset, Sabbath evening, and the measured melancholy note fell upon their ears, the old and familiar signal that some spirit had just left the body, "Keep still, while I count." So by keeping pace with the number of strokes she learned the age of the deceased. "Forty-one, who is it?"

"It must be Mrs. Morgridge," said Margaret. "I

heard that she was sick, but did not think she was going to die. Poor little Arthur!"

This sigh for one of her beloved pupils was supported by no contributions of her friends, and the subject, like those to whom it owed its rise, died away. The family never said much about death, whether they feared it and did not wish their peace disturbed, or were indifferent to it and felt moved to no words, or were prepared for it and needed no admonitions, nothing in their manner would leave us the means of determining.

Monday she resumed her duties; Tuesday afternoon, she was advised by the Master that it was expected the school would be suspended on account of the funeral. She went to the Judge's, who lived on the North Street, a short distance from the Green, with her friend Isabel. There was a large collection, including the remotest inhabitants of the town. After prayer by Parson Welles, the coffin was taken into the front yard, and laid on the bier under the trees. Sunlight and shadows, fit emblems of the hour, flickered over the scene, not more breathless, hushed and solemn, than were the voice, step and heart of the multitude. The voluminous velvet pall thrown back exposed a mahogany coffin, thickly studded with silver buttons, ornamented with some gilt armorial tracery, and having the name and age of the deceased on a silver tablet. The citizens approached one by one to take a last look of the remains, then sunk away into the silently revolving circle. The mourners presently came out and indulged a tearful, momentary, final vision; the lid was closed, and the covering folded to its place. On the coffin were then laid six pairs of white kid gloves, one for each of the pall bearers, and a black silk scarf, designed for the clergyman.

The bier, carried on the shoulders of four young men, was followed by the relatives, when came the citizens at large, two and two abreast. The bell began its slow, far-echoing, heavy toll, and continued to sound till the procession reached the graveyard.

This spot, chosen and consecrated by the original colonists, and used for its present purpose more than a century, lying on the South Street, was conspicuous both for its elevation and its sterility. A sandy soil nourished the yellow orchard grass that waved ghostlike from the mounds and filled all the intervals and the paths. No verdure, neither flower, shrub, or tree, contributed to the agreeableness of the grounds, nor was the bleak desolation disturbed by many marks of art. There were two marble shafts, a table of red sandstone, several very old headstones of similar material, and more modern ones of slate. But here lay the fathers, and here too must the children of the town ere long be gathered, and it was a place of solemn feeling to all.

As the procession approached the grave, the men took off their hats; the four bier-men lowered the coffin by leathern straps, then each in turn threw in a shovelful of earth; next Philip Davis, the Sexton, taking the shovel into his own hands, standing at the foot of the grave, said in form as follows, "I will see the rest done in decency and order." Parson Welles, as the last obsequial act, in the name of the bereaved family, thanked the people for their kindness and attention to the dead and the living, and the procession returned to the house of the Judge.

Some lingered behind to revisit the graves of their friends; Margaret and Isabel also staid. It was, as we have intimated, a spot without beauty or bloom, like many others in

New England; but in New England affections are green remembrances and enduring monuments; tears that mausoleums cannot always command were freely shed on this dry orchard-grass, and the purest purposes of life were kindled over these unadorned graves. The drunken Tapleys from No. 4 moved in a body to a corner of the lot, where four years before was laid their youngest child, a little daughter, marked by a simple swell of dry sod scarce a span long, and there at least they were sober.

Margaret alone had no friends there. Isabel took her to the grave of one of her early companions, Jesselyne Ramsdill, only child of the Deacon's, an amiable and beautiful girl who was cut off by that scourge of our climate, consumption, in her fifteenth year, wasting away, like a calm river, serene and clear to the last. As objects of curiosity, were the old monuments, made as we have said of red sandstone, now gray with moss, bearing death's heads and cherub cheeks rudely carved, and quaint epitaphs, and the whole both sinking into the earth and fading under the effects of time. Alas! who shall preserve the relics of *these* old Covenanters!

The next week, being at the Master's, he showed her a piece of brown parchment inscribed with the following words, which he desired her to translate:—

"Universis Quorum interest.

"Attestamur Bartholomew Elliman in Actis Societatis dictæ Masoniæ ex ordine fuisse inscriptum, &c.," the substance of which being, that he was a worthy member of the Masonic Lodge of the Rising States. He condescended also to explain the seal of his watch, a huge cornelian cased in gold, dangling from a long gold chain, which had attracted the attention of her earliest years. He said it was "Azure on a chevron between two castles argent, a pair of compasses somewhat extended of the first, &c.;" in fine he told her, that as the Masonic Fraternity were about to consecrate a Hall in the village, it would be quite impossible for the School to keep, and perhaps altogether pleasant for her to witness the ceremony.

On the appointed day, with Isabel, she repaired to the Green. The procession, of two or three hundred, formed from the Crown and Bowl. It exhibited what has been called a "splendid parade" in the "gorgeous attire" of the men with their freshly powdered hair, white gloves, aprons and stockings, their standards of crimson and gold, the pictured gradations of office, and the showy paraphernalia of the mystic institution. There passed before the wondering eyes of our novitiate, Captain Eliashib Tuck, Grand Tyler, with a drawn sword, leading the march; her friend the Master of the order of Worshipful Deacons, with staves; Brothers bearing a gold pitcher of corn, and silver pitchers of wine and oil; four Tylers supporting the Lodge, garnished with white satin, and which, so the Master gave her to understand, was the identical Ark of the Covenant, constructed by Bezaleel and presented to Moses; the Right Worshipful Grand Master, Esq. Weeks, who bore the Bible, Square and Compasses on a crimson velvet cushion; the Chaplain, the Rev. Mr. Lovers, of Brandon, in his robes.

The Hall, which was the object of this convocation, covered the second floor of a building recently put up for town occasions on the east side of the Green. The door was decorated with emblematical figures, the floor had a mosaic coloring, heavy curtains of crimson and gold shaded the windows; on the walls were blazoned sundry hieroglyphics, the Sun and Moon, a Cock, Coffin, Eye and Star; there were also the plummet, mallet, trowel and an armillary sphere, and in the centre stood too marble pillars, understood to be Jachin and Boaz. The procession entered and marched three times round the room; at the first turn, the Grand Master, facing the East, said, "In the name of Jehovah I dedicate this Hall to Free Masonry;" then he pronounced it sacred to Virtue and Universal Benevolence. A prayer and anthem succeeded, when an Oration was pronounced by the Chaplain.

"Free Masonry,"—we make a brief extract from the address of the reverend speaker,—"is the most perfect and sublime institution ever devised for conferring happiness on the individual, and augmenting the welfare of society. Its fundamental principles," he continued, "are Universal Philanthropy and Brotherly Love; its pillars are Faith, Hope and Charity; its end Virtue and Happiness; Religion is its Sister, its Creator is God. Its constitution is coeval with that of the world; from the Divine Architecture of the Universe are derived its Symbols, and He who said, Let there be Light, proclaimed the solemn Dedication of our Order.—Free Masonry," said he, "confounds distinctions, and is insensible to rank; owning a common affiliation of the race, it distributes its beneficence to all, and honors the meanest with its fellowship. It treats none with contempt, and pardons the imperfections of the weak. The distant Chinese, the rude Arab, and the accomplished European will embrace an American, and all sit together at the same table of fraternal confidence and affection. Unconstrained by local prejudice, unswerved by the rivalries of party, spurning alike the claims of sect and the limitations of country, we know no preferance but virtue, no sanctity but truth, in whatever clime, or amid whatever fluctuations of outward life they may appear. Our Association relieves misery and shuns revenge. The tears of Widowhood it wipes away, the pangs of Orphanage it soothes, and by its hands are the stores of Destitution replenished. It curbs the fury of War, and multiplies the blessings of Peace. The sign of a brother, even in an enemy's camp, subdues our animosities and sheathes the sword.—We have been accused," such were the closing words of the discourse, "of conspiring against the liberties of mankind, it is slanderously reported that we are leagued with the foes of law and order to demolish the fabric of society. Were Napoleon a Mason, as he is a Warrior, where he has drenched the earth in blood he would have strewed it with flowers, for wasted cities would have arisen Temples to Virtue, for Ministers of Wrath driving before them the horror-stricken nations, we should behold Angels of Mercy keeping watch over their happy homes, our Melodies would drown the notes of the Clarion, and the race, instead of closing with the ferocity of ensanguined battle, would this day meet in the embrace of Universal Brotherhood!"

The speaker took his seat amid great applause; a hymn was then sung commencing thus,—

"Hail Masonary! thou Craft Divine!
Glory of Earth, from Heaven revealed!
Which dost with jewels precious shine,
From all but Masons' eyes concealed!"

A collation succeeded, consisting of fruits and cakes, and since, on a previous day, at a funeral, spirituous liquors were freely dispensed, we are only just to the times and to this festal company, in adding that wine and brandy formed a conspicuous part of their entertainment. Three additional grand marches around the Hall finished the scene; strangers retired, and the Brotherhood were left to their private affairs.

Shortly after, with Deacon Ramsdill and his wife, and a large number of villagers, Margaret was invited to an evening party at Esq. Beach's. This gentleman lived on Grove Street, in a house of the new style, very large and high, having a curb roof with dormers, and perforated all over with windows like a pepper box. The parlor was thought to be elegantly furnished, in its mahogany side-board garishly bedecked with decanters of brandy and wine, silver cups and tankard, a knife-case, and having underneath a case of bottles brass-trimmed; a bright Kidderminster carpet; light Windsor chairs; a Pembroke table, now degenerated into a common dining-table; and, what caught the eye of the Pond girl, more than all, superb hangings. These represented the South Sea Islands as conceived by the original discoverers. The sides of the room opened away in charming tropical scenery, landscapes and figures; the people, their costume, habits, sports, houses were brought into panoramic view, as also appeared their innocence and simplicity, their native and rural enjoyments and peace, now, alas! to be seen no more by those who shall again visit them. These occupied Margaret so long she well nigh trespassed upon the courtesies of the hour, and Deacon Ramsdill was obliged to recall her to her fellow-guests. There were dancing, card-playing, much spirit-drinking, and more warm political talking, very warm indeed, so fervid and life-imbued, in fact, as to engross all things within itself; and Margaret became a devout listener to what for the instant appeared topics the most lofty, and interests the most momentous; nor could she be diverted until the Master had thrice trod upon her toes, and engaged her in a game of backgammon.

The School, in the estimation of its teacher, was going on finely. Her scholars were ductile and inquisitive, many phased and many-minded, and their proficiency in the Spelling Book was only equalled by their attachment to herself. A single instance of discipline sprang from a rude attack made by one of the larger boys, Consider Gisborne, on one whose helplessness appealed strongly to Margaret's sensibilities, Job Luce. She ordered the offender to sit an hour on the girl's side of the house. In enjoyment and fidelity three weeks were nearly spent.

Yet the coolness with which the people at large originally admitted her services was fast ripening into positive dissent. Some boldly proclaimed her unfitness for the station, others clamored for the restitution of the old Mistress, Hester Penrose. Deacon Ramsdill was the first to break to her the no less surprising than depressing intelligence, and Master Elliman confirmed the suspicion that she would be obliged to quit the School. Parson Welles was considerate enough to suggest the propriety of an investigation of the case; which, however, she would have done well to avoid by a voluntary relinquishment of her post; but she was over-persuaded by her friend Isabel, one of those who always hope for the best, and consented to abide an issue.

The study of the Parson was the appointed scene of trial, and that room which in her girlhood Margaret had surveyed with strong delighted curiosity, was now shaded to her mind beyond the stains of tobacco-smoke and time on the walls. There lay the great mysterious books that she had importuned the Master to give her access to, but from which on one pretence or another he had still kept her, and now they seemed about to be forever banished from her grasp. Above all was the reverend presence itself, the grave person of the Minister, a conflicting union to her eye, of extremest sacredness and extremest profanity, a sort of corporeal embodiment of all unreality with which the lessons of Master Elliman were calculated to fill her mind; and when she saw that strange being soberly lay aside its pipe and as soberly put on its glasses—that single act affected her with a twinge of fright, which was not lessened at all by contact with Isabel, who sat next her shaking with awe and alarm. In addition, rumor of what was afloat having drawn a number of people to the place, their faces frowning, sneering and laughing, increased the complexity of her sensations.

The nominal charges were reduced to two heads; first, omitting to use the Primer; and second, harsh and unreasonable treatment of Consider Gisborne. To this was appended a supplement that had its full weight, that she did not attend Meeting on the Sabbath, and that she played with her scholars; and the whole was ridden by the insinuation that she had shown partiality to the crumple-back, Job. On these several and various matters she could make no defence, and she attempted no reply. Her friends, who under other circumstances would gladly have remonstrated in her behalf, felt constrained to abandon the case, and could do no more than secretly condole with her disappointment.

"Touching the unfortunate youth," said the Parson, "he suffereth from that sin which we do all inherit from the Fall. The compassion which you have exhibited toward him would be counted a token of gracious affections in the regenerate mind. But continuing unregenerate, the danger is great that you will reckon it meritorious, and thus by adding to your good works, increase the probabilities of your condemnation, for truly the Bible saith, The sacrifice of the wicked is an abomination to the Lord. But," he continued, addressing her with a direct interrogation, "will the Mistress wholly deny to impart the godly instruction contained in that little manual?"

"I cannot use it," replied Margaret, with a tolerably firm accent, yet faltering in every muscle.

"Therein are to be found," resumed the Parson, "the great truths of evangelical faith and practice."

"I know nothing what it means," she added, "and I could never consent to teach it."

"Truly," exclaimed he, "their eyes are blinded that they cannot see. What saith Master Elliman on the matter?"

"Yea, verily," replied the Master, "as the Lord hardened the spirit of Sihon, King of Heshbon, and made his heart obstinate, that he might deliver him into the hand of Israel, so is it exemplified in what we now behold."

"She's a drop stitch," said one woman, who had been busy during the proceedings footing a stocking. "She has cast her band if she is a spinner's daughter," was the simultaneous comment of another woman. "She ought to have put in a straining brace before she ran her roof so high," observed Mr. Gisborne the Joiner. "She had better learn of her daddy how to mend her own ways aginst she comes down to patch up our'n next time," said Mr. Cutts, the Shoemaker. "How hardly have we escaped from the hands of the Philistines!" ejaculated Deacon Hadlock. "We have a small account against you at the Store, some pins and ferret I believe," said Deacon Penrose, "hope you will call and settle before you leave."

"You have lost your title, and we must call you Molly

again," said Deacon Ramsdill, as they left the house; "but you stuck to your pint, and mabby it's as well. I see 'twas nater, and you couldn't give it up. The Lord knows what'll come of it, but if you follow nater, he'll take care of you. There is more in things than we old folk have thought of, and if you young heads can find it out, for one I shall be glad. You have eat your crib and broke your halter, but there is a good deal of feed out of the stable. Fences last the longest when the logs are peeled; you are pretty well stripped, but I guess you won't give out any quicker. The children have nater, and you and they would get along smart enough together; the old people are chock full of their notions and politicals, and I don't know as you could do better than to let them alone. I was afraid at the start how the matter would turn. About Consider, he is not a nateral bad boy, only it went agin the grain to be put among the gals; and he took on dreadfully, and his people thought he had been most killed. But it was because *you* did it, Molly, yes because *you* did it; if any body else had done so, he would not have said a word; but he liked the new Ma'am, I've heard him say so, and when you punished him it broke him right down; that's nater agin, clear nater. Hester might have thrashed the skin off his body and he wouldn't have cried boo. Then you know, some people's geese are always swans, so we thought when our little Jessie was alive; yes, yes. God knows how hard it is to help setting a good deal by one's children. But, Molly, you musn't judge the people too harsh; they are just like gooseberries, with a tough skin and sharp pricks, and yet there is something sweet inside. Remember too he who can wait hath what he desires."

Tony, the negro barber and fiddler, who had been hovering about the Parsonage during the trial with considerable concern, and still hung on the steps of the party as they walked up the street, at length ventured to address Margaret and ask her if she would not go to his shop and have her hair dressed. She politely declined.

"Your brother Chilion has done great favors to this gentleman in the musical profession," continued the negro, "and if the Mistress would let him try the tongs on her, it would make great commendations. It an't Tory now, and there isn't nobody else in the world that I would see suffer if I could help it, and the Mistress was a most handsomest dancer, and Chilion tuned my fiddle." Margaret was too much occupied with other reflections.

"You had better go," said Deacon Ramsdill; "it is as good to a man to do a favor as to get one. Tony has a feeling nater, and he mabby would serve you when nobody else would, and will take it hard if you deny him.—Isabel will go with you, and he would like to show you his shop."

Margaret yielded. The Barber, whose function was no unimportant one to the villagers, had his apartments set off in a manner for which such quarters have been famed from time immemorial. The window shutters that concealed his treasures during the night published them by day, standing along the front of his shop as advertising boards, whereon appeared a list of articles to be purchased and services done. Within was a conspicuous assortment of the exquisites of the day,—"King Henry's Water," "Pink and Rose Hair Powder," "Face Powder instead of Paint," "Hemmett's Essence of Pearl for Teeth," "Paris made Pomatum," "Infallible Antidote for Consumption," "Elixir Magnum Vitæ;" etc., etc.

Margaret taking her seat in the tonsorial chair, delivered herself into the hands of the professor. "What a head!"

exclaimed the negro, "what a figure she would make, Miss Belle, in the great world if she was only a little dusted! I have had Madam Hadlock four hours together under my hands, when she was fixing for a ball, where I also had the pleasure to attend her four hours more. After she joined the Church I lost that honor. The Sacrament, Miss Belle, makes bad work with the profession. I am as the Master says A. B. Android Barberosum, S. T. D. Societatis Tonsorum Dux, a great man you see, and Parsons, Judges and Masters, as Master Elliman says, bow down to me.—"

"Is that your method!" said Margaret, really shrinking beneath the resolute application of the artist's hands. "You make my head ache."

"Indeed," replied the negro, "'tis a most fashionable pain, Runy Shooks will sit it out by the hour. You won't need a cushion, but a little powder, Patent Lily gives such an etiquette—"

"Nothing more, I thank you."

"I can't use the tongs, you are all in curls now. What shall we do, Miss Belle? A roller, toupee—that's Paris."

"What!" said Isabel, "I thought you didn't belong to the French Party, Tony."

"Oh, no, I'm all Jacobin, all Federal, all Lumination, only I an't no dum Tory. The Lady's father was a Tory, wasn't he? Well, they won't hurt me now. They were good heads, all of them; I use to get five pounds a year out of Col. Welch's. Let me comb it up over the top, and bring these back locks in front?" "No, no," said Margaret. "You shall be welcome to one of my silver spangled ribbons to tie it with." "Let it be as it is." "Ha! ha! who ever heard of a lady's hair being as it is? That isn't the fashion at all. A lady wouldn't live out half her days.

We use to set it up a foot high; but that was before the War. Since that time, taste, as I have heard York gentlemen say, has slided. I have heard ladies say they couldn't go to meetin' a Sunday, or improve on the sermon, because they were not in fashion. We are a means of grace, as Master Elliman says. So I must bring this curl here, and this one here, and let them be as they was. Well, this gentleman declares upon his honor, Mistress looks as beauteous as the great Queen Anne on the wall. She will not disprove a little Hungary Water?" "No." "Thank the Lady Margaret, thank her. No pins, no spangles, no tye-top, no beads,—Miss Belle so too,—well, upon my soul!"

"Simplicity becomes us best, you know, Tony," said Isabel. "Ma always said those were most adorned who were adorned the least. So you will not feel bad, I know you won't."

"This gentleman D. D. Devil of a Doctor,—for you must know we use to perform surgery, phlebotomy, and blood-letting, till the other professors came in, and they have well nigh propelled us,—this gentleman, A. B., S. T. D., D. D. see the toilette every day going down, and expect the great Napoleon will eat the Barbers all up; but he declares Mistress Margaret the most grandiloquent head in all the country—hope no offence, Miss Belle."

"None at all," replied Isabel; "you know we always said Margery was beautiful, and she is good too, and good folks will bear to have any thing said to them, and not take it as flattery, but only truth, Ma says."

The Barber held up a looking-glass, and Margaret saw her hair not essentially affected by the professional endeavor, still as before parted on the top, and hanging in thick frizettes, which the operator had done his best to smooth, gloss and arrange. "Tell Master Chilion," said he, as the young ladies left, "one of my fiddle-strings is broke and the board out of order, and he is the only gentleman this side of the Bay can fix it, as things ought to be done. Do the Mistress take a box of the Patent Tooth Wash."

Margaret finished out the week with Isabel, and Saturday afternoon left for Mr. Wharfield's, where she was invited to make a visit, and two of whose children had been under her tuition. The Quaker lived on the Brandon road half way between the Village and No. 4. Turning from the South Street, she crossed Mill Brook and rapidly commenced the ascent into a more elevated region. Beneath, on the right, hidden among trees and shrubbery, flowed the Brook; farther to the north-west rose the beautiful green-wooded summit of the Pond, with her favorite Indian's Head towering above all; on the left, by alternate gentle acclivities and precipitous bluffs, sloped the long hills away to the skies. A high flat brought her to the house of her friends, who were farmers, and as we say well-to-do in the world.

Where she intended to stop a single night, her abode was protracted nearly a week. The habits of the family were simple, their manners quiet, and tastes peculiar. Their enjoyment seemed to consist in listening to her, they strove to make her happy by receiving what she had to say, they watched her with the interest approaching to awe of those who beheld in one what they described as the "inner workings of the spirit," and from whom they looked for some surprising evolutions. Their children were thrown continually in her way that they might catch the inspiration with which she seemed to be endowed. Troubled at last as her friends imagined with a desire to go home, they would no longer detain her, and gratefully dismissed her.

If she were depressed at all by the events of the School, the treatment of the Quakers was certainly fitted to reassure her ; and with whatever melancholy she may have first thought of returning home as it were disgraced from the Village, this was qualified or displaced by the second thought that it *was* her home, that there were her best friends and purest pleasures—and she trod on with a firm step and considerable buoyancy of feeling.

She traversed No. 4, known in her vocabulary as Avernus, and not inappropriately named. In addition to every aspect of blight and waste that could conveniently be combined in a human dwelling-place, the geese, those very agreeable articles in their proper use, but the greatest enemies of road-side beauty, like the locusts of Egypt, had discriminated and polled the green grasses and more delicate flowers, and left only may-weed, smart-grass and Indian-tobacco, perennial monuments of desolation ; an offence for which they had long since been banished the Pond. Hogs lay under the cherry-trees by stone-walls, crabbedly grunting like bull-frogs, muddling the earth and wallowing in the mire. Leaning well-sweeps creaked in the scant gardens. She encountered a file of children, with hair thoroughly whitened, and face as thoroughly blackened by the sun, kicking before them the dry dust of the road in clouds. Sheep with fettered legs wandered from side to side restless and forlorn. An overturned wood-sled, lying outside of a barn-yard fence, and protecting within its bars a collection of white flowering catnip, was a solitary point of beauty. A bevy of yellow butterflies flying before her and lighting on the road, then flying and lighting again as she advanced, at last whisking off and forming themselves into a saucy waltz over a black pool of water, where they were finally dispersed by the incursion of a pair of blue-spotted dragon-flies, afforded her some diversion.

A pink in a pewter mug standing on the window-sill of one of the low ragged houses, Mr. Tapley's, she would fain turn aside to see ; a little girl, Dorothy Tapley by name, appeared, awkwardly enough with her fingers in her mouth, and said it was hers. Margaret laying hands upon it, asked if she might have it. The girl immediately lifted her fingers from her mouth to her eyes and began to cry. Margaret inquired what was the matter. Dorothy gave her to understand that when her little sister Malvina was sick, and Miss Amy, with the Parson, came to see the invalid, she wanted a pink that Miss Amy had pinned on her breast, and that having got possession of it she would not part with it, but kept it by her, and died holding the wilted stem in her hand ; whereupon she, Dorothy, went to the Parsonage and begged of Miss Amy a root of the same flower, and that in the mug was it; that she had taken much care of it, and would on no account let it go.

This conversation through the window reaching the ears of Mistress Tapley, who was at work in the back shed cutting up cheese-curd, brought her into the room. The mother—not a very tidy looking woman, having a knife in one hand and a snuff box in the other—confirmed all the child had said. Margaret told them she was glad they valued the flower so, said she would not think of taking it, and asked for a draught of water. This produced a fresh demonstration on the part of these people, the mother averring with undisguised emotion that they had used their last drinking utensil for the pink, that they drank rum from the bottle, that the gourd was broke, but she should be welcome to drink as the rest did from the bucket.

"You help her, Dorothy; she won't git away your posy; she han't forgot how much we done for her when she was lost in the woods."

They went through the house into the back shed. That back shed! cheese-room, dye-room, sink-room, airy, piazza, hen-roost, cupboard, wardrobe, scullery, with its soap-barrel, pot of soap-grease, range of shelves filled with rusty nails, bits of iron hoops, broken trays, hammer, wedges, chizel; tar-pot, swill-pail, bench, churn, basket of apples, kittens, chickens, pup, row of earthern milkpans drying about it—take it for all in all we shall never look upon its like again!

At one end was the well, its long sweep piercing the skies, its bucket swinging to and fro in the wind. Dorothy leaped up and caught the bucket and hauled it to Margaret, who grasping the pole was about to draw it down hand over hand. She paused to look at what was below her. The mouth of the well was shaded and narrowed by green mosses and slender ferns; which also covered the stones quite to the bottom, and bore on every leaf and point a drop of water from the waste of the bucket. Below the calm surface of the water appeared a reversed shaft having it sides begemmed with the moss-borne drops, which with a singular effect of darkened brilliancy shone like diamonds in a cave. Through a small green subterranean orifice she could look into nethermost, luminous, boundless space; a mysterious ethereal abyss, an unknown realm of purity and peace *below* the earth, the faintly-revealed inferior heavens; and she beheld, too, her own fair but shadowy face, in the midst of all, looking up to her. Anon a falling drop of water would ruffle the scene, and then it eddied away into clearness and repose. Such was the rare vision that detained her, and made her pause with her hands still grasping the pole.

"What are you doing?" said Dorothy. "I am thinking of your pink," replied Margaret. "I thought I could see Malvina in the well sometimes," added the girl, "but there is nothing there only some fishes Biah put in last summer." "At any rate there is good water there, and we will see if we can get some," said Margaret. The bucket was drawn up, dripping to the curb, where Dorothy steadied it, while Margaret drank. Margaret sat on the long bench to rest herself, and told Dorothy Chilion would make a box for her pink. Dorothy gave her the better half of an imperfect geniton apple, the best she had, and Mistress Tapley with unwashed hands hurried into the garden, that is to say a small unenclosed spot, where they raised a few vines, and got a watermelon, and with the same versatile and economical member, broke it in pieces, which she divided between Margaret and her daughter.

Going on her way, she passed pastures and extensive forest-skirted uplands crimsoned over with the flowering sorrel; and large fields, planted as it would seem to mulleins like nursery trees, with silvery leaves, rising into tall gold-tipped pinnacles; she saw bull-thistles, like a phalanx of old Roman soldiers of whom she had read, suddenly fallen into disorderly mutual combat, piercing one another with sharp malignant spines. The air of the place tainted as it might appear from the vapors of the Still, whose fires waited not for midsummer heats, was yet sensibly relieved by the sweet-scented vernal grass mingling with the odors of new-mown hay from the meadows or lots on the margin of the Brook; she saw, also, women with blue and brown skirts, naked arms, and straw hats, raking and turning hay among alders and willows, that yet flourished in their best mow-lands. From loads of brakes, a lazy substitute for grass, that went by, regaling her with a rich spicy fragrance, she was saluted by the slang and ugly mirth of the drivers. Men and boys were seen going to the Tavern for their eleven o'clock, and in the sun before the house lay Mr. Tapley, boosily sleeping, with his bare head pillowed on a scythe-snath.

She was not sorry to turn into the Delectable Way, a name by which she had enlivened the road from Avernus to the Pond ; and perhaps on the whole it never seemed to her more pleasant. She had often traversed it with the rum-bottle, baskets of chestnuts and bags of yarn, she had been carried over it by her brothers, once she was borne up it in the proud arms of an exulting populace. It was steep, narrow, rough, winding. It had contributed to the elasticity of her muscles and vigor of her heart. Now it glowed with wild-flowers, which the lavish fertility of nature pours into every open space. It was a warm day, and the sunbeams were strongly reflected from the gray pebbles and glassy grit of the road, but a breeze from the valley and another in her soul, gave her endurance and self-possession.

She was going home, and this, however such a home might seem to many of her readers, was, we have reason to believe, in her mind an endeared consideration; she had been disappointed in the School, sadly, greviously; her heart was wrung in a manner that only a schoolmistress can know; it cannot be told. She nevertheless consoled herself with calling to mind how much her scholars loved her, how kind some of the villagers had been to her, and she might have decided the matter at once by reflecting how utterly impossible it was, all things taken together, to have maintained a generous footing with the people at large; she was encompassed by those subtle and exquisite ministries of nature that can be enjoyed at every period of life and are capable of reaching the most desponding, and which operate to mitigate the sense of sorrow, and impart lustre to our most temperate enjoyments. There was besides an unnamed, undeveloped feeling in her own breast, welling and provoking, partly inquisitiveness, partly wonder, partly logic, partly thoughtfulness, partly she knew not what, that heightened the interest of all things. This feeling, we have cause to believe, was allied in character to what it approximated in moral place, that which had been sported between her and the Master as "Anagogicalness," whereby seems to have been intended any or all kinds of profundity of uncertainty; seems, we say, for the compiler of this Memoir professes to know no more of the matter than any of its readers.

On a side of the road was the cow-path winding among sweet-fern and whortleberry bushes, where she a little girl used to walk, and even hide under their shade. The great red daddocks lay in the green pastures where they had lain year after year, crumbling away, and sending forth innumerable new and pleasant forms. On a large rock grew a thistle, the flower of which a yellow-breeched bee and a tortoise-shelled butterfly quietly tasted of together. Farther off, in the edge of a dark green forest, twinkled the small sunflower, like a star. She walked on with a bank of beautiful flowers on either side, golden-rods, blue-vervain, flea-bane, and others, which she saw come up in the Spring, watched from month to month, and would yet behold giving food to the little birds in midwinter, and which had become a part of her yearly life. A thin stream of water emerging from a copse of fox-colored cotton thistle and high blackberries, ran across the road. The sky was blue above her, relieved and variegated by mares-tail clouds, from which some would augur a rain, and over her left shoulder paled the midday moon. Her path in some places was carpeted with the tassels of the late flowering chestnut. A pig in a yoke starting from the bushes scampered before her as for dear life, its ears shaking like poplar leaves, and dashed out of sight into the bushes again. The birds having finished their spring melodies gave themselves up to the quiet enjoyment of the season they so delightfully introduced, and were no otherwise observable than in an occasional rustle among the trees. She made a nosegay for Chilion of yellow loose-strife, purple spearmint, pale blue monkey flower, small white buds of cow-wheat; and a smaller one for Rose, a stem of mountain laurel leaves, red cedar with blueberries, and a bunch of the white hard-hack, a cream-like flower, innerly blushing.

While thus employed, there appeared in the road before her a gentleman, who seemed to have just issued from the trees, and whom she fancied she had seen retreating within doors at the Tavern, as she came by, and who, if it were so, must have hastened across through the woods while she loitered on the way. The face of this gentleman was strikingly marked by a suit of enormous black whiskers that flowed together and united under his chin. His age might have been four-and-twenty; his eye was black and piercing, but softened by an affectionate expression; his look was animated, and a courteous smile played upon his lip. His dress was more elegant than that of the young men of Livingston, a scarlet coat delicately embroidered with buff facings, a richly tambored waistcoat, lace ruffles, white silk breeches and stockings, and a round brimmed hat. He addressed her with deference and urbanity, and asked if he might have the pleasure of accompanying her up the hill. "I am rambling about the country," said he, "and pursue whatever is novel and interesting, and hope my presence, Madam, will not disoblige you? This is a bleak place, and I should think you would sometimes lack for variety." "It is a very beautiful spot to me," she replied, "and—" "Indeed," said he, "I did not mean that it was not beautiful, only there are so few people here,—yet perhaps you are one who has the felicity of being contented anywhere. A boquet! What a rare profusion of flowers. The atmosphere is redolent of sweetness. Most charming day this." So they talked of the weather, the season, the place, till they reached the summit of the road. Before they came in sight of the house, the gentleman suddenly stopping, said, "Might I venture to hope, Madam, if in my rural strolls I should chance again to encounter you, it would not be disagreeable?" "What is your name, sir?" said she. "I am—Anonymous, Mr. Anonymous;—does not that savor of the romantic, of which I see you are passionately fond?" "All wind-fall comers here seem to be without names," said she; "but there is really so little in a name, that I do not care much about it." "Are there other strangers besides myself here?" he asked. "Yes," she replied, "we have one who would be anonymous at first, but she allows herself to be called Rose now, though she is so frail she can hardly support any name." "Rose, Rose," rejoined he with a repetition, "that is a very pretty name indeed." Politely bidding her good morning, he went down the hill.

Margaret hastened home to recount her misfortunes, intelligence of which must have preceded her, and enjoy the commiseration of her friends. Bull with Dick on his back ran out to meet her,—the only member of the family who did not know what had befallen her, and whose expression of unmingled delight gave her a momentary deep pain in the way of contrast, and yet in the end tended to reassure her and bring her back to her former state. After dinner she went to the Widow Wright's to see Rose, whom unfortunately she found plunged in the deepest melancholy, and the more distressing for that it could render no reason for itself. Margaret strove by every effort to compose her friend, but in vain. She remained a while, but found her own tenderness fully reciprocated, that Rose was pained because she was pained, that she increased what she endeavored to dispel, and thus without the possibility of gaining intelligence or affording relief, she could do more than embrace the sad one and go home.

Shortly afterwards, as she was occupied one morning with a book in the shade of the woods near the Delectable Way, she was aroused by the arrival of Mr. Anonymous. "Have you read Cynthia?" said he, after concluding the compliments of the hour. "I saw it at the village the other day," she replied. "It is a charming novel," said he. "I do not know as I am capable of understanding it," she rejoined. "I mean it is a delightful thing to toss off a dull hour with. Are you never afflicted with any such?" "Not often." "Are no dangers to be apprehended in a place like this?" "I never have any fears." "I see you know how to diversify your time. As you would walk, Madam, let me assist you. Allow me to remove that bit of brush from your path." "I thank you, Sir, I never mind the trees." "I am tempted to help you over that rock." "These rocks are no more formidable than our kitchen doorsill." "How rich these woods are in flowers!" "Indeed they are." "The most beautiful are not the most esteemed." "I fear they are not." "With great justice the Poet writes,—

'Full many a flower is born to blush unseen!'"

"That is well said. I find new ones every Spring, and there are many yet hidden in the dark abyss of the earth." So talked they a while, when the young gentleman again took an abrubt but civil departure, acting it would appear on the principle that short visits make long friends.

Margaret was obedient to her parents and faithful to the house, so that she was allowed many indulgences, the chief of which consisted in leisure for her own pursuits. She rose early, did her work with spirit, and her enjoyment suffered but little from the exactions of her mother or the domineering of Hash. A peculiarity of fog-scenery as observed from the Head, a phenomenon in its perfect development occurring only two or three times a year, took her to that point. The fogs arising from the River lay wholly below her, dispersed like a flocculent ocean over the interval between the Pond and the Mountain beyond. As if an entire firmanent of purest white clouds had fallen into the valley, these masses of mist were piled in chaotic beauty, and into them the sun poured its intensest beams. Like a silver flood they rolled before the winds, they overran the high grounds of the Pond, and swept the base of the hill on which she stood. They were an organic lustre sublimated wool, spiritualized alabaster; they glowed like snow-flames. It was to summer what snow is to winter, a robe of whiteness thrown over the face of the earth. It was not often she could *look down* upon the fogs with the pure dry air about her. She had been *in* them, sailing on the Pond or traversing the woods, when they seemed to fall from the sky and drizzled rain-like over the earth; now she was over them, and could command their extent and grandeur.

Higher and higher they rose, till only the top of the Butternut and the peak of the forest were visible. She fancied that the visions of her dreams were composed of fogs, and thought she saw fair Ideal Beauty as it were *precipitated* in them chemically, and becoming animated, like the Beautiful Lady. A new Venus, of whom she had read, was indeed sprung from this foam; and she looked when she should swim for the Butternut, as for a green island, and she would run down and embrace her; at the same moment, a great black crow flew up from these bridal waves, a true make-shift for Vulcan.

But a more substantial apparition engaged her attention. At the edge of the platform on which she stood arose an enormous pair of whiskers, speedily followed by the well dressed young gentleman to whom they belonged, Mr. Anonymous, who, for some reason unexplained, perhaps because it savored more of the romantic of which he was an admirer, had chosen a very unusual and almost inaccessible route to the summit of the Head. Apologizing for his intrusion, he hoped he had not disturbed the tenor of the young lady's reveries. "I cannot be disturbed by one who enjoys the scene," replied Margaret. "The fog is uncivil," added Mr. Anonymous, "it has quite drenched me. If it would clear away I think there would be afforded a very charming prospect. I wonder I had not sought it out before. Yet the view which the place itself affords, Madam, is unimpaired, and would richly repay clambering up a much rougher way." "I fear you must have fatigued yourself," said she, "you missed the path." "It matters little how I came, since I am well here, and in the presence of so fair an object." "I am glad to have an associate in contemplations like these," answered Margaret. "Perhaps, Sir, you can aid me in resolving the exceeding mystery of all these things." "I should be most felicitated to join you in any thing." "That beauty and our beauty, how are they related?" "I see your beauty, and I scarcely think of that." "But there is a connection, I feel it. The beauty that is in me either gives or is given. Or there is some cause that creates both, and unites them like musical chords." "Your beauty, most enchanting lady, since you lead me to speak of it, consists in symmetry and color, those eyebrows, your forehead, your lips, that dark curling hair; it brings me near to you. Nay, pardon my presumption." "Do look at that pile swimming through the mass, like a polar bear!" "Nay, loveliest! I can look only at thee." "Then I will go away; there is enough besides to look at." "Beauteous being! do not leave me. Do not shun the person of one who adores you." "Adores me! Ha! ha!" "I kneel at your feet, sweet Madam, allow me to take your hand." "More mystery still! What is there in my hand?" "May I be so presumptuous as to believe that with your hand you would also bestow your heart?" "I havn't any heart." "Have I vainly cherished the hope that my person had made some impression on you?" "What, your clothes?" "O, you will not trifle with me. Your manner has been such as to inspire the hope that my feelings toward you were reciprocated." "I would not trifle with you. I thought you better dressed than the young men hereabouts. But do see how the Mountain shines in its dewy robe!" "Be not so severe; do not retreat from me; render some condescension to my poor plaints." "I know not what you desire." "Yourself, Madam, is the supremest object of my wishes. Allow me to press your fingers to my lips." "I cannot stay here, Sir, I shall leap off into the Pond." "O, fairest of creatures, be not so cruel. Blame me not if I reveal I love you, never before unfortunate if you prove pitiless, never before happy if you prove kind." "See, the mists are fast rising, we shall be thoroughly wet if we stay much longer." "Dissipate, Madam, the distressing apprehensions your words create. My purposes are legitimate, I offer you marriage, I offer you a fortune. Our banns shall be published in the neighboring Church the next Sabbath." "I must own, Sir, you do sadly disturb me now. Your presence is becoming an intrusion." "You will slip from the rock, you will fall into those hideous waters." "Beautiful waters, and I could almost wish to drop through the beamy air into them." "I will not approach you nearer; I will abide at a distance, till you say the dear, dear word that shall make me happy." "Do not be afraid of me. I would make the birds and toads and every thing about me happy." "I protest my designs are honorable as my sentiments are invincible. Consider what I shall bestow upon you."

Now what should appear but our old friend Obed, tearing his stalwart knobby frame through the bushes, and being somewhat short of sight, a defect that was aggravated by the prevalent haze, wholly mistaking the nature of the scene. Seeing Margaret, as he thought, driven to the verge of the precipice by the violence of the man whose fervid exclamations he had confounded with demonstrations of a more fatal character, he made a tempestuous lunge at the fellow and trussed him in his long arms. In the struggle that ensued, both fell and rolled down the hill, performing a kind of horizontal waltz, through briers, over rocks, quite to the bottom. Margaret running after, screamed to Obed to quit his hold, but in vain; they finished the descent before she could overtake them. The face of Mr. Anonymous was not a little bruised and his dress soiled; nor did Obed escape without some little damage. Pluck and his wife ran out at the alarm, Margaret proffered the unfortunate gentleman every assistance in her power; but as if disposed to withdraw from observation, he made a very rapid retreat, forgetting even his customary civilities in the hurry of departure, and was seen no more at the Pond.

CHAPTER II.

MARGARET.—MR. EVELYN.—CHRIST.

We would come nearer to Margaret; we have kept too much aloof. What she denied to Mr. Anonymous, she will grant to her readers, who, as a parent, have watched about her from her babyhood,—a more intimate approximation. And if Isabel spoke correctly when she said Margaret could bear the truth, she can certainly bear to be looked at, a distinction not mortifying to most young ladies. She denied that she had a heart; has she any? If she has none, unlike most young ladies, in another respect also she differs from many of her sex and age—she can make good butter, which she did this very morning, churning it in the cool dawn, working it out, salting it, and depositing it in a cellar which, if it possessed no other merit, boasted this at least, that it was cold and free of flies. It has been intimated, and may come up again for affirmation, that Margaret was brought up on bread and cider and bean porridge. This, however, must not be taken too literally. The facts in the case are these, sometimes the family kept a cow, and sometimes they did not. But to our purpose.

This morning, after churning and breakfast, she went out to a favorite spot, a little below the house, on the Delectable Way, lying in the shade of the eastern forest. If Bull followed, it was rather from habit than necessity, since she was wont to go where she listed, unattended, relying chiefly upon a pair of pretty strong arms, and whatever defence against danger is to be found in not fearing it. It is here, precisely in this morning retreat, that we propose to take a look at her. The place she has chosen, characterized chiefly by forest associations and aspect, opens to the south, where are visible the Avernian hills, and to the zenith, where is the everlasting sky. No sound, save the solitary crowing of a cock in some distant farmyard or the barking of a fox in the slumbering woods. Near her indeed is a drowsy kind of music box, in a bed of yellow brakes, inhabited by innumerable crickets and grasshoppers, that keep up a perpetual lulling murmur. She holds in her hand a book, or rather her arm lying on the ground the book lies there too, closed on her fore-finger. The book, we shall see, is an old one, so very old, its leathern back has changed into a polished mahogany hue; it is in Latin, and the title anglicized reads, "The Marrow of Theology, by William Ames," a Dutchman. Down the hill a little ways, in a pasture of solemn rocks and gaudy elecampane, are very contentedly feeding two red cows. Whether she *saw* these or not she looked at them, and now her eye lifts upwards. What *we* looking upwards see is a group of clouds, massive and dense, with white tops, dark cavernous sides, and broad bases deepening into a bluish leaden color, having their summits disposed about a common centre, and forming a circular avenue, at the end of which lie boundless fields of fairest ultramarine. We can hardly tell what she does see. Let us look at her eyes and see what she seems to see.

We shall discover if we keep a good memory that those organs have changed since her childhood. *Then*, her eyes perceived with briskness and disposed of their objects with ease. The external world made a rapid transit through them, enlivened and graced her spirit, and returned; and since material substances are by this process transmuted into moral emotions, and the nerves of the face are sympathetic throughout, a beautiful flower for example, borne in on the optic nerve, would come out an irradiation of joy generously covering the countenance. *Now*, a world has been created *in* her eyes; outward objects no longer pass immediately through, but are caught and detained, as it would seem, for inquisition. Some are seen to sink with a sullen plunge into the dark waters of her soul; some she seizes upon and throws out among the waste things of the earth; others again get in by stealth, creep round upon her nerves, come out and sit on her eye-winkers and lips and play their old pranks of beauty and joy; anon some fair large object, that she suffers to pass, floods her spirit and drowns out every thing else; a full proportion of these objects, it would appear, are assigned to the region of the Anagogical. We cannot say she is "sicklied o'er with the pale cast of thought," yet her expression is subdued if it be not positively sober, with a mixed aspect of fervid aspiration and annoying uncertainty. The clouds have shifted their places and forms, the cows quietly feed on, and she betakes herself to reading. The click of a horse-foot on the stones of the Delectable Way arouses her, the cows look up, and so does she.

Strangers in Livingston frequently visited Indian's Head for the sake of its fine scenery; they went to and fro taking little notice of the inhabitants, and with extreme consideration avoided laying upon them the slightest burden of civility or attention; and Margaret, accustomed to these transient manners, would have suffered the present to pass as an ordinary instance, save that, with a stranger man on horseback, she saw little Job Luce—little he was, though older than when she first knew him—on the pommel of the saddle in the arms of the rider; and when they were over against her in the road, Job caused the man to stop. "That's it," said Job, "that's the Pond." "I don't see any water," replied the man, "nothing but a rock and a woman." "That's Margery," reiterated the boy, "and that is where she sits, and I find her there most always." "Is she the Pond?" asked the other. "She had always rather be in the woods than in the house," continued Job, "she pricks flowers into her bonnet instead of ribbons, and likes to hear the birds sing Sundays better than Zenas Joy, the new chorister."

Meanwhile Job, lowered from the horse, stood holding by the snaffle, and insisting that the gentleman should likewise dismount. His manifest anxiety brought Margaret also to the spot. "That is Margery, do stop and see her—here, Margery, is a billet from Isabel."

"I overtook this little fellow on the way," said the stranger "and as he seemed but a sorry traveller, I thought my horse could better do that office for him."

"If you will stop, I guess she will go with you up the Head, you have been so good to me," said Job, with renewed earnestness.

"I should be very glad to see you, Sir, if Job wishes me to," said Margaret. The young man left his horse among the trees, and walked with Job and Margaret to the spot occupied by the latter.

"Since you have been so fairly introduced," said he, addressing Margaret, "I ought to make myself known; Charles Evelyn—Judge Morgridge is my uncle—perhaps you are acquainted with his daughter Susan?"

"I am not," replied Margaret, "but I have heard my friend Isabel Weeks speak of her. This is Job Luce, one among the very few friends of whom I can boast in the village."

"He seems very much attached to you," rejoined Mr. Evelyn, "so feeble, to walk so far to see you. He said there was some one at the Pond who knew almost every thing and loved him very much."

"I do love Job, poor boy, he has but few to love him, and his love for me produces a cyanosis, as Mr. Elliman, my old Master, says, whereby we do not see things clearly, and so he thinks very highly of me, as I know I do of him."

"She knows Whippoorwill," said Job, "and that is more than the Parson does, if she don't go to Meeting."

"I know nothing," replied Margaret.

"Have you no home, no father or mother?" asked Mr. Evelyn. "Do you live in these woods?"

"There is our house behind the trees yonder," said Margaret; "there are my father and mother; there is my brother Chilion; I have books, a squirrel, and a boat; the trees, the water, the birds all are mine, only I do not understand all."

"The Master," interposed Job, "said she understood Latin as well as Hancock Welles who has gone to College."

"Yes indeed," rejoined Margaret, smiling, "I can say as he did once, when pursuing me in the woods he was overtaken by a bear, 'Veni, vidi, victa sum.' I am lost in my gains; every acquisition I make conquers me."

"The vici," replied Mr. Evelyn, "is a rare attainment. It is easier to know than to be masters of our knowledge;—I see from your book you are exploring an abstruse subject through what some would regard an abstruse medium. Theology is not always rendered plainer for being put in plain English. Do you find it cleared up in Latin?"

"My teacher," answered Margaret, "says Latin is the

tongue of the learned; and so, most curiously, to convict me for a fool as it would seem, he commends me to my studies in it. I asked him some questions, and he gave me this book, but not so much in the way of a reply, I ween, as a repulse. I can construe the sentences, distinguish the supine in u; but, the ideas—gramercy! I had as lief encounter a troop of bull-beggars, or undertake to explain the secrets of the nostrummonger that lives above us. I am caught by my own fish, as brother Nimrod says, and dragged into an element where I pant and flounder as any strange creature would in ours."

"Mammy says," explained Job, "it is because Margery is proud, has a natural heart, and won't bend her will down, and so she lost the School. But she isn't proud to me; she used to lead me home all the way from School. Hester Penrose, the other Ma'am, never would touch me or speak to me out of school; and when we were in, she only spoke hard to me, and whipped me, because I caught the grasshoppers that flew in and stopped to hear Whip-poorwill—I could hear it in the windows. She wouldn't give me a ticket either, for all I got my lessons well.—Arthur Morgridge said I got them better than he, and he had a ticket."

"Your mother, Job," said Margaret, "and Deacon Ramsdill don't agree; he applauds me for having a nateral heart, as he calls it, and says he hopes my will never'll be broke; he says a broken will is no better than a broken back. But, of what we were speaking, Mr. Evelyn; are you familiar with these ideas, these things, these what-nots? Or are you, like all the rest, only a dainty, white handkerchief sort of a traveller among the hills?"

"I have dabbled a little in a good many matters," replied the young gentleman, "and if there be any points that trouble you, more than as likely as not it will be found our troubles are not dissimilar, only it sometimes results that difficulties of this sort once fairly stated are dispelled ; the attempt to give them form annihilates them—they pass away in the breath that pronounces them."

"A fine prospect, indeed!" responded Margaret. "I shall be able to discharge the Universe at a whiff! But soberly, here is the source of all my perplexity, a quid and a quis. The book, as you see, discusses without satisfying the case. It is 'Quid sit Deus,' or "Quis sit Deus,' what is God, or, who is God. He, that is the Master, says I did not put the question right at first, and nulla vestigia retrorsum, I have been going wrong ever since. We have quis'd and quid'd it together, till my brain whirls and my mind aches. Who is God? I will ask. 'Do you intend,' he replies, 'entity or form? If the first then you should say, What is God; Who is not What, my child. Language has its rules as well as that whereto it applies. Informal language on formal subjects is altogether contrary to logic.' Good Heavens! say I, I don't know which I mean. 'Then do not talk until you know what you are talking about; let us finish this game of backgammon.' To complete my distress he has given me this book! There is one pretty thing in it, the little boy with a girlish face in the frontispiece. He is holding up a big book *before* the door of some temple. Would the *book* would remove, then we could enter the mysterious place. Alack-a-day! 'Where there's a secret there must be something wrong,' good Deacon Ramsdill says, and I believe it."

"Look here," said Mr. Evelyn, "Father Ames touches fairly on these topics. '*Quid* sit Deus, nemo potest perfecte definire,' *what* God is we cannot perfectly define; but '*Quis* sit explicant,' who he is his attributes sufficiently make known."

"Read another page," said Margaret, '1 Tim. vi. 16, Lucem habitans inaccessam,' &c. What is referred to there seems very mystified indeed. The only Tim that I am acquainted with is our neighbor's horse."

"Don't speak so—you astonish me. That is language addressed by the apostle Paul to a young man whose name was Timothy. 'God dwelleth in the light which no man can approach unto.'"

"I did not intend any harm, I had no idea there was any feeling in the matter. The Master and the Parson are always bringing in some name, Aristotle, Moses, Scotus, Paul, or somebody, whom they make responsible for what they say, and commit themselves to nothing, laughing and smoking in the mean time. They are both as 'amfractuous' as he says I am, and as 'anagogical' as our little friend Job."

"I don't know what that is," observed the boy, "but I do know Whippoorwill, and that I shall die of it. But Margery don't believe the Parson, and she won't read the Bible."

"My troth!" exclaimed the young man. "There are more things in heaven and earth than are dreamed of in my philosophy, and more in Livingston than I had imagined. Did you never read the Bible?"

"No," replied Margaret. "The Master has endeavored that I should never see one, and the first book he put into my hand when I asked him about God was Tooke's Pantheon. There was a great book marked Holy Bible on the outside at Deacon Ramsdill's; there were some singular pictures in it, and some singular reading, but not of a nature to tempt me to look far into it. Only I remember laughing outright when I came to something just like what Pa calls his Bible, and the good Deacon took the book away. Pa's Bible is some leaves of a book hanging by a string on the chimney, and consists of names beginning with Adam and ending with Duke Magdiel, and he always uses it, he says, when he christens his children. It is suspended, also, you must know, directly over his rum bottle; and he says he reads his Bible when he drinks his rum. That is our Bible."

"Mammy gave you a Testament once," said Job.

"The Master took it away," replied Margaret. "He said I was not old enough to understand it, or something of that sort."

"She doesn't go to Meeting either," added Job.

"Do you not indeed?" asked the young man.

"It is not quite true that I never go," said Margaret. "I have been to a Camp Meeting and at Parson Welles's Meeting."

"Only once," said Job.

"I could hardly wish to go a second time. Every thing was turned topsy-turvy; flowers became an abomination; for walking the streets one was liable to be knocked down; people had on gay dresses and sepulchral faces: no one smiled; the very air of the Green grew thick and suffocating; sin lurked in every spot, and I couldn't do any thing but it was an abomination. I was glad to get out of it, and escape to the Pond once more, and breathe in brightness and love from our own skies. No, we never go here; Pa was put in the stocks for hunting his cow one Sabbath, and he swears we shall not go. I frighten you, Sir, and you will have me put in Jail right off."

"If I am frightened," said the young man, "I can hear all you have to say, and would much prefer you should not interrupt yourself."

"I was young then, and these are old impressions which

have grown perhaps somewhat sour by keeping, and I might not feel just so now. At the Camp Meeting—have you ever been to one? Well, I need not recount that. The Preacher I could never forgive, only he was so kind to me when I was lost in the woods. That was the pink of what the Master calls puppetry, a hornet's nest of harlequins, saints bacchanatizing. When I told the Master of some of my accidents on these holy occasions, for in one instance I liked to have been sent to jail, and in another, to have been crushed to death, 'Ne sutor ultra crepidam,' said he, 'you are a shoemaker's daughter; mind your own business, and stay at home next time;' so I did. Nimrod once took me to an ordination at Dunwich, where the Leech, who contrives to be every where, accompanied us. It was more like training-day than any thing else. The town was full of people and soaking in rum. At the Church I was wedged in an impassable drift, but managed somehow to crawl out like a stream of water through their legs and feet. The Widow found means to introduce herself and me with her to the dining-hall. Such things were enacted there as would not disgrace the bar-room at No. 4. Pa, when he is drunk, has far better manners than those sanctiloquent wigs exhibited. It was altogether the richest specimen of 'deific temulency' you ever beheld. The side-boards were emptied half a dozen times, tobacco smoke choked the air, and to finish the play one gray old Punch with inimitable gravity said grace at the close. The exercises of the day were rounded off by a ball in the evening, and that was the best of the whole, save that the ministers were not there to give the occasion the zest of their jokes and laughter—I supposed at the time they were in a state of aquacœlestification, and could not dance. But O! O! O! Job, dear Job, I love you, Job! Why do I, a poorer wretch, speak of these poor things?"

This exclamation was followed by tears that fell drenchingly and hot on the face of the boy whom she clasped in her arms. Job turned up his mild blue eye to her and said, "Margaret, Whippoorwill sings, and Job don't cry; I swing over the brook when the boys tease me, and the bubbles take away the pain; I hear a pewee in the woods, Margaret, that sings when the Whippoorwill is gone. I love you too, Margaret, and Job's love is good, the little Mabel says. If there were no innocent hearts, there would be no white roses, Isabel says."

> "There were two birds sat upon a stone,
> Fa, la, la, la, lal, de,"—

Margaret began, saying, "Come, Job, sing too," and they both sung,—

> "One flew away, and then there was one,
> Fa, la, la, la, lal, de;
> The other flew after, and then there was none,
> Fa, la, la, la, lal, de;
> And so the poor stone was left all alone,
> Fa, la, la, la, lal, de."

"Now, Job," she said, "we will go and get comfrey root for Chilion's drink, and burdock leaves for drafts to draw out all pains. We shall detain the gentleman."

"The detention is rather on my part," said Mr. Evelyn. "Yet I am truly unwilling to have you go."

"I shall only offend you if I stay," said she.

"I have learned," he replied, "never to be offended with any human being."

"Then you are the strangest of all human beings, though I agree with you, and find myself small place for offence. Androides furentes create a sensation of the ridiculous more than any thing else."

"You seem," continued he, "to be sincere, however mistaken; and I am not a little interested in what you say."

"Are *you* sincere?" she asked. Are you not simulacrizing? Yet I wrong you, Sir, I wrong myself. It confesses itself within me, that you are in earnest."

"That is Whippoorwill," said Job.

"It is the voice of nature," said the young man.

"I am not," added Margaret, "so brook-like as I used to be, when neither rock nor night, inundation or ultimate disemboguement disturbed my little joyous babble. The beauties and sweetnesses, the freedom and health that surround me do not so perfectly satisfy me. I have not much of the 'acquiescentia cordis' of which Father Ames speaks. My squirrel, Dick, has been rolling about in his cage these many years, and is contented with it as ever. I, forsooth, must explore the cupboard whence my food comes, dig into the well-head whence my water flows, anatomatize the hand that caresses me. There seems to be something *above* the people in the village, something over their heads, what they talk to, and seem to be visited by occasionally, particularly Sundays, making them solemn and stiff like a cold wind. Is it God! What is God? Who is God? Heigh ho hum—let me not ask the question. Is it Jupiter or Ammon? Is it a star? Or is it something in the state of the weather? Going to Meeting Sundays the Master calls a septenary ague, universal in these countries. Yet the matter is deep and penetrating as it is anagogical."

Why do you not speak with the people," said Mr. Evelyn, "and discover the nature of their emotions and thoughts?"

"My sooth! I had rather lie here on the grass and read the Medulla, dig roots, card and spin, clean dye-tubs, pick geese, or even go for rum—any thing, any thing. Vox populi vox Dei, he says, but it must have a very strange voice. The hygeian gibberish of the Leech is not half so bad; nor that stupendous word, honorificability, he used to make me spell, half so unintelligible. It all runs of sins and sinners, the fall and recovery, justification and election, trinity and depravity, hell and damnation—they have an idiosyncrasy of phrases, just as the Free Masons have, and Tony, the Barber, and Joyce Dooly the Fortune-teller have; then there are experiences and exercises, ah's and oh's, sighs and laments, as if we were about to be burned up—and indeed they say we are, at least our family; and Pa laughs so about it all, and the Master while he seems to join in with it, only turns it to ridicule. Isabel says she is growing tired of it, though she is not apt to complain of any thing, and has already been admonished against keeping company with the wicked Indian, as they call me. She says that those they call sinners are some of the best people in the world, that theological distinctions do not conform to any thing that exists in nature. The Master says that piety is the art of concealing one's original character, and that churchmen are those who have attained the greatest proficiency in that art. But let me hear what you would say. I have 'polylogized' quite long enough. Are you a student for the 'sacred ministry,' a class of young men in whose behalf the Dutchman says he has prepared his Marrow!"

"I am not. But the subjects to which you refer possess a value that engages all professions and all minds. I have a Bible in my pocket, or a part of one."

"What! Are you bibbleous too?"

"Bibliopalous, you mean."

"No, bibbleous. When one comes to our house with a flask of Old Holland, or a bottle of rum, we say he is bibbleous, and has a Bible in his pocket. Pardon me. I am unbridled as the winds. You seem to be drawing upon me, and I give way here within, till every, the most transient, feeling escapes."

"I know what it is to become the sport of impulses, and will not condemn you for that."

"Speak, Sir, and I will listen quietly. I can trim myself to patience when it is necessary."

"You have heard of the Savior of the world, Jesus Christ?"

"Till I am sick of the name. It sounds mawkish in my ears."

"You do shock me now," said Mr. Evelyn with some feeling. "You cause me grief and astonishment."

"I pray your mercy, Sir! What have I done? Your look frightens *me*."

"That you should speak so of Him who to my soul is most precious."

"I am sorry to have distressed you."

"You have distressed one who is dearer to me than my own life."

"Speak that name again."

"Jesus Christ."

"What, my own Beautiful One? Christ—yes—that is his name. I had almost forgotten it. I have thought only of *him*. The name is associated with whatever is distasteful in the world. It is Christ, Jesus Christ. Is he not beautiful?"

"He is described as fairer than the sons of men."

"And you, Sir, know him and love him, and your innermost sense is alive to him? You are the first one who ever showed a deep natural sensibility to that One. I have distressed you and him through you, and myself in him! Therein lies my closet garnered being." Saying this Margaret turned her face away.

"It is Whippoorwill," said Job to Mr. Evelyn. "Don't speak now."

That gentleman waiting a while in silence, was obliged, by direct enforcement, to renew the conversation.

"Tell me," said he, "what is the meaning of this? Here is a greater mystery to *me* than all this strange world can offer to you. By what secret affinities are you bound to him who is my life? How have you come to know him in this heart-felt manner? Like Nathaniel has he seen you under the fig-tree?"

"No," said Margaret, turning herself, and speaking with composure, "it was under those trees yonder in what we call Diana's Walk."

"What, that you literally saw him?"

"It was a dream. He, the Beautiful One, called Christ, filled one of the dreams of my childhood. He spoke to me, he took my hand, he kissed me, he blessed me."

"Tell me about it."

"It was some years ago. Its remembrance fades, then brightens again. Sometimes it bubbles up within me like a spring, sometimes it spreads away into a deep calm surface like the Pond. It haunts me like a summer cloud. In my sensibilities it lies and stirs me up to weeping. Forgive me a thousand times that I should have been so wanton. When you spoke of him in such a way, I was suddenly flooded with emotion such as I cannot describe. Isabel and Job know of it, but they do not precisely answer to my feelings. Indeed at the moment you come up I was endeavoring to form out of the clouds some likeness to what I had seen, the One himself, the Cross, the Dove; I gazed into the heights of the blue sky for some apparition. I beguile the uncertainties of my thought by the creations of my fancy. But that comes not, and the clouds veil over those infinite distances. He said if I loved, I should know. I do love, how little I know!"

"But do, if it pleases you, give me the particulars of your dream."

Margaret repeated what is already in the possession of the reader, and recounted parts of other dreams. "But," said she, as the conversation went on, "I thought this was for myself alone. It has been kept in my own life. Is he, Christ, great, is he general? You, Sir, seem to know and to feel him, though you say you have had no dreams. He has been a strange beautiful flower in my garden, and so he exists in yours. What do these things mean?"

"Your question raises," said he, "a long train of reflection. Let us be seated, and we will go over the matter with that care which it deserves."

"No, indeed," replied Margaret, "I would not trouble you to that extent now. Job promised that I would go on the Head with you, it is time to start—I must be at home, and help about the dinner."

"Where is the cake for Egeria?" said Job.

"I guess she will have to be content with the grasshopper music, or she may lie down in the shade as the cows do," answered Margaret. "I did not tell you, Sir," she added, "that this spot is consecrated to the nymph whom the old Roman was wont to visit, and when we go away we sometimes leave a cake or piece of bread both as an oblation and for her dinner, and will you believe it, Sir, when I return, *it is all gone.*"

They proceeded towards the eminence called the Head. Seeing Chilion moving leisurely in the direction of the water, Job importuned to go and sail with him, and Margaret with Mr. Evelyn went up the hill.

"How very beautiful this is!" said the young gentleman, "there, here, and every where."

"Look down *into* this water," said Margaret, standing on the rock that overhung the Pond, "if your brain is steady enough. This the Master calls Exclamation Point. I have wished to drop into that splendid cloud-flowing nadir, and if I am missing one of these days you will know where to find me. You are sober—well, look off into the mountains yonder. That is Umkiddin. You will not blame a passion I cherish for climbing that sunny height, and laying hand and heart in the downy blue."

"No, I could not. But see that point of rock around which the water bends, with a great tree overshadowing the distance. So I admire a river, not so much in its expanse and full tide as in the turns and angles, where it loses itself within green shores and sinks away under the shade of cliff and forest."

"'Loses itself'!" replied Margaret, repeating the word with some emphasis. "There you have it again. Lost, gone, vanishing, unreachable, inappropriable, anagogical!—I used to sit here in my merry childhood and think all was mine, the earth and the sky. I ate my bread and cider, and fed the ants and flies. Through me innumerable things went forth; the loons whooped me in the water, in my breath the midges sported, the sun went down at my bidding, and my jocund heart kindled the twilight. It now flies away like a bird, and I cannot get near enough to put any salt on its tail. Then I owned so much my losses were of no account, and though I could not reach the bottom of the Pond, I saw the heavens in it, and myself sailing above them. In the darkest night, with our red tartarean links, Chilion and I have rowed across the Pond, and sniggled for eels, and so we conquered the secrets of those depths. I have cried too in my day, I have an unkind brother and a profligate father, and what with the wretchedness of those

I love and their wickedness, my own heart has been duly tortured, and these swollen veins have been bled with weeping; but I seem also to have lost the power of tears. Those, like the days of good Queen Bess, are gone, and how shall they be recovered?"

"Have you no faith?" asked Mr. Evelyn.

"'Faith'! That sanctiloquent word! That is what the Widow Luce dins me with."

"Faith, trust, confidence, repose, seeing the invisible, relying upon the spiritual, having an inner impersonal inhabitancy. In that alone I am happy and sustained. Would you were thus happy."

"I wish I were.—But faint heart never won fair lady. I do not quite give over—I am happy, none more. So in the same moment that I am worried I am at rest. How is this? What many-colored streams flow through us, blood-red, and woolly-white! Are we divided off like sheep? has each feeling its fold? Through our skies sail two sets of clouds, one to the North, one to the South? Even now while I speak all I feel, there is more in me than I can ever speak. What harmony circumscribes the whole? In what are pain and pleasure one? I will not ask you; I am happy; greater simpleton that I am if I were not. Much I have lost, much remains, more comes. My dreams have a place within me; and all the books I have read. My home is every year more beautiful, the trees more suggestive, the birds more musical, the bees more knowing. Roots grow in new ways every summer, and snow falls in new forms every winter. There is more in churning than most people think of. Time is regenerative, and new births occur every hour. The gritty Earth, alumen and silex, spring up in what is beautiful as thought. I have also many and improving visitations, and much select company. I told you of Egeria; then there is Diana's Walk in the woods, and close upon the edge of the water you see some graceful white birches; those are the Nine Muses. Brother Chilion is our Apollo. In the house we have St. Crispin for the shoemaker. Brother Hash, the Master calls Priapus; the Leech we call Dea Salus, and the road to her house has received from the Master the name of Via Salutaris. Religion he says is an anagogical parenthesis, because it must be spoken in a lower tone of voice. No. 4 I called Avernus, and the road to it Descensus Averni, but coming up, he would have it that it was the Delectable Way. The Head is called Mons Bacchi, but our cistern I call Temperance. The Hours dance round me in snowflakes, Naiads and Dryads inhabit our woods and water; in one of my haunts I can show you the Three Graces. That island with a large elm in the centre is Feronia's, where I often go. The Head I told you the Master called Bacchus's Hill, and sometimes our whole region goes by that name, and the Pond he says he has no doubt is the reappearance of the river Helicon into which some fabled Orpheus was changed, and whose waters were a long time hidden under ground: so we sometimes call our place the Lake of Orpheus. To which divinity we are on the whole consecrated, I hardly know; but for my part, I prefer the musical, to the tippling god. Then the fair lady of my dreams sometimes comes to me with her pale beautiful face. I have also one at the Widow's, but whether she be a phantom or a reality I know not, a girl like myself, also pale, sad and beautiful, whose smile is an enchantment, even if I know not her hidden self. Am I not happy?"

"It may be so," answered he, "but in a manner different from the 'world.'"

"Another word that I do not understand! What mean you by the 'world'?"

"People about you, men and women in general."

"If you mean the villagers, the No. 4's, Breaknecks and Snakehills, I know I differ some from them. They drink rum, and I do not; they are unkind one with another, which for the life of me I never could be. Their Anagogics indeed I wholly fail to comprehend, their Meetings, Catechizing, Freemasonry, Trainings, Politics, Courts, Jails, and all that."

"Your religion is so different from theirs."

"Bless me, I have no religion; and Bull defend me from theirs! Albeit, as Deacon Ramsdill says, we must eat a peck of dirt before we die, and perhaps I must make mine out in their religion!—I *have* offended you; it is just as I told you I should do, if you talked with me."

"I repeat, that you cannot offend me, only you must allow what you say to make me somewhat thoughtful. You said you wanted to clamber up the blue mountain yonder, and are ready even to leave your pretty Pantheon for that acquisition. That is religion, even if you had not thought it."

"No, never would I leave my 'pretty Pantheon,' as you call it. But I should like to thrust my fingers between those two blues, that of the hill and of the sky. There Christ has come to me; in celestial skyey softness has *that* vision appeared. No one like the Beautiful One has ever visited my dreams, my thoughts, my aspirations; and I have nothing about me I dare call Christ. There is sometimes a cloud that stretches from Umkiddin to the moon when it rises, like a turkey's tail-feather—whence comes it? to what serene eternal bird does it belong? is it part of the wing of Christ under whose shadow I may lie? is it the trail of the beautiful goddess, Venus?—I know not. No, I cannot leave my Pantheon, and I long for what I have not; and that is religion, you say. Your definition differs somewhat from my tutor's, and by it, I am quite religious! ha, ha! Prithee, tell me, Sir, who are you? Are not you 'the world'?"

"A sorry part of it, I fear; yet removed enough from it neither to drink rum nor disturb the peace of others. I do keep the Sabbath and go to Church; I do not say the Creed, or belong to any train-band. Most people, I confess, are degraded by their piety; I do believe there is a worship that purifies and ennobles."

"You confound and delight me both. I know not what to say. The horn is blowing for dinner, and I am glad something befalls to put an end to the perplexity, Won't you stay and have your dinner with us? I will introduce you to my home and spinning-wheel."

"I am engaged at the Village.—May I have the pleasure of seeing you again, Miss Hart?"

"Miss Hart!"

"That is your name, I believe."

"Yes—only I was never called so before, and it sounds strange. If I do not give you more pain than pleasure, you are welcome to see me when I am to be seen. I have a good deal to do. Can you break flax?"

"I fear I should bungle at it."

"Then I fear Ma would not like you. If you could help me get thistle-down, or rake hay, I should be glad to see you. I would not pain a toad, I hope I shall not you.—Where is the Bible you spoke of, if it does not make me laugh to ask you?"

"You shall have it if you will promise me not to laugh when you read it."

"I never made a promise in my life; only I will try."

"It is not the whole Bible; it is the New Testament, so called. I hope it will please you."

"I don't know. 'A clouted shoe hath oft-times craft in it,' Deacon Ramsdill says, and there may be some good in the Bible."

"We have had fine luck," said Job, meeting them from the boat, as they descended the hill. "Six white perch, eel-pouts, and shiners a plenty."

"Carry them all to your mother," replied Margaret, "and mind you give Whippoorwill a taste. There is my Apollo, not so fair, perchance, as his namesake, but he is as good. He is lame, you see, withal, and in that resembles his prototype; and this stone of my heart becomes melodious when he plays. Mr. Evelyn, Chilion."

"How do you do, Sir?"

"Quite well, at your services, Sir," replied Chilion.

"What springal is that has kept you from helping me?" said Brown Moll, coming to the window with a tray full of hot potatoes, as Mr. Evelyn and Job turned down the road.

"A fox after the goslin, hey?" said Hash, who, with his father, arrived at the same moment. "I saw you on the Head."

"I guess he has lain out over night," said Pluck. "He looks soft and glossy as your Mammy's flax of a frosty morning. Now don't take pet, Molly dear."

"She swells like a soaked pea," added the old woman "What's the matter, hussy? I should think he had been rubbing your face with elm leaves."

"Never mind, Molly," interposed her father. "Better play at small game than stand out. You are the spider of the woods. Spin a strong web; you are sure to catch something."

"She looks as if she had been spun, colored and hung out to dry," said her mother.

"By time!" exclaimed Hash, "I smell potatoes. Give us some dinner."

"Speaking of spinning," said Pluck, when the others were gone in, "you know how to use the wheelpin—keep the thread taught and easy in your fingers, mind the spindle, then buzz away like Duke Jehu;—only if he is a dum spot of a lawyer or a priest, weave him into a breeches-piece, and I'll wear him, I be blown if I don't; and when he is past mending, I'll hang him up for a scarecrow, blast him!"

After dinner, Margaret took her boat and went to the Island called Feronia's, remarkable for its great elm. She threw herself on a bed of mosses under the shade of the tree. "Patience, Silence, Feronia, Venus, O Mother God! help thy child!" she said, or ejaculated with herself. "I, Icarus, with waxen wings, am melted by the light into which I fly! I, Euridice, am in hell! my Orpheus bore me out a little ways, left me, and I am caught back again! How cold I grow! Let me lie in the sun. Dear clouds, sweet clouds! let me shine and be dissolved with you! O Christ!—Relent, thou iron soul of the skies, and speak to me!—My little boat, where is the glad bird-child you used to carry? Still the same, the oar, the seat; the water the same, rocks, woods; waves sing their eternal lullaby, boxberries keep their unchanging red, shadows embrace me as if my heart were free.—How I twattled, skurried! 'Miss Hart!' Miss Pan, Miss Bacchus, rather. Now I grow hot again. Who, what am I? Quis, Quid! God and I alike anagogical. Who or what is he? Let me get it right this time. Who is Mr. Evelyn? His What is what? What is his Who? The What! Lucem inaccessam, light inapproachable. Rose, too, the same.—How kind his words, how gentle his voice, how mild his looks how benign and forbearing in all things! And yet sanctiloquent, and yet so different from others? What is 'the world'? Is he it? Is he like me? Why am I not it? I will see how this matter looks in the water, let me quench my hot limbs."

Drifting along in her boat, she bent over the water,—"Molly, dear," said she, "is that you? Your face is red and feverish. Go to the Widow's and get some balm tea. —Can't you keep cool down there? The sun shines there as well as here. Your hair wants combing, your dress is disordered, Neptune's sea-dog's would be ashamed of you." She left her boat and clothes on the shore, and immersed herself in the grateful water. She returned to the island; she said, "I will lie down under the tree; sleep is better than knowledge, a bed kinder than God, the shadows more beautiful than Truth! Or, Mr. Evelyn, is rest given us wherein we find ourselves and all things? Pardon me, Sir." She slept a long time, and awoke refreshed and regulated, resolute but subdued; with an even hand and quiet temperature she rowed homewards, and went about such duties as domestic necessity or customary requisition imposed.

In the evening she went to see Rose, and while she made no mention of Mr. Anonymous, she found she had much to say of Mr. Evelyn. Rose embraced her with a silent, night-like tranquility, and kissed her lips fervently, which was nearly all the response she made. The sad girl shone out if at all, like the moon through dark clouds, that are only the darker for the brightness behind them. "death," said she, diverging into a train of thought seemingly suggested by what Margaret related, "Death will soon end all. In the grave we shall lie. and the beauty and strength of existence shall perish with us. I only ask, Margaret, that I may be buried side by side with you. The worm devours alike the fairest visions and the most dismal forebodings; decay shall feed sweetly upon your ruddiness and vigor, your nobleness and benignity. A princely offering are we to annihilation. I murmur not, I dread not; with the serenity of angelic love I submit to the all-o'ersweeping fate. In your arms to lie, with you to die, I smile as I sink into the eternal rest. Yet live on, Margaret, while you may; fill your golden cup, it will never be too late to drink it, even if death seizes you in the act."

END OF VOL. I.

www.ingramcontent.com/pod-product-compliance
Lightning Source LLC
LaVergne TN
LVHW020215110826
845151LV00003B/722

* 9 7 8 1 4 2 5 5 3 3 9 9 1 *